WHITHER THOU GOEST

What does it feel like to touch the tip of your tongue to the back of your teeth and know someone else's tongue is literally inside yours, tasting what you taste, sliding where you slide, pressing where you press?

What does it feel like to know someone breathes the air flowing into your mouth and lungs? Hands inside your hands, caressing with you as you touch your forehead, your eyelashes, your lips?

What does it feel like to know anytime you want it, your legs and breasts and belly can fill with the aching presence of a man for whom you would have given your life?

For Claire Islington, knowing he is inside her, shimmering bene̶̶̶̶̶̶̶̶̶̶̶ enough. It will never b̶̶̶̶̶̶̶̶̶̶

MARY BETH BASS

FOLLOW ME

LOVE SPELL NEW YORK CITY

LOVE SPELL®

May 2005

Published by

Dorchester Publishing Co., Inc.
200 Madison Avenue
New York, NY 10016

Copyright © 2005 by Mary Beth Bass

ISBN 0-505-52634-4

The name "Love Spell" and its logo are trademarks of Dorchester Publishing Co., Inc.

Printed in the United States of America.

Visit us on the web at www.dorchesterpub.com.

ACKNOWLEDGMENTS

For Dave, who walked across the Brooklyn Bridge at midnight to tell me I was beautiful.

And for lovely Rebecca, Ben and Sam, who put up with Mrs. Malachite, lame snacks and mismatched socks, and cheered me on anyway.

Thanks to the brilliant, generous women of CoLoNY. And to my supportive friends and family. A forever thank-you to my editor, the insightful, amazing Christopher Keeslar. Thank you so much, Rebecca—for your pink pen and helpful donkey drawings, for your fierce dedication to clarity, and for your long hours of help. I couldn't have done it without you. And deepest thanks to my critique partner, Anne Elizabeth Davidson, for reading more than anyone should ever have to read, for listening and understanding, for Dove chocolates and curly hair, and most of all, for seeing through the haze and making it possible.

FOLLOW ME

Chapter One

"Wait until you see the room," Ian whispered, kissing Claire's neck.

His breath warmed her ear, which was still stinging from the cold November night, and a buzz of something near to pleasure spread through her like an opening hand. She leaned back onto his narrow, strong chest. He smelled like soap and leather. Claire closed her eyes and silently repeated the mantra she'd chanted to herself on the drive from Boston to Dorset, Vermont.

It wasn't real. It wasn't real. I'm not the same person I was then. It wasn't real. He wasn't real.

Ian reached around Claire's waist and opened the door. The brush of oak against carpet purred a throaty welcome. Claire stood passively, her arms limp at her sides, her hands flaccid against the hard muscles of her thighs. Ian pushed her out of the way and walked into the dark room. He switched on a desk lamp: a Tiffany style dragonfly pattern in predictably enchanting blues and greens.

I'm not the same person, Claire repeated to herself in the doorway.

1

"Come on in," Ian said, pulling her inside. "Isn't it great? I requested a room with a fireplace." He kissed her nose. "It's supposed to snow."

Claire half-smiled at him and glanced around the country-life fantasy décor: cozy fabrics, fluffy pillows, antique furniture; a veritable gingerbread house. What could be more enticing?

"It's amazing," she said breathlessly. Her heart pounded in her throat. She tried to remember the breathing exercises she'd read about in the waiting room of his office before they left today.

He opened the suitcase on the bed and started unpacking. "Call the front desk and ask about our dinner reservations, will you, honey?"

Claire stood motionless, staring fixedly at the fireplace and the narrow rolltop desk.

"Are you okay?" Ian asked. "You look pale."

"I'm fine," Claire said brightly. She slid her bag off her shoulder.

She was being stupid. It was in her head, all of it. She had to let it go, to stay with what was real, to believe in what was true. Thank God Ian didn't know anything. He was devoted to her but exceedingly leery of anything unconventional. Claire wondered sometimes if that was why Toby had fixed them up. *Ian Gilbertson, the noble guardian saving fragile Claire from the strange and inexplicable.* She smiled to herself.

"Don't worry about me," she said. "I'm fine. What's the restaurant called?"

"I don't know," Ian said. "You picked it out, remember?"

"Oh, yeah. Um, Beckwith Tavern," she said. "They're supposed to have the best crab cakes in New England."

"Are you sure you're okay?" he asked. "You sound weird."

"Yeah. Yes," Claire repeated emphatically. She kissed him on the mouth.

Ian was adorable, with kisses that tasted like milk and wiry stamina beneath his cashmere sweater. She was crazy. This was what she'd always wanted, a committed, loving relationship with no games or unpredictability. "I love you," she said.

He beamed, kissed her softly on the forehead and went into the bathroom.

"I'm gonna take a quick shower," he said and closed the door. The faucet screeched like an old brake before Claire heard the water come on. "Don't forget to call the restaurant," Ian called out over the rushing sound.

"Okay," she shouted back.

Claire sat on the four-poster bed and kicked off her shoes. They landed on the carpet with a thud like windfall apples. The room was quiet. Thick plaster walls kept out noise from the hall and other rooms. Claire wished Ian sang in the shower or talked to himself. She drew up her legs and tucked her feet under her skirt. As reliable as breath, the memory of that night seven years earlier lingered outside Claire's consciousness. The crack of an eggshell could bring it all back. She never told anyone, not even Toby, how present it still was, how real *he* still seemed.

Claire concentrated on the shush of running water. Ian was a lather-rinse-repeat kind of guy, and he washed every inch of himself twice. She slid off the mattress and shoved the suitcase into an armoire carved with cherubs. She could do this. She wasn't a baby and it had been a long time ago. But *he* grabbed her stomach like a hand made out of butter and climbed inside her, up to her mouth, where she could taste him like sugared air.

Forget it. She wasn't ready.

She cursed and shook him off.

"Hey!" Claire called out. "Can I come in?"

"What time is the reservation?" Ian asked.

"Damn," she muttered.

"Did you call?" Ian asked when she didn't say anything.

"Yes," she said, dialing the front desk.

"Well? What time is it?"

"Thanks," Claire murmured to the innkeeper. "Seven-thirty. We have an hour and a half."

"Then come on in, baby."

Claire took off her clothes, threw them on the bed and opened the bathroom door. Even thick steam in a cold bathroom couldn't hide Ian's lusciously formed body, his long, lean muscles, slim hips and beautiful chest. She could hardly see the white scar on his butt, the result of a battle with a younger sister over bathroom privileges and a forgotten, still-hot curling iron. He'd hated his scar until Claire told him it kept him from being too unattainably perfect.

"Hey, hottie," she said.

"Come here, you." Ian folded her into his warm, wet arms and kissed her. Milk and summer and sweetness.

"Mmmmm," he murmured and kissed her neck.

She felt him rise against her and suddenly wanted to swallow him whole. He lifted her up and pressed her into the cool, slick tile. Good, she thought as she felt him grow harder inside her. Good, she thought, breathing heavily, his mouth at her breast. She turned her head in relief as he climaxed, always on the same sweet, low, almost tuneful moan.

He nuzzled his face to her neck. "Let's skip dinner."

She smiled and kissed him. "You say that now, but in a few hours, when every restaurant is closed, you'll be starving and you'll want those crab cakes."

He ran his hands down her waist. "You're right."

Claire washed her hair, calling to him while he dried off, "This is New England, baby, not New York. We go to bed early here."

After her shower Claire sat on the toilet to brush her hair, and to watch Ian shave. She loved the glide of the razor and the sexy, man-in-the-morning scent of the shaving cream.

"Are you staying in here to watch me shave?" he asked.

"No, you egomaniac," she teased. "You're not that cute. I'm waiting for the mirror."

"There are two mirrors in the bedroom, miss. And no

steam to fog them up." He kissed her nose, then rinsed his face.

A wave of melancholy caught Claire off guard. She brushed it away.

"Don't look so grim," Ian said, patting her head. "The mirror is yours."

He left to get dressed.

I'll be fine, she told herself, massaging lavender-scented moisturizer into her arms and legs. *I won't be alone, that's all. I'll fall asleep before he does. I won't be alone.*

She put on her makeup and opened the bathroom door.

"Do you want to take a walk before dinner?" Ian asked. "The town is lit up for Christmas."

"Sure," she said. "I'll be ready in a minute."

He checked his appearance in the oval mirror above the washstand. "I'm gonna go downstairs and ask the innkeeper about cross-country skiing tomorrow."

"Um . . ." Claire tried to keep an edge of sudden panic from her voice. "Wait for me."

"Claire, I'm hot. I want to go outside for a minute."

"Okay," she said quickly, embarrassed to be so needy. "I'll be down in a second."

He kissed her softly on the mouth. "Thanks for keeping me company in the shower."

"You're welcome." She squeezed Ian's hand and didn't even think about how he was almost never hot.

"I'll meet you downstairs," he said, and left.

Claire sank into the pink love seat in the bay window. She wouldn't think about it. A long time, seven years, had passed; she was a different person now, in a different place. Claire ran her tongue over the back of her teeth and breathed slowly. She'd sworn she would never return to Vermont.

She didn't want to think about why she had come back. It was smarter to avoid that kind of self-examination, no matter how insistently it shrieked to be heard. You didn't have to scream back. You simply had to ignore it, or shove it down.

The six-over-six glass panes on the other side of the

storm window rattled in the cold air. Claire shivered and got up to don what Ian called her "dress-up uniform": big black boots, black tights, a short black skirt and a sweater as green as the lady's lake. She checked her reflection in the window. The few tentative snowflakes had begun to increase their number.

They should have taken her car. But Ian had insisted four-wheel drive was unnecessary. He'd recently gotten a silver sports car that suggested local highlights and recognized your voice, and he'd wanted to test it out. Ian had grown up in Florida. He'd moved to Boston from New York City a year and a half ago.

Toby Cavanaugh, Claire's best friend since college, had introduced her to Ian last Christmas. At school she and Toby were inseparable, and even now Claire felt more comfortable with him than with almost anyone else. He was a successful photographer who'd made a name for himself with a controversial, outrageously sexy fragrance ad that catapulted a tiny cosmetics company, Nymphidia, into the big leagues. Toby had plucked Ian from the shoot of "Eminently Eligible in Boston," a popular annual cover article in *Back Bay* magazine and set him up with Claire.

It was snowing harder, thick enough to catch handfuls in the air. The squall shifted direction; then apparently deciding it liked where it was, shifted back. Claire leaned closer to the window. She let the cool air stream into her skin, then pressed her forehead hard onto the window, as if she could drink in clarity from the circle of wet cold on the glass.

Seven years and it still seemed like yesterday. What the hell was wrong with her? Why didn't she have any resistance? She never should have come here. It was a huge mistake. If she couldn't get away from the sense of *him* in Boston, where she had work to distract her and Toby to stop her, how the hell did she think she could escape the thundering heat of his presence here? Here, at the Black Hound Inn, not ten miles outside Dorset, she had seen him, smelled him, *slept with him*, for God's sake.

Claire heard distant screaming. Not now in this hotel room, but then. A sharp wave of panic spun in her chest. She turned around to see the doorknob twist.

"Hey," Ian said, opening the door. "What's taking you so long? I've been downstairs for fifteen minutes."

"Sorry," Claire said, jumping away from the window. "I couldn't decide what to wear."

Ian shook his head. His sleek brown hair swayed so rhythmically in response it might have chimed. "You only brought three outfits. And they're all the same."

"I know." Claire grabbed her coat and purse and smiled apologetically. "Let's go."

"I have a surprise for you," Ian whispered as they walked down the curved, carpeted staircase.

Claire laced her fingers through his, and squeezed his hand. "What?"

"We're not going for a walk," he said. "I changed the reservation." Ian grinned broadly in an apparent anticipation of Claire's reaction. "I called Toby," he announced as if this would explain everything.

He stopped in the middle of the stairs. "Did you know there's no cell phone coverage in Dorset? I had to use a credit card on the front desk phone."

"I know," Claire said. "They like it that way. Why did you call Toby?"

"For you." A mischievous grin sat strangely on his flawless face.

He led Claire down to the lobby.

"I wanted to know what your favorite place was when you lived up here." He leaned in and kissed Claire's forehead. "I'm proud of your taste. *Yankee* magazine raved about it."

Claire stepped away from him. She rubbed the back of her neck underneath her merino wool sweater and tried to dispel a creeping sensation of unraveling order. "Since when do you read *Yankee* magazine?" she asked. "And New Englanders don't *rave*, or have you never noticed our legendary reserve?"

7

"You're not reserved with me," Ian said, kissing her neck and curling his tongue softly around her earlobe. "But when you are, it's sexy."

Her heart pounded.

Thinking the fierce increase in her pulse rate was his doing, Ian hummed and opened his mouth on her throat. Claire concentrated on steadying her breath. She rested her hand on the curve of his hip.

He pulled her closer. "We're eating in a private suite at the Black Hound Inn," he whispered. "If we ever get around to dinner."

In an emotional echo of the shock that sits between the instant you see a terrible cut and the moment the pain hits you, Claire felt nothing.

Ian finished kissing her, then grabbed her waist and leaned back to assess her response. "Come on," he said. "They're expecting us in twenty minutes." He glanced at his watch.

Claire still couldn't feel anything. But the connection between the imagined blood on her hand and the real, approaching pain in her heart was rapidly knitting together.

"Come on," Ian purred soothingly, like he had a secret they both knew but never talked about. "It'll be fun."

Claire swayed where she stood. A tendril of heat danced inside her. The familiar brush of warmth swept away the panic squeezing her chest, making her feel solid and real. Ian looked strangely far away, as though she were seeing him through hundreds of glass doors, some thick and mottled. Claire breathed slowly and deeply, tasting the smoke in the air filling her mouth. She allowed the sense of *him* to wash through her like a drug.

How bad would it be to let go?

The heat spread rapidly to her fingers and settled in her mouth like a slow kiss. She welcomed the enveloping sensation of his mouth: his lips swelling inside her lips, his tongue whispering to hers, simultaneously inside of her and separate from her. It was a pleasurable sensation, so seductive Claire ignored the danger of losing the understanding of what was real.

Ian stepped closer and stroked Claire's cheek. "It will be fun." His voice was gentle and careful. "You trust me to know what's best for you, don't you?"

A piercing awareness that Ian knew something he couldn't know sounded a severe alarm in Claire's heart. She couldn't go back.

Memories she needed to burn drifted threateningly to the surface. Half in this moment with Ian in the vestibule of an old hotel, half in another moment long ago but everpresent, Claire straddled the narrow, ornate, carpet runner and chose.

Ian's eyes were kind and his arms were strong as he circled her slender shoulders. She had to feel safe. She had to choose refuge.

"Okay," she consented.

The kiss in Claire's mouth melted away. She didn't try to retrieve it.

Outside, the snow couldn't fall fast enough.

A steady rain fell outside the window of the alcove, which served as Harcourt Abernathy's study. His wife Kate's wedding ring lay on top of his desk. He turned the small silver band over in his broad palm, then flipped it onto the tip of his index finger. It was an old-fashioned poesy ring, a type popular during the fifteenth century. He'd had it made by a silversmith in London. An orpine he'd sketched for *Larkey's British Botany* had been expertly carved around the ring and the words, "Love is enough," were engraved inside.

Kate had adored it. The memory of her face when he proposed made it hard for him to breathe. How was it possible he would never see her face again? How was it possible Kate would never again whisper his name? Five months had passed since his wife's death, and Harcourt still could not believe it to be real. The moment of Kate's death replayed itself endlessly in his mind, each repetition wet and fresh, as if her death was only just occurring. And he relived the horror as if it was newborn.

The light scent from the open inkwell reached his nostrils. He squeezed the ring, then placed it back on the desk and began a letter to his sister Anna, who lived with her husband and three children some fifty miles outside Ledwyche in Warwickshire.

Ledwyche
14 April 1824

Dearest Anna,

I hope this letter finds you and your family happy and in health. I miss your presence more than I can say. I do not think I shall ever regard landscapes, or English painters, quite the same way now that Julia has shown me the terrible errors of all painters before our age. I am sure Mr. Constable would be gratified to know he has so devoted an admirer.

Having you—and Elizabeth too—in Ledwyche last autumn helped to make a trying time pass more easily than it might have. A renewed awareness of how much our small family means to me makes what I have to ask all the more difficult.

I have received a third correspondence from Mr. Nathaniel Pickney. He has once again entreated me to journey to America and to join him in the planning of a public garden in the city of Boston. I have decided to accept if you will consider taking Celia for the duration of my stay. Mr. Pickney assures me I shall not need to remain in America past the summer's end. He plans to continue his studies in Paris in September. I regret having to ask you or Lynmouth for any favor that may prove inconvenient even to the smallest degree.

Hopefully the weather shall be pleasanter in May than it has been this April. I cannot recall a season as hot and dry, save the strange summer of your fifteenth year when several trees in Nottingham Park lost all their leaves until the rains came. Do you remember? As for Ledwyche, we have rain today for the first time since the beginning of March.

I trust you and Lynmouth and the girls are well. How does Julia progress on the pianoforte? Has she mastered the Beethoven sonata? Is Rebecca still convinced a pirate's treasure lies buried near the well? Kiss them both and baby Mary for me.

You will be happy to learn Celia is much improved. On Kate's suggestion, she's begun drawing a book of alphabet letters for Mrs. Miller, who is teaching her son William to read.

Harcourt sucked repeatedly at insufficient air and clenched his jaw. The scream, which had reverberated in his head since the moment of Kate's death, strained like a demon to escape his mouth. The effortless tone he had affected for Anna's sake clawed at his insides. An impulse to destroy something shot up inside him. He dug his fingers into the seat of his chair until it subsided and he could breathe again.

He felt himself at the mercy of a wild, possessive grief. Anything, an innocent remark, the scent of wine, a thread of music, enraged him irrationally and instantaneously as if he'd been struck in the face by an invisible fist.

Nausea convulsed in his throat. He pressed the heel of his hand to his brow, closed his eyes and forced himself to exorcise Kate from his memory. She would not leave him. He stood up and began searching the bookshelf for the copy of John Lindley's *Rosarum Monographia* she had given him before they were married.

"Do you like it?" Kate asked. "It is Mr. Lindley's."
Harcourt made no reply.
"He was employed by Sir Joseph Banks," Kate said. "He worked in his library."

Harcourt kept his fingers pressed lightly to the book's marbled boards. "Yes," he said. "I know."

"I've written a verse from Milton's Arcades *on the title page," she said. "I hope you do not mind. My family has a habit of inscribing any book which is to be a gift."*

It seemed she was attempting to hide her fondness for him in an increasing rapidity of speech. Harcourt smiled to himself and kept his eyes on the inscription.

"The lines reminded me of the morning we spent together in the fritillary meadow," she said.

She directed her attention to the pattern of dappled sunlight on Dr. Cowpe's desk. "I hope I am not too bold to have given you a gift. You have been very kind to me."

Harcourt read the verse aloud:

> "O'er the smooth enameled green,
> Where no print of step hath been,
>> Follow me as I sing,
>> And touch the warbled string.
> Under the shady roof
> Of branching elm star proof,
>> Follow me;"

The scene drifted from his memory.

Later, after they were wed, Kate had confided that his voice was poetry itself to her. *Warm, low and endlessly varied as an unexpected brook in a dark forest*, she'd murmured in his ear before kissing him and sliding under his body in their bed.

Follow me, the poem begged. Follow me.

Harcourt closed his eyes. The rain slowed, changing the tenor of the air. He went back to his letter to his sister.

Celia has grown considerably more thoughtful and modest. She shall give you no trouble, at least not of the sort we might have expected in years past. She has been a greater comfort to me than I could have imagined, though she still lights up impossibly at the first measure of "Sir Roger de Coverley."

Write me with your answer as soon as it is convenient. Remember me to Lynmouth and my darling nieces.

Yours affectionately,
Harcourt

Harcourt picked up Kate's silver ring once more. For a mad moment he thought of swallowing it like a mythic creature who swallows a loved one to protect himself from harm.

The wind rattled the casement. He shut it tight.

It wasn't a matter of moving forward. It was a matter of not standing still, not rotting in place like a Narcissus transfixed by memory. Harcourt had entered a new world unwillingly five months ago, but there was no turning back. He had to learn how to walk and think and breathe again. He tucked the memory of Kate into himself like a promise or a secret, and if she breathed somewhere, somehow again, he'd breathe forever inside her.

Chapter Two

The snow lightened as Claire and Ian drove through the stone gateposts of the Black Hound Inn. The large white house was built in the soothingly symmetrical style of the Colonial period. Each twelve-over-twelve paned window glowed in merry, cinematic light.

The Black Hound was reputed to be prodigiously haunted, even for famously ghostly New England. Slamming doors, objects disappearing, footsteps and airy shadows were all to be expected during a stay at the two-hundred-year-old inn. Guests who never heard a moan or rattle or felt the chill of an unexplained presence left the venerable hotel disappointed.

The front door swung wide as Claire and Ian pulled up. Ian opened Claire's window.

"You'd better park near the barn," Mr. Moulton, the innkeeper, called out from the porch. "We're still putting sand down in the parking lot."

Ian waited for Claire to get out, then drove toward the gray barn.

God, Claire thought, staring at Mr. Moulton. Please don't say anything. Please pretend you don't know me. *Please.* Understanding flashed in the innkeeper's round eyes and he smiled amiably. Thank heaven, Claire thought.

"Welcome to the Black Hound," Mr. Moulton said warmly. His booming, friendly voice always made Claire think of spiced wine. "There's hot cider in the library. And Stephen will help you with your suitcases if you'd like." He held open the front door.

"We're only here for dinner," Claire said, avoiding his eyes as snowflakes blew down the neck of her sweater and melted on her skin.

Mr. Moulton glanced at the sky. "Where are you staying?" he asked, glancing dismissively toward the barn and Ian's little car.

"Dorset," Claire said.

"Well, you'd better eat quickly then," he said. "Once the snow starts in earnest you'll have a hard time getting back in that car. We have room, if you want to stay."

"We'll be fine, thanks," she said. "Hey," she called to Ian, who was walking up the snow-dusted brick path.

"Suit yourself, Miss Islington," the innkeeper said.

The name hit Claire's ear like a smack. Even though she didn't want Mr. Moulton to acknowledge her, she almost wept when he didn't call her by her first name. Why the hell was she always running away from the same thing she was running toward? She searched the muscles of her shoulders for a brave posture, nodded at Mr. Moulton and walked inside.

Mr. Moulton waited for Ian, then followed them both into the center hall.

Ian shook the snow off his hair and shoes and handed their coats to the coat check woman. "Did you know this place is supposed to be haunted?" he said to Claire. "A guy outside told me he stayed here when he was a kid and he lost a pack of baseball cards. When he checked in this afternoon those exact cards were on the nightstand. *And no one put them there. Spoooooky,*" Ian wailed like a Halloween bowl that howls when you take a piece of candy.

Claire smiled, but her teeth were chattering. Had Ian heard Mr. Moulton call her by name? He hadn't given any indication that he had. Claire knew Mr. Moulton wouldn't tell Ian anything about what had happened, but panic about being here was starting to line her throat like a virus. "This must be the hostess," she said, half-successfully pretending her heart wasn't slamming against her rib cage. She grabbed Ian's arm.

A young woman with an I'd-rather-be-anywhere-than-here expression walked over and gestured to the wide staircase. The three of them climbed up to the suite. The pretty hostess seemed bored by Ian's baseball card story and monster noises. She listened politely until he was finished, then lowered her voice to gossip about celebrity couples who had eaten—and more—in the intimate rooms.

Claire stood in the open doorway and avoided looking at the fire blazing in the fireplace. *No, no, no,* she thought. *I can't walk into this room. I can't breathe this air.* The bed had been moved to a place nearer the window and the piano was gone, but otherwise everything was virtually the same as it had been seven years ago. Claire breathed slowly. She tensed every muscle to subdue the anxiety clawing at her chest. "Damn! I forgot my purse. Give me the keys, hon. I'll go get it."

"You don't need your purse," Ian said, flushing at the hostess, whose semi-scandalous tale Claire had interrupted.

"I know," she said. "I mean, I do. My hand lotion's in there and my hands are dry already from the heat in the car. I'll feel better if I have it."

Ian had a don't-go-crazy-on-me look in his hazel eyes, which turned greener whenever he felt embarrassed or threatened. "Fine," he said curtly. "I'll get it."

"No," Claire said. "You parked the car and you're all dry.

I'll get it. Besides, Florida boy," she cooed, caressing his chest, "you can't take this weather."

Ian raised an eyebrow, but his eyes mellowed. "I should go outside without my shirt on for that. But it's so snowy and I just bought these shoes." He gave her the keys and grinned.

"I'll be back in a sec," Claire said. She nearly tripped trying not to run down the stairs.

She panted as she ran for the car, grateful for the cold air chilling her nose and mouth. She should just get it over with and tell Ian, she told herself as frigid air bit her ears and made her eyes water. He'd understand. That was what he was good at. Right? That was what she loved about him. Why she'd chosen him. She would tell him. Something bad, something very bad, had happened to her here seven years ago. Coming tonight brought it all back.

The cold burned Claire's cheeks. Her breath puffed like cotton candy out of her mouth. She stopped running. Why the hell had Ian brought her here? Toby never would have told him what happened. And he never would have recommended coming to the Black Hound. So what the hell was going on?

Claire closed her eyes and pressed the heels of her hands into them. More than anything she wanted to go home, drink an enormous cup of coffee with a serious shot of Bailey's and hide under a blanket until none of it seemed real anymore. If she screwed up this relationship with Ian, Toby would never take her seriously again.

She was babbling. Internally. Not a good sign.

Claire unlocked the car and the weird voice greeted her: *"Hello, Dr. Gilbertson."*

Why was it so grating that Ian had programmed his car to greet him as Dr. Gilbertson? Hadn't he earned the right to be called doctor? Claire grabbed her big Dooney and Burke bag and told herself to shut up. *Stop thinking. Close that door in your head until you're home. It's not safe here.*

She walked slowly back to the inn, concentrating on the crunch of her boots on the gravel driveway. She stopped at the foot of the broad, gray porch steps. Maybe coming here was a good thing. Maybe being back after seven years would finally convince her of the truth: She'd had an emotional breakdown brought on by the shock of her beloved grandfather's death, and by loneliness, and being young and alone in a strange town. Maybe she'd never be able to fully commit to Ian until she accepted that it—that *he*—a hard, hot flush in her hands, mouth and heart, had been nothing but a hallucination of something she thought she desperately needed.

Snow fell on Claire's face and melted on her cheeks. Despite her vow not to, she looked up at the window of the suite. No one looked back at her.

Not that anyone would have.

She was weak. Weak and stupid. And in danger—again—of losing herself. She cursed under her breath.

"Claire!" Ian called out from the porch. He took off his sweater and ran down to her.

"What the hell are you doing?" he asked. "It's freezing."

Ian draped his clove-colored cashmere over her shoulders. "What's wrong with you?"

Claire shivered. "I don't know," she stammered, "why Toby would have told you I wanted to come to this place." She bit down on her lip to stop her teeth from chattering.

"Claire," Ian said softly, "come inside."

"I had a kind of bad experience here a long time ago," she said.

"I know," he answered.

He crossed his arms over his thin shirt. "The whole thing was Toby's idea. Vermont. This inn. You know I hate the cold. At least on the Cape it was only supposed to rain this weekend. We could have gone out to dinner and seen a movie. There's nothing to do here." He shuddered. "Come on. We can talk inside."

18

"Wait. What?" Claire grabbed his arm. "What do you mean he told you?"

"I called Toby to tell him how things were going and he suggested we eat at the Black Hound Inn," Ian said. "He didn't tell me what happened to you here. Only that coming here with me would help you move past whatever it was." Ian stamped his feet to stay warm.

Claire didn't feel the cold anymore, which was obviously considerable because Ian began vigorously rubbing his arms. "Toby *told* you to take me here? Because it would be *good* for me? And you didn't ask me? You didn't ask me what happened? Why I never wanted to come back? Am I some kind of rescue project for you?"

"Claire," he said. "Stop it. It's freezing. Come inside." He turned and stomped up the stairs to shake the snow from his shoes.

"Wait a minute," she said.

"No, Claire. I'm going in. I wasn't trying to upset you. I only listened to Toby because you, unmistakably, value his opinion over everyone else's. Let's go."

She trudged up the wooden stairs, snow falling down her neck.

"Wait!" Claire whispered hoarsely once they were inside the crowded lobby. She felt her eyes flash. "Don't be angry with me for being upset when you and Toby have been acting like some nineteenth-century duo deciding what's best for someone too delicate to know her own mind! You should have asked me. You should have talked with me first."

"You could have told me," Ian snapped back. "You knew we were coming up here. You could have said no." He turned away, an expression of disgust darkening his features.

Claire swore silently at herself for being self-destructive. Ian was the best thing that had ever happened to her. She fought against a sudden sense that a snake undulated furiously inside her spine. *I'm not giving in. I can't do this again.*

"You're right," she said. "I should have told you." Claire pressed her tongue to the back of her teeth and steeled herself against the serpent now biting at her heart. "I'm sorry."

She'd apologized and Ian softened. He wasn't angry anymore. Spent feelings slid off him like shedded skin. Thank God, Claire thought, beginning to calm down, ready to close herself up in his arms. *Why can't I just let it go?*

Ian took her gently by the shoulders. "You have to know I trusted Toby because you do. You have no idea how often you defer to him or talk about him."

Claire stood frozen, the roar of the huge furnace vibrating beneath her feet.

"You do, honey," he said, brushing the snow off his sweater, still draped over her. "We can go back to Boston if you want."

A waiter carrying a tray with champagne and two glasses walked upstairs. Claire watched him knock at a room near the top of the hall. A young man in a thick, white hotel bathrobe opened the door and let him in.

I'm not going to destroy this relationship, she told herself.

Ian wrapped his hands around Claire's waist and pulled her against him.

Claire laid her cheek on Ian's chest for a minute. All she needed was time to breathe.

I'm an idiot, she thought and stepped back.

"We don't have to go," Claire said firmly, forcing a genuine smile to her lips. "By the time we'd get back every place would be booked, and I want you to have a good dinner."

A puppyish grin warmed Ian's handsome face. The hostess who had dismissed his ghost story checked him out before going into the kitchen. Claire waited for the round window doors to swing shut.

"But I don't want to eat upstairs in that suite," she said. "Let's wait for a table down here. Okay?"

Ian exhaled but smiled again. "Okay."

FOLLOW ME

Twenty minutes later they were seated. The table was practically in the doorway to the lobby, but they had a good view of the fire.

"I'm getting the pheasant." Ian closed his menu and looked happily at Claire.

"I'm gonna have the pappardelle," Claire said. "But can I please have a bite of your mushrooms?"

Ian winced.

"You can put it on my plate," she said. "I promise my fork won't be anywhere near your food."

"Why don't you just get the pheasant yourself," he said quietly.

"I don't like pheasant," she said. "And I read a review that raved about *heavenly roasted chanterelles*."

"I thought New Englanders didn't rave about anything." Ian grinned, but Claire heard irritation in his voice.

"I guess the critic made an exception for these particular mushrooms," she said.

Ian turned sullenly to the fire.

"Okay," Claire said. "I'm sorry. I know you hate to share food. I won't push you."

He smiled weakly and drank his wine.

Claire leaned back and watched a couple in their eighties who were sitting next to each other in a banquette against the wall. The woman, whose lovely face and bright blue eyes still held traces of her youth, gently touched her companion's arm and whispered something. The man smiled softly and patted her hand. Claire turned to Ian. He was engrossed by a young couple arguing over whether to send back an overdone steak and didn't see Claire.

She nudged his arm. "Did you see the dessert at that table?"

"Claire," Ian said, abruptly pulling his arm away. "You don't have to worry. I'm not going to make you tell me whatever happened here."

Claire didn't say anything, but she knew if she wanted to commit to Ian she'd have to tell him someday. It wasn't the kind of thing anyone would want to find out after it was too late. She must have worn her distress nakedly on her face, because Ian took her hand and clasped it gently.

"I'm sorry I didn't talk to you first," he said.

As cliché as it sounded, Claire knew at least three women who would experience spontaneous orgasm if the men they dated apologized or admitted they were wrong. She needed a kick in the head.

Ian ate his food in order: first the pheasant, then the cranberry relish and finally the chanterelles, one of which he surreptitiously placed on the rim of Claire's plate when she was watching the snow fall. He ate like a pleased little boy in a nursery rhyme who has gotten just what he wanted for supper.

"You haven't touched your wine," he said, eating his last bite of mushroom and laying his fork neatly on the plate.

"Well, I thought I'd drive back," Claire said. "You can drink."

"Babe," he murmured. "I'm really sorry. I had no idea you'd be so upset."

But he didn't ask her what had happened. Not that she would have told him the whole story if he had asked, but why didn't he want to know? She'd want to know.

You're a spoiled and ungrateful girl. The voice of Mrs. Norrison, the woman who had cared for Claire the summer her grandfather went to Oxford, hissed in her ear. It was a dismal, cranky season for both Claire and Mrs. Norrison. No one had ever called her spoiled. Lovingly raised by her grandfather after her parents died in a car accident when she was a baby, she'd never experienced dislike from an adult before. She'd begun to worry then that she was spoiled. She was certain of it now.

Ian was good and kind. Handsome. Smart. Sexy. A doctor, for God's sake. He was a poster boy for eligibility. And Claire loved him. He made everything simple and uncomplicated. He made her feel safe. This was going okay, she said to herself. Wasn't it? No one who looked old enough to have been at the inn seven years ago seemed to recognize Claire. Or if they did, they didn't care. And she felt nothing. No mouth in her mouth. No hands in her hands. She felt nothing that would make anyone's hair stand on end or their hearts open and then break. Maybe, as usual, Toby was right. Maybe coming here with Ian would finally be the thing to drive away the demons of the past so she could have a future.

"I wanted to ask you something," Ian said, breaking into Claire's thoughts. He was sitting up straighter than he had been a minute ago, and an impenetrable expression of confidence gelled on his delicately chiseled face.

Claire felt a thick sense of déjà vu.

"How would you feel about taking our relationship to the next level?" he asked.

"You mean living together?" Claire asked, pushing the remainder of her pasta to the side of her plate.

"No." Ian didn't look apprehensive, just pleased and sure of Claire's answer.

"Really?" she asked, stopping him before he had a chance to respond. "Six months ago you didn't know if you wanted to stay together at all."

"I know." Ian, smiled with a certainty that flirted with arrogance.

"I've done a lot of thinking since then, Claire, and . . ." He stopped and beamed at her. "We *work* together. We give each other enough room and enough attention. We have a great sex life. We almost never fight. No one needs anything else."

A sudden ruckus upstairs caught the attention of the other diners near the door, and they glanced up to see what was going on. Ian kept his eyes on Claire, concerned with nothing but their conversation. His intense focus was part of what made him such a successful surgeon. You couldn't distract him.

"I'm a slob," Claire said.

"I thought about that," he said. "We'll have a room in the house just for you. You could put anything in there we don't need but you want to save. It would be your sanctuary of clutter."

Claire said nothing.

"Or we could think of something else. All I'm saying is—" Ian grabbed her hand with a virility that usually preceded vigorous sex. "This feels right to me. I know it feels right to you."

She didn't know what to do but smile ridiculously.

Ian relaxed his grip, then took both her hands lightly in his. "I know what you need, Claire. I'll stay out of your way when you want to be alone. I'll be there when you want me. And I'll never ask for anything you can't give."

Claire began to feel dizzy and disconnected, as if she'd drunk enough wine to spend the next day puking, her head heavy on a cold tile floor.

Two waitresses hurried down from the disturbance upstairs. One of them looked briefly back, then both disappeared into the kitchen. A heavy bang of roughly moved furniture followed their exit.

"I know what you give me, Ian," she said. "But what do I give you?" Claire almost never called Ian by his name. It sounded ill-fitting in her mouth. "What do you need from me?"

Ian leaned back and glanced upstairs at the loud crash of something falling. "I love you, Claire."

She wanted to scream. *Why? Why me?* When it seemed in her heart of hearts she fit an image of what Ian thought he wanted, a girl who needed to be taken care of and sheltered from the world, a fragile girl who spoke Latin and Greek but couldn't find her way around Boston even before the Big Dig. She would have asked him, but at that moment a wooden side chair flew over the railing and broke in half on the lobby floor.

"What the . . . !" Ian jumped out of his seat and ran to the lobby.

Claire turned herself off, stuffing her head with dreamt-of white noise. The moment took on the unreal, slow motion of a car accident where you become an out-of-body spectator because you cannot possibly be a participant. She needed something to hold on to, but nothing seemed corporeal. *Turn around,* she thought. *See if* he's *there.*

No, she said to herself through clenched teeth. *I won't. I can't go there. I can't be there. If he is there, I can't see him. Not here. Not now. Not ever.*

The noise dissipated and real time flashed back solid and unmistakable. Claire's hands were freezing. She tried to massage some feeling back into them. In two days they'd be home and she'd say yes. Of course she'd say yes.

Claire's heart pounded so violently, her hand shook when she picked up her wineglass. She put it down without drinking any. She couldn't think straight in this place. On the way home she'd tell Ian what had happened and then say yes when they were in bed. She hadn't had any caffeine since early this morning, and now she had such a craving for coffee she felt like a drug addict.

A waitress in her fifties squeezed past. Claire tried to grab her attention and ask for coffee, but the woman either didn't hear her or ignored her, and inched closer to the doorway to get a better view of what was going on.

"This is nothing compared to what happened six or seven years ago," the woman said to the younger waitress who followed her.

"A girl went crazy upstairs," she said. "She locked herself in the suite and wouldn't come out. She tried to set herself on fire. She screamed and screamed and screamed. I don't know how she didn't burn to death. I told Mr. Moulton we should bring a priest or shut the room off. But he said no. He said the ghosts are part of what keeps people coming and always have been. If once in a while somebody doesn't like it, or if one of the ghosts gets mad, it'll soon be all right again. Crazy old man. He sometimes drinks with them, you know. Sits in that room upstairs with a brandy and talks to the air."

Claire saw the girl shudder and then heard her whisper, "I'm quitting."

Claire's pulse pounded hard in her ears until she couldn't hear anything but the rushing sound of her own blood. The slow motion returned. She sliced at it.

Ian came back and sat down heavily.

"What happened?" Claire asked, fighting to stay present.

Ian took a hard gulp of wine. "Some guy found his girl-friend in bed with someone else and freaked out. Where's the waitress?" Ian searched the room frantically, as if dessert was essential to restoring his sense of equilibrium.

"Did anyone get hurt?" Claire asked. She breathed slowly and kept her teeth closed together.

"No," Ian said. "Thank God."

He couldn't catch anyone's eye and gave up. "But you wouldn't believe the way people are talking," he said. "They're disappointed it wasn't a ghost, actually complaining about it. As if betrayal was mundane."

The green in Ian's eyes flickered. "What are you doing sitting here?"

"I don't know." Claire wanted to throw up or run away, to shove her face into the snow until she couldn't feel anything.

Ian's eyes did not soften.

"Listen," she said, anchoring herself to this chair, this moment. The slow motion began creeping back. "I want to think about what you said."

"Why?" Ian barked.

"I just don't think we're ready," she said. "And I don't want to ruin things by—"

"You'll never be ready." Ian stood up. "I'm getting the check."

"Wait!" she said.

Ian spun around. The green in his eyes flashed like a slammed door. "What!"

Claire didn't retreat. "It's not fair," she said quietly. "You're not giving me a chance—"

"A chance! A chance for what? A chance to wake up one day and say, *'Oh yeah, he was a good guy. I should have snapped him up when I had him.'* I'm sorry, Claire, but I'm better than that. I've put a lot into this relationship and I deserve something more in return than, *'I'm afraid we'll ruin it by making a real commitment.'* That's *bullshit* and I'm sick of it!"

Ian wended his way roughly through the crowd in the lobby to get their coats.

Claire breathed deeply and rubbed the back of her neck. Toby's voice rang in her ear.

You don't want to be free of your obsessions, Claire. You cling absurdly to them, like security blankets, long after they cease to be useful, if they ever were. And you'll never be free to be anything else until you accept this and let it go.

Claire couldn't breathe. They never should have come. She knew something like this would happen. Why hadn't she said something? Why didn't she just say no? Did she really want to relive the horror of that night? What the hell was wrong with her? She had to make a decision. She had to choose: stay scared and stuck in a seductive dream or be brave and have a real life.

"I am not avoiding commitment," Claire said, still seated when Ian came back. "I just don't want to be impulsive about—"

"Impulsive? We've been dating for almost a year, for God's sake. Do you know how many women would kill to be in your shoes, Claire? I am everything every woman says she wants. I'm successful. I'm sensitive. I apologize when I'm wrong. I listen. I'm reasonably good-looking."

As stressed as she was, Claire couldn't help smiling slightly.

"Don't patronize me," he snapped. "And don't fucking smile at me when I'm angry." Ian sat down and folded their coats on his lap.

27

"I'm sorry," Claire said. She gestured to a waitress. "Two regular coffees, please."

She turned to Ian. "Do you want dessert?"

"No. Yes. Apple pandowdy," he said to the waitress, who took the order and left.

Claire gave Ian a few minutes to calm down. She stirred cream and sugar into the coffee that had come blissfully quickly.

"I'm not asking for a lot of time," she said. "But I don't want to say yes just because you asked me."

"I didn't realize merely posing the question made saying yes so abhorrent." Humiliation, like tiny emerald chips, flashed in his eyes.

"That's not what I meant and you know it," she said. "I want to say yes—and you should want me to—because it's the right decision for both of us. Neither one of us is built for divorce, Ian. I want to be sure."

"I *am* sure," he said coldly.

"Okay," she said and turned away.

The pastry came. Ian ate deliberately and silently.

The crowd in the lobby broke apart and drifted into the rest of the hotel. Claire turned to watch. She overheard Mr. Moulton talking to the chair thrower about the police. He laid his huge hand on the young man's shoulder and leaned in closer. Mr. Moulton saw Claire watching him and smiled at her.

No, Claire thought, *no. I can't think about that. I can't think about him, or you, or anything else that happened that night. I can't. I can't.*

Mr. Moulton nodded almost imperceptibly and returned his attention to the man under his hand.

I can't, Claire thought decisively. *I won't. I'm not that person anymore.*

Ian finished the last of the fruit and crust. He turned a penetrating gaze on Claire.

Claire took a long breath.

"This is not the way," she said, trying to hide a gigantic

clot of uneasiness with a mollifying tone. "Or the place I want to remember as where you proposed."

"Well, it's too late for that, isn't it?" Bitterness pierced Ian's mellifluous voice, but self-assurance overpowered it. He shot Claire an intense glance, as if everything between them depended upon her understanding what he wanted. And he was not going to ask for it.

Claire shifted her body to face the fire, which flickered so merrily, for an absurd moment she expected to see a night-capped grandfather reading from an oversized book, children spilling off his lap and a sleeping Newfoundland dog at his feet. She drew in a deep breath and held her wineglass in both hands.

Ian waited.

She began. "When I was twenty-three," she said, "I tried to kill myself in that suite upstairs."

Ian paled, clearly not expecting anything like this.

"The police came," she said dispassionately, separating herself from the memory. "I spent six months in a hospital. Then I moved back to Boston." She swallowed half the glass of Bordeaux.

"Claire," Ian said. "Oh, my God. I'm so sorry." He grabbed her hand and stroked it urgently, as if he could erase everything bad in the world. "I'm so sorry. I didn't know. You can't believe I would have taken you here if I had known. You have to believe that."

"I know," she said.

Letting her hand rest in his, Claire put up a wall to block everything that had happened that night: the fire, the screaming and every sensation and conversation leading up to it. A thick wall, which nothing, no memory, no heat, no kiss, no connection could pass through. Claire sealed up her soul and her spine. She locked the great stone teeth together and waited for the terminal bang.

Distractedly, she searched Ian's face, his beautifully shaped features—like a poet's—for a sense of herself apart from his conviction that he would always know what she wanted, what she needed, what was best for her.

Ian leaned over and kissed her hands, then both her eyes. He smelled innocent and untried.

"I'm sorry I didn't tell you before," Claire said flatly. "I just didn't know how."

"Shhhhh," he soothed. "We don't have to talk about it."

The check came.

Claire pulled her chair closer to his and buried her face in his shoulder, pressing her eyes to his hard muscle. Ian wrapped his arm around Claire and held her while he signed his credit card slip.

"Baby," he murmured as he slipped the pen into the plastic sleeve. "It's okay. Let's go home."

Chapter Three

Harcourt Abernathy dipped his pen into the ink bottle and began a letter to his seventeen-year-old sister Celia.

Black Hound Inn, Vermont
31 July 1824

My dear Celia,

I am writing from a delightful inn near Mr. Pickney's brother's home in Dorset, Vermont, where I shall stay for the remainder of my American adventure. My rooms are spacious and comfortable and offer a pleasant view of the avenue and the road beyond. The estimable innkeeper, Mr. Moulton, has a voice like mulled wine, and the mysterious air of a man with a tragically romantic past. The inn boasts delicious wild game and excellent claret, of which you know I am exceedingly fond. The wild beauty of Vermont's landscape surpasses its charmingly descriptive name.

Mr. Pickney and I have failed, for now, to persuade the authorities of the usefulness of a public garden (to say nothing of the essential utility of Beauty), but I remain convinced of the merit of the plan and hope, for Mr. Pickney's sake in particular, that it succeeds eventually. Mr. Pickney is keenly disappointed, although he tries not to show it.

I am afraid I may disappoint you, my dear Celia, for I find I am not up to the task of describing the latest fashions, as displayed by American ladies, in a manner which might meet with your exacting standards. However, in anticipation of what I can only imagine will be your immediate inquiry upon receipt of this sad confession, I will answer that American women, as of this date, must content themselves with the *Ladies* magazine. There is no American periodical for fashionable ladies as far as I can tell.

I do not wish to entirely disappoint you in your rather fervent appetite for all things American, and thus I have sketched a young lady of Mr. Pickney's acquaintance. She is dressed in a gown, which her mother assured me is positively the latest fashion, in a shade of green I felt might become you. The original I made as a gift to her mother, but I am sending you a copy in watercolor so you will be able to appreciate the gown.

Anna has written to tell me Mr. Edward Stackpoole has come to Everdon more than thrice to call upon you.

Harcourt returned the pen to the inkstand and walked to the window. Outside on the lawn, two boys played roughly with a patient Newfoundland dog. Harcourt pressed his forehead to the cool glass pane.

He couldn't bear the thought of Celia marrying yet. He wanted everything to be the same when he came home. He wanted time to stand still. Still enough that he could reach into the fabric and pull Kate back to him. A knock at his chamber door freed him from having to follow this weak-minded thought any farther.

"Abernathy!" Nathaniel Pickney's lilting cadence rang from the hall.

Harcourt opened the door.

"Good morning," Pickney chimed. "I hope you'll forgive the intrusion, but a cousin of mine, Robert Southey—like the poet, no relation—has expressed a fervent desire to meet you."

"Is he interested in the plans for the public garden?" Harcourt asked.

Pickney's face darkened momentarily. "Not at all, I'm afraid. He's a physician. When I mentioned your name in reference to the garden he asked if you were the same Harcourt Abernathy who illustrated an English monograph on putrid pox."

As if a hand had closed instantly and crushingly about his throat, Harcourt struggled for a moment to breathe, then managed a neutral expression before speaking. "I am he."

Pickney's ruddy face brightened. "Splendid. For the past few months Southey's been corresponding with the author of the monograph, and he would like very much to discuss it with you."

Panic like a poisonous vapor rose inside Harcourt. "Is Mr. Southey here now?" he asked.

"Yes," Pickney answered. "I am afraid you English are right about the brash enthusiasm of the American. When I told him of our acquaintance, Southey was quite eager to meet you. He's waiting in the parlor now. Will you come?"

"Of course," Harcourt said brightly, gathering the armor of civility about himself. "I shall finish my letter later. I've run out of tales with which to amuse my sister, at any rate."

Harcourt turned his back to Pickney and walked slowly to the desk. With a shaking hand he closed the ink bottle and slipped the unfinished letter into a leather case.

He turned to face Pickney and smiled. "Done."

Pickney held open the door. "The family of the young woman Southey hopes to marry lives in Dorset."

33

The men walked down the stairs to a broad center hall and into a large parlor with a cold fireplace.

In a frozen moment in which the air seemed corporeal, solid enough to bite into like a joint of meat, Harcourt spied the monograph opened to the illustration of a pock-marked torso.

"Southey," Pickney said, "meet my friend, Mr. Harcourt Abernathy."

Whatever pleasantries transpired, Harcourt was cognizant of nothing but a rapidly unraveling sense of order within himself. While Pickney and Southey chatted, he held to a fixed expression of pleased interest. Tales of Cowpe's correspondence and the contents of the monograph passed through his consciousness like hot thread through a cold needle. Southey leaned closer to where Harcourt sat near the empty fireplace and turned the open book so the illustration faced its artist directly.

"I am curious about a colleague of Dr. Cowpe's," Southey said, "who is referred to obliquely but with an unmistakable measure of delicacy and intimacy, as if the colleague was a woman. If I did not know Cowpe's devotion to his wife and family, I would suspect him of forming an attachment to a brilliant female physician, if such a person were commonplace."

Harcourt smiled, though his heart pounded so violently he had to clench his teeth to keep them from chattering. "I dealt exclusively with Dr. Cowpe," he said calmly. "I am unacquainted with any of his colleagues." He turned toward the hearth and swallowed the scent of long-dead fires. "The perithisis monograph was my sole venture into medical illustration. I am primarily a botanical illustrator." He returned his gaze to the two men, then glanced beyond to the hall, where Mr. Moulton stood speaking to a serving girl. "Ah, there is the innkeeper."

Harcourt rose to take his leave. "He has promised to show me his wine cellar."

Pickney and Southey stood up.

"It was a pleasure speaking with you, Mr. Southey," Harcourt said. "Pickney, I shall join you for dinner. Good day, gentlemen."

As he walked across the nearly empty parlor, Harcourt was seized by a pervasive sense he was swimming across a wild ocean and the innkeeper was a life vessel. Ridiculous, he said to himself, never taking his eyes off Mr. Moulton's black waistcoat and rough muslin shirt. The brief expanse between the parlor doorway and the hall where Mr. Moulton stood seemed to extend itself to the point of impassability, though it was shorter than the distance between the front door of his house in Ledwyche and the street.

Unrequited, *unrequitable* longing to see Kate, to smell her, to hear her voice, captured him utterly and stopped him where he stood. Was he to go mad in a foreign country? Was he to lose all sense, all sense of self, in an orgy of grief that would not abate? What weakness made him insensible to the order of things? Everything dies. Why could he not accept it?

The innkeeper, who had stolen upon him without his notice, laid a hand on Harcourt's shoulder. The heat from the man's broad palm seeped into him like a calming drug.

"Mr. Abernathy," Mr. Moulton said. "Come with me."

"Come with me, Claire," Ian urged, hurrying her out of the hotel the next morning. He'd checked them out earlier. Neither of them had slept much the night before.

The road out of Dorset was slippery. Ian said almost nothing. He kept his hands closed tightly around the black leather steering wheel, occasionally flashing Claire a concerned glance. She answered with an I'm-okay smile before turning back to watch the bare, brown trees fly past the car window.

"Deer," Claire warned.

"I see," Ian snapped back, his voice taut with concentration.

"There are usually more, so slow down," Claire added.

Ian slowed the car. It fishtailed a bit. Two more deer darted across the road.

"Do you want me to drive?" Claire asked, knowing she risked him pissed off with injured pride.

"No."

When it was clear no more deer were coming, Ian slowly accelerated.

They spent the next few hours in near silence. Ian hated the radio, and he hadn't put any of his CDs in the car yet. The snow on the ground thinned as they got closer to Boston. Broad brown swaths of dead grass and mud lined the highway. Claire glanced down at the empty space around her feet on the immaculate gray floor mat, then closed her eyes. *Damn*. She sighed and turned to Ian, a little apprehensive about breaking his moody silence.

"What," he said as soon as he felt her eyes on him.

"I forgot my purse," she said.

He cursed quietly. "Where?"

"Not in Dorset," she said. "At the . . ." Claire clenched her teeth, irritated by her trepidation. "Where we ate."

"We'll have to call," Ian said, resignation making him sound older than he was.

"Don't call now," Claire said, touching his hand. "There still might be icy patches."

"I don't have to use the cell," he said in the same tight voice he'd had since they awoke. He pushed a series of buttons and the speakerphone came on.

"City and state, please."

"Where was it?" he asked Claire. "Never mind. Dorset, Vermont."

"It's not in Dorset," Claire said.

"Shhhh!"

"What listing?"

"The Black Hound Inn."

The phone connected him.

"Black Hound Inn, Mr. Moulton speaking."

"Good morning, this is Dr. Ian Gilbertson. My fiancée

and I ate at the inn last evening and she left her purse behind. Has anyone turned in or found a caramel-colored leather Dooney and Burke bag?"

"Hello, Dr. Gilbertson. How is Miss Islington?"

"She's fine, thank you," Ian said brusquely. "Has anyone turned in the bag?"

"Yes, I have it in my office. Someone turned it in last night after you left, and I thought it too late to call. When I tried your hotel this morning you and Miss Islington had already left. I'll send it to her right away—excuse me, there's something I must attend to."

Mr. Moulton hung up.

"He didn't ask for your address," Ian said, shaking his head and pushing redial. "Shit. Now we have no coverage." He exhaled heavily and shifted in his seat. "Maybe he'll look in your wallet."

"I don't think so," Claire said. "I'll call when we get back."

"Listen," Ian said. "I have a lot of paperwork to catch up on. I don't want to stay up late tonight."

"Fine," Claire said. "Why are you telling me?"

Ian opened and closed his fingers on the steering wheel and didn't say anything.

"I don't have to sleep over," Claire said, realizing what he meant. "Toby has a key to my apartment."

"But you don't have any money," Ian said. "Or credit cards. Or ID. Or your bank card. And it's Sunday. What are you going to do for food?" The muscles around Ian's mouth tightened. "I wish you would think, Claire."

"Toby has a copy of everything in my purse," Claire said quietly.

"What?" Ian asked.

Shame crept through Claire. She set her teeth and breathed deeply.

"After the hospital and all the medication I had some memory loss," she said. "I kept forgetting things."

Claire watched Ian's long fingers rhythmically clasping and releasing the steering wheel.

"Toby has a key to my apartment," she said. "He also has a bank card and a copy of my license—so I have the number if I need it. I don't have any credit cards."

"Toby has your bank card?" Ian said. "He doesn't have your PIN number? Does he?"

Embarrassment heated Claire's skin. She slipped her fingers beneath her jacket collar and rubbed the back of her neck. Six months ago, in a moment of supremely foolish let's-always-be-totally-honest-with-one-another cuddling, Claire told Ian she and Toby had slept together once. She'd said it to highlight how much better things were between the two of them; that she and Toby were best friends, but she and Ian were lovers and lucky to be so happy. Ian didn't see it that way and walked out. They'd almost broken up. He was still hypersensitive about her relationship with Toby.

"Yes," Claire said quietly. "I forgot it a few times. He's on my account."

"Toby's on your bank account?"

"His name's not on my checks, but yes."

"I don't believe it." Ian shook his hair out of his face.

You don't understand, Claire thought. *I needed help. Toby helped me.*

"Toby doesn't need any money, Ian," she said.

"Yeah, but you don't need . . ." Ian stopped himself and clenched his teeth.

Claire saw his jaw muscle flex.

"How often do you lose your keys?" he asked.

Often, she thought. Probably eight or ten times last year. "Once in a while."

"I don't know what to say," Ian said.

He pulled off the Mass Pike onto Huntington. "Fine. I'll drop you off at Toby's apartment." Ian held his hand tentatively above the horn while a fat white Lexus slowly climbed to the speed limit. "Shouldn't you call him at least, to make sure he's home?" Vexation tainted his beautiful voice.

Claire picked up Ian's cell phone and dialed Toby's number.

The girl de jour answered. Claire explained the situation and asked if she could stop by to pick up her keys.

"Are you Claire?" The girl's voice was thick with sleep.

I told you who I was when you answered the phone, Claire thought, irritated by Toby's taste in women. He chose with his dick.

"Yes," Claire said.

"You already told me," the girl slurred. "Sorry. I just woke up. Toby's not here."

"I know," Claire said slowly. "I don't need to talk to him. I just need my keys."

"Oh. Okay."

Have long have you been modeling? Claire thought bitchily.

"I'm sorry I sound so spacey. I found out yesterday I passed the Bar. My sister Miranda and Toby and I stayed out way too late. I drank more than I drank in three years of law school." The girl exhaled heavily.

Claire closed her eyes, bit her lip and vowed not to be so judgmental.

"I found your keys," the girl said. "I'll leave the door open. The keys are in the silver bowl on the front hall table. I'm going back to bed or to the bathroom floor. It was nice to talk to you. Lock the door behind you."

Early the next morning Claire woke to the sound of her name stuck in someone's throat. Frightened, she sat up and listened.

Nothing. A dream. She rubbed the muscles of her neck and waited for the ache of *his* presence to drain out of her. She concentrated on the high-pitched shush of Ian's shower and got out of bed. Claire shook her hands and feet and pulled on an old white robe. She knew Ian had slept over because he felt guilty, but she was grateful he had. After being back in Vermont she didn't trust herself not to fall into useless, unrequitable longing when she was alone.

And now, apparently, she was thinking in made-up words. *Unrequitable.* Great. Pretty soon she'd forget all pretense of sanity and talk to the air.

She stumbled into the kitchen and started the coffee. Someday she'd get a French press to extract the optimum flavor, but until then she'd have to be content with exceeding the recommended number of ground tablespoons and heating the mugs.

She set the table with herb-colored, rough fabric placemats from Pottery Barn and thought idly of a boy she'd known in grade school. He'd made the mistake of confiding a fear of napkins, more a terror than a fear from the panic in his voice.

I'm afraid they'll get stuck in my mouth and suck up all my spit and I won't be able to breathe.

Along with the others at the lunch table, Claire had stared for a moment before throwing wadded napkins at the boy, who left the cafeteria. Later, when she was home and her grandfather was in his study with the door closed, Claire stuffed paper napkins into the hollows of her cheeks and under her tongue, and held them there until her mouth was dry as cloth.

Ian came into the kitchen and placed his phone on the counter next to his apartment keys. He kissed Claire on the head. "What's up with you?" he said. "You look a million miles away."

Any guilt stemming from the events of the weekend had apparently vanished from Ian's consciousness, as if what was past had never existed.

Embarrassed and annoyed, Claire smiled artificially. "I was just thinking of this kid I knew when I was little."

"First love?" Ian teased. He poured himself a cup of coffee and vanilla soy milk, then sat next to Claire. He smelled of soap and shaving cream and the hair around his ears was still damp.

"No," Claire said. She closed her hands together and rubbed the carved orpine on the antique silver ring she always wore.

"Well, what were you thinking about?" Ian asked, unfolding the *Globe* onto the table."

"It's silly," Claire said, letting go of the ring and lacing her fingers together. "Stupid, really. He was terrified of napkins."

Ian looked up from the headline. "What?"

"He was afraid they were going to get stuck in his mouth," she said.

"That *is* stupid."

Claire knew Ian had no tolerance for weakness he didn't understand, but it pissed her off anyway.

He opened the paper to finish the article he must have started after he went running earlier that morning.

"I know," Claire said. She stared out of the kitchen door through the living room to the white brick building across the street. What kind of person is as frightened of a ludicrous idea as he is of an actual threat? she thought.

"Your thinking is so tangential," Ian said after he finished his coffee and the paper. "I'll be home late tonight. Call me if you're not too tired from work."

"Okay," she said in a weird little voice that sounded appallingly like a kitten's. "Have a good day." She lifted her face to him. Ian smiled possessively and obliged her with a chaste kiss.

He left. The door smacked shut behind him.

Claire heard him say good morning to her downstairs neighbor, Mrs. Nathan, before he headed for the T. She thought again of the little boy—arms around his half-closed lunch box, determinedly fleeing the flurry of napkin balls—but she was still in the kitchen, her kitchen, of her apartment. Memory, even benign and toothless, did not transport. But she knew that. She did.

She got up to clear the table.

I wonder what he meant by tangential.

41

The vacuous nature of her question scalded Claire's ears, but it was easier this way. Vapid was preferable to crazy. Wasn't it?

Claire turned too quickly and smashed her knee on the sharp corner of a chair. She swore under her breath and switched on the radio to a station with an insipid boy/girl DJ duo and ear-piercing music. She wanted a bass to pound in her chest or an adolescent wail to drown out her thoughts. Nothing but inane chatter about CONTESTS and CASH! She murmured a second profanity and turned the radio off.

It was going to get easier. If she could just hold out a little longer, try harder to forget, he, or the memory of him, would fade and die off.

"Fuck!"

Claire screamed the only word in English that had blood in it, the only word with life and weight and scent. She was still screaming when Mrs. Nathan knocked on the door to see if everything was all right. Claire snapped to attention as if she had a spring in her head.

"I'm fine, Mrs. Nathan," she said roughly, her throat scratched from screaming so loudly. "I just broke something. A vase."

Mrs. Nathan had a voice like a nosy neighbor on a forty-year-old sitcom, but she had big eyes and full lips and walked like she'd had an orgasm every adult day of her sixty-something years. "Are you sure?" she asked.

"Yes," Claire said. "I'm fine. I'm sorry."

Mrs. Nathan waited. "Well," she said. "Next time whisper it like everyone else."

"Sorry," Claire said.

The word and the rebellion tied to it cleared Claire's head. She did the dishes, drank more coffee, then took a long shower.

She was dressed, but her hair was still damp when she called Toby's studio. She squeezed the wet ends in a towel. It had been six years since she'd cut her waist-length hair, but she still occasionally reached for it.

Toby's phone rang repeatedly.

I'm going to be coolheaded, Claire told herself. *I'm not going to be bitchy or preemptively aggressive.* Preemptively. That wasn't a word either.

Damn. Why was he taking so long to pick up the phone? After four cups of coffee and a steaming shower Claire didn't feel any less on edge. *"Like cures like,"* she'd told Toby once when he sarcastically questioned her practice of calming down with a stimulant. *"It's the philosophy of homeopathic medicine."*

"Ah," he'd said. *"Self medicating, are we? Always a good idea. Do you ever think you're wrong, Claire?"*

"Hello." Toby answered the phone.

"What the *hell* were you thinking!" she said.

So much for coolheadedness.

"Welcome back, Claire."

Toby sounded pissed rather than contrite. They were off to a flying start.

"I'm serious, Toby," she said. "Really. What the hell were you thinking, telling Ian to take me there? What am I anyway, the number-one patient at the Toby Cavanaugh Hospital for Unstable Women?"

"What are you talking about?" Toby asked. He muffled the receiver while he talked to someone at the studio. "Just a minute, Claire. Let me take this in my office."

She heard a door close.

"What are you talking about, Claire?" he asked again in an even voice. "Take you where?"

A lump thickened in Claire's throat. She held her mouth shut to stop her lips from trembling. It was one thing to go behind her back to try to help her, however misguided the attempt. It was something else altogether to lie to her face about it.

"Don't you dare lie to me, Toby," she said, too upset to care that her voice was shaking. "Not about this."

Toby sighed heavily. He had to be sick of this sort of thing. She knew she was.

43

"Don't lie to me," Claire repeated.

"I don't know what you're talking about, Claire," he said slowly.

She bit her cheek until she tasted blood. Fine. If that was how he wanted to play it, she'd play along.

"The Black Hound Inn," she said. "Are you satisfied? You got me to say it. Did you think saying it out loud would make it all go away?"

Toby was silent.

Claire held her tongue and waited.

"Ian took you to the Black Hound?" he asked quietly.

Claire heard Toby's long fingers rake through his thick hair. She listened to him pace the floor of his office and waited, trying to figure out what was going on.

Toby cursed quietly, then put the phone back to his mouth.

"Are you okay, Claire? Why didn't you call me? I thought you went to the Cape."

Claire leaned back and laid her head against the white kitchen wall. She felt dizzy and grabbed the lip of the counter to steady herself. Fractured images of a dark, wood-paneled room and a bloodied man on the floor swam in her head. Claire shut her eyes and opened her mouth wide enough for an ocean of air to pass through. He started inside her, blossoming like a flame from the center of her soul to fill her with his body. It wasn't enough. Claire closed her eyes tighter until stars disappeared and blackness hummed in her ears. She reached for the rough wool of his coat and smelled the scent of wood fire in his hair. He wrapped his strong arms around her and held her away from the betrayal and the lie.

He whispered something in her ear, but Claire couldn't understand what he said. His words came faster, doubling and tripling over themselves like radio stations crossing over one another. Claire held tighter. She clung to him, but he was pulled away.

She opened her eyes and gasped. *Too close,* she thought, *way too close.*

"Claire!" Toby said, alarm in his voice. "Take a breath. Breathe slowly. I'll be right over."

"No," Claire said. "It's okay. I'm okay."

"I'm coming over," Toby insisted.

Claire sucked in a mouthful of air and looked at the clock on the stove. Fewer than three minutes had passed since she called Toby; what had felt like a lifetime had not been more than a few seconds.

"I'm okay," she said. "Really. I just thought—"

She shook her damp hair, opened a bottle of water and drank from it.

"Ian said he called you and you told him to take me there," she said. "Because it would be good for me." Claire took another drink of the water.

Toby cursed again. This time she heard it clearly.

"How could you have thought I would *ever* do anything like that?" he asked, hurt in his voice. "I'm the one they called to meet you in the hospital. Remember? I'm the one who took you home. Why would I ever send you back there when I saw what I saw?"

"I'm sorry," Claire said. "I know. But how did Ian know anything about it if you didn't tell him?"

"I didn't tell him anything," Toby said. He paused again.

Claire drained the water.

"Before you left for what I thought was the Cape, Ian called to tell me he was going to propose," Toby said. "He wanted my advice on a romantic place to do it. He remembered me talking about the Reluctant Panther in Manchester, how sexy it was, how great the food was. I told him Vermont would be a bad choice. I told him you'd lived in Dorset and had had a bad experience there. He pressed me for the story."

"What did you say?" Claire asked.

"I didn't know what to say. If I didn't say anything, he

45

might ask you," Toby said. "And I didn't want that. I told him you had a bad breakup in Vermont."

"How did he know about the Black Hound?" Claire asked.

"I don't know."

They both were quiet. Claire knew Toby still wanted to come over.

"I'm okay, Toby," she said. "Really."

He didn't say anything.

"I'll come to the studio later," Claire said, "and you can see for yourself. All right?"

"Okay."

"I've got to get to the store," she said. "It's got to be almost ten."

Toby waited for a second. "Call me when you get there."

The suffocating irony of needing someone to be there for you and then resenting the invasive attention infuriated Claire. She breathed deeply and pushed it away.

"I'll call you," she said without a trace of impatience. "I promise."

"Okay," he said.

"I'm fine, Toby," she said. "Really I am."

"Okay," he answered, sounding at last as if he believed her.

Claire glanced at the clock on the stove. "It *is* almost ten. I've got to run."

Toby hesitated.

Let me go, Claire thought.

He said good-bye and hung up.

Claire threw on her coat and gloves and ran downstairs. *God, I hope no one's waiting,* she thought as she ran up Beacon Street toward Charles.

Chapter Four

Claire owned a flower store called Arcades. She had named it after a Milton poem of the same name. Her favorite verse, which ended with the lovely plea "follow me," was inscribed on the frontispiece of a botany book that had belonged to her grandfather. *Rosarum Monographia* was a lush antique history of roses. Claire had spent hours as a child leafing through the hand-colored illustrations and fantasizing about roses and gardens.

She turned onto Charles Street and saw Ian standing outside her store. She walked faster.

Ian glanced down at his watch, then smiled at Claire.

"You're late," he said, kissing her head. He stood back while Claire unlocked the door. "A package came from FedEx," he added.

Claire struggled with the lock and tried to catch her breath.

"I signed for it," he said, leaning against the building. "It's from Vermont, if you can believe it, but I don't think it could be your—."

Claire snapped her head up from the door and faced him.

"What?" Ian pushed the door open, strode inside and flipped on the lights.

Claire stood in the doorway.

He laid the package on the counter and turned around.

"What?" he said again, sounding annoyed this time.

"Nothing," she said. Claire clenched her teeth and shut the door behind her. "What are you doing here?"

"I had two cancellations this morning," he said, smiling, "so I thought I'd go get you a coffee and surprise you."

"Where's the coffee?" Claire asked.

"I saw you weren't in yet so I decided to wait." The slenderest threads of guilt flashed in the green speckles of Ian's eyes.

Claire didn't know what to say. Or, more truthfully, she didn't want to talk about it, any of it, the lies, the fire, the half confession, Ian's passive-aggressive proposal. She had to keep treading water until she was separated from all of it and could think rationally.

"I took a long shower," she said curtly, pulling off her honey-colored leather gloves. "I lost track of time."

Claire was stunned to see confidence light Ian's face once more.

He grinned at her. "Let's open the package. I can't believe it got here so fast." As he spoke, Ian pulled a silver pen knife from his jacket pocket and sliced open the clear plastic tape.

"I can open it," Claire said, still standing a few feet from the door.

"Why is it so heavy?" Ian asked, taking her purse out of the box.

Claire drew her fingers together inside her coat sleeves and rubbed her thumb over the silver ring on her right hand. She watched Ian unlock the clasp and open her bag.

"What the hell is this?" he asked, pulling out what looked like a very old book. He held it gingerly by a single corner, as if the book or its contents might contaminate him in some way.

"What is this?" he repeated. Disgust curled his lip as he opened it. "What is that creepy old man sending you, Claire?"

Claire swallowed an overwhelming impulse to grab the book, but she said nothing, still frozen to the spot where she stood near the door.

Ian flipped roughly through the pages.

Claire bit her tongue.

"It's a monograph," Ian said with a mixture of disbelief and disdain in his voice. "On measles or something. No. Perithisis." He gazed up at Claire again. "Why would he send you an old medical book on an eradicated disease?"

She didn't reply. Ian's eyes narrowed, as if she'd done something she shouldn't have.

Claire avoided his gaze and stared in out-of-place concentration at a basket of silk fumitory. Her feet started to feel hot, as if the store sat above an enormous furnace. Heat rose up her legs and spread through her chest and arms. She felt suddenly, weirdly substantial. It wasn't erotic or protective. It didn't feel like someone else at all. But there was definitely someone, or something, inside Claire, and it made her feel solid and present.

"I talked with Toby this morning," Claire said, the strange sense of power replacing her nearly perpetual urge to apologize whenever she and Ian were together.

"And?" Ian asked, keeping his long fingers wrapped around the book's tattered binding.

Claire crossed to him. The floor creaked under her. She took the book from his hands. "You can't treat me like a baby, Ian."

He stiffened and stood up straighter. "What are you talking about?"

"You know what I'm talking about," she said. "The Black Hound. How did you find out?"

He exhaled, deflated a bit, then stared into the refrigerated case. "It was a lucky guess. I read about Vermont inns online and picked the one I thought you would have liked the most."

Claire didn't say anything. The air in the room stilled.

Ian stared angrily back at her. "You could have told me! I don't know why you keep secrets from me, Claire. I don't know why I try to help you." He moved past her and stomped toward the door. "Get your own damn coffee."

"Ian!" Claire said, following him.

"I'll call you later," he shouted and slammed the door.

The stringed bells clanged. Claire closed her hand around the vibrating brass and held it.

Shit, she thought, then remembered the monograph on the counter. She'd never seen it before. Why would Mr. Moulton send it to her? She sat behind the cash register and slid a framed daffodil print out of the way. She opened the book on the cool green Formica. A letter fell out onto the floor. She picked it up. The paper was lovely and the handwriting elegant and precise as calligraphy.

Dear Miss Islington,

I hope this letter finds you well. The monograph was left behind after your last visit to the inn, and since then I have been uncertain about whether, or how, to return it to you. When I saw you alight from the car last evening I hoped for an opportunity to return the monograph to you in person, but you seemed uneasy about renewing our friendship and I have no wish to bring you any further pain.

I remain your servant,
Martin Moulton

Miss Islington, Claire noted bitterly. She re-read the letter, then dropped it on the counter. The heavy paper clicked lightly on the cool green surface.

Mr. Moulton had not come to see her in the hospital after the fire, or if he had Toby never told her about it. After she got out she was initially too hurt and angry to call Mr. Moulton, and later she was too embarrassed. Maybe he was embarrassed as well, and that's why he hadn't tried to contact her since the fire. He had been in the room the night before. He'd spoken with the man whose memory haunted her now.

In the hospital Claire had begun to question whether Mr. Moulton really had seen him, or if, like the rest of what happened except for the fire, she had only wished he had. That night Mr. Moulton had looked like himself but somehow not himself, as in the unquestioned reality of a dream until daylight makes none of it seem possible.

She had always secretly wished Mr. Moulton would one day come to her rescue and say, *yes, it did really happen.* If he did; *if he said yes, there was someone in that room with you . . .* Claire bit her lip. Her pathetic desire frayed at the edges. She saw the words fall from the sentence, dissolving in the air. *I am such a fool,* she thought. *Ian totally pissed me off. And later on Toby is going to hover like a nursemaid.* She couldn't breathe.

The rest of the day crawled like the minute hand on a geometry class clock. She could hardly keep her eyes open. It was just two weeks before the official Thanksgiving and Christmas holiday rush, and hardly a single customer had walked in all day. Even for I'm-sorry-I-slept-with-someone-else apology roses. Maybe everyone was home cocooning in preparation for the stress of the upcoming season.

Claire re-read Mr. Moulton's letter and skimmed the monograph again, hoping to recognize something in it. She hadn't seen it before; she knew that. It wasn't there the night *he* came into her room as she put out an ember that had leapt onto the hearthrug—

Stop it, Claire said to herself. *Stop it. Dwelling on it only makes things worse.*

He waited below the surface of her weakening resistance. She held him off and hated herself for it. But letting him in, letting him swell inside her, letting herself acknowledge his presence only painfully reminded her of what she couldn't have.

He licked the back of her teeth and Claire felt his lips buzz in hers.

But that was all it could ever be. If she wanted to, she could lock the door and lie on the couch in the back of the store and let him breathe inside of her. She could close her eyes and open herself to the sense of him warm and heavy on top of her, and hard and hot inside her. But she couldn't see him, couldn't touch him with her eyes open, couldn't hear his voice if she tried to listen. So what was the point? Almost Everything was not the same as Something.

Claire shivered even though the radiator was hissing madly in the corner. She had to figure out how to let him go. And when she did, she had to find the strength to go through with it.

She glanced up at the glass door. A man peered in, then walked by. Claire stood up and walked around. She flipped through the pages of the monograph again, stopping at a passage describing the early symptoms of putrid pox. She loved vernacular names for diseases: bloody jack, dropsy, putrid throat. The voice of the writer describing the sudden change in behavior of an unidentified old man made Claire's heart beat faster. She brushed her hair behind her ear and sat down on the needlepoint-covered chair.

A wash of dream-memories Claire hadn't thought of since childhood came back vivid and intense. A beautiful house with a lawn that stretched out to a thick wood. Lovely clothes. Playing hide-and-seek with a cousin who tore his pants and cut his bottom. The boy hid in the garden until dark, afraid to tell anyone he'd ruined his clothes. Claire thought of a sister, and their soft blue box for hiding secrets. She remembered spacious rooms filled with books bound in smooth leather, lined neatly in fat rows on heavy shelves.

Claire snapped the monograph shut and choked on the resulting cloud of dust. She panicked perversely for a moment, thinking Mr. Moulton had become a drug dealer in his old age and sprinkled a hallucinogen in the pages. *Great,* she said to herself, still choking on the dust in her throat; *now I can add paranoia to my expanding list of mental afflictions.*

Claire walked to the fake mantel over her shop's unusable fireplace and turned the antique white ormolu clock so she could see its face. Almost four. This day was at a standstill.

Ian hadn't called back. Though he had been the one to storm off, and she hadn't done anything, he was probably still pissed.

The clock chimed. An ache of emptiness cracked open inside Claire. She shook her head and grabbed a water bottle from the tiny fridge beneath the countertop. She drained the water and ran her hand over the back of her neck. A familiar sickening panic squeezed her chest and throat. Was she blacking out again? *Was* there something in the dust of the book? Hadn't she read something in one of those *Worst Case Scenario* books about hallucinogenic mold spores in old books?

Get a grip on yourself, she thought, standing up and sucking in a cleansing breath. She'd known Mr. Moulton since she was a baby. He was a good guy, compassionate and kind. He'd even tried to help the man who threw the chair over the balcony that night with Ian. She had seen Mr. Moulton in the lobby, talking to the man, laying his bearlike hand on the distressed lover's shoulder. She glanced at the monograph, still open on the end of the counter.

Why had he sent it to her?

And what was she supposed to do with it?

Mr. Moulton left Harcourt in the center hall of the Black Hound and went into the parlor. He spoke briefly with Pickney and Southey before he returned. He led Harcourt to an alcove and motioned for him to sit on a red velvet sofa in a wide bay window, which overlooked a small garden. Harcourt sat.

"Forgive me, Mr. Moulton," Harcourt said. "I did not mean to give the impression I required anything of you other than a means to extricate myself from an uncomfortable position."

The innkeeper smiled and clapped a hand on Harcourt's shoulder. "I brought you the book," he said, holding the monograph for Harcourt to take. "I explained your situation to Pickney and his kinsman. They each regret causing you any uneasiness."

Mr. Moulton seemed to take no notice of what had to be an expression of shock on Harcourt's face. "You should have told them," the innkeeper said gently. "They are good men." He patted Harcourt's broad shoulder.

Conflicting emotions heated the skin of Harcourt's face. In order to avoid any unanswerable questions from Mr. Moulton, he turned to the window and stared at the meadow beyond the garden.

"Take the monograph, Mr. Abernathy. It will help." The innkeeper laid the monograph in Harcourt's hand, smiled again, bowed slightly and left the room.

Harcourt leaned against the wall and exhaled heavily. How Mr. Moulton knew about Kate or what he thought he knew about her seemed irrelevant. He didn't want to think. He couldn't feel anything but desperation to rid himself of every emotion. Harcourt eyed the meadow, now empty of children, with its path to the wood beyond. He rose from the sofa, taking the monograph with him, and walked outside.

He needed air and movement. Out of doors he could think and breathe. He left the walled garden of the Black Hound Inn and crossed the meadow leading to the wood. Trees clustered at the edge. Harcourt plunged into the lush green forest, glad of the dark. Kate's voice pulled gently at his ears and filled his mouth. He climbed over twisted tree roots and stones half-buried in the soft ground, but he could not run away from her. Memories of the day he'd seen Kate for the first time, blew through his heart like notes in a pipe. He couldn't hold on to them and he couldn't escape.

One year earlier, on the sixth of May, Harcourt Abernathy strode toward the village of Ledwyche in the throes of a black mood he couldn't have shaken off even if he'd wanted to, which he decidedly did not. The exercise of the morning had done nothing to ease his restlessness, and a compulsion to run until his legs gave way still gripped him. He cursed himself for feeling more like a sixteen-year-old boy than a man of twenty-eight.

The entrance to the village appeared over the hill sooner than he wished to see it. From the village gate he saw Dr. Thomas Cowpe charging up Beckwith Street at twice the speed of any other passersby. Unfit for pleasant conversation, Harcourt watched with dread as his good friend approached.

"Abernathy!" Cowpe said, almost pouncing upon him. "Are those the sketches? May I see them?"

"What? Now? On the street?" Harcourt asked, his jaw tight. He had the illustrations in his valise, along with sketches he'd made in the meadow that morning, but he had no desire to pull them out here.

"Mr. Ishingham is almost come," Cowpe said.

"The coach from Warwickshire is not due until half past three," Harcourt reminded his friend. He placed his hand at Cowpe's back and attempted to usher the man down the street.

Cowpe would not be moved.

Harcourt dropped his hand. "Surely we may permit ourselves the luxury of walking the short distance to your office."

"I do not wish to be caught unaware if the coach is early or ahead of schedule," Cowpe said.

"Four hours ahead of schedule?" Harcourt said incredulously. "Cowpe, calm yourself. These are preliminary sketches, at any rate. Mr. Ishingham will most certainly have his own ideas about the monograph and what should be illustrated."

"Please," Cowpe nearly begged.

Harcourt sighed and shook his head. "Very well." He handed Cowpe the twenty or so drawings.

Cowpe exhaled, and then beamed approvingly as he turned the leaves depicting cross-section diagrams of healthy and diseased lung tissue and the distinctive red skin lesions, that characterized putrid pox. "Excellent," he said, smiling. "What did you use as a model?"

"I have the works of Vesalius and Morgagni in my library."

Cowpe shot Harcourt a quizzical glance. Harcourt knew Cowpe wondered that he should have a library at all in a house so small.

"An inheritance," he said tersely.

"These are very fine," Cowpe said. "Precisely what I expected."

Harcourt smiled ruefully to himself, despite his foul temper. If Cowpe had been so certain of his abilities, there would have been no cause to prove it before the physician arrived.

Cowpe's housekeeper ran up the dusty street.

"Dr. Cowpe," she said breathlessly. "Mrs. Cowpe has had me looking for you for three quarters of an hour. Not five minutes after you left this morning, a lady came to call—a Miss Ishingham."

"Miss?" Cowpe drew back abruptly, as though a vial of smelling salts had cracked in half under his nose. "Surely you mean *Mr.* Ishingham."

The woman screwed her lips together and chewed briefly on the bottom one. On a good day she had little tendency toward mirth, and a running hunt for Dr. Cowpe on a hot May morning was not the start of a good day. "Begging your pardon, sir, but I think I can tell a miss from a mister. She is a miss, and a lady to boot, sir. Mrs. Pegler told me she arrived last night by private carriage with a very proud lady's maid beside her. She has been waiting in your office since half past nine."

Harcourt smiled at the housekeeper and kept his eyes fixed on hers. Small and ripe, she looked like a vibrant actress permanently miscast in a lifeless role.

"Good morning to you, Mr. Abernathy," she said in a very pretty voice and fixed a lock of hair that had escaped her bonnet. "If you don't need me, Dr. Cowpe," she said, returning her attention to her employer. "Mrs. Cowpe will be wanting me. Jenny, the housemaid, is ill. Again. And we are short of hands."

"Of course," Cowpe said. "Thank you. You may return home."

She walked back toward the Cowpes', albeit at a gentler pace than she'd left it.

"*Miss* Ishingham?" Cowpe repeated. "Do you suppose her to be Mr. Ishingham's sister? Or perhaps his daughter? But who would send a lady in his place?"

Harcourt had a sudden, visceral conviction that Miss Ishingham was neither sister nor daughter, but he dismissed it as a consequence of his mood.

"I cannot say who Miss Ishingham might be, but it seems you must hurry to your visitor, Cowpe, and I to Miss Abernathy. My sister Celia is, I think, still abed. She is mourning the absent affection of some village swain whose name she will not for her life divulge to me."

"I had intended you to meet with Mr. Ishingham as soon as he arrived," Cowpe said.

"But it is not Mr. Ishingham who waits for you," Harcourt snapped. He needed physical companionship of a kind he was unlikely to find satisfactorily in Ledwyche. He took a moment to calm himself, then said, "Forgive me. Of course I shall accompany you."

Chapter Five

As they made their way to Cowpe's office, Harcourt regretted trampling on his friend's good nature. He was striving to think of how to set things right when he remembered a Miss Ishingham he'd met in London a few years earlier.

"Ishingham," Harcourt said, as they stood at the open doorway of Cowpe's office. "I knew the name sounded familiar, but I couldn't place it. I painted a portrait of a Miss Ishingham in London. Lovely girl. Lovely. Lydia Ishingham."

They entered the office to wait for Cowpe's guest.

"There were two Miss Ishinghams I was to paint," he said. "Katherine was the name of the other. But she demurred, refused actually, to have her portrait done. It seemed to vex her mother, but it made me like the thought of her. It was she I envisioned when I painted her sister. Katherine Ishingham. Might she be the same?"

"It's Kate," a bright female voice said, startling him. "I do not care for Katherine. I cannot help but be reminded of poor Catharine, the overfond wife of Henry VIII who dressed in yellow and danced all night upon the news of her death. I much prefer Shakespeare's Kate. Before she was tamed, of course."

Harcourt turned, and Miss Ishingham fixed her gray eyes on his. She had clear, creamy skin flushed with pink; glossy brown hair and lovely, if not quite beautiful, features. The intelligence and passion in her gaze reached inside him and awakened a part of Harcourt he'd thought was dead. For a long moment he was conscious of nothing but a ferocious desire to kiss her.

"I am Dr. Cowpe," Cowpe said calmly. "And this is Mr. Abernathy." Cowpe stood apart from Miss Ishingham and seemed to regard her with the kind of caution one observes when in the proximity of a wild beast.

Painfully aware he was caught in a trap of sensation divorced from reason, Harcourt swallowed Miss Ishingham's scent: lavender, spring air and some indefinable fragrance that reached to the core of his body. He smiled and extended his hand.

"Mr. Abernathy," she said. "I am happy to meet you."

"Miss Ishingham." Harcourt shook himself imperceptibly, he hoped, and recaptured his composure. "You are then the same Miss Ishingham who refused to allow me to paint her portrait? Were you pleased with your sister's?"

Miss Ishingham's face colored and she glanced away from him, to the doorway.

"Your portrait is among my family's most beloved possessions," she said quietly, returning her attention to him.

Before he could inquire after her sister, Miss Ishingham gazed intently at him, pleading for something he could not identify. Harcourt held back his inquiry and turned to Cowpe, who seemed unable to believe that in the place of his Warwickshire physician stood a woman.

"Would you like to sit down?" Harcourt offered Miss Ishingham after a moment of silence. He guided her to the chair nearest the light from the window.

"Thank you," she said.

"Dr. Cowpe," Harcourt went on after the doctor still hesitated to address his guest, "Miss Ishingham has traveled a great many miles to speak with you, and I am certain she is anxious to begin. I shall not intrude any longer. Good day to you. A pleasure to have met you, Miss Ishingham."

"Wait." Cowpe bore the expression of one awakened from a drunken stupor by a pail of water.

Harcourt stood half in sunlight, his fingers on the cold doorknob. He waited for Cowpe to indicate what he wanted. An uncomfortable silence lingered.

"Dr. Cowpe," Harcourt said, "Miss Ishingham waits. If there is something you require of me, ask it now or allow me to take my leave."

"Stay," Cowpe commanded.

Harcourt felt his eyes flash. He clutched the door.

"Please," Cowpe begged.

"Do not leave on my account, Mr. Abernathy," Miss Ishingham said. "You are welcome to hear what I am come to say. Perhaps Dr. Cowpe requires your assistance."

Cowpe turned before her words vanished from the air. His lip quivered and he seemed prepared to address Miss Ishingham in anger. Harcourt felt obliged to remain if only to look out for her, though she seemed a young woman more than capable of looking out for herself.

"You'll forgive me, Miss Ishingham," Cowpe said, "if I am too forward, but the coincidence is so striking I cannot help but question." He pulled a chair from behind the desk and sat closer to her.

The sun shone on Miss Ishingham's neck, and Harcourt saw pink splotches of protest dot her skin. She held tightly to the book on her lap. He moved to stand between her and the window; blocking the heat of the sun. She relaxed, and softened her grip on the book.

"I am expecting, as we sit, a Mr. Ishingham of Warwickshire," Cowpe said. "Are you in any way connected to him?" Cowpe leaned in and waited. "Are you acquainted with a physician called Ishingham?"

Harcourt stepped closer: near enough to smell that her hair was scented with orange blossom water, and to see that she did not shrink at all from Cowpe's threatening posture. Miss Ishingham drew in a deep breath, which seemed to surround her with a sense of renewed purpose. Harcourt began to worry that Celia was right, that he had been alone too long. Desire he could taste began to cloud his thinking. Miss Ishingham relieved him of his reverie.

"I am K. Ishingham," she said.

Dr. Cowpe leapt back as if from a fire.

"It was never my intention to deceive you—" Miss Ishingham said.

"But you have," Cowpe protested hotly. He rose suddenly from his chair and paced the room, as if searching for anything with which to occupy his hands. "I'm of a mind to demand your instant departure!"

"I shall leave as soon as you wish, Dr. Cowpe," Miss Ishingham said quietly, remaining in her seat. "But your letters revealed a man of boundless curiosity. I ask that you remember the spirit of our correspondence and hear what I am come to say."

"The 'spirit of our correspondence,' Miss Ishingham, was predicated on the—foolhardy as I am now most painfully aware—presumption that we two were equal."

Without the interference of the sun, the pink spots returned to Miss Ishingham's pale neck. She shifted forward as if to rise but leaned back suddenly. "Was there anything in my theory as I described it to you that indicated we were not?" she asked defiantly.

Cowpe paled, then flushed. "Do you mean to insult me, Miss Ishingham?"

"I might ask you the same question."

Cowpe turned sharply and clasped his hands together behind his back.

"Forgive me," Miss Ishingham said, her voice drained of anger. "It is not my intention to insult you, nor was it my intention to deceive you into believing I was someone whom

61

I could not be." She slid her hands beneath the book. "I had not expected you to return my letter with so much sympathy."

She drew closer to Dr. Cowpe. "When I realized what might be accomplished—in spite of the exceptional situation—I could not refuse your request for help. Please, hear what I have to say, and I shall abide by whatever you wish."

"How did you come to this?" Cowpe pleaded. "How did you come to write me? What brings a woman here?"

Miss Ishingham turned away from Cowpe and kept her gaze to the floor.

If she raised her head but a little her eyes would meet his, Harcourt thought. For a reason he could neither fathom nor dismiss he had the sense she desired something from him, approval or understanding, before answering Cowpe's question. What could he do when he did not know what she wanted or why she had come?

He knew what he wanted, and it was not as simple as a comfortable night in a woman's bed. Harcourt desired something he could not speak of, something that haunted his dreams and made him long to run until he could hardly walk. He stepped nearer to Miss Ishingham's chair and breathed deeply and slowly. If he was free to desire, surely she could explain what she wanted and why she had come.

Miss Ishingham breathed in the end of Harcourt's exhalation and raised her head. The idea of his breath in her mouth stirred him more intensely, and more physically obviously, than he was prepared to reveal in Cowpe's office. With effort, Harcourt filled his head with visions of uneaten breakfasts and dying flowers. The danger passed. He fought not to think of anything of his in her mouth.

Miss Ishingham turned to Dr. Cowpe.

"Since childhood," she said, "I have been possessed by a desire for knowledge—specifically, knowledge of the workings of anatomy and disease. My father, who is himself a physician, encouraged my curiosity and permitted me to sit with him as he did his research. Gradually my quiet company grew to an engaged companionship. Eventually he became my teacher and I his pupil. In time, he allowed me to research on my own and work with him in a kind of partnership."

Cowpe started visibly.

Miss Ishingham hesitated. When Cowpe did not interject, she continued, "Last spring, after a period of uncharacteristic mirth, Mr. Standish perished of perithisis. When I saw the same strange joviality manifest itself in others who later developed the disease, I suspected an early indicator and wrote to you."

"But Miss Ishingham," Cowpe said gently, "surely you cannot have expected your"—he struggled for a moment—"your sex to have gone unnoticed by me or by anyone else." He gestured to Harcourt, who remained behind her.

"I have not forgotten Mr. Abernathy," she said, swiftly running her fingers over the back of her neck.

For Harcourt it was as if she had touched him, and the reaction he had been fighting a moment earlier ignored the breakfast and the flowers and screamed internally for attention. He took in a mouthful of air as quietly as he was able and shifted his position. The imagined breakfast on the table kept transforming into a woman on a bed, surrounded by bowls of strawberries and cream. Harcourt concentrated on the pockmarked surface of the whitewashed walls and willed himself not to think of her.

"Though I allowed you to assume I was a man, the established aim between us is unchanged," Miss Ishingham said. "I ask you to read my research and reconsider your offer to me. My father has written a letter delineating his reasons for permitting me to come and work with you."

"Miss Ishingham," Cowpe said, visibly struggling to keep hold to a gentleness in his tone and in his manner. "Your revelation and your proposal are so far afield of my expectation of the nature of this meeting that I must confess I am at a loss. I cannot, under any circumstance, consider my request to engage you in partnership. You were wrong to have written me. Wrong to have come, no matter what the possibilities for good."

Harcourt watched Miss Ishingham spread her hands on the dull brown cover of her book. She rose to her feet.

Dr. Cowpe waited far too long before rising with her.

"May I see your notebook, Miss Ishingham?" Harcourt asked, immensely relieved not to hear any hint of desire in his voice.

"Please, Abernathy," Cowpe said in a slightly strained voice. "Do not indulge Miss Ishingham's hopes. They are misguided."

"I am merely curious," Harcourt explained. "She did, after all, move you initially." He opened the book and examined pages filled with a neat, sure hand. He had never told Cowpe, but he had been engaged to illustrate a physician's monograph on another occasion. It ended badly, and without pay for months of work. It seemed the doctor had used another man's research and claimed it as his own. It was his poor and mistaken interpretation of the information that gave him up. Even without a thorough knowledge of medicine, Harcourt could see Miss Ishingham did not suffer the same fate. He closed the book.

Miss Ishingham did not shrink or retreat. Rather, she seemed to stand taller and more powerfully in the room, as though she would not apologize for intelligence or foolish courage. Harcourt's pulse beat in pleasurable discomfort in every part of his body, his mouth, his hands, the hard muscles of his stomach.

"You do yourself a disservice, Cowpe," he said. "At the very least, curiosity shall plague you, rendering your company unfit for I cannot say how long. So you shall do me a disservice as well by refusing."

Harcourt saw from the corner of his eye Miss Ishingham smile almost imperceptibly. That small gesture echoed fiercely within him. For a moment he lost his place in a study of her gently pretty countenance. He held out the notebook for Cowpe. After hesitating briefly, Cowpe took it.

"Mr. Abernathy is a better man than I, Miss Ishingham," Cowpe said, sliding the book under his arm. He walked to his desk and arranged his papers so the angles of each stack were mathematically precise. "Still," he said when everything was in order, "I believe your intentions to be honorable, in spite of your deception. I shall read the notes and I shall answer your father's letter. That is all I can offer."

"My intentions are honorable, sir," Miss Ishingham said. "And my theories as sound as when you believed me to be *Mr.* Ishingham."

She pulled on her gloves.

"After you have sated your curiosity, you may return my notebook to the Horn and Powder. Do so before tomorrow evening, please. I shall leave for Warwickshire on Saturday morning. Thank you for your time and good day to you. Good day to you, Mr. Abernathy."

Harcourt crushed an impulse to pursue her as she left the office. He watched through the window as Miss Ishingham walked down Beckwith Street.

"Deception." Cowpe paced about the room. "Unbelievable deception! What sort of man encourages his daughter to study medicine? It sickens me to think of what she must have been exposed to." He turned her notebook rapidly over in his hands, as if daring the volume to force him to open it. "I shall not need your sketches, Abernathy. There will be no monograph."

"Why?" Harcourt asked. "Because she cannot have the answer you seek, or because she might and you cannot accept it?"

"Damnation, Abernathy, I am not a radical like you."

The appellation stung, returning Harcourt instantly to the reason he'd left London. Delicious desire fell away, replaced by a cold fury that had not abated in the ten years since he'd seen his grandmother's house.

Cowpe was oblivious.

"Though I have, as a matter of course, discussed medical matters in the presence of a female patient," Cowpe said, still pacing the room and running his fingers through his thick, dark hair, "I cannot abide the idea of listening to a *woman* hold forth her own, most assuredly, inferior theories on the subject." He threw the book onto the desk. "What the deuce does it matter if she is everything she appeared to be from her letters? I cannot take on a woman as a partner. It's immoral. You know that."

Harcourt exhaled sharply. "I do." He crossed to the door, desperate now for the refuge of the woods, to be alone until he could empty himself of desire and anger. "I shall take my leave of you now, Cowpe. Miss Abernathy is sure to be in a state of distraction if no letter has come."

Harcourt hadn't been tempted by anyone or anything in so long, the fierce hot clutch at the floor of his body unsettled him. He tried to ignore a tenacious desire to hold steady when he had every intention of leaving. Pulling in air like smoke from a cigar, he turned to Cowpe. "Tell me, if you don't mind, what you think of the research."

Cowpe glared at the notebook in disgust. "I cannot even tell you if I shall read it at all. Good day."

Harcourt walked out onto the bright street and headed reluctantly for home.

The phone rang and Claire jumped from her seat. The monograph fell from her lap and landed on its spine. She answered the phone and bent down to pick up the book.

"Good evening, Arcades," she said. "How may I help you?"

She worried something might have happened to the book, and checked it for damage.

"I'm sorry," Ian said on the other end of the line.

"What for?" Claire asked cautiously. She closed the book gently and laid it on the counter.

Ian sighed. "For blowing up at you like that," he said. "You had every right to be angry."

Claire turned on the CD player. Beethoven piano sonatas. Good. She took a deep breath. "It's okay," she said. "I know you were trying to do the right thing. Let's start over."

"We'll forget it ever happened," he said. "Okay?" Ian's voice recaptured its velvety assuredness. "I've made a reservation at Sonsie," he said.

This was a peace offering of an extravagant kind. Sonsie was practically next door to Avenue Victor Hugo, Claire's favorite antique bookstore. She knew Ian's pattern. After they ordered some fabulously delicious meal he would pretend to go outside and make a call. When he came back he would give her a lovely, expensive, rare book, and everything would be all right. They could forget anything else ever happened.

"I only want what's best for you, Claire," he said when she didn't respond to the dinner idea.

Claire ran her finger down the rough spine of the monograph. The tempo of the sonata sped up. The pianist's fingers seemed to fly over the keys.

"I love you, Ian—" she said.

"I love you too," he interrupted.

"I know," she said, biting her tongue.

She couldn't say it. God, she was so passive! Why couldn't she just speak truthfully with him? Why couldn't she simply say: You want what you think is best for me, but you can't know what that is because *I don't know* what it is. Why the hell did she lead him on and allow him to think she was something, someone, she wasn't? It was reprehensible.

"What is it?" he murmured sweetly, probably thinking he already knew the answer.

Whatever that was.

"Nothing," Claire said, her throat tight with frustration over her paralyzing passivity. "I'm tired. Hardly anyone's come in today, but I'm exhausted anyway."

"We can go out another time," Ian said, sounding disappointed.

The pianist on the CD kept up the accelerated tempo. Claire concentrated on the rapid movement of the music. What difference did it make if they went out tonight or not? "No. I'm fine. I'll take a bath or something."

Ian sighed in relief. "I'll pick you up at seven-thirty. Or you can meet me there at eight."

"I'll meet you there," Claire said.

"Fine," he said brightly, sounding ready to go. "Did you ever figure out why that innkeeper sent you the monograph?"

"No," she said. Claire glanced down at the calf bound book and opened it.

"Did he think it was yours?" Ian asked. "Or mine? Did you ever tell him—when you were there before—that you love old books and things like that? Maybe he remembered and thought you'd find it interesting."

A chill spiked up Claire's spine, followed almost immediately by a shallow wave of nausea. "I have to go, honey," she said abruptly. "I'll see you tonight at Sonsie. Bye."

She hung up the phone with a shaking hand.

If Mr. Moulton had seen the man Claire had almost died trying to save, why hadn't he come to the hospital and told people what really happened? Why didn't he talk to her about it so she would know she wasn't crazy? She opened her hand over the monograph and rubbed the dry cover. *There's not going to be a genie,* she thought, chastising herself for her stupidity. If she wanted answers, she'd have to get them herself.

Claire picked up the phone. She dialed the Black Hound but hung up quickly before anyone answered. If Mr. Moulton hadn't seen anything, if she had dreamed the whole thing up, she wasn't ready to know or accept that yet. Mr. Moulton was the last link to the possibility that it had all been true.

If it was true, if she had met the love of her life and he

had disappeared in a fire, the monograph was a link as well. Mr. Moulton said it had been left behind.

He hadn't said *she'd* left it behind.

Claire opened the book to the title page.

Perithisis; A Case for Variolation. By Dr. Thomas Cowpe with diagrams and illustrations by Harcourt Abernathy. 1824.

Harcourt Abernathy.

The night in the room at the Black Hound Inn when he sat nearly speechless beside her in front of the fireplace, he'd said he was a botanical illustrator.

Harcourt Abernathy.

The sound of the name thrilled Claire like remembered music. She felt whole and present.

Harcourt Abernathy.

What if that was his name? He'd never told her his name, even after she'd blurted out hers in embarrassment the next morning.

Harcourt Abernathy. 1824.

Was it a ghost, or a man from another time, she'd met and fallen in love with in Vermont seven years ago? A man she connected to and made love with. She'd watched him disappear after getting burned in a fire she couldn't feel or smell until it was too late.

Claire covered her eyes with her hand, then ran her fingers to the back of her neck. She turned to the book once more, re-read his name and remembered him. Sparkling brown eyes like coffee in candlelight. Dark blond hair streaked with gold. A powerful chest, and muscular arms and legs. A low-slung voice like an unexpected brook in a dark forest. And an amazingly soft, lush mouth.

If Harcourt Abernathy was a ghost, he was made of solid, sexy, extremely sensitive flesh.

Claire closed her eyes. The first kiss. Just the first kiss, she told herself. She wouldn't linger too long in the memories of that night. That kiss hadn't felt like any first kiss Claire had had before or since. It felt knowing and familiar. Beyond infatuation and first bliss. A kiss that instantly reached inside all of her.

And him as well.

Claire shuddered and pulled herself out before she got lost in the memory of him. She glanced around her store. Foliage and flowers were everywhere. Fresh flowers. Dried flowers. Flowers on prints and pillows. Candles scented with honey and roses, raspberry mignonette, vanilla heliotrope, lavender, jasmine and orange blossom. She breathed in the fragrance of the room.

A ghost. Who loved her. If only for that night.

That was better than crazy.

Wasn't it?

Chapter Six

Claire stood on tiptoe in her small, clean white bathroom and checked her lipstick in the mirror. Good enough, she thought, though she wasn't crazy about the plummy color.

Her childhood best friend Linda's voice buzzed in her ear. *Cherries-in-the-Snow™, that's the shade for kissable lips. When I grow up I'm gonna work for Revlon and make up names for lipstick, but I'll always wear Cherries-in-the-Snow™ when I want someone to fall in love with me.*

A few years later Linda had her heart broken by a thirteen-year-old boy whose name Claire had forgotten. The lipsticks Linda made in her bathroom bore names like Heartbreak and Despair. They were dark, romantic colors. The following fall, red "Despair" helped Linda win the boy of her ninth-grade dreams. Claire and her grandfather left Ohio that Christmas and moved back home to Boston. She and Linda lost touch.

Claire flipped her lipstick tube over and read its name: Veritas. What the hell did that mean? That the purplish hue revealed the true you?

The front door rang.

"It's me." Ian's voice fizzed on the intercom.

Claire buzzed him in and opened her apartment door.

"I thought I was meeting you there," she said as Ian climbed the red-carpeted stairs in the hall.

He kissed her. "You look beautiful."

Ian walked into Claire's apartment and laid her mail on the kitchen table. "You should get the super to fix your mailbox. Anyone could go through your mail. The box was wide open when I walked in." He looked Claire up and down. "Are you ready?"

Claire ran her fingers over the back of her neck. "I have to get my boots," she said. She went into the living room and pulled her black boots out from under the couch.

Ian picked up the monograph from the piecrust-edged table near the door. "You should have this table refinished. It looks terrible." He laid the book's spine in his palm and let the monograph fall open over his fingers.

"Careful," Claire said, irritated by his disregard for her things.

Ian glanced up. "Why did he send this to you?"

Claire slipped her feet into her long boots and started to lace them up. "It was left in the room when I stayed there seven years ago. Shit." She put her finger in her mouth.

"What?" Ian asked.

"Nothing," Claire said. "I cut my finger on the hook."

"Let me see," Ian said.

Claire took her finger out of her mouth. "It's fine. I'll get a Band-Aid in a second."

Ian tossed the book back onto the table.

"Hey!" she said.

"Sorry," Ian said. "Was it your book?"

"No," Claire said, sucking her bleeding finger.

"Well, whose was it?" Ian asked. "Why did—what's his name, the innkeeper—think it was yours?"

"I don't know," Claire said. She stood up and took the monograph from the table. "I'm gonna get a Band-Aid. Then we can go."

"Let me see it again," Ian said.

Claire thought he meant her finger. She held it up, but he pulled the monograph from her as if she were a child and her opinion didn't matter.

He sat on the couch.

She stared at him. How could anyone be so oblivious? she thought. And what the hell is wrong with me? She sighed in disgust and walked toward the bathroom.

"I failed a test on perithisis in an infectious diseases class," Ian called to her. "It was the only test I failed in med school."

Claire stopped in the hall and listened to him page through the book.

"This monograph is probably worth something, you know," he said. "These plates are hand-colored."

Claire came back into the living room. "What is perithisis? I can't remember."

"How did you ever know about it?" he asked.

Claire sighed and pulled on the ends of her hair.

"Oh, sorry," Ian said. "I always forget. You went to med school for what, a year? Six months?"

"A year."

"Thank God," Ian said. "Medicine would never have suited you, Claire." He clapped the book shut. The noise chimed in a pair of wineglasses in front of the window.

Claire winced.

"Did you get the Band-Aid?" he asked.

"Why?"

"What do mean why? Your finger." He laughed. "How do you get through a day, Claire?" He crossed over to her and kissed her head. "I'll get the Band-Aid."

"Why wouldn't medicine have suited me?" Claire called to him.

"Oh God, Claire," Ian shouted from the bathroom. "You're too . . . I don't know. Fragile."

She took the monograph off the couch and put it in her bag. He came back with Neosporin and a Band-Aid.

"And delicate." Ian smiled and wrapped the bandage around her ring finger. "Why do you always wear this ring?"

Claire pulled her hand away. "I bought it in Vermont after I got out of the hospital." She bit her tongue and grabbed her long black coat out of the jammed hall closet.

"Surround and consume," she said.

"What?" Ian asked.

"Perithisis," Claire said. "Surround and consume. The virus surrounds the cell like a boa constrictor, then eats it."

"You're adorable," Ian said. "I don't know anyone who knows more arcane trivia. I love you." He wrapped his arms around her. "Let's go."

Ian pulled her into the hot hallway. "You should tell your super to fix the heat. It's too hot in your building."

Claire let herself be led down the stairs, then outside to Newbury Street and the restaurant.

Avenue Victor Hugo was closed. Forever. They had an online store, but the actual space was shut down. How could she not know that? It was a few blocks from her apartment. She used to go almost every day; how could she not have known it closed?

She was right about the peace offering, anyway. Halfway through a delicious dinner Ian gave her a lovely, pale blue, cloth-bound volume of *Days With the Romantic Poets; Byron, Shelley, Clare, Ishingham, and Keats*.

"It's beautiful. Thank you," she said, opening and paging gently through it. She smiled at Ian's pleased expression. "Oh! 'Ode to Eurydice.' That was my grandfather's favorite poem. He read it to me every night when I was little."

For a moment Ian looked different: open and vulnerable and hopeful. Tightly held possessiveness vanished from his hazel eyes. Claire smiled at him. She felt as if she could breathe.

"I'm glad you like it," he said quietly.

Ian was still grinning sweetly when his beeper went off. He glanced down at it. "I have to take this call," he said, standing up. "Order me the ginger-pumpkin pudding with the maple whipped cream." He took his phone out of his pocket. "I'll be back in five minutes."

Claire smiled and watched him walk to the enclosed vestibule. She slid the poetry book into her bag and took out the monograph. The first illustration of a pockmarked hand was in the middle of the introductory chapter defining perithisis, commonly called putrid pox.

"Shut up!" a man whispered audibly from a table near the window.

Claire glanced up to see a very red-faced young man seated across from a sexy, round, blue-eyed, twenty-something. The woman took his hand and turned to face the center of the room.

"Be quiet. Jen, please," he begged in a whisper. "You're embarrassing me." His face turned Bazooka Joe bubble-gum pink and he couldn't stop smiling. The girl held up her left hand.

"Jack Green loves me, Boston," she shouted. "And he wants to marry me and—"

Jack Green leaned across the table and kissed her. Jen threw her arms around his shoulders.

Claire realized she was staring. She couldn't stop smiling and hid her mouth behind her hand. Maybe it was the excellent Bordeaux or maybe it was seeing two people so unabashedly in love, but a stripe of giddy pleasure unfurled down her spine. With a pop like a Christmas cracker, her senses thrust into overdrive. She could smell more, hear more, see more, *feel* more.

Now would be the time to go home and take a long bath with a hot book. She ran her tongue over her lips and behind her teeth. Now would be the time to go home, take a bath and dream of Harcourt Abernathy. Bright, intelligent eyes, amazing mouth, powerful muscular chest and a big fabulous—

Okay, Claire thought, finishing her wine in a hard swallow. *Get hold of yourself. You're in a public place.*

She felt *his* hand run over the back of her neck and reluctantly shook him off. *Not here,* she thought. The sense of his hands moved down her waist and to the hard curve of her hips.

Seriously, she thought in a more severe tone, *not now.* He ran his finger down her spine.

Later.

Claire sucked in the restaurant aroma of garlicky steak. She shook herself free of him for the time being. She concentrated on watching Ian pacing and talking on his little silver phone. She filled her head with here and now, then turned and glanced back at Jack and Jen.

They were still kissing passionately. The boy's youthful ardor and the girl's intense affection swam strangely in Claire's head. Whatever thread connected her to the present moment disintegrated like cotton candy in a wet mouth. She closed her eyes and saw the blissful pair of lovers float, kissing like a Chagall pair, out of the restaurant and into a moonlit garden.

The dreams of Claire's childhood and the people and places in them swelled in her head. She felt dizzy. She shouldn't have drunk any wine before the food came. But it was only one glass.

Ian was still talking intently and pacing in the small hall.

Claire opened the monograph to the frontispiece. She read *his* name and traced the path of his tongue on the roof of her mouth. Harcourt Abernathy. If she asked him, would he take her with him? Could she spend the rest of her life in love with a ghost?

Crazy, she thought. *Don't go crazy.*

Was she drunk after a single glass of wine?

She shook her head and her hands, then drank Ian's water. When had she become such a lightweight?

How could Ian still be talking? It seemed like a half hour or more had passed.

She felt dizzier and a little sick.

Harcourt Abernathy, she thought.

A circle of heat rose in her chest. She breathed slowly

and tried to concentrate, but she felt disconnected and out of place.

"Show yourself," she begged.

Nothing.

A heavy wave of vertigo and nausea swelled inside Claire. "Show yourself or talk to me or leave me the hell alone."

Her head was heavy and she couldn't see clearly. Ian looked a million miles away and she couldn't hear anything in the room. *No!* She could hear too much. The echo of every noise that had ever emanated from this space sounded simultaneously. Hundreds of voices, animals and machines, wind and rain, all vied for this single corner of the aural universe.

Claire gazed around the room. No one saw her. She might as well have been an ocean away. She laid her head on the open book, closed her eyes and wished she was home.

"Quiet!" Kate Ishingham whispered harshly, not trusting the cover of night alone to keep the secret she had unexpectedly come to share. "If you wish to avoid discovery, you must keep silent."

"Oh, but you're hurting him."

"*Please,*" Kate implored, "please keep quiet. I am not hurting him. I am cleaning the wound and sewing it up to prevent infection. If you wish to keep your position, Jenny, you must stay quiet. If you cannot, you must return home and allow me to tend to Mr. Greeley."

Silently, Kate directed the young woman to hold the candle nearer to the wet slash across Mr. Greeley's hand, all the while keeping a watchful eye on the entrance to the walled garden.

Footsteps sounded on the gravel path. Kate's heart jumped into her throat.

"Miss Ishingham," a decidedly male voice called out in a tone at once protective and outraged.

Kate leapt to hear her name. She accidentally pressed the needle too deeply into young John Greeley's palm.

"Damnation." He grimaced, squeezing his eyes shut.

"Forgive me, Mr. Greeley," Kate said. "Mr. Abernathy?"

Jenny swore a terrible oath and ran from the garden, tripping over a tree root.

"Take care, Jenny," Kate ordered. "You've frightened her away," she said sharply to Mr. Abernathy, who had just walked into the garden.

"Miss Ishingham," he repeated pointedly, his face unsmiling and his brown eyes flashing in the silver moonlight.

Kate steadied herself. She had not forgotten the sheep-eyed swoon she had nearly fallen into this morning, but she was not a fool. Mr. Abernathy was no different than Dr. Cowpe and quite certain to share his opinion on a woman performing any tasks but ribbon-wearing and child-bearing.

Harcourt stared at the stripe of blood glistening on Greeley's palm then raised his eyes to Kate. "Take Mr. Greeley to my house. It's very near. The light in this garden is insufficient."

Kate's jaw dropped as Mr. Abernathy took Greeley's uninjured arm and ushered him out of the garden.

In the open air of the street Greeley appeared to be younger than Kate had thought.

"What were you doing out at such an hour, Greeley?" Harcourt asked as Kate followed them.

Greeley stared down at his half-sewn wound and grimaced. "I'd rather not say, Mr. Abernathy. If that's all the same to you."

Harcourt did not alter his sober countenance, but Kate saw flecks of liquid light return to his eyes. "If you insist on courting Jenny Easton, you must first get her father's permission," he said sternly. "You do intend to marry her, do you not?"

"I do, Mr. Abernathy. I do," Greeley insisted, the pink of his cheek fluctuating madly. "But her father says she's too young. She gets good wages from the Cowpes and I have nothing until my apprenticeship is up in a year. Then I shall open my own shop. Mr. Beedle is old . . ."

Harcourt smiled slightly.

"I'm sorry to say it, sir, but he is, and Ledwyche'll always need a good blacksmith." Greeley stopped walking. "Then Jenny'll have me."

A shadow fell over Harcourt's countenance. Kate turned toward the darkened shop window and blushed. She too suspected the round, emotional Jenny had already *had* John Greeley.

"Leave her alone then, John," Harcourt said. "Until you can marry her."

"I can't, Mr. Abernathy," Greeley protested quietly. "I'm afraid she'll have another before I'm ready."

They reached the door of a honey-colored stone house fronted with a profusion of flowers. A housekeeper, who must have heard them coming, stood in an open doorway. She glared reproachfully at Greeley, then stepped aside.

"Bring Mr. Greeley a brandy, Mrs. Week," Harcourt said, "And bring Miss Ishingham a cup of tea. Or would you prefer brandy?" he asked, turning to Kate.

Kate smiled at him in spite of herself. "Tea, thank you," she said to the housekeeper.

Inside, brightly polished paneled walls and a beamed ceiling shone in the light of a huge fire. The room smelled of roses and lavender. Harcourt brought a pair of oil lamps to a round table with a piecrust edge.

"Thank you," Kate said.

He stopped and smiled at her, so slightly it was hardly a smile at all. Like an answer to a call, a swift pleasure unfolded inside Kate. The desire to drink in the air surrounding Mr. Abernathy captured her. She inhaled and smiled back, then took Greeley's hand and held it to the light.

Greeley swallowed more of the brandy than he'd intended. He choked loudly while Kate finished stitching his hand.

"There," she said, wrapping the wound in clean white cloth.

"Go home now, boy," Harcourt said. "Stay away from Jenny until you can marry her. She'll wait for you."

Greeley rose unsteadily, more likely from a throbbing in his hand and the events of the night than the brandy. "I shall try, Mr. Abernathy," he said weakly.

"Good," Harcourt said, squeezing the boy's shoulder.

"See Dr. Cowpe within the week about your hand," Kate said. "And keep it clean until then."

"I will," Greeley said. "Thank you."

Harcourt closed the door.

Kate stood in the firelight and met his eyes. Mr. Abernathy might have taken many unfeeling, reasonable steps this evening, but he took none. Few men she knew did what was right in defiance of what others might think.

"You were very kind to that boy," she said. "At a time when I am certain he has few allies in his or Jenny's family. Even your Mrs. Week treated him with icy contempt."

Harcourt smiled slightly again. "Mrs. Week's dearest friend is Jenny Easton's mother," he said softly.

"Ah," Kate said.

Greeley was gone and Mrs. Week had retired. No sound, save the crackle of the fire, echoed. Through an open door in what looked like a study lit partially by the moon, Kate saw paints and brushes and vases of flowers. The heady scent of lilac drifted in.

"How did you come to tend to John Greeley's hand?" Harcourt asked, leading Kate to sit nearer the fire. He did not need ask where she had learned to treat a wound so deep, or what she thought she was doing sewing up a young boy's hand as though it was a Christmas goose, nor did he seem offended she had done so.

"My chamber at the Horn and Powder is above the garden. I was reading at the open window when I heard Miss Easton and Mr. Greeley. She was crying, pursuing him as he walked. I heard her say something about Mr. Greeley bleeding. No one came to help. I took my kit and a candle and left to find them." Kate took a sip of her cooled tea. "He cut his hand climbing out a window at the Cowpes'."

"This night?" Harcourt asked, incredulous. "I spent all of the evening with the Cowpes'. I heard nothing."

"I suspect," Kate said, "that Mr. Greeley and Jenny are quite adept at the art of silent entry and exit."

Harcourt gazed at her intently, his dark eyes blazing in the bright light of the fire. Kate stiffened and finished her tepid tea.

"Thank you very much for your kindness, Mr. Abernathy," she said graciously. "I must return to the inn. If Mrs. Gardner awakens to find me absent, she will have the vicar, the magistrate, and the earl of Oxford searching the hills."

"Permit me to escort you, Miss Ishingham," he said. "It is nearly midnight."

"I know I ought to, Mr. Abernathy," she began coolly.

He said nothing. But he waited, with that enigmatic, searching gaze. Kate felt a blush of heat curl at the nape of her neck. His acceptance of her skills and ambitions had pleased but not shocked her, though perhaps it should have. But to wait for her decision, instead of insisting that he knew better, struck a clean blow at Kate's conviction that she knew more about people—especially men—than they knew themselves.

He seemed glad to take her in, anxious neither to stay nor go.

The swirl of heat moved to Kate's chest. The distinct sensation that he could see through her was so intense and new, Kate felt utterly naked. A blush rose, coloring her cheeks.

He did not avert his eyes or smile condescendingly. He stood, breathing softly in the glow of firelight, comfortable and content in his own skin.

"Very well then, Mr. Abernathy," she said, completely uncertain of the right course of action but unwilling to leave him just yet. "I shall gather up my kit."

Every instrument was returned to its proper place. Kate

hoped she had also successfully composed herself, and her thoughts, into some semblance of what had previously been an unshakable order. She breathed deeply, then turned to him. "I am ready."

"You have no pelisse?" he asked.

" 'Tis a warm night, Mr. Abernathy, and the distance to the inn is not far."

"Let me at least fetch a shawl of Miss Abernathy's," he begged.

"Thank you, Mr. Abernathy, but I am content as I am."

He smiled slowly, took his coat and motioned to the door. "As you wish," he said quietly.

Kate savored the hum his voice teased out in every muscle of her body and realized he had somehow made her small victory his own.

The temperature of the air outside had dropped considerably. Without speaking of it, Harcourt removed his coat and draped it over her shoulders.

He wore nothing now but his white shirt and dark blue waistcoat. Kate could not help but notice his powerfully muscular frame. A sudden, intense wish to be touched by him darted through her as though it met no boundaries of bone or muscle or better judgment. Heat from his body still clung to the wool coat. The wish to feel his hands on her waist flicked its silver tail. Kate shuddered and tasted the smoke from his fireplace in the air.

"Miss Ishingham," he said, "shall we be off then?"

A second blush ripened over Kate's face and chest. She'd never been so grateful for darkness. She must look as if she'd been bathed in strawberry cream.

"Of course," she said. "Forgive me."

They reached the gray stone inn sooner than she wished.

She thanked him for his kindness and closed the heavy door behind her.

A rush of cold air, like someone had opened a door, chilled Claire. She squeezed her eyes more tightly closed.

Was she still blushing? Someone grabbed her shoulder and called her name. She clenched her teeth and searched for the scent of spring and the woody smoke of a tavern chimney. The hands shook her. Her name sounded as if it were under water. She breathed in the dust of the book and held on to it like a life raft.

A glass of claret caught the firelight in the dining room of the Black Hound, and splashed its scarlet reflection on Harcourt Abernathy's hand. He listened to Pickney and Southey argue over the feasibility of a public garden and drummed his fingers on the clear crystal stem of his wineglass. Pickney's ringing voice kept him from too closely heeding the screaming chaos in his brain.

"Abernathy knows I'm right about this, Southey," Pickney said brightly. "Am I not right, Abernathy?"

"He is right, Southey," Harcourt said. "Irrevocably, incontrovertibly right."

"He is buying your supper," Southey said, a broad grin lighting his athletic face.

"He is that," Harcourt said, and smiled.

The conversation continued, without his input, in the same jocund vein. The more time passed without Kate, the larger the hole in his heart grew. It gaped at him from the center of his soul like an open mouth. What could he have done differently? He couldn't have stopped her from going to London. But he could have forgiven her for going before it was too late.

Harcourt swallowed the remainder of his wine and gestured for more. For one night at least he would deaden his regret with drink, and silence the wail that had sounded unbroken since the moment of her death.

After a time, uncounted glasses of claret began to soften Harcourt's comprehension of his surroundings. He knew he sat in the dining room of the Black Hound Inn, and that the commodious establishment stood in green, very green, Vermont. He knew the men engaged in intense conversation before him were Nathaniel Pickney and Robert Southey, but he still knew himself too well. The wine had not yet deadened his sense of himself and the memory of Kate.

Southey's brash voice broke in over Harcourt's sensory inventory.

"I knew I would have her from the moment I heard her voice," Southey said. "She sat with her sister in a corner of her father's house and her voice touched my heart. When I crossed the room and spied her enchanting face I knew she would be mine or I'd have no other."

Pickney, who had no wife and no intended, turned to Harcourt in mock sorrow. "Southey's done for, Abernathy. Absolutely lost to us." He poured all three of them more claret.

Harcourt paused before finishing the glass.

Sometime later, he could not say when, Southey and Pickney went to smoke outside. The air was too close, they'd said, and invited him to join them. He knew he must have declined their invitation for he sat in the large room alone.

In the absence of the distraction of Southey's ardent heart and Pickney's good humor, the excess of wine excited rather than shrouded memories of Kate. Harcourt walked toward the cold fireplace to shake himself free.

Mr. Moulton met him there. "You can't force yourself to forget, Abernathy."

Harcourt turned too swiftly and nearly fell. Mr. Moulton caught him by the elbow.

"How do you know?" Harcourt asked in far too naked a voice. "How do you know what I have lost, what I am trying to forget? For that matter, how do you know I am trying to forget anything at all?" He knew he was swaying slightly. He planted his feet on the stone hearth and steadied himself. "Who told you?" he begged, clutching the mantel.

The innkeeper laughed like a ship's bell. "It's your face that gives you away, Abernathy. That and your bold attempt to drink yourself to death in my inn." He clapped Harcourt lightly on the shoulder. "No man drinks that much wine who isn't trying to forget something."

Harcourt sucked in the scent of cold stone and stale chimney smoke.

Mr. Moulton stepped nearer and smiled kindly. "It doesn't work, at any rate. Not in one night it doesn't." He took the claret from the table. "Go outside. Have a smoke with Mr. Pickney and Southey." He led Harcourt to the porch, handed him a cigar and closed the wide oak door.

Pickney and Southey were nowhere to be seen. Harcourt pocketed the cigar and gratefully breathed in the crisp night air. He nodded at a gentleman and his wife who walked past him and into the inn. A lingering fragrance of lavender reached for him and he swallowed it. The lush scent returned him to the night he'd walked Kate to the Horn and Powder after she had tended to John Greeley's hand.

If he had accepted then that he loved her, if he'd been more honest with her from the beginning about his failings, if he'd asked for her hand sooner than he had, would Kate still be with him? What choices could he have made that would have saved her? He would give anything to make them now.

Miss Ishingham closed the door at the Horn and Powder. Harcourt stood for a moment and breathed in the last of the lavender from her hair into his mouth. As he walked home he thought of the deft movements of her graceful fingers and how beautifully she'd treated Greeley's hand, how she'd come to the aid of strangers on a dark street when no one else had paid any heed.

The wind picked up and Harcourt put on his coat. It smelled lightly of her. A surge of desire wended its way inside him. He walked faster, glad of the cold. He didn't want to want her. Not this much.

He sucked in cool, damp air until it replaced the taste of

lavender. The order he had carved out for himself and his sister Celia was still tenuous and vulnerable. As much as he wanted the pleasure of a woman's company, he didn't want to need anything he couldn't bear to lose. Miss Ishingham had captured too much of his imagination, made him feel too close to the man he'd been before he'd lost everything. A vision of her sitting at his fireside flashed before him and an involuntary shudder licked his insides. With a mixture of relief and sorrow he sighted his house and quickened his pace.

Harcourt craved peace with a visceral urgency. He grasped at it, as a drowning man reaches for the jetsam of a sinking ship. Miss Ishingham, sensual without even knowing it, and as different from any woman in Ledwyche as a castle to a cottage, had threatened that peace before he'd had time to mount a defense. Relieved to find no one else in the house awake, he climbed the stairs and got into bed.

Miss Ishingham's lovely face taunted him. He tasted her scent in his mouth and an ache that would not let him sleep swelled feverishly. He shuddered and closed his fingers around the hard shaft of his sex. It pulsed like an animal in his hand. He stopped moving his hand and tried to steady himself.

He hated to be at the mercy of anyone. When he had a woman he was in command of his feelings and hers. His desires and hers.

The sudden image of Miss Ishingham's hand on him now, instead of his, shot through him. He moaned and closed his fingers more tightly on himself. He didn't want to need anyone this much. He stopped again and tried to concentrate on other women he had known, other women he had had; lovely, willing, desirable women. He closed his eyes and ran his hand up and down as fast as he could bear. He filled his mind with other women, other faces. Not hers.

Desire flamed inside him. He moaned in desperation to release it.

Miss Ishingham's face, her body hot underneath him, flashed like lightning in his mind. Her hands on him. Her mouth on his. Her mouth on him. He moaned and moved his hand faster over his pulsing.

Her body, her breasts round and pink, her legs wrapped around him, her heat tightly clasping and releasing him. His hand stopped. He cried out, and longing for her poured from him in violent throbbing relief.

A long time later, when he could steady his breath and his heart had slowed to an ordinary rhythm, he fell asleep. He awoke several times, hard and hot and wanting her more than before. Each time he released his longing for her, it came back harder and more urgent.

Harcourt rose as the sun softened the morning sky. He wanted to walk the five miles to and from Easton's farm before breakfast. He was determined not to let longing for one woman master him. *He* would be the master over his desires and his emotions. He had pledged long ago not to subordinate himself to any idea or any man.

And certainly not any woman.

Chapter Seven

Before departing for the Easton farm Harcourt stopped at his sister Celia's open bedchamber door. She was awake uncharacteristically early and sat on her bed, cradled in heaps of muslin and Apollo gold silk. Mrs. Week patiently gathered the discarded dresses and ribbons.

"I do not want an ordinary man!" Celia mourned to her sole female intimate, unaware that Harcourt stood just outside the room. "I long for a hero. A man larger, braver, nobler than an ordinary man. Handsome. Kind. Fierce in the face of danger. A man true as a knight."

"And your Master Stanley is such a man," Mrs. Week said dubiously.

"Yes," Celia wailed, pressing her tearstained face into her pillow. "He is. But I am not worthy of his attention." The word "attention," muffled and wet, was nearly lost in the depths of the feather-stuffed bolster.

"There, there," Mrs. Week soothed. "If you are not worthy, dove, Mr. Leonard Stanley is no knight."

"But he is," Celia cried. "More than you or anyone in Ledwyche shall ever know!"

"Calm yourself," Mrs. Week said. "You look a terrible sight, your lovely face all red and damp. What will Mr. Abernathy say if you spend another half day in bed?"

"I care not at all what Harcourt thinks. He has never been in love and I don't think he ever shall be. He cares for naught but work and for tiresome talk with Dr. Cowpe." She gazed dispassionately at the clothing Mrs. Week had laid at the foot of the bed. "My heart is breaking. Truly breaking."

"Your heart shall heal," Mrs. Week clucked. "In the meantime, do not judge Mr. Abernathy too harshly, or Master Stanley too well. Remember, dove, every man is a hero to the one who holds his heart."

Harcourt left Celia to the care of Mrs. Week and walked downstairs, hungry for the open air.

The hands stopped shaking Claire. She felt a pillow supporting her head and a mattress under her back. Hungrily, she reached for the lavender scent of home. The memory of Harcourt's hand slowly tracing the length of her spine ignited her senses. She opened herself and remembered. His breath spilled down her neck as he murmured a name that didn't sound like hers but couldn't have been anyone else's. He pressed his forehead to hers and his hair fell over her brow. Her nipples hardened and brushed up against his chest. She lifted her hips to meet his. He was hard as iron between her thighs. She squeezed her legs together and felt the beat of his pulse against her skin. He buried his face in her hair spread over the pillow.

A slamming door smashed like a rock through glass in Claire's brain.

She sat up quickly. She had no idea where she was.

"You passed out," Ian said.

Claire stared at him. Why was he here? Why wasn't he at home? He had no right or reason to be here. Did he? What had happened? Where was Harcourt?

Ian laid her back down.

"Why?" Claire asked.

"You passed out at the restaurant," Ian said calmly. "Toby's here. He's going to stay with you. I had an emergency call and I have to get to the hospital."

Ian gently opened Claire's lower eyelid and shone a tiny light into her eye.

"You're not taking any medication I don't know about, are you?" he asked. "Anything that might react with alcohol?"

"No," Claire said. "I . . ."

Toby walked into the room. Relief tightened Claire's throat. She felt immensely glad to see him standing in the doorway. Toby was always exactly, reliably, what Claire expected him to be.

"Hi," she said in a tiny voice, immediately ashamed to sound so small.

Toby crossed to her bed and sat down on the end.

Ian studied her for a minute more. "I have to go. I'll call you tomorrow." He turned to Toby. "Thanks." He left.

Claire couldn't stop herself. "Oh God, Toby."

"Shhhhh," he said.

She fell into his arms. Claire *hated* to cry. She clenched her teeth until her jaw hurt. She squeezed every muscle against letting go. She hadn't cried at all since she couldn't stop crying at the Black Hound seven years ago, when she'd wanted to scream until blood poured from her throat. At the hospital they gave her medicine to make her stop. Then she'd felt nothing.

Claire bit her cheeks and balled her fists, digging her nails into the flesh of her palms.

"Don't," Toby said. "Don't close yourself off to me."

Claire couldn't hold on any longer. She let go and wept until she had nothing left.

"It's okay," Toby said when she finally stopped sobbing.

Her head ached with a clotted burn that stretched her skin, making her face feel like a hot balloon about to pop. "I'm sorry," she said haltingly.

"Don't be," Toby said. "Now, tell me what happened."

Claire stiffened in his embrace. She dreaded having to

tell him. What would she say, anyway? It hardly made sense to *her*.

Toby pulled back abruptly and held Claire at arm's length. "You promised! You *swore* to me. You swore you would forget about it." He jumped up and began pacing the room like a caged tiger. "Jeez, Claire! You weren't in Vermont for twenty-four hours and look what happened!"

He stopped pacing and took a deep breath. "I'm sorry. It isn't your fault." He sat next to her on the bed. "Tell me what happened. And we'll move past it."

Crying so hard must have released something, because Claire began to feel less disconnected to the real world. She easily breathed all the air she needed. For the first time in as long as she could remember she didn't want to apologize for anything.

"Ian said you were holding on to an old book," Toby said. "He said he could hardly get it out of your hands. What was it?"

Claire swung her legs over the side of the bed and accidentally kicked Toby in the knee. "Sorry."

His brushed off his pants. "It's okay."

Claire stood up and checked herself in the small, rectangular mirror above her dresser. She smiled and glanced back at Toby on the bed. "Thanks for not telling me I look like shit."

Toby grinned slightly. "You're welcome."

Claire ran her hands through her hair and sat on a wooden chair with a sage-and-silver–striped cushion. "Thanks for coming."

"Stop it," he said, kindness lighting his already lovely eyes.

Claire smiled. Toby always made her feel he could fix anything. He would have made an excellent doctor.

"You're avoiding my question," Toby said. He kept his glance fixed to hers.

"I know," she said.

"Well, don't."

"It was nothing." Claire got out of the chair and walked into the bathroom.

Toby followed her. "Don't lie. You're terrible at it."

Claire splashed water on her face. The cold bounced off her skin, not reaching the heat inside her. She rubbed her face with a thick green towel. Her skin reliably tightened and stung. She pressed her fingers to her cheek, then turned to Toby. "I need you to be open-minded."

He sat on the closed toilet. For a second Claire marveled at how Toby, who looked like a movie star, made every gesture and position attractive. "You're the only man—the only person—I know who looks good sitting on the toilet."

"Don't change the subject, Claire," he said. "Why wouldn't you let go of the book?"

"I didn't want to."

"Nice try. Come on."

Claire leaned against the counter and massaged rosewater moisturizer into her arms. She raised her hand to her face and breathed in the lush floral scent, evocative of everything that kept her awake at night, of why she'd never let go of the monograph now that she had it. The monograph, she thought, the realization dawning on her slowly. That was part of what was making her feel better, having something tangible that had belonged to *him*.

The frayed edges of Claire's friable connection to the world around her began to weave themselves together. And the peace she felt in dreams fell over her waking life. If she could tell the story of what happened in Vermont, and accept that it had happened, she could begin to move on. She could live the life she was meant to live.

Claire drew in a long breath. It entered her lungs cool and cleansing as peppermint. "The night we stayed at the Black Hound . . ." She shouldn't have said *we*. Her teeth buzzed and her hair stood on end. Trying to ignore an increase in her heart rate, she swallowed the powdery lavender fragrance in her apartment

"That night someone left a book in the room," she said.

"The innkeeper sent it to me after Ian and I came home last Sunday. It's a nineteenth-century monograph on a disease called perithisis. It was written by a Dr. Thomas Cowpe."

Toby stood up and almost smashed his head on the glass shelf above the toilet.

"And illustrated by Harcourt Abernathy," Claire said.

For an instant, Toby's features squirmed, his hair grew darker and his face filled out a little. "What are you staring at?"

A shiver in his voice made Claire believe he knew the answer.

"Your face," she said.

Toby reddened. *"Please."* He turned toward the open door. "Don't." He exhaled heavily. "Do you mind if I make myself some tea?" He didn't wait for an answer.

"Go ahead." She watched him walk through the living room.

He stopped at her desk and arranged her piles of papers so the angles of each stack were mathematically precise. "I know who Harcourt Abernathy is," he called back to her.

Claire's heart jumped into her throat. She stood in the doorway and stared at him.

"My dad collected nineteenth-century prints and engravings. Harcourt Abernathy was his favorite botanical illustrator after Sydenham Edwards. He had me photograph his whole collection when I was in high school."

Toby pulled an antique silver inkwell to a more symmetrical position on the desk, then disappeared into the kitchen. "He sold the entire collection before he died. It broke my mother's heart."

Claire heard the whoosh of water, the clang of the teakettle onto the burner and the click, click, click, of the gas lighting.

Toby came back to her room.

He looked like himself again, but whatever stress he'd experienced today had risen to the surface of his face. He ran his fingers though his thick dark hair and stood impatiently in front of Claire. "Why did an old book on a rare disease freak you out so much?"

"Because it was in the room that night," she said.

"So what?" Toby picked up a tiny white ceramic cat Claire kept on her dresser. He played with it, tossing it back and forth between his hands.

"Don't drop that," Claire said softly. "It was broken a long time ago. You can see the cracks. Be careful."

He shot her an I-dare-you-to-say-that-again glance.

Claire rested her fingers on his arm. "Let's go see if your water is ready." She walked toward the kitchen and beckoned him to follow.

"Wait!" Toby said. "Stop."

Claire turned around.

"What difference does it make if the monograph was in that room?" he asked, ridiculously shaking the white cat at her. "There must have been a lot of things in there: a bed, a rug, chairs, lamps, sheets, towels. What are you going to do, Claire, go up to Vermont, collect the contents of that room and erect a shrine to *something that happened only in your head?*"

Toby sighed convulsively and stepped closer. "It wasn't real, Claire. You had an emotional breakdown. You spent six months of your life in a hospital. It wasn't real."

He sat on the green striped chair. "Whoever you thought you saw, whatever—whatever thing you thought you experienced—did not happen, except in your head." Toby dropped his temple to his palm, then ran his hand over his hair. "I should have told Ian what really happened," he said to himself. "He never would have taken you if he had known."

Claire bit her tongue. It would be easier if it *wasn't* real, she thought. Or if she could take a pill to make the sense of *him* disappear so she could have a regular life.

She took the little cat gently from Toby.

He grabbed her hand. "It's my job to watch over you,

Claire. I don't ever want to see you—" He stopped himself and looked out the dark window. "I don't ever want you to go through what you did the night they took you from that room."

Claire held Toby's hand in both of hers. "I won't let that happen again. I promise."

He opened his mouth to argue.

"I know I promised before," she said, interrupting him. Claire let go of Toby's hand and tried to think of how to be true to herself and honest with Toby at the same time. She didn't quite know. "I want to stop pretending."

The tension on Toby's face melted. He exhaled heavily. "You don't know how happy it makes me to hear you say that, Claire." He pulled her close to hug her.

"What time is it?" he asked, stepping back to check his watch. "Do you want to go out? I'm starving. Is Summer Shack still open? I could go for cherry-stone seviche."

"It's freezing," Claire said.

"I know," Toby answered in an endearing mix of pleading and sheepishness. "You could get fried clams and French fries."

"I don't know," Claire said, craning her neck to scan the frigid blackness outside the window.

"I need to talk with you about something and I don't want to do it here." Toby's voice sounded oddly uncertain. He rarely asked Claire for anything.

"Sure," she said gamely. "I'll take a quick shower."

"How long are you going to be?" he asked. "I'm tired."

"You said you were hungry," Claire said. "I don't care if we go out."

Pleading edged out embarrassment in Toby's clear eyes. "I want to."

"Okay," she said. "I won't be long."

Toby went into the living room and lay on the couch.

"Don't fall asleep," Claire said.

"Claire," he said, "have you ever known me to fall asleep

anywhere but my own bed?" Toby stretched his long legs on the faded damask upholstery. "I've been sleeping badly." His voice broke over a heavy yawn. "I can't remember any of my dreams. You know I always remember them. I wake up feeling weird and exhausted."

Claire walked into the living room and stood over him. He smiled at her and closed his eyes.

"You can fall asleep if you want to," she said.

"I'm just resting my eyes," he said.

Claire grinned. She walked to her bedroom and closed the door.

Harcourt closed the front door of the Black Hound Inn and walked up the wide center staircase. Memories of the morning Kate had come to his house to care for Celia chased him, grabbing for his heart and tearing apart any resistance he had left. The chamber door shut behind him. The slam resounded in his head. He stared at the fat, full moon in the window and poured himself more wine. Images, like floating pictures, danced before him: Celia's uneaten breakfast, Kate's calm attentiveness in the face of his frenzied impotency, Kate's lovely face in the filtered moonlight. He drained the wineglass. A numb heaviness blurred the edges of the dark room, but the memory of that morning, and the long day and night that followed—they remained fixed in his brain, clean and sharp as cut glass.

Harcourt Abernathy opened the morning paper and glanced up at Mrs. Week. He'd returned from his walk nearly an hour earlier. "Is Miss Abernathy still in bed?"

Mrs. Week did not answer.

He put down his knife and glanced disapprovingly from the tray in the housekeeper's hands to the untouched breakfast laid out on the table for Celia.

"Did you take breakfast to her, Mrs. Week?"

"She's heartbroken, sir," the housekeeper pleaded. "She says she cannot come down today."

"This shall not stand," he said. "I have tolerated this nonsense for three days. I've listened to her heartache. I've allowed her to stay in bed and mourn for that Stanley fellow. I have—regrettably—permitted her to ignore her lessons. But I am finished. Get her up, Mrs. Week. Get her up, get her dressed and send for the tutor."

"Very well, sir."

Mrs. Week, who loved Celia as her own, stood for a moment in the doorway, apparently reticent to subject her pet to the cruelties of breakfast downstairs and the horrors of arithmetic lessons, which would do a pretty girl like Miss Abernathy no service whatsoever.

Harcourt sighed and rose from the table. "I shall do it myself. Send for the tutor and take Miss Abernathy's breakfast to Mrs. Miller for her children."

He quietly opened the door to his sister's bedchamber. Surrounded by bedclothes, Celia looked more like a child than a young lady of fifteen. Her face was bright pink and her hair curled softly around it. If Harcourt stared long enough, Celia became the lovely child she was before both their parents died.

"Wake up, Celia," he said gently. "It's time to throw off this nonsense and come downstairs."

He gently shook her to rouse her. "Celia." Her narrow shoulder was so hot he drew back his hand before touching her again to make certain he wasn't mistaken.

Mrs. Week entered the room to help Celia dress.

"Miss Abernathy is ill," Harcourt said, his calm voice belying the panic coursing through him as hotly as fever coursed through Celia. "Send for Dr. Cowpe. And send away the tutor when he arrives."

Claire got out of the shower and listened for any signs of movement in the living room. Nothing but soft breathing and street sounds outside. *Toby did fall asleep*, she thought. She pulled on a bathrobe and walked into the living room.

Toby started slightly but didn't wake. He slept with his

brow furrowed and his arms crossed. *How can anyone sleep with such an expression of impatience?* Claire thought. She took a white down comforter out of a wicker basket on the floor and covered him with it.

"Thanks for staying with me," she whispered. She kissed his head and went back to her bedroom and turned off the light.

Cowpe strode into the tavern of the Horn and Powder as the innkeeper's widow came laughing from the kitchen. "Mrs. Pegler," he said, "I wish to speak with Miss Ishingham. I hope she has not yet returned to Warwickshire."

Kate stood on the stair. "Dr. Cowpe."

Mrs. Pegler turned coolly to an elderly man, who was the sole patron of the tavern this morning, then re-entered the kitchen.

"Thank you for coming early in the day," Kate said. "May I expect a response for my father?"

"I am true to *my* word, Miss Ishingham," he said pointedly.

Kate allowed the implication to pass. "And I am grateful to you, Dr. Cowpe. May I have my notebook, please?"

Cowpe hesitated.

Kate bit the inside of her lip. She could hold her tongue, could she not? She hadn't responded to his insult, had she? But why did he falter now? Was he formulating a lecture on delicacy? Should she prepare for an anatomy lesson on the smaller, softer female brain: an organ given to emotional rule and unacquainted with reason?

Her cousin Charles's last words before she left home rang in her ears: *"With every privilege you possess, Kate, why do you devote yourself to vile matters, to things of which no woman should ever speak, no less spend her life contemplating? You, who should be an example to those beneath you, are a disgrace. I would rather you had gone to Scotland with the son of a tanner than to know what I know now!"* Kate sighed and pushed away any shame. Coming to Ledwyche might have been a mistake, but she was grateful at least to have learned the lesson on her own.

Cowpe held her notebook and kept his eyes downcast for a moment longer. When he raised his head he looked kinder.

Kate felt a stab of pity.

"I'm sorry," he said, "but I simply cannot agree to such an arrangement. Your work was exactly as you described. Superior, in truth, to your description of it. I had to constantly remind myself a woman wrote it." Cowpe exhaled. "But I have a family to think of, Miss Ishingham—a wife and children. The scandal of my working with you and the ensuing gossip would make their lives uneasy and difficult. I am sorry."

Deprived by his gentle confession of the compensatory pleasure of despising him, her anger diminished. "Thank you." She took the notebook from him. "Thank you for reading it and thank you for coming to speak with me this morning."

Cowpe smiled.

Kate hadn't noticed until now how handsome he was, possessing the face and manner that feeds many a maid's dreams of love and marriage. Not hers however; she dreamt of work, not wifehood.

"A safe journey home, Miss Ishingham," he said. "Remember me to your father, if you will. I studied with him in Edinburgh."

"My father remembered and thought well of you, Dr. Cowpe," she said. "Did he not mention it in the letter he wrote you? It was for that reason he permitted me to come to Ledwyche."

Before Cowpe had time to reply, Nell Easton, Cowpe's maid Jenny's younger sister, ran into the tavern.

"Dr. Cowpe," she said. "Mama needs you. She says it's twins. She's always thought so, but they're not coming. The midwife has gone to Oxford for her daughter. Mama told her to go. She said she could deliver two babies and feed the rest of us at the same time."

"Tell your mother I shall be there presently," Cowpe said.

"Please do not wait on my account," Kate said.

Cowpe took her hand and held it for an instant. "Good-bye, Miss Ishingham. Safe journey."

Kate saw a flicker of what looked like regret in his eyes. Though she had been naïve about Cowpe's willingness to flout convention for the possibility of good, she had not been wrong about his ambition and curiosity. If she had been a man this would have proved a fruitful and happy partnership. The door opened again and sunlight flooded the room.

John Greeley ran in, startling Mr. Gedge, who had nearly fallen asleep at his table. The old sheep farmer dropped his tankard, splattering ale all over the floor and walls.

"Dr. Cowpe." John Greeley caught his breath. "Miss Abernathy is ill."

"What is the matter?" Cowpe asked.

"Fever," Greeley replied. "Mrs. Week said you should come straightaway."

"Tell Mr. Abernathy I shall come when Mrs. Easton's child is safely delivered," Cowpe said. "In the meantime, ask Mrs. Week to keep Miss Abernathy comfortable."

"I don't know, sir," Greeley said. "She was crying about it being her fault and insisting I bring you straight to Miss Abernathy."

Cowpe sighed and turned to Kate. "Miss Abernathy is a willful girl, apt to feign illness to get attention. Mrs. Easton would only ask for help if her life depended upon it.

Kate could see Dr. Cowpe did not like to have to choose between two people who needed his care. She dared to suggest, "My kit is in my chamber. Mr. Abernathy's house is very near here. If you would like, I could see to Miss Abernathy and wait with her until you are free." She turned to Greeley, who stood shifting his weight from foot to foot. "Good morning Mr. Greeley."

Cowpe's attention shot to Greeley's neatly bandaged hand.

"Good morning to you, Miss Ishingham," Greeley said, sounding embarrassed to have been acknowledged by her.

The vexation of the day rose to the surface of Cowpe's face. He ran his fingers through his thick dark hair and stood impatiently in front of Kate. "Get your kit, Miss Ishingham. And come with me."

Chapter Eight

Dr. Cowpe and Kate arrived to find Harcourt at Celia's bedside, her small hand in his. "Cowpe," he said hoarsely. He gazed through Kate as though she weren't there.

"If you will permit it," Cowpe said, his voice thick with reluctance, "Miss Ishingham has offered her assistance. I must tend to Mrs. Easton. Her confinement is over."

Harcourt nodded, then turned to his sister.

Miss Abernathy looked worse than Kate had expected. Her skin was red and dry and her face was swollen.

"Forgive me, Mr. Abernathy." Mrs. Week's voice came from the open doorway. "I thought it was lovesickness. She talked all morning of Mr. Stanley and her broken heart."

"It is not your fault," Harcourt said, keeping his attention fixed on his sister. "It is no one's fault."

Cowpe counted the pulse in Miss Abernathy's wrist.

"Will you bleed her, Dr. Cowpe?" Mrs. Week asked.

Cowpe laid his hand on Celia's brow.

Suddenly Celia sat straight up and stared at Harcourt, addressing him in a strong voice. "Why do I have a teapot for a brain, Harcourt?" She said this twice and lay back down.

Harcourt's fingers whitened at the knuckle as he gripped the edge of his chair.

"She must be bled," Mrs. Week whimpered from the doorway.

"Dr. Cowpe," Kate said softly, as if he were the only other person in the room, "are you familiar with theories on fevers and the dangers of excessive bleeding? My father has been corresponding with a French physician who has been closely observing hospital patients and recording his observations."

"What of it?" Cowpe snapped impatiently. "What competent medical man does not record what he observes as well as what he experiences?"

Kate glanced quickly at Miss Abernathy. She reined in an impulse to snap back at Cowpe for not allowing her to finish. She took in a deep breath. "He has begun to theorize that excessive bloodletting weakens the patient, rather than the disease." Kate ignored a barely concealed squeak of disapproval from Mrs. Week. Several patients had left her father's care when they discovered he employed bleeding as a last resort rather than a first choice. As she spoke, Kate laid her hands on Celia's feverish flesh. "Shall we wait before bleeding her?" she asked, instantly regretting the word *we*, which seemed to stab Cowpe's ear.

The doctor ignored Kate and addressed Harcourt, who seemed not to hear him. "I have begun to note a connection between deteriorating conditions in patients, especially among the sickest of them, and too much bloodletting." He flashed a hot glance at Kate, then turned to Mrs. Week. "Bring cool water," he said. "I shall not bleed her."

He turned back to Kate. "Stay with Miss Abernathy until I return. If she worsens, send for me."

"I shall," Kate said.

Harcourt had not taken his eyes from his sister, as though by his attention alone he could help her. He hated nothing more than the corrosive effect of powerlessness.

103

"She'll be all right, Abernathy," Cowpe said gently, laying his hand on Harcourt's broad shoulder. Harcourt shuddered.

"Dr. Cowpe," Kate said as he walked toward the door, "should you not wash your hands?"

Cowpe blinked in astonishment.

"My father learned from a Scottish midwife long ago never to come to a childbed unclean," she said.

Cowpe trembled with bruised masculine pride.

"You wouldn't want hands that had been in the stables to bring your food," she continued, "and thus you should not let unwashed hands usher life into the world."

Cowpe furiously ran his fingers through his hair. He turned to an untouched basin in the room and thoroughly, angrily, washed his hands. "Keep Miss Abernathy comfortable," he snapped at Kate and left for the Eastons'.

Mrs. Week returned with more water and clean muslin. Kate soaked the strips of cloth in the water and rubbed Celia's arms and face and neck.

"Thank you for staying on," Harcourt said roughly, not looking at her. His words strained in his throat, as though he kept a struggling heart locked in a cage.

"Of course," Kate said.

"I too thought it a self-made malady," he said. "Brought on by fancy more than any real cause." His lip rose. He clenched his jaw and stroked Celia's fingers with his thumb. "My sister has kept to her bed for three days." He breathed deeply and shuddered. "She is fifteen." Harcourt gazed up at Kate for the first time since she arrived. "Fifteen."

"When she wakes you must try to persuade her to take a little cool broth or tea," Kate said quietly.

Mr. Abernathy appeared not to hear her. The spirited man who'd sprung to her defense in Cowpe's office, who'd taken her and Mr. Greeley into his house when most would have barred the door, seemed utterly incapable of action. Kate watched him continue to stare desperately at his sister. Nursing was a woman's responsibility, but Mr. Abernathy seemed not to care that she had come to Ledwyche to act as a physician.

Kate dipped a piece of cloth in the cool water Mrs. Week brought. "Help me," she said calmly. "Lay this cloth over her head and replace it when it warms."

Harcourt stared at Kate for a moment, then laid the wet cloth across Celia's brow, seeming ineffably grateful for something to do.

The day fell away and darkness poured in. Celia worsened. Cowpe was sent for but could not come. Kate administered one half grain of tartar emetic, in the hopes of lessening Celia's febrile excitement. Celia wrinkled her nose and shook her head, but she swallowed it. Mrs. Week brought in a light supper. Harcourt refused it.

"You should at least take some tea, Mr. Abernathy," Kate urged gently.

"Miss Ishingham," he snapped in a raw voice, "you do not know me. I admire your skills and am grateful beyond what I can express for what you have done today, but do not put yourself in a position to care for me." The hard carved muscle of his arm, exposed where he pushed up his sleeve, pulsed in tense undulation as he pushed himself noisily from the chair.

Kate sighed and rubbed her eyes. She felt as if she hadn't slept since she left Greydon Hall. "If you do not care for yourself, Mr. Abernathy, you shall be unable to care for your sister. Sorrow robs us of strength. Do not risk your health for a display of pride."

Did she mean to insult him? he thought. In his own house? While Celia lay in danger? Harcourt rubbed his tongue over the back of his teeth as he considered what to say. "My sister is all I have in the world, Miss Ishingham. Whether I take tea or food tonight or tomorrow shall have no bearing, neither good nor ill, upon her recovery." His voice was rising and he could not stop it. "Attend to Celia," he growled through clenched teeth. "Not to me!"

He left the room.

Kate shook her head and exhaled wearily. She wondered why women were always accused of not mastering their emotions.

Celia stirred and started to gag. Kate quickly raised her to a sitting position. She vomited all over herself, and Kate as well.

"Who are you?" Celia asked in a voice like a very young child's.

"My name is Miss Ishingham," Kate said. "I have come to help Dr. Cowpe." She took the remainder of the dry cloth on the bedstand and cleaned the vomit from Celia's chest.

Celia looked surprised and frightened. "Where is Harcourt?"

"He shall return. Shall I help you change your gown?"

"Where is Harcourt?" Celia asked again, shivering.

Her brother's footfalls sounded swiftly on the stairs.

"Harcourt," Celia cried, holding out her arms.

"I am here," he said. "I am here." He stroked her cheek and brushed the hair from her face.

"What happened?" Celia asked.

"You are ill," he said, glancing from Celia to Kate. "Forgive me, Miss Ishingham."

"Think nothing of it," she said, but his devotion to his sister moved Kate more than it should have, and she had to turn away for a moment. "Now," she said brightly, swallowing any trace of sorrow in her voice. "Mr. Abernathy has returned. Will you permit me to help you change your gown? You are trembling."

"What happened to you?" Celia asked. "Your gown is filthy. And that color is wrong for your complexion."

"Thank you for the counsel," Kate said, smiling. "Perhaps I shall not wear this gown again."

"You should not," Celia said in complete earnestness. "Devonshire brown does not suit you at all. With your light eyes you should wear celestial blue or pomona green."

Celia was as placid as a sleepy baby as Kate pulled the gown from her and replaced it with a clean, warm robe.

Harcourt turned away but stayed in the room. Celia had grown more womanly than he liked to admit. He helped Kate change the linens. Celia fell asleep the moment he tucked the soft coverlet around her.

"Would you like a change of clothes, Miss Ishingham?" he asked. "Miss Abernathy's older sisters left several gowns here for her."

"Might there be something in celestial blue?" Kate asked, a smile brightening the corners of her vivid blue-gray eyes.

Harcourt grinned slightly, feeling at ease for the first time that day. "I feel certain of it."

"Then thank you, Mr. Abernathy," Kate said. "I should very much like to change."

When he came back with the clean blue gown, Harcourt stood for a moment in the doorway. Miss Ishingham sat at Celia's bedside, checking her pulse and laying her hand on Celia's cheek. Moonlight, filtered through the great beech tree outside, shimmered like a fairy ocean on the coverlet. Miss Ishingham turned to him and smiled.

It was a very strange time to want to kiss a woman, but Harcourt had never wanted to kiss anyone more than he wanted to kiss Miss Ishingham now, in Celia's gently lit chamber. He wanted to feel Miss Ishingham's mouth soft on his. He wanted to feel her open and let him inside to taste her. Miss Ishingham gazed at him, then lowered her lashes and returned to Celia.

The thin, sky-blue silk hung coolly over Harcourt's bare forearm. Soon the dress would cover Miss Ishingham with little between it and her soft skin. Would that he was the one to drape it over her firm round breasts and the swell of her hips. He could nearly sense her beneath him, pressed up to him in that intoxicating mix of hard and soft flesh.

Celia sighed deeply and Kate folded the coverlet more snugly around her. Absurd and terrifying, Harcourt thought, trying to stave off hunger for her. Joy and sorrow fall forever upon one another, vying for dominance. He handed her the gown.

Miss Ishingham returned his gaze and smiled slightly, a tiny wry glance that made him think she guessed his thoughts and felt no shame because of them. Whether or not she returned his feelings he did not know. She took the gown and left the room to change.

Harcourt sat at Celia's bedside and closed his eyes. Miss Ishingham had been right: He should have eaten something. He felt dizzy and exhausted. He longed to run for the meadow and lie beneath the wide sky until clarity replaced chaos and he could master his thoughts and feelings again.

After a few minutes he heard Miss Ishingham's feet on the floor of the landing. A second shock of desire flared before he could stop it. It wasn't a matter of any woman, soft and compliant, meeting his hard body with an unfolding and anticipation of her own. It was this woman, beneath him, around him, pressed against him.

Harcourt set his jaw and tightened every muscle against the thought of her, for to want a woman above everyone and everything threatened to release a chaos in his soul he could not bear.

The fear of scandal opened its swallowing mouth and murmured in his ear. It was one thing to support the idea of a female physician. After all, he was a rational, forward-thinking man, and Miss Ishingham had already proved her superior intelligence to her father, and to Cowpe, though Cowpe wouldn't admit it. But it was a damnably cursed decision to let such a person into one's family. Wasn't it? He must not allow his too-soft heart to influence his mind. He must think of Celia. Who would want to marry a girl with no money and a doctor for a sister-in-law? He must think of appearances.

The whisper had solidified into the vital, angry, musical

voice of his grandmother. Harcourt swore a terrible oath and pushed violently away from Celia's bed.

"Is everything all right?" Miss Ishingham asked in alarm, running into the room. She crossed immediately to Celia and laid her hand on her cheek.

Harcourt watched with an ache of conflicting emotions tearing at his heart. *Weak and soft,* his grandmother's voice continued to snap at him. Knowing that a fear of scandal was keeping him from pursuing the only thing he wanted since that same bone-deep terror had destroyed his family did not free him to take Kate as his own. A more insidious fear stood in its place like a parasite in the heart of an animal. If he had what he wanted, if Kate was his, she would disappear like his father and mother. Damnation! He *was* weak. Stunted, and stuck in a howling adolescent moment from which he could not break free.

Harcourt stared uncomprehendingly into the room. Before he knew what was happening, Miss Ishingham slipped her hand under his arm and led him to the chair near the window.

"You look exhausted, Mr. Abernathy," she said gently. "Please sit down."

The sense of her soft, strong hand under his arm and the sound of her voice caressing his ear echoed through every muscle of Harcourt's body, as if this moment had happened before and would continue to happen again. The solidity of her connection to him, and his to her, rippled out like rings on a lake. Moonlight spilled down her sky-blue gown, making it appear that she stood in a place where daylight mingled with the night.

Claire rolled over and opened her eyes to a splash of moonlight on her bed. She got up and tiptoed into the kitchen. Toby was lightly snoring on the couch. Claire was struck by an image of him standing at someone's bedside, striving to do the right thing. She shook her head and opened and closed the cabinets and refrigerator. She wasn't hungry, but a craving for sensation pricked her all over like a thirst inside her muscles.

Padding quietly into the living room, Claire took a vial of lavender oil from a shelf of dried flowers in silver bowls. She took a clean white pillowcase from the armoire near her open bedroom door and poured a few drops of oil on it.

With a glance at the soundly sleeping Toby, Claire walked back to her room. She dropped her underwear and brown T-shirt on the floor and slipped on a sky-blue nightgown. It fell like water over her breasts and hips. She slipped the scented pillowcase onto her pillow and slid into bed. The lush, powdery scent of the lavender filled her mouth and nose.

"Charles!" Kate said, as her cousin stepped from a coach in front of the Horn and Powder the following morning. Before she could say another word he crossed the footpath and grabbed her hand.

"I have come to bring you home," he said.

Kate pulled away from him with enough violence to seize the attention of anyone not already gaping at the handsome, beautifully dressed young poet. She had made arrangements to leave Ledwyche in a few days, but she felt her feet root themselves into the dirt of the street. "Upon whose inclination? Yours or my father's?"

Charles ignored her question. He nodded imperiously at a wide-eyed young woman who appeared to be on the verge of ecstatic collapse.

"Come inside," Kate commanded. She turned to enter the inn. "Come," she repeated when he did not follow. "Or we shall stand here all forenoon while fluttering maids gather like pink storm clouds of adoration."

Charles frowned but obeyed. "I see your journey to the brink of disrepute has not softened your tongue," he said when they stood inside the tavern.

"And I see my father's decision has had no bearing on

your willful supposition of your unvarying rightness on every issue."

"I did not come to engage in a nursery battle, Kate," he said wearily.

"Why then did you come?"

"To save you from yourself," he said heatedly. "If your good father is too set apart from the world to see what irreparable harm you bring on yourself and our family, I have no choice but to take it upon myself to act for him and for you."

Mrs. Pegler stood near the kitchen, shifting her weight from foot to foot.

Kate guessed the innkeeper had decided to give Charles a moment before demanding he order something or take his business elsewhere. With his light brown hair and a face like John Kemble in his prime, Charles Ishingham commanded breathless awe from every woman who crossed his path.

"We shall have to sit," Kate said, "and you shall have to drink, or we must return to the street."

Indignation flashed so swiftly across Charles's fine-cut features, Kate swore she heard a snap like a fairy whip.

"Let us sit then," he hissed through clenched teeth. He gestured to the innkeeper for ale. "Where is Mrs. Gardner? Why are you alone?" Charles seemed suddenly grateful for the tankard of ale dropped noisily in front of him, for he drained it as Kate answered.

"She has gone to make arrangements for our return trip," Kate said coolly.

Charles leaned back and sighed in relief. Kate felt a sting of regret that she had spoken harshly. She knew he had what he believed to be her best interests at heart.

"I am happy to know you have come to reason and given up your . . ." Charles chewed for the right word. "Your adventure." He pulled his chair closer to hers and spoke softly. "It is not that I have no sympathy for your yearnings to make a man's way for yourself in the world, Kate. It is not your fault your father treated you like a son instead of a daughter and never taught you to understand a woman's place, where her happiness must and should lie."

Kate breathed deeply. "I have not *come to reason*, Charles, for I never left it."

Anger stole the color from his cheeks. "Tell me you have declined that man's offer."

"I have not," Kate answered.

Charles paled. "He has not kept his word after meeting with you? Has he?"

Kate said nothing.

"Have you given any thought, any thought at all, to the shock you must have given this unsuspecting doctor when you arrived?" Charles asked. "I do not wish to think on his humiliation when he comprehended the way in which you deceived him. A woman physician! The idea is unthinkable." He exhaled forcefully, as if Kate were a naughty child and he a governess at the end of her wits. "More than that, it is immoral, Kate, you know it is, for an unmarried woman to have intimate physical contact of any kind with men, however noble your intentions might be. I shudder at the thought of it. For some reason, your father indulged this . . . this interest of yours while it was maintained at home but you have overstepped yourself. You must end this madness, Kate. Now. Come home and find a husband before what you have done is found out."

"Charles," Kate said quietly, "you cannot know—"

"I assure you, Kate, I know far better than you your place in the world and how woefully ill-prepared you are to take it." Charles rose noisily from the heavy wooden chair. "What you do not know—"

"*Please!*" Kate said, with more feeling than she intended to reveal. "Allow me to speak. Permit me to defend my position this once. I shall not speak of it again. As a gentleman you owe me the honor of respect, no matter what you think of my opinions."

The muscle of her cousin's jaw flickered. "Forgive me."

"You mistake me to think I disregarded the probable outcome of this endeavor. I understand my place and his far better than you ever shall. I never imagined Dr. Cowpe would be easy with my deception." She hesitated. "I signed my letters K. Ishingham. He of course assumed—"

"What else would he assume?" Charles exhaled quickly, and clasped his fingers behind his back. "Continue."

"What you do not know," Kate said, "what you cannot understand, is Dr. Cowpe's devotion to medicine. His ambition and passion, and his ability to treat disease. How many people, Charles, in your circle, in Town and in Warwickshire, do you know who have lost their lives or their loved ones to putrid pox? What should I do when I know I might help Thomas Cowpe find an answer to this plague? Shall I stand by mute and ashamed because I was born a woman? Should I withhold information that might hasten or complete his search because I am female? Come to me, Charles, when someone close to you, someone you hold tenderly to your heart, finds their arms and legs and neck covered with shiny blood-red spots, and then tell me I should come home and find a husband before I am found out."

"But, Kate—"

"If Dr. Cowpe declines my offer to help him—and I believe, regrettably, that he shall do so—I will return home. But I do *not* want a husband. And I will not abandon a life's work because of a misguided and fearful conviction that a woman's anatomy renders her brain useless." Kate rose and stepped dangerously close to her cousin. "The only anatomical feature that makes you and me different from one another is neither connected to, nor in any proximity of, the brain."

Humiliation like tiny emerald chips flashed in Charles's hazel eyes. "You are lost to me, Kate," he said softly. "And I am verily sorry for it."

Kate bit back sudden, unwanted tears.

Charles walked away from her but stopped at the tavern

door. "What you are attempting is foolish and dangerous. And I do not accept it. You shall return to Greydon Hall altered and pained, whatever you experience." Charles gazed directly at her. "If I were a different sort of man, I would force you to come with me."

Kate clenched her teeth against a sadness she did not expect to feel. "If I were a different sort of woman, you would be able to."

"Then that is the end of it, Kate," Charles said. And he left her in the tavern alone.

The next morning Claire woke up feeling angry and upset. The ugly red light glowing in the apartment across the street irritated her. Wind howled through the window seam and a foul, frat-boy pukey smell seeped in beneath it. Gross. She shivered and stuffed an old brown towel into the crack. She was already tired of cold and it was only November.

Claire walked into the kitchen and took two bags of coffee, one flavored, one strong, out of the freezer. Frigid air chilled her skin. She slammed the freezer door shut and her front door opened.

"What the . . . ?" she said. She took a meat tenderizer from the rarely used utensil jar and walked into the front hall.

"Ian!" she said, lowering the steel tenderizer to her side and feeling stupid. "What are you doing here?"

"Why is Toby still here?" Ian asked, dropping Claire's newspaper on the front hall table and gesturing to the couch.

"Shhhh," Claire said, beckoning him into the kitchen. "He's still asleep."

She gently closed the kitchen door behind them. "He fell asleep when I was taking a shower," she said, measuring coffee into the coffeemaker.

Ian frowned and looked out the kitchen window into the living room. "Whatever," he said sulkily.

"Whatever?" Claire repeated. "What are you? Twelve?"

Ian whipped his head back to look at her, pissed off.

"Sorry," Claire said reflexively. She stepped back and turned on the coffeemaker. Why did she always try to make herself agreeably small with Ian? She sighed and reveled slightly in the comforting sizzle of the coffee dripping into the pot, then opened the cabinet to get three mugs. "How did it go last night?" she asked, hoping to distract Ian from being jealous of Toby, which was so absurd Claire didn't bother to defend herself or him.

Ian's delicate features fell into a soft grimace. "Badly." He shifted all his intensity to Claire. "How are you?"

"I'm fine," she said. "I don't know what happened to me last night. I hadn't eaten much all day. Maybe I drank the wine too fast. Hey," she said, turning away from the open cabinet door to face him. "Where's the monograph? Toby said you had it."

Ian grunted, took off his black cashmere coat and sat down. "I left it in my car. I'll give it to you later." He opened his hands onto the table. "Are you seeing anyone?"

"What?" Claire stammered. "No! How can you ask me that?"

Ian squinted at her. The brown in his eyes swallowed every trace of green. "No," he said wearily when he realized what she meant. "Not like that." He glanced distractedly around the small galley kitchen. "Would you pour me some grapefruit juice?"

Claire filled a glass and handed it to him.

Ian drank the pink liquid. "I meant, are you seeing a therapist?"

"What for?" Claire asked.

"What do you mean, what for?" Ian laughed condescendingly.

Claire blushed and ground her teeth together. Ian pushed away from the table and stared at the still-dripping coffee.

This is going to be nice and awkward, Claire thought, watching Ian glare at the pot as if he could force it to brew faster.

Toby stirred, and swore under his breath in the living room. A moment later he pushed open the kitchen door and banged into Ian.

"What the . . . ?" Toby said. "Sorry. I didn't know you were here. It's not eight yet, is it, Claire?" He pointed to the clock on the stove.

"No," Claire answered. "That clock is always wrong." She picked up Ian's wrist, checked his watch and set the clock. "It's six-thirty."

Toby sighed in relief and took a cup out of the cabinet. "Sorry about the door," he said to Ian.

Ian nodded his head grumpily.

Toby maneuvered past him and poured himself a cup of coffee. He sipped it, then made a face and stirred in cream and sugar. "God, Claire, you make your coffee strong. Did you sleep okay?"

"Kind of," Claire said, pouring coffee for herself and Ian. "How about you?"

"Terribly." Toby turned to Ian. "How did it go at the hospital?"

"Shitty," Ian said putting vanilla soymilk into his cup. He exhaled heavily and sat down. "How did it go here?"

Toby glanced at Claire. "Fine."

The muscle of Ian's jaw pulsed. "Thanks for staying with her."

"You're welcome," Toby answered.

Toby lined up his placemat with the edge of the table. Ian glowered into his soy-milky coffee. Claire finished her own coffee and put her mug down too hard. Both men jumped a little.

"Sorry," she apologized, wiping up the caramel-brown drops on the scrubbed wood countertop. "Listen: I'm fine. And I don't want to talk about it. I don't see a therapist anymore," she said to Ian. "I don't need to. Thank you both for helping me, but I'm really okay."

She put her mug in the sink and rinsed it out. "You guys can stay and eat breakfast. There are Wolverman's English muffins in the fridge, and butter and marmalade." She wiped off the rest of the counter. "I have to get dressed and get out of here. I'm giving a lecture on nineteenth-century vernacular portrait painting tonight. I've gotta pick up my slides before I open the store." She kissed Ian on the cheek, squeezed Toby's shoulder and ran to dress.

Chapter Nine

Harcourt rose noisily from the red velvet chair in his chamber at the Black Hound. He threw a glass of wine down his throat and choked on the burn of it.

It seems I have regressed to the self-addicted state of a fourteen-year-old-boy, he thought morosely. *Unable to recover from the sorrow of a lost love, I sit and stoke the fire of memory, hoping to achieve blessed insensibility.*

He opened the window and hungrily breathed the air. Kate would never have allowed him to wallow so mournfully. Indeed, if she could see him now, drunk—but not drunk enough, he thought—and mired in grief, she would have urged him to act and not to drown in self-pity. The idea that he had become like a petulant young boy would have amused her.

The cool air on his skin and the idea of Kate's presence cleared Harcourt's head. He filled the basin and washed his face. Water dripped down his neck and onto his collar. He rubbed his face dry with a cloth and took off his coat.

The fire had nearly gone out. Harcourt added more wood. He sat and watched the flames and listened to the

118

pleasant crackle and hiss of green branches. The homey fragrance of smoke filled the room, and a sense of ease he had not experienced in nearly a year softened the ache in his heart. Memories of the earliest days of their courtship washed over him. He breathed her in and closed his eyes.

Claire locked the front door of the Arts and Antiques Society behind her. The lecture had gone well. Everyone loved the slide of a beautifully dressed, handsome young poet with an intense expression in his hazel eyes and light brown hair romantically curling over his alabaster brow. Claire grinned to herself. Charles Ishingham had been her grandfather's favorite poet. She loved this unsigned painting because it seemed to capture a very human mix of petulance and vulnerability. Claire crossed to Acorn Street and walked down the steep hill. She pulled her scarf tighter around her neck and savored the sensual thrill of the cashmere gloves Ian had given her last January. A hot guy, at least three or four years younger than she was, almost bumped into her.

"Sorry," he said, smiling.

Claire met his flirty glance and grinned back. A sting of vitality warmed the surface of her skin. She felt dangerously, uncharacteristically confident.

"Shit!" She tripped and had to grab the doorknob of someone's house. She let go of the door and slid her foot back inside her boot. Not *uncharacteristically* confident, she corrected herself. But it had been a very long time since she had felt that way. The hot guy spun around at the bottom of the hill. He smiled at her again, then turned down Charles Street. A thread of recklessness wound its way up Claire's spine. She felt it open in her fingers and spread across her back. It wasn't the sense or the memory of Harcourt; it was different. It made her feel powerful. And she liked it.

Kate watched Mr. Abernathy stride toward her and savored a reckless thrill that would have terrified her mother.

119

"Miss Ishingham," he said, bowing slightly.

"Mr. Abernathy, how lovely to see you!" He seemed taken aback by the enthusiasm of her greeting in relation to his own. Kate felt her cheeks redden, but she had to tell someone. "I am waiting for a carriage to convey me to Fretherne."

A quizzical expression stole over his face like an unexpected spice in tea. "Are you acquainted with Mrs. Ansley?" he asked.

"Not yet," Kate said. "I know nothing more of her than that she is Mrs. Cowpe's aunt."

Curiosity flitted across Harcourt's masculine countenance. "You have me at a loss."

Kate ignored the blush on her cheeks and blazed forward. "I think we are friends, Mr. Abernathy."

Fear flashed in his eyes before it surrendered to a covetous glance, immediately swallowed by cool amiability. Kate hardly had time to register the changing emotions and implications. The heat of the blush dropped to her throat, making her long to taste something she could not name. She breathed deeply. She must keep a closer watch over herself in Mr. Abernathy's company. A flash in his dark eyes or the scent of his hair robbed her of her sense of purpose, replacing every thought in her head with the idea of him.

"Please continue, Miss Ishingham. We are indeed friends." He said this kindly, but a breath of unease lingered in his voice.

"I am glad of it," Kate said clearly, recapturing herself.

His strong features shifted again. He gazed directly at her for a moment. He might as well have brushed his fingers along her spine. As in a game, in which a small object is tossed between a pair of players, Mr. Abernathy offered and took back secrets. Each gift and retrieval left a mark on Kate as permanent as a scar and as pleasurable as a kiss.

"You have captured me in a moment of delight," she said, then instantly regretted her familiarity. She tried again to focus on the subject at hand.

"Delight," he echoed. "You have been in Ledwyche only a few days and you have already experienced delight."

His musical inflection of the word *delight* enlarged its meaning for Kate.

"I envy you," he said.

Kate temporarily lost the understanding of how to express herself. To be heard above Charles and Lydia, Kate had learned to pitch her voice clear as a clock chime, but now she could not find that timbre. Mr. Abernathy's deep, sure notes resonated through her skin. She devoured the word *envy* from his lips like a warm strawberry.

"Envy me?" she said. "You are curious, Mr. Abernathy. I do not know anyone who would envy me. Certainly no woman, at any rate. But my delight suits me better that any offering I can imagine."

"You have my attention," he said, and led her to the shelter of a small alcove near Carbury's shop, away from the clatter of passing carriages. He had both dreaded and counted upon her leaving Ledwyche. For even in the dusty air of this alcove, the scent of her hair curled around him like fragrant smoke and he could hardly think past the idea of his mouth on hers and a slow slide inside her. He smiled and she beamed joyfully at him. Had he been eighteen instead of eight and twenty he would have leaned closer to see if she would retreat. And if she did not, he would have drawn nearer, his hand at her waist, aching to rise to her breast. He would have pressed against her, her back at the cold stone wall, her mouth opening to let him in.

"I have you to thank," she said softly, as though they stood alone in a quiet drawing room.

"I?" he asked, relieved to feel curiosity ease the crush of desire.

"Yes," she said. "For without your suggestion Dr. Cowpe would never have read my notes."

"He has read them?" Harcourt asked.

"He has," she said triumphantly. "And for the good he believes we can accomplish together, Dr. Cowpe has accepted the terms of our initial agreement."

Harcourt stepped back in astonishment. "Without constraint?"

"None at all," she said. "Save I am to keep the nature of our work a secret and act as a private secretary."

"And you agreed to this?"

"I have." Satisfaction blazed in her gray-blue eyes.

Miss Ishingham seemed utterly unaware of the remarkable nature of her *delight* or its likely effect upon him or anyone else.

"Are you not concerned with scandal or gossip?" he asked. "If you act as though you are a physician, there will be people who will not speak to you or allow you into their homes. And what of Dr. Cowpe? Have you thought about how this *partnership* will affect him and his family?"

Kate breathed deeply. *This* cleared the seductive haze from her head. Mr. Abernathy sounded like Charles. On more familiar ground, she stepped nearer to him. "Is it your opinion then, Mr. Abernathy, that I should be concerned with scandal, and who will not ask me to tea? Who is marrying whom and who has fifty thousand per year: These are the only questions with which I am to occupy my thoughts? And if I *can* think beyond money and marriages, if I *can* help save the lives of these gossips who would scorn me, I would do well to do otherwise, and pretend my brain is merely a pedestal for the choicest French bonnet?"

Harcourt straightened his position. Desire sharpened and fell into clarity. "You are fond of your own voice, Miss Ishingham. And as I am neither your father nor your brother, the security of your reputation is of little personal consequence to me. If I have offended you, forgive me. It will not happen again."

The pink on her face slipped down the skin of her throat, below her collarbone to her breasts, and he was seized by the maddening paradox of wanting something and loathing it at the same time.

"There is nothing to forgive, Mr. Abernathy," she said coldly, but fire still shone from the coal-black center of her eyes.

"I have not finished," he said. "Although I have no obligation to you, Miss Ishingham, beyond a simple human compassion for your well being, I have an obligation to Dr. Cowpe. He and his family are very important to me. His young daughters are like my own, and with their reputation I am very much concerned."

A quiver danced over Miss Ishingham's pink mouth. She bit her lip to stop it. "You misunderstand me, sir. I am not coldhearted; nor am I ambitious to see my name blazoned in the public sphere. Dr. Cowpe and I spoke at length about the necessity of protecting his and his family's reputations. I do not seek acknowledgment. And I affix no value to achievement for the sake of public opinion. What I wish is for the freedom to work as I please without interference or obstacle. And to continue what I have begun."

She stood taller and breathed in the close air of the alcove.

"Where you differ from your friend, Mr. Abernathy," she said, "is in your flexibility of thought. Dr. Cowpe found a way to reconcile his duty to his family with his duty to medicine. If my theory proves to be true, lives will be saved. If for you the possibility of scandal is too high a price to pay for those lives, you are not the man I imagined you to be."

He expected her to leave, but she didn't. She waited—for what he did not know, but he couldn't think, couldn't respond and couldn't leave. The memory of his grandparent's betrayal and his mother's death sliced at the edges of his consciousness. He steeled himself against it.

Despite her indignation, Kate felt her heart soften in the face of Mr. Abernathy's obvious distress. "I would never allow any harm to come to Dr. Cowpe or his family," she said in a gentler tone. "He has given me the opportunity to achieve everything I should ever hope to achieve, and for that I shall be forever in his debt."

A smart black phaeton stopped in front of the Horn and Powder. "Is that Mrs. Ansley's carriage?" she asked.

"It is," he said.

"Mrs. Ansley has invited me to stay at Fretherne until my partnership with Dr. Cowpe is ended," she said.

Harcourt escorted Miss Ishingham to the coach and watched her leave with a sense of fear he could not banish and desire he could not escape.

Ian was in New York for a conference. He and Claire talked every day on the phone. Today, Claire had landed two huge weddings for late spring. And this morning, *Horticulture and Home* magazine called to say they wanted the series of articles she'd written on historic garden restoration.

The clock on the shop's fake fireplace chimed. Six o'clock. Claire walked to the door of Arcades and glanced outside. No one looked interested in buying flowers. She locked the door.

Ian still hadn't returned the monograph, but that was okay. When he came home she'd get it back. Maybe she'd go to England early this spring, before the wedding rush. She could learn something about Harcourt Abernathy and what he'd illustrated. Maybe she could find out where he lived and where he was buried. She could make some sort of peace with the idea of him and what had happened to them in Vermont. Maybe that was all he wanted from her.

Claire massaged her neck. She'd been feeling great, but she'd been sleeping terribly. After Sonsie and her drunken embarrassment she'd kept Harcourt out of her mind, but she hadn't slept well. She couldn't remember any of her dreams. She slid her hand from her neck to her tight shoulders. She probably needed a new pillow.

Claire crossed the small space of the store and turned off the lights. Snow had begun to fall. She watched as already lovely Charles Street was transformed into a movie set or a Currier and Ives scene. The phone rang. She ran back to the counter to answer it.

124

"It's me," Toby said.

"Hey! How are you?" Claire asked. "Did you see the snow? Isn't it beautiful?"

"Just a minute, Claire," Toby said. He answered a question before coming back to her. "I haven't been outside all day. Sorry. Listen, can you meet me at Boston Pizza Kitchen at eight tonight?"

Claire heard muted demands, followed by staccato replies from Toby, who was obviously still at the studio. "Sure," she said. "Is something wrong?"

"No." He sighed. "I'm just really busy."

Claire waited while Toby re-explained a concept to a scabby-voiced man. "Are you sure you're all right? You sound stressed."

"I'm fine," he snapped.

"Okay," she said. "I just—"

"Claire," Toby said, interrupting her in an unnaturally high voice.

"What?" she asked, a little alarmed.

"Please don't be late," he said and hung up.

Two and a half hours later, Claire ran down snowy Boylston Street. "Shit, shit, shit," she chanted as she tried not to fall in her ill-chosen heels. She'd taken a bath and talked to Ian, who'd said he thought he'd be home on Wednesday. Then she'd fallen asleep for almost an hour. "Shit!" she said one more time as she ran into Boston Pizza Kitchen, a noisy, trendy dive, at eight forty-five.

Toby was sitting alone in a booth.

"I'm so, so sorry," Claire said breathlessly, pushing her hair away from her face. "Ian called. I lost track of time. I'm really sorry."

"Forget it," Toby said. But he didn't get up as he usually did when Claire walked into a room. He poured her a glass of white wine.

"What's going on?" she asked. She sipped the wine. "Oh, my God. What is this?"

"Chassange-Montrachet," Toby said, smiling. "I brought it. Delicious, isn't it?"

His warm grin dissolved.

Claire took a deep breath. "I'm really sorry."

Toby didn't respond.

"I know I shouldn't be," Claire said, "and I wish I weren't, but I'm late a lot. Why was it such a big deal tonight?"

"Claire!" Toby said. "Claire," he repeated, modifying his tone. "I don't ask you for anything."

"Toby, I—"

"Stop!" he said. "I'm not complaining. I love you. Who you are. The way you are. I don't need anything from you except to know that you're around and okay. I need you to be there."

What the hell is going on? Claire thought. "I *am* there for you."

"I know!" Toby's voice rose slightly, echoing the weird tone he'd had on the phone.

"I'm sorry," Claire said. "I won't interrupt. Go ahead." She spoke softly, meaning to soothe him, but instead she seemed to provoke him further.

"Just show up on time," Toby snarled. "Pay attention to what time it is and be where you need to be when you say you will."

"I will," she said.

"Fine," he said. "Let's just stop talking about it and order." He swallowed his wine slowly and deliberately.

"How was your day?" Claire asked.

Toby put his menu down. "What's going on with you?"

"Me?" Claire asked. "You're the one who's acting crazy."

Toby ran his hand swiftly through his hair, then spread his long fingers over the scratched tabletop. "What is going on?" he repeated.

"Nothing," Claire answered emphatically. She rubbed her neck and Toby sat up taller. Every straight woman and gay man in the place turned a little. Most of them probably

126

didn't know anything about Toby except that he was dis-
armingly handsome.

He ignored the subtle staring and leaned closer to Claire.
"Are you still obsessing over Vermont?" Toby asked this
question carefully, as if her answer decided something.

Panic grabbed her chest for an instant, but she pushed it
away. "Actually, I've been feeling better about it." She drank
her wine. "God, this is so good. What? I thought you'd be
happy." She put her glass down too hard. "I am."

"I *am* happy," he barked crankily. Claire jumped.

"I'm sorry," he said, sighing. "I had a hellish day." He
craned his long neck to capture the attention of the moody,
kohl-eyed waitress.

Claire sat up straighter. She took off her silver ring and
played with it.

"I don't mean to be an asshole," he said, softening.

"I know," she said, patting his hand.

"What's on your ring?" he asked, taking it from her.

"*Sedum telephium*. Orpine," she said. "Love Restorer," she
added in a silly voice.

Toby reached out to pour her more wine. "How are
things going with Ian?"

She held her glass for him. "Thanks. Things are going
pretty well. I mean, he's been in New York all week, so I
don't know what that means, really." Claire drank the wine
and savored the soft burn as it slipped down her throat.
"Why were you so upset that I was late?"

Toby stared through her.

"What *is* it?" she asked gently. "What do you want to tell
me? I'm not made of glass, Toby."

"I can't do this anymore," he muttered. He pushed away
from the table and gazed intently at her. "I've met someone.
I've met someone, and it's serious. I've never felt like this
about anyone."

A screamed obscenity, followed by peals of laughter,
came from the bar. "I dropped my *cell phone* in my *beer!*"

Claire turned away from Toby and concentrated on the shrieking woman, who shook a tiny phone, splattering beer on her friends. A deeply hidden chunk of self-knowledge fell on Claire's lap. Toby was *her* guy. She didn't *want* him; not sexually, anyway. But she didn't want to share him with anyone either.

"Oh, my *God!* It's broken! I'm gonna hafta get a new phone!"

"Claire. Did you hear what I said?" Toby asked.

Claire looked away from the squealing and cursing. "Yes," she said in an oddly chirpy voice. "What? Were you afraid I wouldn't be able to handle it?"

"Well, you don't seem to be handling it," Toby said, staring into his wine.

"Why shouldn't I be able to handle it? We're not dating," she snapped. "Do you think I don't remember what an unmitigated disaster our one night together was?"

"Okay," Toby said, sitting up straighter and looking away from her. "Fine."

Claire closed her eyes. What the hell did she want?

"I don't know what you want from me, Claire," he said.

"I know. I'm sorry," she said quietly.

"Don't apologize!" he said. "I don't want you to apologize."

"I'm not in love with you, Toby," she said.

He shook his head and glared uncomprehendingly at the next table.

"I'm not," she repeated. "And I don't mean to seem like such a freak."

"You're not a freak," he said, still not looking at her.

"You know what I mean," she said.

"No, I don't. I don't know what you mean, and I don't know what you want," he said. "What I do know is, for the first time in my life I'm in love with someone and all I can think of is how the fuck Claire is going to handle it!"

Claire cringed. Toby was the most important person in her life, and she was driving him away. "I'm not in love with you."

"What are you, then? Why am I so terrified of being happy when I'm with you?"

Claire leaned back in her chair. She couldn't think straight. She couldn't think at all. She wasn't in love with Toby. She knew that. She knew that a long time ago. So why did she care if he had someone? What was she so afraid of losing?

"I don't want you to be afraid to be happy when you're with me, Toby," she said. "You saved my life. You made it possible for me to find myself in the world again, and for that I am forever grateful."

"You're not going to lose me, Claire," he said.

"And I'm not going to fall apart because you have your own life." She bit her cheek.

The intensity in his eyes softened.

"I mean it. Whatever debt you thought you owed me is more than paid. I want you to be happy." Claire licked the sharp wine taste from her mouth and breathed deeply. "So, what's she like? What does she do?"

Toby hesitated. Claire grabbed his hand across the sticky table. "Come on. You'll never know how strong I am until you give me a chance. What's her name?"

"Miranda Douglas," Toby said, trying not to smile when her name came out of his mouth. "She's an actress. Red hair. Amazing face. I met her in Scotland. She'd just finished a remake of *That Hamilton Woman*. You know: the Vivien Leigh movie about Horatio Nelson and Emma Hamilton?"

Claire grinned. "I know what it is. Wait a minute: You went to Edinburgh in September. You've been keeping this a secret for four months?"

"I didn't know how serious it was at first," Toby said. He played with the position of the slender olive oil bottle and the grainy ceramic salt dish. "And then I didn't know how to tell you."

Claire squeezed his hand. He beamed. "Tell me more," she said.

The waitress came.

"Let's order first," Toby suggested, poring over the artfully stained menu, probably seeing it clearly for the first time that night. "What do you want?"

"You know what I want," Claire said. "I always order the same thing here." She smiled at the waitress, who looked terminally bored. "Could you come back in a minute? We're not quite ready."

"Wait." Toby held out his hand to stop the waitress from leaving, then turned to Claire. "Why don't you get something different tonight? Expand your horizons."

"All right." She glanced over the menu. "I'll have a slice with leeks and a Bluebird bitter."

"Beer?" Toby blurted out as if Claire had asked for a bowl of grog.

"Yes." She closed her menu. "I'm really happy for you, Toby."

"You don't know how glad I am to hear you say that." He spread a plum-dark smear of the previously untouched tapenade on a piece of crostini and topped it with soft goat cheese. "I'm sorry about before. Not telling you about Miranda was driving me crazy."

"It's okay." She bit her lip. "Did I react exactly the way you thought I would?"

Toby reddened.

"Don't worry." She took a bite of his crostini. "The crazy part of our relationship is over. I'm going to be better about everything now. No more obsessing, no more fainting in public, no more making decisions based on fantasy."

Toby's handsome features brightened. "Don't be so hard on yourself."

"Don't chicken out with me," she said.

He dipped his bread in the olive paste and gazed at her.

"What are you thinking?" Claire asked.

"Would you ever consider going back to med school?"

"What! What the hell made you bring that up?"

"I promised your grandfather I'd keep trying," he said.

Claire shook her head and ran her fingers over the nape of her neck. An electric flicker of Harcourt's fingertips suddenly buzzed in hers. She froze her heart until the sensation dissipated, then turned her attention back to Toby. He'd gotten along famously with Claire's brilliant, eccentric grandfather. "You know that's never going to happen." She searched the room for the waitress.

"Never say never," Toby said.

"Well, I guess if the 'Byron of Back Bay' is ready to settle down," Claire said, alluding to a hot online gossip article on Toby's legendary pursuits, "anything is possible."

He smiled. "Shut up and drink your beer."

The door blew open and a busboy dropped a tray of dishes. A feathery chill swept through Claire, and she flashed on an image of her grandfather. The summer after her twenty-third birthday he'd kissed her good-bye, and Claire had the premonition she would never see him again. That moment had stilled in her memory. His wild gray hair. His enormous, caterpillar eyebrows. His shabby black sweater. The wonderful scent of books and English Leather cologne. Her grandfather had died of a heart attack two weeks before she moved to Dorset to work on restoring the gardens of the Southey house. Claire swallowed the memory of his death with the rest of her excellent ale and gave over the remainder of the evening to Toby.

He talked a bit about his day, but mostly he mooned over Miranda. Claire sat back; watching Toby's hands meticulously shape the space in front of him as he described the way Miranda had done some ordinary thing, which to him now was amazing and full of beauty. His intense happiness made Claire feel peaceful, as though everything was beginning to be right with the world.

Opening the door to her apartment a few hours later, Claire saw her answering machine light flash, bathing the white kitchen in a watery red glow, too faint to be menacing. She pressed the button and waited for the machine to give the wrong time and date.

"It's Ian, honey. Great news! I got out of having to attend the last tedious dinner and I'm definitely coming back to Boston tomorrow! I love you and I can't wait to see you."

Good, Claire told herself. *Great.*

Despite sleeping badly for the past few nights, she wasn't ready for bed yet. She grabbed the book of poetry Ian had given her and ran her fingers over the pale, blue surface. She opened it and looked for Ishingham's "Ode to Eurydice." Her grandfather had read it to her all the time when she was little. He had loved it, and read with aching emotion in his resonant voice. " *'How beautiful,'* " he would say of the poem, quoting Keats, when he was finished, " *'If sorrow had not made Sorrow more beautiful than Beauty's self.'* " Claire hoped the memory of his voice would help her sleep.

Chapter Ten

Harcourt had just drifted off in the red chair in his room at the Black Hound when a knock at the door roused him.

"Abernathy. It's Moulton." The innkeeper's sonorous voice poured like warm water through the oak door. "I've decided to take pity on you."

Harcourt opened the door and squinted in the light of the innkeeper's candle.

"May I come in?" Moulton asked.

Harcourt nodded and stepped aside.

Mr. Moulton walked into the room. He lit the candle on the table with the flame from his own and set down a bottle of claret and two glasses. He crossed to where Harcourt stood near the mirror.

Harcourt waited unsteadily, but Mr. Moulton seemed unsure of what he wanted to say. "May I help you with something?" he asked when the innkeeper stood silently for an uncomfortable moment.

Mr. Moulton cocked his head and looked Harcourt up and down, as if surveying his aptitude and capabilities for some closely guarded task.

Harcourt shuddered a bit and inhaled the dry air in the room. "Forgive me. I've had rather too much wine.

Mr. Moulton kept to his examining posture and said nothing.

Feeling increasingly ill at ease, in addition to a threatening throb in his head, Harcourt slipped his hand into his pocket and pulled out Kate's ring. The silver band caught the candlelight. Moulton's eye shot to it like an owl's.

"Your wife's?" he asked quietly.

Harcourt breathed deeply and nodded. He closed his fingers around the ring.

"May I see it?" Mr. Moulton asked.

Harcourt hesitated before dropping the ring into the innkeeper's open hand.

Mr. Moulton held the ring to the light. "Orpine?"

"It is," Harcourt said.

Mr. Moulton smiled. "Culpepper said of orpine, 'The moon owns this herb. It cools any inflammation upon any hurt or wound and eases the pain of them.'"

Harcourt eyed Mr. Moulton, bewildered by his strange behavior. The wine was making his head swim, and he felt decidedly unready for any discussion of the venerable seventeenth-century physician Nicholas Culpepper, though Kate would have stayed up half the night to talk of the merits of herbs or the history of medicine. "Thank you for the claret," he said, "but I've had more than my share."

Mr. Moulton flipped the ring over in his palm, then gave it back. He clapped Harcourt gently on the shoulder. "Good night."

"Good night, Mr. Moulton." Harcourt shut the door behind the innkeeper and dropped his head into his hands. He pressed his fingers to his now seriously throbbing forehead. *What time is it?* he thought, searching the room for a clock. The moon was still high in the black sky, and the air outside was silent. He poured himself a glass of claret but did not drink it.

The monograph lay open on the bed. Harcourt grabbed it, sat down to read and spilled wine on his shirt.

"Damnation!" he cursed and jumped out of his chair. The monograph fell from his lap. He cursed again and went into the anteroom to change his clothes. Clouds obscured the moon in the upper panes of the window, looking for a moment like snow. A branch ignited and crackled loudly in the fireplace of the main room.

Harcourt pulled on a clean white muslin shirt.

A woman's voice cried out. A pounding thump followed immediately, as if she was attempting to put out an ember smoldering on the floor.

Harcourt ran into the room. A woman knelt in front of the fire, hitting the floor with a heavy cloth. She glanced at him, hardly seeming startled at all.

She stood up.

Harcourt stumbled back.

"I'm sorry," she said. "They must have double booked us."

"What?" he asked. Harcourt heard his own voice as if from a distant stone passage.

The woman was dressed in a strange scarlet gown with naught for sleeves but silk strands, slender as raspberry canes, over her pale shoulders. The thin fabric clung to her shape like wetted muslin of an earlier day, but at her chest it opened into a *V*, revealing the round firmness of her breasts.

"Double booked us," she repeated. "Because of the snow. No one can get out."

He didn't say anything.

"Would you like me to leave?" she asked. "Maybe there's another room."

He couldn't answer.

"Are you all right?" she asked. The woman moved into the firelight. Her face was illuminated in the glow.

"Kate?"

"What?" she asked, stepping closer with a quizzical expression on what was undeniably Kate's face.

Harcourt took a breath to repeat her name when a snap of comprehension split open in his head. He stepped back toward the door. "Forgive me. You resembled . . . for a moment . . . someone I knew."

Delight flashed in her gray eyes. "No one's ever told me that before. I don't look like anyone in my family. I'm Claire Islington." She stretched out her hand.

Was he to take it? To hold it? To kiss it?

Standing before him was the woman who had shared his bed, and who held his heart for eternity. Now she introduced herself to him as though he had never seen her face. She smiled.

Harcourt felt dizzy. He took Kate's small hand into his larger one and was surprised to feel a strong grip as she shook his hand briefly, then released it. He was aware of his own hand as it fell like a leaf to his side. He could think of nothing to say. Surely the claret had taken him over and he was at this very moment lying in an inebriated heap on the carpet, or slumped in a stupor in the red velvet chair. A second snap of awareness clicked in Harcourt's fogging brain and he spun to see if the chair was still there.

It was. But it appeared to be newer somehow. Thick varnish suffocated the ebony arms and legs, and a more garish scarlet velvet graced its plumper cushions.

"Are you all right?" she asked.

No, he longed to shout. *Where am I? Why don't you know me?* Harcourt took in a long, shuddering breath, and before he knew what she was doing, Kate, the woman who called herself Claire, the woman standing near him smelling seductively like his wife, slipped her hand under his arm and led him to the couch in front of the fireplace.

"You look ragged," she said, helping him to sit.

"Wait!" he demanded and leapt unsteadily to his feet. "What are you doing here? How did you come to be here?"

She gazed at him calmly, as Kate might have done, never rising from the couch. "The snow. Remember?" she asked softly. "The inn double-booked us. Everyone is stuck here. The weathermen predicted rain and, foolishly, we all believed."

Harcourt felt her surveying him. He tried to stop swaying.

"Why don't you sit down?" she said gently. "If you're uncomfortable with my being here, I'll ask Mr. Moulton if he can find someone who'll share a room with me."

Claire, *Kate,* gazed down at the couch and ran her hand over the heavy damask upholstery. Harcourt watched the movement of her slender hand and stopped swaying. The effect of the wine began to drain from him and he breathed in the smoky air of the room along with the floral scent of her hair. She raised her eyes.

"I think Mr. Moulton thought that since this is a suite we'd have enough room and enough privacy." She sat up straighter and folded her hands on her lap. "I don't mean to be so casual. I'd put on a bathrobe, but I don't have one. And Mr. Moulton doesn't stock those fluffy white hotel bathrobes. I think he finds them to be too indulgent somehow." She gazed down at her hands. "I'm sorry. I babble when I'm nervous and I feel like I'm making you nervous, so that makes me nervous. Damn," she said, then covered her mouth. "I'm sorry."

Harcourt smiled. *Kate,* his Kate, somehow existed again. Now. An ocean away from Ledwyche. She sighed nervously. He swallowed her breath from the air and sat down beside her.

"What are you smiling at?" she asked, grinning back at him. "Do we know one another? Have we met before?"

"I don't know," he answered, savoring the chance to sit near her. "Perhaps." Harcourt turned away, so as not to alarm her with too close a study of her face. And her body. Ripe and lush in that impossibly thin gown. He sucked in the air and turned back to her. "Have you always lived here, in Vermont?"

"Oh, I don't live in Vermont," she said. "Well, I do now— or I will for a year or so, anyway. I live in Boston. I'm up here for work." She pulled her knees up to her chest and wrapped her arms around them.

Harcourt looked down and saw her bare feet peek out from the scalloped hem of her gown. He longed to lean down and kiss each toe. *Kate,* Claire, drew in a deep breath.

She slipped her feet beneath her and leaned away from him. "My grandfather died in September."

"I'm sorry for you," Harcourt said. He moved to take her hand, then retreated.

"Thank you," she said. "I should have been prepared for it, but I wasn't. He was eighty-three. I thought he would live forever. I had to get out of Boston for a while to clear my head." She sighed again and seemed to take up more space in the room. "Mr. Moulton is an old friend of my grandfather's. He got me the job restoring the gardens on the Southey estate."

Snap.

Harcourt jolted back on the couch.

"Do you know about the Southey restoration project?" she asked.

He shook his head in disbelief.

"Robert Southey was a wealthy nineteenth-century doctor who had amazing gardens," she said. "His cousin was a frustrated public planner who used Southey's enormous grounds to live out his Olmstead dreams of landscape design. The gardens were extraordinary but far too expensive for Southey's descendents to maintain. Two years ago the family donated the land to the state with the understanding that it would be a park and museum."

The expression on his face must have been one of utter astonishment.

"I'm sorry," she said, blushing. "I must be totally boring you." She tossed her long brown hair over her shoulder. "I'll shut up."

"No," he said, biting back an impulse to brush an errant lock away from her face.

She blushed a deeper pink and kept silent for a while. Harcourt watched the play of firelight in her hair.

"Sorry about this ridiculous nightgown," she said suddenly. She picked up a handful of the voluminous skirt, then dropped it. The fabric spilled like scarlet water over her round thighs. He shuddered and pressed his tongue hard to the roof of his mouth.

"I think I must have had delusions of a snowbound romance," she said, still not looking at him. "My friend Toby bought this thing for me. I never wear anything like this."

She picked up the silky cloth again and rubbed it between her fingers. " '*Red as pomegranate seeds,*' " she said, releasing the gown from her grip.

"What?" Harcourt asked.

"The nightgown color," she said. "That's how the ad described it. A little over the top, don't you think?"

He didn't know what to say.

"I guess they're trying to appeal to the woman who dreams of Persephone or has a thing for the Underworld," she said, grinning.

A heady mix of salved grief and intense longing swept through Harcourt like a pleasure fever. He smiled at her. If this was a dream, he did not want to wake. She smiled back at him, then touched her cheek to see if she was blushing. Desire opened its searching hand inside him. He was glad of the darkness in the room. He shifted his position on the couch, conscious that if she looked closely at him she would see hard evidence of how much he wanted her, and he did not know what she would do. More than anything he didn't want her to leave.

"Thanks for not thinking that Underworld reference was too weird," she said, sliding her feet back onto the floor. "It's not really 'red as pomegranate seeds' anyway. Pomegranate juice has more clear pink in it. This is kid's-toy fire engine red."

He continued to stare at her.

"I have to stop talking," she said. "Can I have a sip of your wine?"

She gently took the wineglass from his hand. Harcourt hadn't noticed until now that he was holding the half-spilled glass of claret. She took a sip and handed it back to him.

"I'm sorry," she said. "You're not germ phobic, are you?"

"What?" he asked, embarrassed to feel grateful that she had drunk his wine. "I can't say I am."

She smiled playfully and took the glass again. "Pathogens are everywhere anyway. Washing your hands is the best defense against most of them."

She drank the wine, leaving a little in the glass for him. "A friendly drop. Besides," she said, handing it back, "exposure strengthens your immune system. Children raised in slightly dirty houses get sick far less often than kids raised in lick-off-the-floor houses."

She ran her hands over her legs.

Blood rushed to his groin. He shifted uncomfortably and tried not to think of her beneath him.

"My grandfather was a classics professor," she said. "Great books. Cluttered house."

Harcourt sucked in air. Claire rose suddenly from the couch.

"What is that amazing scent of coffee?" she asked.

Harcourt couldn't smell coffee. He couldn't smell anything but her, and he didn't know how long he could last this close to her without touching her.

She walked toward the door. The fabric curved around her thighs and her behind as she strode away from him.

His shaft throbbed in anticipation of release. He wanted to swallow her.

A fortnight after Dr. Cowpe had agreed to take her on as a research partner, Kate walked into his office.

"Miss Ishingham," Cowpe sang out from the well lighted room. "Good morning."

"Good morning, Dr. Cowpe." Dr. Cowpe's enthusiasm reminded Kate of her father, though Cowpe looked nothing like the brilliant, eccentric Lord Greydon. Dr. Cowpe was handsome in a way that made both women and men turn their heads. Her father had wild, long gray hair and enormous, caterpillarlike eyebrows. She gestured to her notebook on the writing table, opened to the section on the gamekeeper's fatal bout of perithisis. "Will we begin with Mr. Standish today?"

"Yes," Cowpe said. "He is your milkmaid, after all."

Kate felt a thrill at the reference to Edward Jenner, the Gloucestershire doctor who had discovered a path to protection from smallpox by using pus from a dairy maid suffering from cowpox. She sat at the large, leather-lined, mahogany writing table Cowpe had purchased for their use together.

"You have not yet told me, Miss Ishingham, why Lord Greydon discounts your theory," Cowpe said.

Kate sighed. "My father believes it too imprecise. He contends that joy can be attributed to so many causes it is nonsensical to link it to perithisis. The potential origins of happiness are too diverse to be applied as an indicator of disease. Even for so striking an example as Mr. Standish."

"What of your observation that every person to fall victim to perithisis in the wake of Mr. Standish's case displayed the same signs of light euphoria in the weeks prior to onset?" Cowpe asked.

"His argument is the same," she said. " 'Take a cross section of the same number of villagers in the same period,' he said, 'and note that all of them, at one time or another, feel happiness, as well as despondency, frustration, contentment, longing. And these no more indicate putrid pox than a display of mild bliss does.' "

Cowpe stood up and crossed the room to the window facing the busy street. "Tell me, in as precise detail as you can recall, what you observed in Mr. Standish."

"In the spring of my twenty-first year Mr. Standish came upon me in the orchard," Kate said. "I was reading Sydenham's theory on epidemic constitutions under the cover of a needlework of leeks I was embroidering as a gift for my father."

Cowpe crossed his arms and leaned into the sunlight on the whitewashed walls.

"Jack Standish had been gamekeeper at Greydon Hall before my father was born," Kate said. "He was a milk brother to my grandfather, and he was a mean, small-hearted man." She smiled. "My cousin Charles thought him to be a devil who turned into a green-winged creature at night and stole children from their beds." She leaned closer to Cowpe. "When Old Jack sat near me I am ashamed to say I felt such revulsion I thought of running back to the house."

She opened her hands onto her notebook. "After making gentlemanlike inquiries into my family's health and commenting on the beauty of the day, Mr. Standish began to converse with me on matters of his own life." The strangeness of the encounter colored Kate's voice. "He talked of games he and my grandfather had played as children. And how much he'd cherished his wife, for she had been the only soul to truly love him."

Cowpe listened.

"After a few minutes of this pleasant discourse," Kate said, "Mr. Standish took his leave. Nearly a fortnight of this strange courteousness passed. Villagers attributed it to Mr. Standish's unheard of appearance at church on the two previous Sundays and the felicitous influence of the new curate. Some thought it due to the uncommonly fine weather or too much drink at such an age, and then it was forgotten. Most of Mr. Standish's acquaintances or friends were dead. No one else cared enough to attach any significance to the change in his personality."

Kate turned over a leaf in the notebook.

"But I could not stop thinking about it," she said. "Why would a man who had been cruel and choleric for the whole of his life suddenly, and without any notable cause, change?"

Kate rose from the chair and walked to the window

where Cowpe stood. "Within a fortnight Mr. Standish developed the telltale spots and the fever and lung congestion. His illness was considered to be a sign of the merciful and just hand of Providence who, having bestowed a final gift, now took Mr. Standish to his deserved end. In the months that followed his death, every person who developed putrid pox showed a period of good feeling and happiness no matter what their true nature. All within a fortnight of the appearance of the pox."

"But Miss Ishingham," Cowpe said, "we cannot frighten every gladsome person with a death knell."

"It's not a general happiness," she protested. "The response is like the effect of strong wine. A euphoric change descends on the person, leaving him like one who has been given a drug of merriment. The mood indicates the presence of an invasive force, which deceives its victims by mirroring the opposite of its purpose."

"To what end?" Cowpe asked, crossing to the door and peering out the latticed window. "Does this period of strange bliss allow for anything more than additional time for effective therapeutics?"

"Not at all," Kate said. "My observation of a kind of incubation period offered me the opportunity to come to what I believe the answer to be."

"And what is that?" Cowpe asked.

"Variolation," Kate said.

"Variolation?" Cowpe repeated, stepping away from the door. "What do you mean? Putrid pox is not smallpox, Miss Ishingham. Perithisis, as I am sure you know, has more in common with consumption."

Kate sighed. She did not need to tell Dr. Cowpe that although Jenner successfully vaccinated two hundred people against smallpox twenty years ago, the conviction that inoculating the healthy with the pus of the sick was blasphemous and dangerous, still raged.

"You do know, Miss Ishingham," Cowpe said, standing up

taller in the sunlight, "there are those in Parliament who would make variolation a felony. In America, in Boston, Dr. Boylston was threatened with hanging for offering variolation to smallpox victims during an epidemic."

"That was a century ago! And why do you omit the essential part of Boylston's story?" Kate asked. "The nearly two-hundred-fifty lives saved by his bravery. Variolation reduces the number of fatalities due to smallpox from thirty per centum to *one*." She stepped nearer to him. "You have exhibited great courage in permitting me to work with you. Do not abandon it before we have begun."

"My courage thus far, Miss Ishingham, has rested upon evidence," he said. "Evidence of the promise in your research. Where you made no reference—none at all—to so revolutionary an answer."

This was true. Kate had made no direct reference to variolation. She'd wanted to be sure of his opinion on the idea. "But Dr. Cowpe," she said, attempting to contain her vexation, "your paper clearly pointed in that direction. Surely you cannot have been unaware of it? It is why I wrote to you and none of the dozen other men to publish on perithisis that year."

"I left it open-ended," Cowpe conceded. "As a possibility among many, not as the sole choice."

Kate said nothing.

"What causes you to be so certain?" Cowpe asked. "My reading of your research led me to believe you were after a quicker diagnosis, which would lead to more effective treatment. Not variolation. What links the presence of a euphoric phase with the need for variolation?"

"Nothing," Kate said quietly. "Dr. Cowpe, I am unmarried and of wealth. I have no obligations. And due to my . . . unconventional upbringing, as you have called it, I have been in possession of uncommon freedom. Unlike you, sir, I have had no office, no patients. I have had nothing but a luxury of time, to study and observe."

She breathed deeply. "In the year that elapsed from Mr. Standish's death until the pox had run its course in our village, I had nothing but time to study perithisis." Kate gazed into Cowpe's impassioned eyes. "As a boy, did you ever long for mythical gifts? Invisibility, like Perseus? Immortality? Flight? Prophecy? Any careful reading of mythology reveals that every gift, like every scientific advance, comes with some consequence. My theory gave me the burden of knowing who would be stricken, and like Cassandra, no one would heed my warnings. I tried to convince my father. I tried to inform the families, but without my father's affirmation, no one would listen. And so I observed and carefully recorded what I saw. I helped to care for the victims when the pox appeared and kept silent about what I knew. But in that year I learned more about perithisis than I have read or heard anywhere. You have read Dr. Jenner's inquiry, have you not?"

Cowpe nodded.

Kate inhaled deeply, then leaned forward. "Did you never wonder if cowpox and smallpox would be the only diseases linked in some way for one to have a curative effect on the other in the form of variolation?"

"What are you suggesting?" Cowpe stepped back so abruptly that he nearly smashed his head on the wall.

"That it is not a singular occurrence," she said. "If cowpox and smallpox are linked, then links of a similar nature must exist betwixt other diseases and causes. What is it about the nature and definition of cowpox that makes it effective against smallpox?"

"You have read Jenner's inquiry," he said. "You know the answer to that question as well as I do."

"Why can we not apply that answer to other diseases?" she asked.

"How do you propose to find a cowpox for putrid pox?" he asked, his voice rising slightly in pitch. Cowpe's handsome face revealed a struggle between fearful skepticism and powerful curiosity.

"The cure lies in the cause," she said. "And the cause of perithisis lies hidden in its makeup."

"And how do you propose we unravel that makeup?" he demanded. Despite an obvious effort to remain calm, Cowpe's mellifluous voice brightened in intensity. "A magic eye? An all-seeing orb? Even a microscope cannot reveal everything. We can theorize about miasma and ill humors and the effects of weather, but the causes of most diseases are yet a mystery, kept by God. Inscrutable and invisible to us. We are theorists and treat the best we can with what we know, but we are limited in our ability to shift the hand of nature."

"I agree," Kate said.

Cowpe sighed in uneasy relief.

"But an untested theory is useless," she added.

Cowpe ran his fingers through his sleek dark hair and re- garded Kate cautiously. She knew the window of time to act was closing. Dr. Cowpe could hardly be expected to abandon all connections to established knowledge after he had pushed the boundaries of accepted practice in tak- ing her on. Kate stood straighter and breathed as confi- dently as she could.

"I scratched pus from a lesion of a victim of a light case of putrid pox into my own forearm," she said.

Cowpe reeled back and grabbed his hair. The practice of a physician testing a theory on himself was not unheard of, but Kate had no degree and she was a woman. She saw Cowpe viewed her recklessness as dangerous and worried he was near to asking her to quit the partnership.

"In the year after Mr. Standish's death, I cared for nearly every person in Warwickshire who contracted putrid pox. I stand before you now, unmarked, unscathed and immune forever to the scourge, which takes nearly as many lives per year as does smallpox. Variolation is the answer, Dr. Cowpe. And you are the conduit that shall make it possible."

"Why me?" he sputtered. "Lord Greydon is arguably among the most illustrious of English physicians and—

obviously, from your presence here today—not a man tied to conventional thought or practice. Why did your father not offer to advance your theory? Why me?"

"My father's two older brothers died from what must have been the kind of contaminated smallpox vaccine Dr. Jenner warned of in his pamphlet," she replied. "Their deaths gave my father the title, and wealth beyond anything he could ever have imagined for himself. And the freedom to do with his life anything he pleased. Forever mindful of the unwitting sacrifice his brothers made, my father joined those who would make variolation a crime and turned a deaf ear to any argument to the contrary."

Cowpe studied Kate intently, as though he longed to pull an answer from her like an invisible thread. Kate watched him fight to balance a need for respectability and a palpable, ravenous curiosity. She waited.

"You have won me," he said, reluctance darkening his previously bright tone. "For now. But if the substance is yours, the structure must be mine. I have lived in the world you have known little of. We must proceed as I lay out, and you must defer to me in all matters but theory."

Kate sighed in relief. "You shall find me compliant, Dr. Cowpe."

"I have not yet found you to be anything of the kind," he said. "But I trust you will be so from now on."

She reddened.

His face softened. "Let us begin."

Chapter Eleven

In the dream, Claire was choking on shimmery fluid clogging her mouth and throat.

"Too late, too late," she screamed. The irises outside the cottage opened their spectral heads, fueled by some fertility drug, some feeding memory cry. And out came rosemary, bled through with powder-blue forget-me-nots. Not vines at all but vinelike, running rampant over the small house, suffocating it, while Claire, on a chair like tiny Alice who cannot grow big enough to break through roof and windows, choked within.

Too late. Too late. Too late. The voice was hers, but she wasn't speaking, her mouth filled with shifting silver. She wanted to crow and caw and cry for help, but the asking would not come. She gasped in silent demands of air want, air lust, air desire until she woke up. Drenched and drowned in sweat in her own bed, her own apartment, her own slippery skin that didn't quite fit, like a dress forced on by a well-meaning aunt.

Her chest felt swollen and painfully tight, her lungs stuffed with echoes and remnants of ineffectual screaming,

148

scarred by the intake of false air, oxygen made for lungs other than her own. *Help me,* she wanted to say but she said nothing. She sat on her bed, wearing a pink nylon nightgown she hated, didn't remember buying, and pulled her knees to her chin. She felt as if she was bleeding, blood and fluid and life pouring from her too loose, ill-fitting skin, but she wasn't even sweating anymore. She just sat, shaking and lost again. Another boat had sailed off, separated forever from the jagged coastline. She sank into the swallowing seabed but was forced back to shore by an unseen fist. The only person she could talk to was Toby.

Claire got out of bed and tripped over the poetry book, which had fallen to the floor. "Shit."

Her hand shook so much her fingers had difficulty making effective contact with the buttons of the phone. The color of the phone shifted from red to green to violet to red again. At first Claire dialed the wrong number and a tremulous, ancient female voice answered.

"Hello."

"I'm sorry," Claire said.

"Hello."

"I'm sorry. I'm sorry," Claire said and hung up to dial Toby again.

"Hello," Toby answered, sleepily, groggily, velvet-voiced, mossy soft and seductive. "Hello. Who is this? Claire?" His voice snapped awake. "Claire? Are you okay? What is it? Claire?"

"I'm sorry, Toby, I didn't know who else to call," was all she could say. Her voice poured into the open receiver.

"Where are you?" he asked. "Are you home? Do you want me to come over?"

She heard a soft, female voice in Toby's apartment.

"I'm sorry. It's Claire," he said. "I don't know. Just a minute."

Toby spoke to Miranda differently than he spoke to Claire: The undercurrent of uneasy anticipation that always lingered in his voice was completely gone. Maybe she really was crazy.

"Are you okay?" he asked Claire.

She couldn't hear herself. She must have been speaking because Toby answered her.

"It's all right. Don't worry about it. I'll come over. No, it's okay. Stop it," he said. "If you didn't want me to, you wouldn't have called. It's okay. Really. I'll be right over." He kissed Miranda and hung up.

Claire walked to the kitchen and opened the refrigerator door. She stood in the blast of cold air until she could breathe again. Toby's presence was only a tease, a shadow of what she wanted, what she couldn't have, what she could never have, like a copy or a photograph of a real thing. But you couldn't reach into a photograph or a song or a painting. You cannot become part of something incapable of accepting you. You couldn't enter a universe without a door. Or open a door without a key.

Toby let himself in with the key Claire had given him a long time ago. He made her tea and read to her: old stories of fairies and dragons and earth and nature, long poems with words out of favor and images steeped in dust. Toby's voice shook them from their slumber.

I dream of infidelity, Claire thought as Toby read. *Not to be unfaithful to you or Ian but unfaithful to me, to time, to life. Unfaithful to all that has been given me. I reject it. I betray it. I long for betrayal. I lust for some other hand, a different voice, a different air to breathe.*

Toby's voice drifted back to her:

> " 'She mounts her chariot with a trice,
> Nor would she stay for no advice,
> Until her maids that were so nice,
>   To wait on her were fitted,
> But ran herself away alone;
> Which when they heard there was not one,
> But hasted after to be gone,
>   As she had been diswitted.' "

150

Enough, Claire wanted to say. *I can't hear any more. I can't take any more.* But she couldn't say it. He had come over. He had left his bed, and Miranda, to come here in the middle of the night for her. She wasn't that selfish. *I can't take anymore,* she thought, shaking still, trembling under his arm, chafing stupidly beneath Toby's generously offered, protective embrace.

"Are you all right?" he asked. "Do you want me to stop?"

"No. Keep reading," Claire said. Once she said it she felt better and gave herself permission to forget for a minute.

Toby read more of the poem: "Nimphidia, Court of the Fayrie," by Michael Drayton.

"You could have been an actor," she murmured.

"Are you okay now?" Toby asked, ignoring her remark and brushing her wild hair from her face. "Are you okay?"

"Yeah," Claire said, knowing how much he wanted to get back to Miranda.

"Someday, Toby," Claire said, sitting up straight and closing the green clothbound book in his hand, "I'll repay you for everything."

Toby kissed Claire's head. "I'm going to go now, if you're all right."

"I am," she said. "Thanks for coming over."

But he didn't leave.

When Claire was in the hospital, Toby had moved to Vermont to be with her. He told her that since he first saw her in the library at school he'd wanted to look out for her. He'd felt it as surely and known it as deeply as anything in his life.

"I'm fine," she said. "I'm sorry I scared you." She grabbed his hand. "I'm not that person anymore, Toby. I'm not going to fall apart and disappear." She squeezed his hand and then let go. "Go home."

Toby got up. "Okay." He waited a minute longer and left.

Claire considered walking over to the Charles and watching the sunrise on the river. The yellow light on the gray water always made her think a bit ridiculously of *Ping*, the story of the duck separated from his family because he couldn't swim to the boat in time.

She got back into bed and leaned against the head-board. Her chest ached. She ran her fingers over her ribs, pressing into the tender muscles. The feather-light, friction-flinty scent of rain on pavement washed in through a crack in the window. Claire drew her knees to her chin. Was this happening because Ian had been in New York all week? Should she just say yes and marry him? Neither of them had mentioned the marriage proposal since they'd come back from Vermont. He acted as though he'd never asked her to marry him and she pretended not to notice.

Her chest really hurt, she thought, rubbing between her breasts, as if she'd been violently coughing or had bronchitis.

Claire got out of bed and wandered to the window. She sat on the unsteady radiator cover and peered out to the empty street below. Toby was probably almost home. His legs were so long, when he walked he swallowed slabs of pavement two at a time. She wondered what Miranda thought of Toby's fierce protectiveness of her. Or if he'd told her they'd slept together once. She hoped he hadn't said anything, because it had been a mistake.

Claire sucked in a long breath. The air seemed to take little, sharp bites of the inside of her lungs. "Ow," she said, holding her chest again. Maybe she was getting sick. But she didn't feel ill, just hurt. And lost.

She missed Harcourt Abernathy. Since the night she'd passed out in Sonsie, she'd pushed away every sense or thought of Harcourt's presence, but more than she could say, more than she wanted to admit, she missed him. She couldn't have a lover, even a ghost lover, and stay with Ian. Ian made sense. Harcourt, most certainly, did not.

Chilled air streamed in through the crack in the window. Claire shivered and stood up. She didn't want coffee. She always wanted coffee. A cotton-bright glow of gathering sunrise settled on the couch. Claire sank into the faded damask cushions and closed her eyes to think of him, if only for a minute.

She started in her chest and thought of what he'd felt like: a circle of heat growing inside her until she'd felt the length of his fingers extending into hers. The way his wild, untamable hair had curled under her smooth hair and the way his hips had pressed hard into her hips. But she felt nothing.

Was he merely a figment of her imagination? Was she just remembering what he had felt like seven years ago? Or a lifetime ago? She wanted to scream. What were her choices to believe? If Harcourt was just a vivid erotic fantasy she was not only a little crazy, but worse; she was without him. If the hot sensation of him filling her with his presence was nothing but an elaborately re-lived memory, then Harcourt didn't want her or need her and would never find her again. If the hot, hard sense of his body swelling inside hers was a memory of a past lifetime then everything—her life, her love, everything she wanted—was impossible to reach.

Dropping her jaw to swallow the emptiness of the air in the room, Claire felt desperate for some tangible, solid connection to him. She walked to her computer to look at pictures of their room in the Black Hound online. After that she would re-read the monograph. She'd read his name and study his illustrations. And then she'd try to release herself from wanting him. Again. She couldn't live this way anymore. She had to commit to real life, and that had to be with Ian.

Claire waited for her archaic dial-up to make its molasses-slow connection and idly tried to remember what she'd learned about putrid pox in med school. *Perithisis is a virus characterized by fever, lung congestion and blood-red pockmarks appearing on the limbs, trunk and neck.*

Doctors thought she had perithisis when she was born. She wasn't breathing. Mucus filled her nose and mouth and the doctor had a difficult time aspirating it out. For days afterward, Claire's lungs filled with fluid and no one could determine the exact cause. Her grandfather said she was a fierce fighter from the beginning. *You screamed so loudly and with such regularity the poor woman in the bed next to your mother's demanded to be moved to another room. You kept the whole wing awake.*

A screeching ring indicating Internet connection startled Claire from her foggy-headed reverie. After a few clicks leading to the wrong Black Hound Inn and a bizarre site she never wanted to see again, it dawned on her: *Of course,* she thought, leaning back in her chair and automatically reaching for a coffee cup that wasn't there. Mr. Moulton was devoutly old-fashioned. Though you couldn't call him a Luddite, he'd never have a website. Claire logged off, listening to the white-noise hum of disconnection.

Ian would loathe Mr. Moulton's website refusal. That kind of stubborn clinging to an unsupportable idea would drive him to distraction. A shaft of sunlight bounced off the monitor and blinded Claire for an instant. She pushed away from her desk and got up to get the monograph. She stopped before she reached her crowded bookcase. Ian still had it. She walked into the kitchen to call him. He wouldn't be back from New York until at least noon, so she'd have to leave a message.

"Claire?" Ian muttered sleepily.

"What are you doing home already?" she asked.

"A colleague drove me home last night, but there was an emergency at the hospital. I got back at four-thirty this morning," he said. "How are you?"

"I'm fine," Claire said. "Go back to sleep. I'll call you later."

"Is something wrong?" he asked, more awake now.

"No." She was sick of seeming so breakable. "There's nothing the matter. I wanted to know if you still had that monograph. Well, you must have it, because I don't. Could you bring it over tonight? Or could I stop by after work and get it?"

Ian didn't say anything. Claire heard him sit up and get out of bed. Except for his front hall, Ian didn't have carpeting or rugs in his apartment. His feet slapped against the highly polyurethaned floors. "Sure," he said evasively. "As soon as I get a chance."

"You don't have to bring it over," she said. "I don't want to bug you on your day off. I'll stop by tonight."

"Claire," Ian barked in an unexpectedly harsh voice, "I got three hours of sleep. I don't want to talk about your book. I'll get it to you as soon as I can. Okay?"

"I'm sorry for calling so early," Claire said quietly. "Go back to sleep. I'll talk to you tomorrow."

"No," Ian said. "I'm sorry. I'll come over tonight. We can make dinner and watch a movie or something."

Claire smiled. "Go back to sleep," she said quietly. "I'll see you tonight."

She hung up the phone. She shifted her weight from foot to foot and massaged the back of her neck. Letting go of Harcourt was the right decision. How could she have a life with someone she couldn't see when her eyes were open? Claire rubbed her chest, which still ached, though much less than before. When she was totally free of Harcourt, and free of wanting him, she'd learn to love Ian the same way. She stepped away from the wall and let go of her chest.

Starting now she would put more effort into her relationship with Ian. It wasn't enough to let go of Harcourt; she had to grab hold of Ian. She pulled a notepad decorated with delicate green fumitory from the counter and began making a list of ingredients for dinner. Lobster bisque, steak au poivre and lemon mousse for dessert. And she'd wear the hot pink corset Ian had given her for Valentine's Day last year. The lacy corset didn't look very good on her and she didn't really like it, but wearing it would make Ian happy because he would see that she'd decided to try to be what he wanted. Claire finished the list, dropped the pen in a ceramic pencil jar shaped like an open suitcase and went to get dressed for work.

* * *

Harcourt had arrived early at the Cowpes' for a party that would include Mrs. Cowpe's brother, Matthew Denton, his wife and Miss Ishingham, whom he had hardly seen in a fortnight, though Cowpe kept him abreast of their progress.

Harcourt read to Emily and Sarah Cowpe in the library while their mother saw to the table. The girls adored him and had begged him to read "Nimphidia, The Court of the Fayrie," by Michael Drayton. The poem told of Queen Mab's flight from Oberon, her husband, to her lover, Pigwiggen.

> " 'Her Chariot ready straight is made,
> Each thing therein is fitting layde,
> That she by nothing might be stayde,
> For naught must be her letting . . . ' "

Miss Ishingham's voice drifted in from the drawing room, where she was introduced to Mr. and Mrs. Denton. Harcourt had read "Court of the Fayrie" so often he could allow his mind to wander. What would he say when they met? How would she receive him? They hadn't parted well. Though he could not regret confronting her over her blindness to the consequences of working with Dr. Cowpe as if she were a man, he regretted her wounded coldness, and he regretted upsetting her.

Emily's restlessness brought him back to the tale. She loved the poem and always tried to hold very still for what he knew to be her favorite verse, in which Pigwiggen, the fairy knight, prepared himself to face Oberon, the fairy king. Whenever he read the description of Pigwiggen's beetlehead helmet Emily could hardly stop herself from squealing.

> " 'His Helmet was a Beetle's head,
> Most horrible and full of dread,
> That able was to strike one dead,
>   Yet it did well become him.' "

"Abernathy!" Mrs. Cowpe's brother, Matthew Denton, had come into the library with a jovial greeting. Denton was tall with red hair, a straight nose and brown eyes—the very image of his older sister Mary, but with a sparkle of mischief in his eyes.

"Denton," Harcourt said, grinning. "You'll forgive me if I sit with your nieces a moment longer; Pigwiggen is preparing for battle." He smiled at Emily, who was clearly displeased by her uncle's intrusion.

"Don't let me keep you," Denton said, winking at Sarah and ruffling Emily's hair.

Emily frowned slightly and smoothed her long curls.

"Now, where did I stop?" Harcourt asked, knowing full well the answer.

Emily concentrated on the dense print and pointed. "Here. 'Yet it did well become him.'"

"Very good, Miss Cowpe," Harcourt said, smiling. "Perhaps you should read the rest to me."

Emily blushed and shook her head. Sarah hummed, having just sneaked her thumb into her mouth under Harcourt's protective arm. He continued.

> " 'He made him turne, and stop, and bound,
> To gallop, and to trot the Round,
> He scarce could stand on any ground,
> He was so full of mettle.' "

"Girls," Cowpe interrupted from the doorway. "Mr. Abernathy must come with me now. Your uncle has come all the way from Painswick to talk with him."

"Oh, no, please, Papa," Emily begged. "Painswick isn't so very far. Please let us hear the next part, only that much. *Please.*"

"Yes, Papa, please just that part," Sarah added, though she was nearly asleep on Harcourt's lap.

"I promise I shall return and finish the poem tomorrow,"

157

Harcourt said. "With your father's permission, of course."

Emily's dark eyes brightened. Cowpe smiled.

" 'It is settled then," Harcourt said, lifting Sarah from his lap and handing her to her father. "Tomorrow Proserpina saves the day."

"Thank you, Mr. Abernathy," Emily said.

"You are most welcome, Miss Cowpe."

Cowpe carried Sarah and held Emily's hand. He sent them to the nursery then excused himself to answer a call from Mr. Gedge, whose wife was apt to imagine all sorts of maladies.

Harcourt moved to join the others.

"Abernathy," Denton said, reclining on the cinnamon-colored couch Cowpe had bought as a gift to his wife. "Perhaps you should have a go of it in London. You read that poem in better voice than any actor in *Tom and Jerry*— though, come to think of it, the play is now called *Green in France*."

"Matthew," Mrs. Cowpe said, "you *did not* see that play."

"Twice," he teased, grinning at his sister.

"Mr. Denton," Mrs. Denton chastised, then turned to her sister-in-law. "Mathew saw it once and swore he'd never see another play."

"Abernathy," Denton entreated, ignoring his wife, "you lived in London. You must have been to the theater. Seen a farce at the Adelphi perhaps."

"I'm sorry to say I had very little occasion to attend the theater," Harcourt said.

"What," Denton said, "not beneath you, is it? I should have thought a great reformer like you would attend low comedy on principle alone." He grinned.

"Matthew . . ." Mrs. Cowpe scolded.

"Mary," he mimicked in a singsong voice.

"Do not vex yourself on my account, Mrs. Cowpe, though you are very kind," Harcourt said. "Mr. Denton, regrettably, is no match for me." He smiled.

"No match for you?" Denton stepped back in mock outrage. "You have offended me, Abernathy. Deeply. But now I remember your reputed skill with a sword. My sister's fine husband tells me you bested every man in your class at both fencing and Latin."

Harcourt leaned back on the carved armchair. "It seems then, Denton, you would be well advised not to incur an advance of verse or steel."

"Miss Ishingham," Denton said, turning to her, "forgive me. You are new to Ledwyche and thus you may be unacquainted with the adventures of our Mr. Abernathy. Botanist, artist, lover of the people, despiser of the peerage. Perhaps you have heard of his legendary feud with *Blackwood's* for their denunciation of Keats, the Poet King."

"Matthew, please," Mrs. Cowpe begged. "Hold your tongue."

"Whatever for?" Denton asked. "I have not offended you, have I, Miss Ishingham? None of us has the blood of a peer in our veins, save Abernathy of course, and he would rather bleed that ancestral liquid out of him. Though you do dote on Mrs. Newington—a great snob if there ever was one."

"I am not offended, Mr. Denton," Miss Ishingham said.

"See," Denton said, raising a reddish brow and laughing.

"Mrs. Newington is not the daughter of a peer," Harcourt said. "But of a very rich wool merchant and the widow of a richer one, and thus she escapes my wrath."

"Mrs. Newington has been most kind to you," Mrs. Cowpe said.

Harcourt gazed curiously at Mary Cowpe. He had never made his loathing of the peerage a secret.

"Overdressed, overfed and idle," Denton pronounced. "Isn't that how you describe the residents of Berkley Square and Cheapside, Abernathy?"

"I am afraid you have offended your sister, Denton," Harcourt said. "And in her own home, too. Perhaps we should

159

cede the floor to a gentler voice. Forgive me, Miss Ishingham, we are too familiar."

"Not at all, Mr. Abernathy," Kate said. What would he think if he knew her father was Lord Greydon? She didn't care. No one, rich or poor, could help their birth. "I am happy to hear of your commitment to reform. It raises my opinion of you."

She gazed at him and smiled slightly. The movement of her pink mouth unfurled inside him with a flicker of pleasurable heat. He lost his place in the room for a moment. Denton's voice brought him back.

"If you are fond of radical ideas, Miss Ishingham," Denton said, smiling, "and if, unlike our noble Mr. Abernathy, you appreciate the art of the theater, perhaps you have heard of the rush to produce a play based on Mrs. Shelley's terrifying *Frankenstein*."

Mr. Denton seemed charming but not foolish, more than likely much indulged in his family. Kate smiled back at him. "I have heard nothing of any upcoming theatrical adaptations of Mrs. Shelley's work, but from the look in your eye, Mr. Denton, I feel safe to assume you intend to relieve me of my ignorance."

Denton glanced triumphantly at his sister, who rolled her eyes and set her teeth. Mary Cowpe was a soft, intelligent beauty, who resembled a young Emma Hamilton. Kate thought she seemed a perfect match for Dr. Cowpe, who had returned to the room and who gazed adoringly at her every time she spoke.

"The English Opera House is in the lead with *Presumption, Or the Fate of Frankenstein*," Denton said in mock solemnity. "But hard at the heels of that illustrious production is one that exceeds the original novel in its power to shock."

"Please, Matthew," Mrs. Cowpe said, "try to control yourself. You are a grown man. A darling boy no longer." She smiled. Denton reddened and returned his gaze to Kate.

"Continue, Mr. Denton," Kate said. "You'll find I am not easy to shock."

Denton grinned slowly, and Harcourt felt a stab of uneasy premonition. Struck by an irrational desire to sit nearer to Miss Ishingham and shield her from whatever Denton had to say, he leaned forward in his chair and tried to catch her eye.

"The play is called *Frankenstein, A Vindication,*" Denton said. "I am not certain whether it means to celebrate or condemn the ideas contained in Mrs. Shelley's mother's appalling work, but the premise is this: Dr. Frankenstein is a woman masquerading as a man. Distraught over the death of her father, a young woman takes over his medical research." Denton waited a moment for a reaction. It did not come. He continued in a more dramatic voice. "The revolting conditions of the work of a physician—I shall spare you the vulgar details—drive the poor young woman mad. It is her father she attempts to reanimate as the monster." Denton leaned back with the satisfaction of an unreformed gambler with a winning hand.

Miss Ishingham paled.

"Ha!" Denton exhaled. "I *have* shocked you."

Before Miss Ishingham could respond, Sarah Cowpe rushed into the room, crying loudly. Emily followed at her heels and pushed Sarah out of the way.

"She *broke* it," Emily sputtered. "On purpose."

" 'I didn't," Sarah protested, sobbing. "It fell from the table. I tried to catch it."

"Emily!" Cowpe said. "You'll cut yourself." He took the shattered remains of a much beloved white porcelain cat out of Emily's hands.

"Come," Mrs. Cowpe said to the girls. "Help me find Jenny. Perhaps Papa can mend the cat." Mrs. Cowpe looked hopefully to her husband, who shook his head and followed her out of the room.

"Perhaps it is meant as a lesson," Denton said, oblivious to both the distress of his young nieces and Miss Ishing-

161

ham. "The perils of forcing an unnatural situation. What do you think, Abernathy?" Denton grinned amiably again.

Kate stared at Mr. Abernathy. Denton's opinions mattered not at all to her, but suddenly Mr. Abernathy's views seemed vital to know. What *did* he think of her and her work? He had been the one to convince Dr. Cowpe to take her seriously. He had allowed her to care for John Greeley's hand, and he had been grateful for her care of Celia, but what did he think of a woman at work in a man's world?

He said nothing. Kate swore silently to herself and stood up. "I am sure you're right, Mr. Denton. Forcing an unnatural situation in art or in science or in life never comes to any good. It is a waste of energy and ends badly for all involved."

Denton smiled and nodded.

"Perhaps I shall ask Mrs. Cowpe if she needs any help," Kate said. "I both broke and mended many porcelain figures when I was an untamed girl." She moved for the door.

"Miss Ishingham," Harcourt said, "wait. Please." He crossed to the room to stand near her. "There is a difference between forcing a truly unnatural situation, such as the creation of life from dead flesh, and advances in science or in art, which no matter how controversial they are at the outset, help society."

Harcourt led her to the center of the room. He felt her tremble under the light pressure of his fingers at her back. He wanted to slide his hand under her gown and pull her to him. He waited until she was sitting on the couch, then sat beside her and turned to the room.

"Twenty years ago Edward Jenner found a way to halt the spread of smallpox," he said. "Although there are still reactionary accusations of blasphemy, lives have been, and will continue to be, saved because of his courage."

Kate glanced down at her hands and recaptured her composure. She hadn't intended to respond so heatedly. He was right about Jenner, of course, and she was grateful he had said it, but the memory of his furious reaction to her acceptance of Cowpe's offer mixed uneasily with how much she longed to see him, to talk with him, to touch him, to have him touch her. She couldn't control her reactions to him. The terror of losing the mastery of her own destiny threatened to close her heart. But the idea of losing her connection to him made her feel as though she were bleeding from the inside.

"Miss Ishingham," Harcourt said quietly, while Denton talked to his sister about his recent trip to France, "the world is not a small place in my eyes." He held her gaze, which seemed to both pull him in and beg him to leave.

She breathed deeply. "Thank you."

He moved to reach for her hand but thought better of it. "I shall never forget your kindness to my sister."

She smiled ever so slightly and turned away from him. He could not read her thoughts.

Dr. Cowpe returned. The party went in to dinner.

Chapter Twelve

"Do you want to?" Rare as an orchid, a strand of vulnerability shimmered in Ian's whispered question.

"Yes," Claire said, opening her palms over his slender chest.

The lobster and steak were sitting in her stomach, making her feel sick. She ran her hands down Ian's ribs. Moonlight caught on the polished orpine petals of her ring. Ian held himself above her. Claire raised her hips to his. He closed his eyes and thrust softly inside her.

Toby was wrong: She was an excellent liar. To herself. But the lies were like a paper city, blown apart every night and meticulously reconstructed every day. Even this, Claire thought as she held herself against Ian, even this elaborate metaphoric thinking was nothing more than another way to cut herself off from the only thing she ever wanted and the only thing she couldn't have: a life with Harcourt Abernathy.

Ian stopped. Claire waited and brushed her fingers idly across the small of his back. He sighed and pushed inside her again. Her ring grabbed at the moonlight. The more he filled her, the emptier Claire felt. A chasm grew in her body and in her heart, a feral ache she could not ease or wish away.

Ian pulled out and pushed himself off her. "You don't feel anything!"

Wet, naked, stunned and guilty, Claire couldn't listen to him. He continued to yell at her. She concentrated on ideas of the rumpled corset on the floor and pink, lobster bisque–coated bowls standing unwashed in the sink, until all she heard was the tension of her jaw in her ear canal.

"I'm sorry," Ian said heavily, softened by her silence. "I don't want to hurt you, Claire. But I can't live like this. I have to know you want me. And I don't. I've tried. You can't say I haven't."

He threaded a goatskin belt through the loops of his black pants and slipped on a cobalt blue shirt. He neatened his hair with his fingers and sat on the foot of Claire's bed. "I'm sorry to leave you this way tonight, Claire, but this is killing me." Ian patted her ankle as if she was an old dog. "I'll call you in a few days."

He stood up and checked his reflection in Claire's gilt-framed Regency mirror. "In the meantime, figure out whether you want me or whether you want to live alone for the rest of your life."

He grabbed his bag from the floor and left.

Claire sat as still as she could on the edge of the bed, contracting every muscle over which she had any measure of control. She squeezed her eyes shut, then pulled her face through her hands and stared into the dimly lit room. She should be angry. She should be furious. Want him or live alone forever; who did he think he was? Claire dropped her head onto her knees. The scent of Ian, and of her, sticky between her thighs, choked her. She stood up.

She wasn't angry. She felt dead, stuffed with emotions and ideas she didn't recognize. She wanted Harcourt. Claire swallowed her desire until she couldn't breathe. She had to run, from Harcourt and longing, from Ian and guilt and from herself. She jumped into a shower. The hot water intensified every sensation until she wanted to tear at her skin.

After she got out and dried off, Claire put on black underwear, black boots, a velvet skirt and an ivory sweater. She paused for a moment at her front door and let the chill of the doorknob fill the well of her hand. Moonlight poured into the living room, making it seem emptier than it was, pooling like mercury in the center of the coffee table. Claire dropped her keys on the piecrust table and sat on the couch.

What the hell was happening? she thought, biting angrily at a lump rising in her throat. She wished she could say that her head swam with a thousand feathery images. That she didn't know what to think. Or what to do. But what she needed gnawed at her back. She'd emptied her bag of self-deception tricks when she opened the monograph and allowed herself to wallow in her childhood fantasy life. And when she'd wanted Harcourt intensely, after she thought she'd begun to let him go.

Claire covered her open mouth with her fingers and, although she sat so still she barely breathed, inside a frenetic energy spun out of control. What was she supposed to do? What could she do?

The answering machine light flashed in the kitchen.

Who the hell had called when she was in the shower? She got up from the couch. She knew she didn't have it in her to talk to Ian, whether he wanted to yell at her or apologize. She padded into the kitchen and pushed the message button.

"Hey, it's Toby. I just saw Ian at Sonsie. What happened? I'm home. Call me."

Claire shuddered. She went into her room and got undressed. She put on a robe and warm socks before calling Toby back.

"Hey," she said when he answered on the second ring. She didn't bother to try to hide the stress in her voice.

"What happened?" Toby asked.

"I don't know," Claire said heavily. She dug her hand into her robe pocket, pulled out a Tootsie Roll, and popped it in her mouth.

"Please don't eat when I'm on the phone with you, Claire," Toby said.

She took the wet chocolate out of her mouth and wrapped it in the paper. "Sorry. I always forget how much you hate that."

"Did Ian leave?" Toby asked.

"For tonight," Claire said. "I guess." All of a sudden she wanted nothing more than to get off the phone.

"Why?" Toby asked.

"I don't know," Claire said irritably. "I don't make him happy. All right?"

Toby didn't say anything.

"I'm eating the candy!" Claire said and put it back in her mouth.

Toby ignored her. "What happened?"

"You know what happened," Claire insisted. "We fight in front of you often enough. I can't . . . I won't . . ." She sighed. "I didn't give him what he wanted."

The Tootsie Roll stuck to Claire's teeth. She spit it into the paper.

Toby waited again.

"Is it over?" he asked, apprehension coarsening the edges of his soft voice.

"No," she said. "I don't know."

"You have to make a choice, Claire," Toby said.

"I don't want to talk about this," Claire warned.

"You have to," he said.

Claire walked into the kitchen and noisily poured herself a glass of wine.

"Drink," Toby said sarcastically. "That's a good idea. That'll keep your head clear."

"Shut up!" Claire said. She instantly regretted it. "I'm sorry."

"It's okay."

Claire let fat silence fall between them again.

"What are you going to do?" Toby asked.

Claire watched the wrong time on the oven clock slowly change. The new number flipped clumsily over the old one like a jointed doll on a music box.

"What should I do?" she asked Toby quietly.

"You should do what's right for you," he said.

"I don't know what that is!"

"Yes, you do," he insisted.

Claire swirled the blood-dark wine in the glass but did not drink.

"You know there's only one answer," Toby said emphatically. "The other choice—no matter how much you want it to be the right choice—is untenable. You'll disappear if you force yourself into a situation that can never be real. No matter how much you want it to be."

Claire felt suddenly sick. She dumped the wine into the sink and watched red spots splatter on the white porcelain basin. A wave of nausea rolled over her.

"Just a second," she whispered to Toby and put down the phone. She turned on the faucet and splashed cold water on her face. There was only one choice. It wasn't even a choice, she thought bitterly, trying not to throw up. She had no control. If Harcourt was real, he came when he wanted to. He breathed inside her and she could feel the tips of his fingers warm in hers when she thought of him. But she hadn't seen him, or clearly heard his voice, since he pushed her out of the fire and fell onto the floor and disappeared. The memory of not being able to help, of not being able to follow him, still cut Claire in half. She lost her sense of place for a minute.

Toby was right. So much time had gone by, and nothing had changed because *nothing could change*. If anything was going to happen, besides exhaustingly erotic dreams or painful memories of watching him disappear forever, it would have happened already. In seven long years nothing had happened. Claire sucked at the dry air in her apartment. The exchange of gases in her lungs seemed to fall short of sufficient oxygen. She picked up the phone again.

"You're right," she said in a humiliatingly small voice.

"I'm sorry, sweetie," Toby murmured.

"Thanks," Claire said, grateful that someone knew what she was giving up. "I'm going to bed."

"Okay," Toby said. "Good night."

"Good night," Claire said and hung up.

Before she fell into bed, she called Ian. She couldn't let everything go. She had to have something to hold on to, no matter how disgustingly pathetic it made her, to herself or anyone else.

Ian didn't pick up the phone. Claire left a beautifully apologetic message. Apologizing was like breathing. *"I'm sorry,"* fell out of Claire's mouth like quarters from a slot machine. What was hard—almost as hard as actually letting Harcourt go—would be telling Ian the truth. That for seven years she'd been completely in love with, had dream sex with, *had almost died for*, a ghost lover whose body she felt but whose face she never saw unless her eyes were closed or she was asleep, save one glorious, terrible night in the Black Hound Inn when Harcourt Abernathy looked and felt more real than anyone Claire had ever seen.

Harcourt had not seen Miss Ishingham since the Cowpes' party. He missed her. In the hope of seeing her again, he agreed to his sister Celia's almost daily request to host a dinner party. Now, re-thinking that hasty decision over a breakfast of cold eggs and dry ham, he listened as Celia described the menu, and waited while she arranged the seating. By Celia's pointedly careful count the party was still one woman short. She glanced up from her half-eaten breakfast and turned to her brother as if struck by a sudden, brilliant inspiration.

"Harcourt, why did I not think of it before? Miss Galvin should round out our little party. The Leightons are at Staithes Court all evening and Miss Galvin is left alone tonight."

When Harcourt agreed to the dinner party he had insisted none but their closest friends be invited. Had Celia suggested Miss Galvin then, he would have refused. Lily Galvin was a charming young woman, but he hardly knew her. Celia avoided his eyes and busied herself with a spray of wilting veronica. Mrs. Week passed by the doorway a third time.

Harcourt shot his attention back to his young sister. She and Mrs. Week had recently become enamored of Miss Galvin, who had come last month from Hampshire to stay with her cousin, Dorothea Leighton. Knowing glances were directed toward him daily, along with subtle hints of a too long bachelorhood and his assured impending loneliness. Celia could not be expected to remain unmarried much longer—she was, after all, now sixteen—and then what would he do for companionship?

"So that's the reason for this party," Harcourt said.

Celia blushed to the tips of her ears. "I don't know what you are talking about, Harcourt. Really, you have such strange ideas." She shook her head and her blond curls loosened. "I hear Mrs. Week calling for me. Perhaps she has a question about the mutton."

Celia flounced off in a very pretty display of indignation. Harcourt waited until she reached the entry to the hall.

"Mrs. Week is on the other side of that doorway, Celia," he said. "She has not called for anyone. Although I am certain she is regretting the incriminating clatter of her boots on the floor."

The distinctive sound of Mrs. Week shuffling away on the tips of her toes made Harcourt smile to himself, but he kept his countenance severe in Celia's presence. "What do you have to say for yourself?"

"Harcourt," Celia cooed like a practiced coquette, "you

spend far too much time alone or at Dr. Cowpe's. You need more."

"Take care, Celia," he warned.

"Well, you do, Harcourt," she snapped, forgetting her artfulness. "You *need* someone. I shall be married myself, soon enough."

He knew better than to counter with: to whom? Did she have a secret suitor?

Celia read his thoughts, raised a beautifully arched eyebrow and continued. "You shall be alone, Harcourt," she said with genuine compassion in her young voice. "And that simply will not do. You are not so very old."

"Thank you," he said.

"You're not," she assured him. "But seeing that no maid in Ledwyche has caught your eye, you might consider it a gift that Miss Galvin has settled on visiting the Leightons at the very moment you are in such great need of a wife."

Harcourt laughed. "Celia," he said kindly, "whenever and whomever I shall marry is my affair and no one else's. Miss Galvin is indeed charming—"

"And comely and accomplished and witty enough even for you, Harcourt," she interrupted.

He took in Celia's lovely, earnest expression. "Your concern for my happiness is commendable and I thank you for it. But I want no more talk of this. Do you understand? Especially not tonight, when Miss Galvin is here."

Celia squealed and then turned away. "As if I would consider such a thing, Harcourt." She sniffed indignantly. "The very fact you could even suggest it shows how very little idea you have of the nature and course of love." She kissed him condescendingly on the cheek. "I *shall* speak to Mrs. Week about the mutton. And do not vex yourself; I shall not discuss Miss Galvin with you again." She beamed mischievously and scampered off.

Harcourt could only assume the imperative mutton question would be instantly forgotten as Celia informed

171

her co-conspirator that the seed had indeed been planted. He sighed and pushed away the eggs. He couldn't wait to see Kate.

That same morning Cowpe arrived late to his office and in a very bad temper. "Paracelsus," he spat when he saw what Kate was reading. "The sorcerer?"

She closed the book. "Surely one can separate his search for the philosopher's stone with his work on the plague."

"Miss Ishingham," Cowpe said, "ours is an age of science. We subscribe to the logic of natural law, not magic."

"I am not proposing magic, Dr. Cowpe," she said. "I am merely suggesting we examine his theory on plague. His success is documented."

"By whom?" Cowpe demanded. "What is there to say other than that the victims did not recover in spite of the sorcerer's help?"

"It is arrogance," Kate said, "to reject a sound idea because you find the source to be distasteful."

"Not distasteful," Cowpe said. "Worthless. Paracelsus is a fairy figure, fit more for poetry than medicine. Would you study Merlin to treat apoplexy?"

"Have you read the research to which I am referring?" Kate asked.

"I have," Cowpe said. "And in my opinion as medical history it teaches how we progressed in fits and starts from Hippocrates to Vesalius to Harvey to Hunter. As historical reference, Paracelsus possesses value decidedly, but as a guidepost to treatment today I would as soon consult Mr. Gedge's aunt the tea leaf reader."

"You will not read it?" Kate asked.

"I *have* read it," he said emphatically.

"I believe there is relevance to be found in it," Kate said.

"Then we are in disagreement, Miss Ishingham. If you wish to pursue your suspicions I cannot prevent you, except to say that your time would be better spent on the task at hand."

The remainder of the day proceeded in the same contentious manner. Whenever Kate thought she'd persuaded him, she found she was mistaken. Cowpe would agree with nothing she said and she would not move from her position. The only break in the hostile silence of the afternoon came when Mr. Abernathy sent word in the late afternoon that the dinner party tonight would be moved from seven to eight to accommodate the needs of an unexpected guest.

The party, Kate groaned internally. She'd completely forgotten. She hadn't spoken with Mr. Abernathy since Mr. Denton taunted her with the idea of a female Frankenstein. She'd planned to offer some excuse not to attend, but she'd said nothing to the messenger. Now she must go. Perhaps she could claim a headache and leave early. She felt decidedly unprepared to see Mr. Abernathy, and to successfully contain her reaction to him when the day and work had been so difficult.

Cowpe went home in the afternoon, still plagued by his black mood.

After finishing her reading and finding nothing of value, Kate began to walk toward Fretherne. The wind picked up. Her loosely tied bonnet slipped to her shoulders. A carriage sped by, splattering her face with thick mud and small stones. Why was it, Kate thought, with the vexation of the day tangling her fingers in the ribbons, she could never tie her bonnet tightly enough? She could sew up a wound beautifully. How was it she could not tie a bonnet? Lydia always said it was because she hated to wear the thing and learned badly on purpose. Kate had cleaned most of the mud from her face and hair when Miss Abernathy ran excitedly up the street.

"Miss Ishingham," Celia said, glittering with excitement, "how glad I am to have met you. I have happy news. Mrs. Leighton's cousin, Miss Galvin, who is come through Michelmas, has been invited to join our little party this evening."

"Ah," Kate said, not comprehending the importance of the tidings.

"She is a delight," Celia said. "She plays the pianoforte beautifully. I was ashamed to play for her, but she was very kind and helped me with my fingering. And she is lovelier than any lady in Ledwyche."

Mr. Leonard Stanley walked by with Miss Sarah Tichborne at his heel. Celia nodded courteously but coolly. Kate saw that Mr. Stanley had ceased to be a knight.

"I look forward to meeting Miss Galvin," she said. "And I am happy you have found her to be an agreeable companion."

"I hope Miss Galvin shall be more than a companion," Celia said. "I have already confided my hopes to Mrs. Week. I shall confide them now to you. I hope Harcourt shall marry Miss Galvin. He has been alone for too long and is in very great need of a wife."

Kate felt this news drop to the bottom of her heart.

"Shall I walk with you?" Celia asked joyfully, taking Kate's arm.

The feeling of dread in her stomach prevented Kate from introducing any new topic of conversation. Not that any subject would have the strength to shift Miss Abernathy from her endless delineation of Miss Galvin's numerous gifts and accomplishments.

"Miss Galvin would suit Harcourt," Celia continued. "She has a scholar's knowledge of botany. Her uncle was acquainted with Reverend Gilbert White. Do you know of him? I did not. Mrs. Week told me he wrote a famous book, *A Natural History of* . . . something, I think. Mrs. Week said it was very popular when she was first married and sold all over the continent."

Kate drew herself up. At the very least she would not spoil Celia's ardent pleasure at the prospect of the party. "Yes. I know of Reverend White."

But Miss Abernathy had already moved past the Surrey naturalist. "And Miss Galvin is lovely," Celia said. "I only hope when I am grown I shall appear half as fetching in a plain morning dress."

Kate's day had progressed from bad to worse in painful and humiliating increments. She waited for some large bird, shot in error, to fall from the sky and land on her head.

"Yesterday at the Leightons'," Celia purred, oblivious to Kate's discomfort, "Miss Galvin prettily begged Harcourt to quiz her on botanical nomenclature, then bested him with knowledge of the language of flowers in English and in French!"

With great relief Kate entered the footpath to Fretherne. The two ancient stone gables had never seemed so welcome. "Thank you for seeing me home," she said to Miss Abernathy. "Shall I ask Mrs. Ansley to lend you her carriage?"

"Our house is not far," Celia said happily. "I should like to walk."

Kate watched Miss Abernathy bounce toward home and went inside.

She chose to wear a dinner dress too plain for her mother's taste, but one she loved, robin's egg muslin, trimmed with velvet orpine at the hem.

When she arrived at the Abernathy house Kate found Celia and a comely brunette, who could only be Miss Galvin, huddled rapturously over a slender, pale blue book.

"Miss Ishingham," Harcourt said when he saw Kate. "Allow me to introduce Miss Galvin."

Wretchedly, Miss Galvin was even fairer upon close inspection. "I am happy to meet you," Kate said.

"Miss Ishingham," Miss Galvin said warmly. "Miss Abernathy speaks very highly of you."

Celia beamed at Kate. In spite of her foul mood Kate could not help but smile.

"What is it you are reading?" Kate asked, gesturing to the volume resting in Miss Galvin's long fingers.

"Days With the Romantic Poets. There is a wonderful new poem within it: 'Ode to Eurydice.' *Blackwood's* has praised it, and Leigh Hunt is rumored to be in raptures." Miss Galvin smiled shyly at Mr. Abernathy.

"Is Mr. Hunt the author?" Kate asked.

"No," Miss Galvin said. "Forgive me, Miss Ishingham. With your name I assumed you were familiar with the poem. 'Ode to Eurydice' was written by Charles Ishingham."

Kate stepped back. She knew Charles had been hard at work since she left Greydon Hall in the spring. But how could he have written and published so quickly?

"Are you an admirer of poetry, Miss Galvin?" Kate asked. Miss Galvin blushed charmingly. Kate felt grim.

"I am," Miss Galvin answered.

Kate suspected Lily Galvin, like so many young ladies in England and abroad, was enamored of Charles as much for his fine face as his delicate verse.

Miss Galvin turned. "What do you think of the poem, Mr. Abernathy?"

"Do not ask Harcourt," Celia warned. "He loathes Mr. Ishingham. I am sorry to say it, Miss Ishingham." She stopped. "Is Mr. Ishingham your kinsman?"

Kate nodded.

"For Harcourt," Celia continued, "if a poet is not Milton or Keats, he is dismissed out of hand like the vegetable peelings of a kitchen maid." She and Miss Galvin both suppressed giggles.

Harcourt's face darkened.

"Tell us what you think of it, Miss Ishingham?" Celia asked, handing the book to Kate.

"I have not read it," Kate said. She opened the book to the first verse, which began with a prophecy of death. In a very few minutes of reading she saw the reason Charles had been able to publish so quickly. The poem was not new. Kate recognized it as one he had completed in feverish haste in the days after Lydia's accident. It had a different title then, and he had improved the form, but the content was the same. Kate looked up to see Harcourt standing near her.

"Well, Mr. Abernathy," she said as calmly as she could, "shall you tell me your opinion?"

"Allow me first to apologize for Miss Abernathy's indiscretion," he said, his eyes flashing with embarrassment.

"Think nothing of it," Kate said coolly, though her heart raced in wounded pride for Charles.

"My opinion of your cousin's work thus far, Miss Ishingham, is not due to any question of whether or not he has real poetry in him, for that he does," Harcourt said. "And he squanders it on half efforts, which are devoured by a female public in love with his handsome face."

The attention of the room had fixed excitedly on the story of Miss Galvin's chance meeting with Lord Wellington in Italy October last. Harcourt directed his interest to Kate alone. "This newest work, however, has changed my view."

Mr. Abernathy did not smile but gazed openly at her, his eyes the color of coffee in candlelight. "As a meditation on love and loss, the poem exceeds all of Mr. Ishingham's early work. His delicate lyricism serves the source myth well. It moved me, Miss Ishingham, deeply. It is my opinion 'Ode to Eurydice' shall make your kinsman's reputation and elevate him from a handsome wordsmith to a poet of substance."

The trials of the day, Cowpe's foul temper and Miss Galvin's inescapable beauty began to melt. Mr. Abernathy's sensual, expressive mouth closed softly into a smile that reached to the depths of Kate's heart. She agreed with his assessment of Charles's work. As the proudest of all the Ishinghams, and the heir but not the son in that tightly knit family, Charles had been the most susceptible to flattery from the right sources. High praise from *Blackwood's* for his first effort, "Pandion," had blunted his fire to challenge himself, and the ravenous readers who bought his poems in record numbers did nothing to dissuade him from an easy rapport with his own talent.

"I'm ashamed to admit I'm in complete agreement with you, Mr. Abernathy," Kate said.

"How can you be, Miss Ishingham?" he teased easily, his dark eyes flashing. "You have yet to read it."

"I meant your opinion of Mr. Ishingham's prior efforts," she said, trying not to raise her hand to her face to feel whether she was blushing. "As for the poem, Mr. Ishingham permitted me to read it in an earlier form three years ago. From the verse I read now I see it remains very much the same."

Mr. Abernathy smiled covetously at her, as if she were a rare book he longed to open and read. Kate had to avoid his eyes. How could she have so little control over her response to him? One heated look and she was ready to run off to Gretna Green. Now she knew she was blushing. She pulled back.

Miss Galvin seated herself near a large candelabrum. It seemed to illuminate her from within; adding fire to her green eyes and making the burnished gold of her gown resemble sunlight itself. "Mr. Abernathy," she purred, "I have brought my copy of *Blackwood's*. Come see where the critic—not unfavorably—alludes to *Endymion*."

Kate smiled. "Go," she said.

Mr. Abernathy crossed to the Aphrodite in his drawing room.

Though Lily Galvin did flirt with Mr. Abernathy, Kate could find no other fault in the young lady from Hampshire. She seemed as kind as she was pretty, intelligent and unafraid to be so. Kate rubbed the back of her neck and stared dully at Miss Galvin, vexed that Charles had published a poem that was dear to both of them without writing to tell her.

Miss Galvin glided to the pianoforte and sat down. Her playing exceeded Celia's delighted description. Kate had rarely heard music played with such insight and emotion. This was too much: a flawless woman, gifted and beautiful.

She bit her tongue, but there was nothing she could say against Miss Galvin, save that the woman was sure to win the heart of Mr. Abernathy.

Kate felt choler nip ferociously at her common sense. She squeezed the back of her neck and turned to Celia, who was sitting quietly while the attention in the room was fixed on the luminous Lily Galvin. "Miss Abernathy, what did you think of the poem?"

Celia's face expressed surprise that anyone but Harcourt would be genuinely interested in her opinion. "I found it hard to understand," she confided. "And what I did understand, I found melancholy." Celia paused. "Harcourt called it a threnody," she said. "It means a grief song. Did you know?"

Kate smiled. Celia Abernathy was a girl with much more to offer than Lily Galvin, no matter how charming the young lady from Hampshire seemed. The little Kate knew of the Abernathys' lives before they came to Ledwyche made her realize how well Harcourt had raised his sisters on his own. For that reason alone he was more intriguing than any other man she knew.

"Such a lovely word for something so sad," Celia said. "Was she very pretty—Mr. Ishingham's cousin Lydia? He dedicates the poem to her."

Grief shot to Kate's throat. She hadn't seen the dedication. "Yes," she said quietly, "Lydia Ishingham was very pretty."

Harcourt watched this scene unfold with interest both for Kate's kind attention to Celia and Celia's newly emerging thoughtfulness. He smiled proudly at his sister, then returned his attention to Miss Galvin, who continued to talk of literary salons in London.

When dinner was over Harcourt approached Kate, who sat alone in the drawing room after Cowpe walked away from her, irritation marking his countenance.

"Miss Ishingham," he said gently, sitting near her on the

silver damask couch. "You have been very quiet. Is everything all right?"

Kate sighed. "Dr. Cowpe and I are at an impasse." She had given up trying to be someone she was not. She was not luminous, witty or elegant. She was nothing like Miss Galvin or Lydia or even young Celia Abernathy. She drew in a deep breath. "I am certain you are aware I do not possess the willingness to submit usually expected of my sex. This has created a temporarily untenable situation."

"Over what did you and Dr. Cowpe disagree?" Harcourt handed Kate a glass of port, which she took from his hand with a distinct awareness of the closeness of his fingers to hers.

"Delicious," she said after sipping the ruby liquid.

He smiled. "I have a secret trove of magnificent wine." Darkness shaded his eyes for an instant, then disappeared. "Please, continue." He drank his wine.

How ridiculous, Kate thought before speaking again, to be utterly charmed by the way a man drinks wine, but she smiled to herself, allowing the thrill to expand inside her like remembered music.

He waited for her to speak again. Kate ran her fingers delicately over the nape of her neck and continued. "You are—I am sure—acquainted with the life and work of Paracelsus," she said. "Dr. Cowpe believes that his emphasis on the mystical and the occult, the homunculus and the philosopher's stone, negates all his ideas."

"I believe the prevailing opinion on much medical theory before our time is that most of it is too tied to sorcery and magic and is of little value unless one returns to the works of Vesalius and Hippocrates," Harcourt said.

"It is folly, though, don't you think?" Kate asked heatedly. "To discard two centuries of work because some of it is wrong or outdated? We cannot be so blind as to assume the prevailing ideas of our own age will last unaltered by advances in theory and practice. Science—and art as well—are in a constant state of change and growth. Only a fool ignores the past entirely!" Kate stopped abruptly and felt her face flush crimson.

Harcourt drew closer to her. "Do not fret, Miss Ishingham," he murmured in a low voice, which made Kate think of an unexpected brook in a dark forest. "I know it was not your intention to call Dr. Cowpe a fool."

"Forgive me," she said, still blushing. "I must remind myself not to speak as freely as I did at home." Kate turned toward where Miss Galvin sat surrounded by an admiring throng. "Miss Galvin is very pretty."

Harcourt put down his wineglass. "She is," he said. "But she is also goodhearted and witty."

Kate whirled back to face him. Harcourt brushed away a sting of guilt. He knew that had not been fair, but he had the answer he wanted. Kate sat near him, dressed in a blue gown trimmed with pale pink orpine at the hem. She was fair, with a lovely complexion and glossy dark hair, but the fire and intelligence that lit her eyes and animated her delicate features, unraveled Harcourt's comprehension of anything else in the room. She didn't seem to know what to do with her hands. He worried he had pained her.

"Miss Galvin is as pretty and as kind as most young women here in Ledwyche," he said gently. "And anyplace else. What of it?"

"Nothing. I suppose," Kate said, a glow still coloring her cheeks.

Harcourt leaned back in his chair to glance across the room at his sister, who gazed at Miss Galvin in rapt attention. "Celia is an exceedingly romantic girl." He moved forward again and smiled at Kate. "Despite my best efforts, she seems to have far too little to occupy her mind."

"You have seen more than admirably to her education," Kate said. Her smooth voice was quiet and low.

Harcourt grinned slightly and turned to the window, where soft night had begun to swallow the day. "She resents me for it."

"Now she does," Kate said. "Wait until she is grown and

can converse easily with anyone. She will be grateful to know so much of the way of the world when she is out in it."

"Ah," Harcourt said, breathing deeply to erase what Celia already knew of the world. "Perhaps you are right."

Kate drew closer. He had to clench his teeth to keep the scent of her hair from invading him too deeply.

"Your sister is good and sweet, Mr. Abernathy, and capable of much more than most will allow of her, until she proves herself."

He didn't say anything.

"And she has you to thank." Kate smiled and wrapped her delicate, slender fingers around the wineglass.

Celia approached, arms locked with Miss Galvin's, barely suppressed giggles on their lips.

"I must take my leave of you now, Mr. Abernathy," Kate said. She smiled and nodded at Celia and Miss Galvin, then walked away, stopping to speak briefly with Cowpe before leaving the room.

"Harcourt," Celia burst out, "whatever are you thinking? You look an ocean away."

"Arithmetic lessons," he said, and tried not to laugh at her thunderstruck expression. "I'm considering increasing their frequency."

Celia opened her mouth to protest, but he stopped her. "Mr. Kipling told me you have an aptitude for complex equations," Harcourt said, grinning broadly. "You need only apply yourself more steadily. Miss Galvin." He nodded, then took his leave to speak with Cowpe.

Chapter Thirteen

Mr. Moulton knocked loudly at Harcourt Abernathy's chamber at the Black Hound Inn. Claire opened the door. *Kate,* Harcourt said furiously, correcting himself. *Kate* opened the door. A fragrant wash of coffee-scented air filled the room.

"I thought you might need coffee," Mr. Moulton boomed amiably. He strode into the room and laid a tray with a coffee urn, a bowl of sugar, a pitcher of cream and two cups on the table.

The scent coming from the silver urn was stronger than Harcourt would have thought possible. Claire, *Kate,* peered into the cream pitcher.

"Mmmmm," she hummed. "Have you ever tasted real Vermont cream?" she asked Harcourt. "You'll never want anything else in your coffee." She smiled happily at Mr. Moulton, who grinned back.

"Miss Islington," he said, and nodded, beaming.

Harcourt stared in silence as Mr. Moulton poured the coffee into the two cups, then swirled in the thick yellow cream. Claire—could he ever think of her that way? He'd

183

have to if he wanted to keep his head clear. *Claire* brought a steaming cup to her face and breathed deeply.

"I love the smell of coffee," she said. She breathed in the fragrant steam once more, then drank deeply from the purple-flowered cup. "You must think I'm strange," she said, putting her cup on the table and handing him the other.

Harcourt took the cup from her, wishing he could take her hand in its place. "Not at all."

Claire smiled at Mr. Moulton. "Thank you for the coffee."

The innkeeper nodded and moved to take his leave but stopped. "Thank you, Miss Islington, for giving me your grandfather's *Works of Byron*," he said, his huge hand on the doorknob.

"Grandfather would have wanted you to have it," Claire replied. "I know he would have. And besides, you know I only love Keats and—because of Grandfather—Charles Ishingham."

Moulton kissed the top of her head. "Good night, Catherine."

"Stop it," Claire said, smiling. "That's not my name. You can't call me that anymore." She pulled away. He walked into the hall. "Good night, Mr. Moulton," she said and closed the door behind him.

Harcourt reached for the back of the chair near the table and held on as if the floor were disintegrating beneath his feet.

"Sorry," Claire murmured, taking another long drink of the hot coffee. "Mr. Moulton lived with my grandfather and me when I was little. I think the Black Hound was being renovated after a fire. Anyway, Mr. Moulton was terrible with names. He always called me 'Catherine the Great' to tease me. I thought it was cool until I found out what kind of person she was." She glanced up from her blossomy cup. "Are you all right?" She stepped around the table to where he stood.

Harcourt's heart pounded in his chest.

She waited.

"I don't know," he said.

Claire breathed slowly. Harcourt watched her breasts gently rise and fall in her scarlet gown. She laid her cool hand against his face and then his brow. He bit his cheek to stop himself from taking her fingers into his mouth.

"You don't have a fever," she said. She pressed her fingertips to his neck. "But your pulse is racing."

He grabbed her hand and held it. "Do you not know?"

"Know what?" she asked, not taking her hand from his.

Harcourt sucked at air, which seemed not like air at all but thick blankets of some choking, noxious vapor. He dropped Claire's hand. "Forgive me." He walked to the corner of the room farthest from her and sat heavily on the piano bench. "I haven't slept well since I arrived." He ran his hands over his knees, then gazed back up. "And I miss my family."

An expression of surprise shot across her face. "You're married?" she asked, stepping out of the firelight.

Harcourt shook his head. He couldn't say aloud—had never said aloud—that he was no longer married. "I have a sister. She's seventeen."

He thought of how much Celia had loved Kate. Claire stepped closer.

"She'll be nearly married by the time I am home," he said. "Though in her letters she promises she'll wait."

"Are your parents . . . ?" Claire stopped talking, then crossed the room and sat beside him.

"My mother and father are dead," he said, gazing away from her. "Celia is staying with our sister Anna until I have returned."

"I'm sorry," Claire said. "I didn't mean to press you."

She turned on the piano bench and faced the keys. As she moved, the gown caught and strained against her breasts and hips. Harcourt brought his hand to his mouth and tried to find enough air to clear his head. *She didn't know. She didn't remember.* What could he tell her: that she was dead, that he was her husband; that he hadn't

185

breathed since she died and could hardly breathe now to sit so near and not touch her, not kiss her? Harcourt got up from the bench and walked to the table. He picked up a cup of coffee and put it down again without drinking.

She turned to him. "Can you play?"

Harcourt poured the last of the claret into his glass and drank it. "I can."

She smiled. "Well, then, since we're stuck here for the night, let's make the best of it."

He stayed near the table.

"I won't bite you," she said.

"I hadn't thought you would," he said.

"Good," she said, grinning. "Will you play something?"

Harcourt picked up the lit candle from the table near the door and sat beside Claire at the piano. He rested his hands on the keys for a moment, then began.

She closed her eyes. "Oh," she said, smiling brightly in the soft gold light. "*Hoffnung.* I love Beethoven."

Harcourt continued to play.

"My Italian is terrible," she said. "But I love the English translation. Do you know it? *'Tell me, my sweetheart, that you love me, tell me that you are mine, and I will not envy the gods their divinity. With only one look from you, dear, you open the paradise that is my happiness.'* " She smiled.

He lifted his hands from the keys.

"Don't stop," she said, gently touching his arm.

Harcourt turned to face her. He pressed his hand into the soft silk cushion of the bench and she threaded her slender fingers through and under his.

"It's okay, she said. "You don't have to play if you don't want to."

He drew nearer to her. She did not retreat. He unclasped his hand from hers and slid it under her thigh. Claire sucked lightly at the air between them and gazed searchingly at him, as if she'd lost something she could hardly remember but that she desperately needed. Harcourt placed his free hand on her knee, opened his fingers over the silk covering her leg for a moment, then took her hand. He turned her open palm to his mouth and kissed it. She nestled her face between her palm and his mouth and kissed him.

Grief and longing exploded inside him. He pulled her closer, her breasts pressed against his chest. Slowly she thrust her tongue into his mouth. He caught it and raised himself above her, pressing his mouth against hers, his tongue inside her. She moaned softly.

Kate, he whispered to himself, *Kate, Kate.*

She slid her hand inside his shirt and stroked the hard muscles of his stomach and the hair on his chest. Harcourt pulled back from the kiss and tried to catch his breath, but she reached up for him and kissed him again, flicking her tongue gently against his teeth. His hair fell across her brow and she ran her fingers down his shirt to his stomach.

His body swelled and ached for her. He kissed her nose, her eyes, her cheek, then pressed his forehead to hers and steadied his breath. From inside his shirt she caressed his waist and the bones of his hip, then slid her hand down and closed her fingers firmly around the head of his shaft, still trapped in his pants. He moaned, then sank down beside her and wrapped his hands around her waist. She opened her mouth on his neck and kissed him.

Harcourt took her breasts lightly into his hands and rubbed his thumb gently across each nipple. She released the swollen flesh and stroked the length of his shaft through the fabric until he almost released himself.

"Stop," he said hoarsely, standing up, struggling to breathe.

"I can't," she said, rising to meet him and kissing him more deeply than before.

He moaned, low and deep and long, then lifted her into his arms. Her bottom filled his hand. He slid his finger up into her sex. Wet and hot, she cried out and pulsed around his finger through the damp fabric of her gown. Harcourt laid her on the bed. She sat up and pulled her gown over her head.

He swayed at the sight of her. *Kate,* his Kate.

She slid to the edge of the bed and unbuttoned his pants. His fully aroused, erect shaft strained painfully against the rough wool. He tore off his shirt as she finished unbuttoning his pants. Gently, her cool hand lifted him from the constraints of his clothes. His pants fell to the floor. She took him into her mouth and sucked, circling the head with her tongue then taking the length of him to the back of her throat.

"I can't," he said haltingly. "I can't hold on if you—"

She licked the throbbing underside. He moaned and held her head, running his fingers through her long dark hair. Harcourt held himself furiously against release, but her soft mouth and darting tongue were almost more than he could bear. When he knew he could hold on no longer, she pulled her mouth from him and lay back on the bed.

He stood still for a moment, waiting until he could continue. She smiled at him.

Kate, he thought, *my Kate.* Slowly, Harcourt lowered his weight onto her. His shaft pressed heavy and hot between her thighs. He took her breast into his mouth and she gasped, pressing her hips hard into his. He circled her nipples with his tongue and stroked her belly down to the soft curve of her hip. Harcourt opened his mouth on her other breast and gently took her firm nipple between his teeth. She sighed slowly and lowered her hips to the bed before pressing herself up against him again.

He slid his hand to her soft hair, caressed the wet, hot center. She cried out and arched her back so her breasts touched his chest. He stroked lightly and rhythmically again.

"*Wait,*" she said, taking his hand away and breathing heavily. "Not like this. I want you inside me."

Harcourt's need for release thundered until he could almost hear it. Kate writhed beneath him and took his shaft into her hand again, stroking desperately and pulling it toward her. The need to be inside her, *to release inside her,* almost blinded him. As gently as he could, he unbound her fingers and thrust slowly into her. At every inch she moaned a song of pleasure, closing her hands around him and pulling him tighter to her. He felt her—hot, wet and soft, closing and opening against him.

He moved slowly. She cried out and rose up to meet him, pressing herself against him. He penetrated to the core of her again. She arched her back and said something he couldn't hear. Why couldn't he hear her? He pulled almost out of her, then sank slowly back.

Her tight muscles clung rhythmically to him and she moaned something low and desperate. Harcourt tried to keep to their slow, steady rhythm, but when she moved faster, he gratefully followed. He couldn't hold on much longer.

"Oh," she breathed in his ear. "Oh," she whispered. "I love you."

He thrust harder, deeper, faster. She called out to him, opening and closing against him in a cascade of release that pulled him in. Harcourt came inside her, thunderously matching her pulse for pulse. Panting, he lowered his chest until he could feel her heart pounding against his.

Still hard inside her, he felt her body convulse around him again.

He kissed her ear. "I love you," he said.

She came a third time. He buried his face in her neck. She wrapped her arms around the hard, damp muscles of his back. He pulled the coverlet over them both. He waited until she fell asleep before pulling out.

The moon rose and splashed its light on Kate's sleeping face. *Kate.* Here. Now. Beside him. If this was a dream, Harcourt never wanted to awaken. He watched her sleep until he was sure dawn had to be coming. He settled next to her on his side and wrapped his arm across her belly. She sighed and nestled against him, her bottom against his lap.

Harcourt pulled her closer. He felt himself fall asleep with his face in her hair.

Claire ran up Charles Street at 9:15 in the morning. Wind off the river plastered her hair to her face. She wiped it out of her eyes so she wouldn't get hit by a car as she crossed Chestnut. Ian hadn't called back this morning, in spite of her beatific apology. She hadn't really expected him to. In the clear light of the morning she wished she hadn't called him. Riding the I'm-so-weak-take-care-of me-train had been losing its dubious appeal since she realized Ian had lied about Vermont.

"Thank God you're here," a breathless woman called out from the shelter of the doorstep at Arcades, startling Claire. "I've been here since eight-fifty."

Claire shot her an apologetic glance, mumbled something lame about lost keys and unlocked the door.

The woman pushed past and strode into the store. "My daughter's getting married." She said this as if no one else had ever decided to get married. "You'd think she would have introduced us a few months ago." The woman shook her head, and a cloud of powder-light, expensive-smelling perfume spilled into the air. "It doesn't matter."

She fingered a rose-and-sage–patterned quilt and sniffed. "Annabelle wanted big," she said, crossing to where Claire stood behind the counter. "Now she wants small. She read about this store in *The Phoenix*. Can you do a wedding in early May?" The woman grabbed Claire's hand. "Say yes."

Claire opened her leatherbound calendar and scanned the filled pages. "We're booked every Sunday in May." The woman colored. Claire glanced down at the pages again. "Where are you having the wedding? And how many people?"

"I don't know. And I don't know," the woman replied. "She's told me nothing except she wants Arcades flowers and Indian food." A gorgeous eyebrow rose. "They met in an Indian restaurant. I don't even know what he does for a living." She shrugged, and a second fragrant cascade filled the shop.

"I can't really tell you anything unless you give me a date," Claire said.

The woman waved her hand and answered a cell phone ringing a tinny degradation of *Moonlight Sonata.* "Just a minute."

"Yes," she piped into the phone. "I'm at the store. I don't know what you expected, honey. Push it up a few months. Get married in October. It'll all be easier. No! All right. All right. I'll call you right back."

The woman set her teeth formidably at Claire. "They're willing to hold it at night in the middle of the week. The young man's father owns a building with loft space or something like that. What about the Thursday after the fourth?"

Claire checked. "Okay."

"Thank you," the woman said, sighing and pulling on red leather gloves. "I'll be back with my daughter in an hour or less." She left in a cloud of Chanel, passing Ian in the doorway.

"Hi," Claire squeaked, embarrassment constricting her throat.

"I got your message," Ian said. "What do you want to discuss? I have an hour before I have to be back." He glanced dismissively around the empty store. "Can you close so we could go to Panini or something? I'm starving, and I haven't had any coffee yet."

"I can't close," Claire said. "You know that."

Ian adjusted his watch. "I don't see why not. It's freezing. It's January. Who buys flowers in January?"

Claire rubbed the back of her neck. "Well, if they didn't, I'd be out of a job, wouldn't I?"

He sighed and sat heavily on striped chair near a print of

Orpheus and Eurydice. "What did you want to talk about?" Ian's tone was distant, and the green flash in his eyes told Claire her excessive answering machine apology had been insufficient. He wasn't an idiot. He could see through her as well as she could see through him. He knew an apology that florid was hiding something. He'd meant what he said when he left last night. Why would he want to stay if she kept herself at such a physical and emotional distance? She'd hurt him.

Claire exhaled and let go of her irritation at Ian's condescending attitude about her work. Understanding that everyone is flawed is part of being able to sustain a successful relationship. You just have to know the flaws you can accept, and the ones you can't. Ian's patronizing attitude and his jealous possessiveness were outweighed by his fierce loyalty and affection.

The equation immediately felt false, but Claire circumvented her instincts and concentrated on the living, breathing man in front of her. *Ian and his flaws are acceptable because he has to be what I want,* she told herself. Claire breathed deeply and made herself believe it. She crossed the store and sat on the chair beside his.

Ian's forbidding posture melted. He took off his camel-colored leather gloves and grabbed Claire's hand. She smiled at him. Ian was a tenderhearted boy in a haughty man's body. She kissed his hands, then laid them on his lap.

"What?" he asked. "What can I do? What do you want?"

Claire massaged the back of her neck, then slid her fingertips to her throat and collarbone. "I have to be totally honest with you, so you know what you're getting into if you stay with me."

Ian drew back and straightened up in his chair. "What are you talking about? I thought we *were* honest with each other."

The stinging awareness that Ian had lied about Toby and the Black Hound pinched Claire's tongue for an instant, but his white lie blanched in comparison to what she had to tell him.

"I wasn't completely honest with you about what happened to me." Claire folded her hands together and spun her silver ring around her finger. "I didn't tell you the whole story of what happened at the Black Hound seven years ago."

"There's more than attempted suicide and hospitalization?" Ian squawked, jumping from his chair. He stared at Claire's hands writhing in her lap. "Why are you always playing with that ring! Did Toby give it to you?"

"No," Claire said slowly, swallowing her annoyance at his reflexive jealousy. "I bought it for myself. In Vermont, after I got out of the hospital." She hid her hands in the folds of her black velvet skirt. "What difference does it make?"

"None," Ian said, exasperated. "None at all." He leaned his long, beautifully dressed body against the counter. "That inn gave me the creeps." He crossed his arms over his narrow chest. "It was disgusting. All those stupid people hoping to see a ghost."

He shivered and walked to the end of the counter, where Claire had left the book of poetry he'd given her before Christmas—*Days With the Romantic Poets; Byron, Shelley, Clare, Ishingham and Keats*. He popped open the blue volume and flipped through it. "Did you ever read this?" he asked defensively.

"I've read it before," Claire said. "And yes, I read it again. I love it. Charles Ishingham is one of my favorite poets."

He tossed it back onto the counter.

"Why are you always throwing my books?" she asked.

Ian glared at her, then shook his head.

"When you get a chance," Claire said, "I'd like my monograph back."

He didn't say anything.

Claire stood up and crossed the room to stand next to him at the counter. "The monograph is part of what I have to tell you." She leaned against him.

193

Ian put his arm around her. "Whatever you have to tell me, whatever happened, we can get through it." He held Claire by the shoulders. "You know I love you, don't you? That should be enough."

"There are things you don't know about me, Ian," Claire said, standing loosely in his tight hold. "We can't get married until you know everything there is to know about me, including things you might not want to hear."

"Okay," he said, sighing. "I'm ready."

Claire turned to a pot of dormant paperwhites she'd been forcing and tried to ignore a strange idea that Ian somehow knew what she was going to say. But he couldn't know. Not everything.

A sense of Harcourt's presence flooded Claire with heat. *No*, she thought, *not now, not anymore. I can't live like this anymore.* Guiltily, though, Claire waited for the pleasurable feel of his mouth in hers. It didn't come. Protection, not pleasure, coursed through invisible veins and arteries of connection. Harcourt swelled like a shield inside Claire. But to guard her from what?

Claire pulled away from Ian. Harcourt's voice whispered, but she couldn't hear what he said. *I can't hear you,* she thought. *If you're trying to say something to me I have to be able to hear you.* Anger and frustration threaded through longing and sorrow.

Claire sucked in air and faced Ian. "Seven years ago when I was twenty-three and my grandfather, whom I loved more than anyone, had just died, I left med school and moved to Vermont to work on restoring the gardens of a nineteenth-century estate. It was April and a late snow blanketed the area for a few days. I was snowed in at the Black Hound."

Ian clenched his teeth, and the muscle of his jaw flickered like a beating heart.

How the hell was she going to say this out loud to someone who hated everything weird and inexplicable? Claire spun her ring. Ian held her fingers and stopped her movement. She gently pulled her hand away. "The inn was over-booked because of the unexpected snow. A lot of people were stranded. I only got a room—or half of one—because Mr. Moulton, the innkeeper you met, was an old friend of my grandfather's and took pity on me."

Ian glanced at his watch and sighed.

I'm not trying to bore you, Claire thought.

"Claire," Ian suddenly, "I don't care who you slept with or what you did before we met. You're not my first girlfriend either. What I care about is now."

Silver and brass bells on a raspberry-colored cord tinkled brightly as the Chanel woman and her daughter blew into the store.

"Delphinium!" Chanel Woman wailed, continuing a conversation that must have began the moment the two women met to come back to Arcades.

The bride-to-be, a soft physical echo of her mother, might have suggested strippers dancing on a flamingo pink–frosted wedding cake for the horror in her mother's voice.

"They're scraggly," the mother whined. "What about orchids?"

"No," her daughter said patiently. "I want delphinium."

"Well, you can't get sweet peas," the mother said definitively. "No one will have them. Why are you picking such wild-looking flowers, honey?"

The bride, whose serious, sensitive demeanor was the exact opposite of her mother's breezy authority, turned to Claire for support.

"I can get sweet peas," Claire said.

"Where?" the mother asked, craning her neck to see the back of the case.

"Not here," Claire said, catching Ian's resentful expression from the corner of her eye. "I share garden space outside the city with two other florists. We grow heirloom and seasonal flowers."

"What about peonies then?" the mother asked, brightening. "Do you have peonies?"

"I don't like the way they smell," the bride said.

"What?" the mother sputtered. "Everyone loves peonies."

"Maybe this is a bad idea, Mom. Our tastes are just so different. I'll come back another time," she said to Claire.

"Honey," the mother whined, stretching the vowels until Claire imagined being able to pick elongated letters out of the air.

"Would you like to see photographs of arrangements from other weddings?" Claire asked.

Eventually the two women settled tentatively on a hand-tied bouquet of French blue hydrangea, white lisianthus, delphinium and sweet peas. And for the flower girls, a garland of ivy threaded with the bouquet blossoms. Reasonably happy, mother and daughter left at ten-thirty.

"Well," Ian huffed, "that took too long." He pulled on his gloves. "I have to get back."

Claire stared at him. He held his teeth and his jaw muscle throbbed back and forth.

"I'm sorry," he said in a gentler voice. "Come to my apartment tonight. I'll be in a better mood. I promise. And I'll listen to whatever you have to say." He kissed the top of Claire's head. "And then maybe we can have makeup sex." Ian winked at her and shut the door, ringing the chain of bells behind him.

Claire leaned back on the counter and stroked her neck muscles. What the hell was that? she thought. She grabbed the leatherbound calendar book and swung around to the back of the counter to put it away. She'd be stronger tonight. She'd tell him outright what had happened with Harcourt, and in the clearest possible terms.

Then Ian could decide what he wanted.

As he lay in their bed in the Black Hound Inn, Harcourt kept his arms tightly clasped around Claire. He whispered to her of the night of the Cowpes' card party, when he'd known she'd be his forever.

* * *

Harcourt Abernathy sat at a card table at the Cowpes' and waited for Kate to arrive. Since she'd left his house last week he'd been able to think of nothing but her. His work for the monograph was almost completed, but he had found an excuse to call at Cowpe's office three times during the previous week, and had been lucky enough to see Kate twice.

Dr. Cowpe was almost scandalously fond of card parties. Though he never played, he hosted just such an occasion nearly every month. Harcourt watched the parlor door for Kate while attempting to discreetly lose to Mrs. Gedge in such a way that would surprise her when she won.

Kate came into the room dressed in a gown of white crinkled silk spotted with white satin and trimmed with black silk roses. Before Harcourt could catch her eye, Kate was surrounded by young Ledwyche ladies anxious to hear of Miss Ishingham's cousin, the poet Charles Ishingham. Did she know him? How often had they met? Was Mr. Ishingham still fond of, "strawberries on a sunny summer hillside"? Could he be as handsome as his portrait?

Harcourt smiled to himself as Kate gracefully answered each fervent inquiry. He remembered her kind attention to Celia. The pleasurable sting in his body, which anticipated her nearness, made him want to open his mouth and taste every drop of air that had touched her skin.

"Mr. Abernathy," Mrs. Gedge's tart, raw quince voice scratched his ear.

"Ah, yes, forgive me," Harcourt said. He scanned the cards in his hand and chose.

Mrs. Gedge's small eyes brightened. She beamed triumphantly to her friends sitting on either side of her. The hand started again, but the game had lost its charm for him.

Kate seemed to have addressed the final vital question concerning her handsome cousin. The young ladies appeared to be satisfied. They returned reverently to the circle of shyer poetry devotees sitting near the pianoforte and tenderly retold the tale.

Kate gazed up at Harcourt as he laid his cards on the table. His dark eyes met hers. He smiled, a slight smile that Kate knew was for her alone. She felt that he had kissed her. With a single glance in that well-lit parlor, Harcourt Abernathy had penetrated all of her. She felt the warmth of his attention spread through her, from her chest to her arms and down to her legs, which seemed to melt beneath her weight. Some hint must have shown on her face, for he hastily excused himself from the card table and rushed to her.

"Are you well, Miss Ishingham?" he asked.

Harcourt's nearness and the concern in his voice swallowed Kate's ability to stand upright. She swayed a little and caught herself on the back of a silver-and-pink-striped chair.

"I should like to take a turn about the terrace," she said, embarrassed by her transparent emotions.

Harcourt escorted Kate out of doors and onto the terrace. He led her gently to the stone balustrade on the eastern side and stood very close to her. "Are you ill? Shall I take you home? Shall I call for Cowpe?"

He was standing so near to her, Kate could smell the sunlit afternoon still lingering in his hair. Harcourt's hand was at her elbow, supporting her. She could not meet his eye. He would know what she felt. He would see it. Harcourt's breath, warm and sweet, melted over Kate's neck and chest.

"Miss Ishingham," he said, "I am very much concerned about your health. Please relieve me by telling me you are well or allow me to call for Cowpe immediately."

"I am quite well, Mr. Abernathy, thank you," Kate said. Her voice in her throat felt like a rain-washed stone. "The air has revived me."

"I am relieved to hear it," he said, sighing and smiling at her.

Kate thought she would never be as happy again as she

was at that moment. The white of Harcourt's shirt the rough black wool of his coat, his strong hands at his side, captivated her intensely: as though no man had ever before worn a white shirt or black coat, or had strong hands, that rested on a rough stone railing waiting to clasp a waist.

The Tichborne sisters began to sing. Everyone in the parlor gathered around the pianoforte. The terrace and the late moon were abandoned by all, save himself and Kate.

"Ah, Beethoven," Harcourt said. "Do you know Italian? *'Tell me, my sweetheart, that you love me, tell me that you are mine, and I will not envy the gods their divinity!'* " The intimacy of the phrase caught him off guard and he turned abruptly to the open terrace doors. "Shall we go inside to better hear the music? There are no finer musicians in all of Ledwyche."

Kate hesitated. Harcourt felt his eyes flash.

"Forgive me, Miss Ishingham," he said, shading his disappointment. "I should not have presumed you to be fond of music."

Kate turned from him and glanced at the disappearing daylight. "I adore music, Mr. Abernathy. And Beethoven above all. But the air is sweet and I cannot bear to remove myself and return indoors yet."

"Then we shall remain here, until you are ready to leave," he said. How he could stand this near to her was past his comprehension.

The black velvet sleeves of her gown crested lightly on her white shoulders. Harcourt watched the gentle movement of her breathing. A sharp wind carrying the first breath of nightfall came up from the west. Servants rushed to close the terrace door. Without thinking, Harcourt encircled Kate with both his arms to shield her from the cold. He pulled her close to him, her face so near to his that her nose brushed his chin.

He kissed her, and Kate melted into him. He kissed her. She laid her light fingers on his chest. Harcourt kissed her and the world disappeared. Her breath quickened. He pulled away gently and pressed his lips to her brow. She laid her head upon his breast. He lived a lifetime in that moment.

Chapter Fourteen

The song finished and Kate took Harcourt's arm. Her soft fingers radiated heat through him as he led her back into the parlor. There, in the glow of candlelight and the bright talk of the revelers, obligation parted them. Harcourt could not imagine how he allowed her to leave his side.

Another game of whist was played, replete with a long tale of past illnesses from Mrs. Gedge, the price of corn from Mr. Gedge and others and Napoleon from still more, but Harcourt could hold no thought in his head but of Kate, and how he could hardly live until he kissed her again.

"Abernathy," Cowpe said when the party was ending, "would you be so good as to escort Miss Ishingham home?"

"I shall," Harcourt said, helping Kate with her pelisse.

Dr. Cowpe briefly glanced at his two friends, then was called away.

"If it is too cold, I shall send for my carriage," Harcourt said to Kate when they were outside.

"I would much prefer to walk," she said. "The night air is invigorating and I have little time to walk during the day."

"Very well then," he said, offering his arm. "We shall walk."

They walked in silence up Beckwith Street toward Fretherne.

"It is not my habit," Kate said, slowing her steady pace, "to shade my meaning, or to pretend to attach myself to an idea I cannot abide."

Fear clutched Harcourt's throat.

"Or to an emotion I do not feel," she said.

Harcourt stopped abruptly. He turned to her sharply, forgetting to keep the truth of his emotions from his face.

"Mr. Abernathy," Kate said, "I do not know how to begin."

"Miss Ishingham," he interrupted, "permit me, if you will, to speak for you. I fear I have offended you and pressed upon you my ardent feelings, which you do not share. Forgive me. I cherish your friendship too much to lose it."

"Mr. Abernathy." She whispered his name roughly, like a last caress, then turned from him and briefly touched the nape of her neck through her bonnet. She exhaled forcefully and faced him.

"You have mistaken me," she said in a strong clear voice. "My feelings are fond, much too fond." She gazed at him, vivid passion lighting the dark center of her gray eyes. "I cannot express my heart to you in words that would be adequate." She massaged her finger where a ring should be and seemed to bite back decidedly unwanted tears.

Desperate to be of some help, Harcourt took her hand and pressed it to his own. Kate laced her fingers through his and drew a deep breath.

"I am not well made to be any man's wife," she continued. "I like my own opinions too well. And I cannot make statements or allusions I do not believe to be true in order to please." She glanced at their intertwined fingers and rubbed her gloved thumb over the back of his bare hand. "But more than that," she said, gazing up into his eyes, "I cannot hide behind another and wait to live till he is with me. I came to Ledwyche to work, and I couldn't sacrifice that privilege. It is as much a part of me as my limbs or my voice or my heart. Indeed, I would not be complete without it."

She pressed Harcourt's hand lightly, then let it fall from her grasp. "I would not be a proper wife for you, Mr. Abernathy. I am far too shocking and improper, and I have no intention to ever be anything else. I fear that the damage to yours and Miss Abernathy's reputations if you took my hand could not be undone. And if I will not abandon my life's work, I cannot ask you to risk your profession or your family."

Kate moved into a shaft of moonlight now penetrating the darkness of the street. "Please forgive my boldness. But it would be folly to pretend that the hoped for end of affection is not marriage." She had finished and now stood shaking in front of him.

Harcourt longed to take her in his arms and wed her, tonight. He clasped his hands behind his back and tried to feel his feet against the soft street. "My dear, dear Miss Ishingham, I am no more capable of releasing myself from my feelings for you than you are of artifice." A breeze blew the scent of lavender from her hair into his mouth. He caught it and ran his tongue over the back of his teeth. "I do not take your reasoning lightly. Or your concern for my sister and my vocation."

The wind blew harder. Harcourt shifted his position to block it. "But as I see nothing improper or shameful in you or your work, I would be untrue to myself if I allowed the possibility of the opinion of others to sway me from your affection." Once he made that statement aloud, the decaying skin of the dread of scandal fell from his heart. He felt free of the events of his past and easily breathed in the cool night air. He stepped nearer and shared the silver pool of light with her. "For in truth, Miss Ishingham, I cannot imagine a day of my life without you. Indeed, I can hardly imagine leaving you at your doorway this night and not waiting at your window until morning."

Kate smiled.

"So you see," he said, returning her affectionate gaze, "I am all too ready to subject myself to more derisive conjecture and tongue-wagging than marrying you could ever engender."

He took both of her hands in his. "Would you permit me to write to your father and ask his permission for your hand?"

"I would," she said.

He kissed her lightly on the mouth, allowing the tip of his tongue, feather light, to slide between her lips. She laced her arm through his and laid her head against his shoulder. He could have carried her to the gates of Fretherne and counted himself the luckiest man in the world.

Harcourt Abernathy woke to moonlight pouring into his window at the Black Hound. Claire rolled over in her sleep and nestled her head under his arm. He kissed her brow and fell back into a blissful sleep.

Claire got to Ian's apartment before he did. Thank God she'd found his spare key before she left work today. She pushed open the heavy front door, which reverently caressed the expensive carpeting. The sharp scent of sterility met her. She brushed the snow out of her hair and checked her image in the large bronze mirror.

Claire straightened her naturally wavy hair for Ian because he preferred smooth hair, but it was growing so quickly recently and she hadn't had time to straighten it or even have it blown out. He didn't like the look of air-dried hair. She ran her fingers through the ends and hoped Ian wouldn't notice the waves. She flipped on the recessed lights, then dimmed them.

His key clicked into the lock and the door opened.

"Hey," he said, coming behind her and kissing her ear. "I like your hair."

"Thanks," she said, running her fingers over the back of her neck.

Ian grinned blithely—beautifully—as if nothing in the world had come between them. "So," he said lightly, "do you want to go anywhere?"

"No," Claire said, bewildered. "I thought I came over to talk."

The muscles of Ian's gorgeous face contracted, and slits of green opened in his hazel eyes. "Couldn't we just forget it, Claire?" he begged, trying not to sound scared. "Whatever it is, I don't care. Whatever you did and whoever you did it with, doesn't matter. What matters is now. We're what matters. Our family."

With a crack like a bullwhip undulating in her spine, Claire stepped back. "We're not family, Ian."

"Not yet," he murmured, confidence smoothing out the green flecks until his dark eyes gleamed like polished wood. "But I fully intend to make you my wife." Ian gathered Claire into his arms and lowered his head to kiss her.

"I had sex with a ghost," Claire said loudly.

He dropped his hands and arched backward. "What?"

"Seven years ago, at the Black Hound, I had sex with a man from another time," Claire said, her heart pounding. "He disappeared. I tried to follow him. He pushed me back. I didn't try to kill myself, Ian. I tried to follow a dead man through a burning fireplace."

Ian stared at Claire. She waited for him to say something. He clasped his long fingers behind his back and walked up and down the long, L-shaped living room. "Okay," he said slowly. His narrow eyes searched the air. "Your grandfather had just had a heart attack, right?" He sounded preoccupied, as if he were trying to solve a particularly difficult acrostic puzzle.

"Yes," Claire stammered, "but—"

"And," Ian continued, as if Claire hadn't spoken at all, "you can't handle stress or feeling abandoned." He stopped pacing and stared at the floor. "Have you had a psychotic episode since then?" he asked, looking up at Claire.

"No," she said. "Wait. What do you mean? Do you mean have I . . . since that night . . . seen a person who should not exist and walked through fire and not gotten burned? No. But—"

"It's okay," he said. "If it hasn't happened again, it probably never will. And you'll have me. I'll make sure you stay on the right path."

"Ian," Claire said. "I don't think you understand." She glanced dizzily around her. For a blurry moment she expected the room to be different: bigger, colder, with a wide expanse of green lawn outside a huge paned window. She shook herself and exhaled. "I wasn't hallucinating. It happened. If I'd imagined it, it wouldn't be such a big deal. If it was an illusion it would be over."

"What are you saying?" Ian asked.

"I'm saying it was real," Claire said, stepping closer to where he stood in the middle of the room.

"Claire," Ian said, in a tone she'd never heard from him, "that isn't possible. Ghosts don't exist. Except in overheated or diseased imaginations."

He stood inches from her face. Claire could smell this morning's soap behind his ears and the tight scent of snow and cold air in his perfect hair.

"And you can't stand in a fire without burning." His voice had thinned to a child's timbre.

Claire sucked in a shallow breath. "His name was Harcourt Abernathy."

"Stop it, Claire," Ian warned, no longer sounding anything like a child.

"The monograph, the one Mr. Moulton sent, *the one you still have,* was his."

Ian said nothing. Claire grabbed her chance. "But it's over." She grabbed Ian's limp hand. "Finally accepting that it was real, that *he* was real—" She bit her tongue, suddenly terrified it might swell until it was big enough to clog her mouth and throat. She swallowed an ocean of air and dove in. "I'm ready to get on with my life. And I want you in it."

Ian avoided Claire's eyes and searched the room.

"If you want to call it off, I'll understand," she said, when he said nothing.

Ian gazed fiercely down, as if trying to tune out additional voices in the room.

Claire sighed. "I couldn't marry you without telling you the truth about me."

Ian locked his eyes fixedly to Claire's, staring at her with a weird intensity as if, simultaneously, he'd never seen her before and had known her all his life. "Okay," he said, nodding to himself. "Okay." He strode into his narrow wood-paneled study and picked up a black portable phone.

"What are you doing?" Claire asked, following him.

He shut the door. She tried to open it. He locked it. Claire waited for a second, then knocked.

"What are you doing?" she asked. "Who are you calling?" She leaned closer to the door and tried to listen. She heard nothing but a hushed, incoherent murmur.

A few minutes later Ian opened the door and gently took Claire by the arm. "Come sit with me."

"Why?" she asked. "Who were you calling?"

"Sit down," he said, leading her to the Italian leather couch in the living room.

Claire started to sit, then stood up again. "Wait. No. Not until you tell me what's going on."

Ian fixed his gaze not unkindly on her. "Tell me again," he begged gently. "Tell me what happened."

"Why?" Claire asked. Anxiety scurried in her lungs like a trapped animal.

"I'm sorry," Ian said softly. "I'm not trying to scare you. I'm trying to understand."

Claire weighed explaining it to him again. It was hard enough to say out loud once.

"People experience psychic phenomena all the time, Ian," she said. "It's well documented." Claire stood up taller and breathed slowly. What did she have to lose? He knew everything now. Telling him again wouldn't change anything. She jumped in. "I'm not asking you to believe; I just wanted you to know. I did then. And I still do." Claire sat next to him on the couch and took his hand. "But I'm not going to let it run my life anymore."

Ian paled. "I . . ." he began, but drew back abruptly and shut the vulnerability in his expression. He put his arm around Claire's shoulders. "Come here." He pulled her close and kissed her head. "Don't worry. Don't worry."

Claire rested her head on his chest for what seemed like a very long time. She had to stop kidding herself. *This is never going to work between us,* she thought as he patted her leg as if it were a kitten. But at least she'd told him. Claire sighed. Ian smelled strangely like ink and starched linen. He continued kitten-stroking her. It was kind of a relief, she thought, knowing they were headed for an unambiguous end.

Claire inhaled expansively again. Her chest felt tight. Now wasn't the right time for a relationship, she thought. She had to find closure with Harcourt and give herself time to deal with losing him. Her hands and feet felt suddenly and intensely hot. For an instant she thought she might be sick.

The buzzer rang.

She looked at the door. Something sounded in her head: a metal latching noise like an iron clasp clicking shut. A stench of warm beer and piss and body odor filled her nostrils. She jumped off the couch, but it was too late. Two men in EMT uniforms were standing in the hallway with Ian.

"Don't be scared," Ian said.

"What?" Claire asked.

She tried to walk away, but Ian grabbed her arm and held it fast.

"You can't do this," she said.

"I have to," Ian said. "It's my responsibility, Claire."

208

"You can't . . ." she stammered. *This could not be happening.* "You can't have me hospitalized against my will," she said slowly, and in as calm a voice as she could summon. "I'm not a danger to myself or to anyone else."

Ian gazed sorrowfully at her as if she were crazy or sick, or too stupid to know what was best for her. Claire pulled her arm from his grip. "You can't!" she shouted in his face.

Ian grabbed her chin and turned her face so she could see his eyes. "For seven years you've been haunted by something that never happened, and it's swallowed your life like a poison," he said. "I'm going to help you. But you have to let me."

"No," she said, shaking her head and trying to pull away. "No."

He closed his long fingers around her wrist. "I called the hospital. A good friend of mine is on call. I explained the situation." Ian turned Claire's face to his. "Dr. Harvey did his residency in Vermont seven years ago." He let go of her arm. "Claire," Ian said, impassioned, "he remembered you. He remembered what happened to you. He agrees with me."

"How could he?" she asked. "What did you tell him?"

Ian nodded to the EMTs. They walked toward the couch.

"Did you lie?" she asked. "You had to. You did. Didn't you? You said I did something I didn't do. Didn't you?" she screamed. "What did you say?"

The technician opened a case on the coffee table.

"No!" Claire shouted, pulling away from Ian, who had pushed up her sleeve. "No." She ripped her arm from his grasp and ran for the door. "I didn't do anything," she screamed at the two men, who caught her before she reached the entryway. "He lied. Ask him. I didn't do anything!"

"It's for your own good, Claire," Ian said, holding her shoulders. "You can't live in a fantasy world. Nothing bad is going to happen. Dr. Harvey is only going to evaluate you. Nothing will happen without your consent. I promise."

Mary Beth Bass

"*This* is without my consent, Ian" she shouted. "*This*," she shouted, shaking her arm held by one of the men.

Ian let go of her and stepped back. "You're not capable of understanding anything clearly right now, Claire."

"*What the fuck is wrong with you!*" Claire screamed.

Ian walked calmly toward her. "You passed out in a public place with no discernable physiological cause. You were incoherent when you woke up. Your behavior is increasingly erratic. And you cannot separate fantasy from reality. I had no choice."

One of the men brought the case to the steps of the entryway and took out a syringe and needle. Claire stared uncomprehendingly. *This cannot be happening*, she thought. *This cannot be happening.*

"Claire," Ian said beseechingly as the EMT popped the needle to the bottle and syringe. "Let me take care of you."

"No!" Claire kicked and scratched at Ian and the EMT, until a sting in her arm sucked the light from the room.

Harcourt brushed his lips against Claire's shoulder blades. She hummed and turned over to him. The moon still hung fat and bright in the sky, fixed to its place in the window, seemingly unwilling to leave so pleasing a situation. He wanted to stay in this bed, in this room at the Black Hound for eternity.

Claire—he could call her Claire, could he not—smiled and ran her hands up his chest. She slid her soft foot between his legs and stroked the big muscles of his calves. He shuddered and his body buzzed with arousal.

She looked down and took his shaft into her hand. It hardened in her grasp. She caressed the length of it, stopping periodically to lightly stroke the pulsing underside with a single fingertip. He moaned softly and kissed her. She opened her mouth and he dove his tongue inside, running it gently over the bone behind her teeth.

Her grip loosened on his already aching erection. He

210

eased her back and climbed on top of her; the hair on his hard stomach brushed against her soft, already wet curls. Harcourt took her breast into his mouth, awakening the soft bud with his tongue. Claire arched her back and writhed beneath him. His sex brushed her skin. She closed her legs and held him. He throbbed between her thighs.

Harcourt lifted his head from Claire's breast, clenched his teeth and stared over her face at the woodgrain pattern of the headboard. He didn't want to release himself over her belly. That thought did not clear his head. He ground his teeth tighter and held on, blasting from his mind the image of his seed shimmering on her soft skin.

She opened her mouth on his chest and ran her fingers down his ribs. He moaned and dropped his head to her brow, breathed deeply and kissed her eyes. In a slow rhythm like music she pressed her hips up to him. Harcourt shuddered and, moaning, raised his body so his face was level with hers and the bones of his hips gently crushed hers.

Her breath was ragged as she reached for him again, but he stopped her hand. "Not yet," he whispered, kissing her ear.

Harcourt kissed Claire from her sensitive neck down to her breasts and belly. She moaned beneath him, running her fingers through his hair. He knelt on the floor, breathed in her scent and slipped his hands under her bottom.

As slowly as he was able, Harcourt slid his tongue inside her wet, hot center, darting it in and out and circling the soft tight bud with his tongue. Claire cried out and closed her fingers around a lock of his hair, pulling hard as his tongue moved in and out of her. He dove in again, pulled out and licked the firm bud until she came in his mouth.

He held on fiercely to his own release as he raised himself above her again and slid his hardness inside her, catching the last vibration of her climax. She throbbed lightly against his pounding erection, which threatened to explode immediately if he didn't pace himself.

211

He concentrated on a hand of cards and the best ways to win and lose, but she grabbed him and pulled him tight against her. That was it. The image of cards fell away like salt in water. Harcourt thrust fast and hard in and out of her.

Claire repositioned herself so they were more tightly joined, bone to bone. Harcourt thrust farther inside her, harder, faster, until he felt the first shiver of her second climax, which pulled on him, until, in a release of hot liquid and thundering ecstasy, he came inside her. The throb and pulse of his climax seemed to last forever. When it was over he lay upon her, nuzzling his damp face in her neck.

His heart smashed in a broken rhythm against his rib cage. Claire ran her hands up and down his back. "Don't," she whispered. "Don't worry."

It didn't matter. It didn't matter that she knew what he was thinking without him speaking of it. It didn't matter that she called herself Claire and hadn't said his name, or for that matter even asked him what his name was.

She laced her fingers through his hair. He raised his head and kissed her. She smiled at him. "I'm not afraid," she said.

The idea that she had anything to fear sliced his heart in half. He couldn't answer her. A sudden conviction that the moment he opened his mouth she would disappear beneath him like a receding tide smacked against his head. He rolled off her and tried to catch his breath. Claire climbed on top of him and held his face in her hands. "I'm not afraid," she repeated.

She kissed him hard on the forehead and got out of bed. "But I am hungry. Do you think it's too late to get something to eat?"

He glanced at the moon in the windowpane. It hadn't moved in hours. He got out of bed and pulled on pants and shirt, a waistcoat and black boots. "I'll see if anyone is still awake." He moved to leave but stopped at the door and turned to her.

212

She smiled reassuringly, as if she read his unspoken thoughts. "Where else would I go?"

He exhaled jaggedly and walked back to where she sat naked and lovely on the bed, moonlight pooling in a silver shadow at her feet. "I don't know how or why you're here at all," he said, unable to do anything but vaguely articulate his fear.

"I don't think we have to know," she said, pulling the coverlet over her shoulders like a cloak but leaving her breasts exposed to the moonlight and his eyes. "But I do know I don't ever want to be anywhere else."

Someone knocked at the door. She closed the coverlet around her like a pelisse and stood up. "I'm going to take a shower," she said, and walked into a closet and shut the door.

"A shower of what?" Harcourt asked as a rush of water followed the squeal of a turned crank.

The knocking continued insistently. Harcourt opened the door. Mr. Moulton walked in carrying a tray laden with a joint of beef, crusty bread and a steaming tureen. The innkeeper lifted his head and glanced toward the closet and the sound of water. Harcourt stared at the food in amazement.

"What is going on?" he demanded of Mr. Moulton.

The innkeeper smiled slightly but said nothing.

"How did you know she was hungry?" Harcourt asked. "How did you know she was here? What the devil is going on?"

The grin on Moulton's face disappeared.

Harcourt stepped back and turned protectively toward the closet where Claire was.

"Forgive me," Moulton said.

"Who are you?" Harcourt asked slowly. "What is the meaning of this?" He backed closer to the closet.

Moulton gazed toward the closet door. "I meant only to help."

"Help whom!" Harcourt shouted.

Moulton inhaled slowly. "Claire. You."

Harcourt pressed his fingers to his brow and shook his head. "I don't understand," he said, glancing back at Moulton. "Who are you? What do you want from me and from my wife?"

The innkeeper cringed. "I'm sorry. But when I saw how grief-stricken you were, I couldn't bear it. I acted without thinking."

Harcourt stared as Moulton crossed to a table where a pair of silver fighting cocks poised in mock battle. The day and night of drinking threatened to extract its violent nauseating price, but he had to keep a clear head. Kate, Claire. *Kate,* Harcourt thought furiously. Kate, his wife, by whatever means it was possible, was here, was with him, and he would do nothing to jeopardize her.

Moulton picked up one of the birds and stroked its silver head. "She wasn't unhappy. She didn't remember." He returned the bird to the table. "I should have left her alone. But she would have remembered. She would have remembered and it would have been too late."

The turned-crank squeal sounded again and the water noise ceased. "You cannot remain here," Moulton said firmly.

"Where am I to go?" Harcourt asked. "Would you turn me out?"

"Don't answer her questions. Say nothing, save you must go; and then leave."

"I will not!" Harcourt said. "I will not leave here and I will not leave her. I'll die before I leave her again."

"It isn't you I'm worried about, Abernathy."

"I will not leave," Harcourt growled.

"And what would you have her do?" Moulton asked. "Live forever in this room? She has been here three days already."

"Three days!" Harcourt protested. "It has been but a single night. The sun has hardly risen."

"Look again," the innkeeper said.

Harcourt walked to the window and peered out. Sunlight sparkled on patches of snow dotting brown grass. People walked to and fro. Women wore men's clothes, and what appeared to be self-propelled carriages, painted in bright colors, shone like paste jewels. As Harcourt stared in disbelief, the scene surrendered to a familiar vision of lush spring green and carriages with horses and women in their own clothes.

"You must let her go," Moulton said.

"I'll be right out," Claire's voice called from the closet.

Moulton waited and smiled slightly, as if he could still hear Claire's bright voice hanging in the air. "Tell her nothing," he said, and left.

"Oh!" Claire exclaimed, coming out of the closet and blinking in the sunlight. "How long was I in the shower?" She'd wrapped a thick white cloth around her body—almost like a Grecian gown—and she rubbed her wet hair with the same heavy white cloth. "Did Mr. Moulton bring breakfast?" she asked, gesturing to the silver tray on the table. "Yay! I'm starving. I feel like I haven't eaten in days." She walked to the table, flipping her long, damp hair over her bare shoulder.

Claire lifted the soup tureen lid and grinned. "Isn't he funny?" She broke off a bit of bread and dipped it into one of the soup bowls. "Who eats soup and cold roast beef for breakfast? When I was little and I didn't want to get up to go to school, Mr. Moulton would insist that he was a ghost and had walked the earth for four hundred years, and that if he could still go out into the world, then I could. I totally believed him and I always got ready for school, happy with my secret that a real ghost lived in my house and liked me." She pulled two chairs up to the table and sat down. "Are you hungry?" she asked, eating a bite of meat.

"Claire," Harcourt said.

She dropped her soup spoon. "You've never said my

215

name," she said quietly, then raised her hand to her face and covered her mouth with her fingers. "And I never even asked you what your name is." She turned away from him and rested her chin in her open hand. "I thought I had. I actually thought I knew your name. But I don't. And I never asked you." She blushed and looked away. "God. What must you think of me?"

He couldn't speak. He was vaguely aware of his breathing, but even of that jagged rhythm he was uncertain.

"What's wrong?" Claire asked, getting up from the table and clinging to the white cloth around her body. "Are you all right? Eat something," she urged, picking up a bowl of soup. "You look pale."

Harcourt slowed and steadied his breath. He walked to her and gently pushed the bowl back to the table. "No," he said softly, lacing his fingers through hers. He didn't want to let go of her hand.

"What is it?" she asked. "Have I done something to offend you?"

He snapped his head up and gazed at her as though he would etch her features on the insides of his eyes. "You?" he asked, taking her face in his hands. "You have done nothing. It is I. I have longed too ardently for something that was not mine to have again."

"No," Claire said. "That isn't true." She threw her arms around his neck. "It isn't true."

Harcourt pulled her close to him. He felt the heat of his body melt into her cool skin. If only he could secret himself inside her. He swallowed as much of the fragrance of lavender and rosewater from her hair as he could hold, and clenched his teeth until he thought his jaw would split from his skull.

"Don't," she whispered desperately. "*Don't*. You'll regret it."

"I cannot stay," he said.

Southey's clear bass rang from the landing. "Pickney!"

Harcourt stepped back and stood between Claire and the door, as if he could shield her from the sound without.

216

"Pickney," Southey bellowed again. "Good morning!"

Claire's gaze shot to the closed door. Harcourt grabbed her face and kissed her, hard and long. She clung to him. He pulled away.

"I cannot stay," Harcourt said in a raw voice. He went into the antechamber where he had first heard her voice. "Do not follow me," he said, and walked through the door.

Chapter Fifteen

Claire's head spun. She felt sick and her chest contracted violently. She ran to the door of the antechamber. The room was empty. She ran back into the larger room. Everything looked the same: the unmade bed, the coffee from the night before, the tray, the meat, the soup tureen still steaming. The fire in the fireplace had not died as she had thought before but instead roared merrily. Claire staggered over to it, mesmerized by the uneven sway of the flames.

Her lover sat in a chair in a room on the other side of where the fire back should have been, his head in his hands, a new, heavy growth of beard on his distraught face, as if he hadn't shaved in days. An empty wine bottle lay at his feet. He glanced wildly around the room, then dropped his face into his hands again.

Claire fell to her knees. He didn't see her. She called out. He didn't hear her. The fire crackled loudly. Claire stared at it. She couldn't feel any heat. She reached into the shivering flames and felt nothing. He sat still as death with his head in his hands. Claire crawled into the fireplace. She felt cold, freezing cold. Her chest tightened, making it harder to breathe. She crawled through the frigid flames until her hand almost reached the hearth in his room, an inexact mirror image of hers. He raised his head and saw her. She saw him mouth the word, "No," but no voice sounded.

He leapt out of the chair and dropped to his knees. She was freezing. Why was it so cold? She felt his hands on her shoulders and smelled burning hair and cloth. *He was pushing her back.* She tried to scream. Nothing came out of her mouth but soft air. She fought against him, pushing as hard as she could. She felt colder. Her fingers stiffened on his chest.

The burning scent became more pungent. She heard him scream and then he pushed her so forcefully, she fell into the room. She jumped to her feet and ran for the hearth, but hot fire had sprung up in the fireplace.

Harcourt staggered in his room. The fire back closed. He couldn't see Claire anymore, but he knew he had gotten her out of the flames. The wine swam violently in his stomach and he couldn't think. He sank to the floor.

Claire saw him fall. His clothes were on fire. "Help!" she screamed. "Help! Someone help him." Her room door opened. She ran for the fireplace. Someone held her away.

"No!" she screamed. "Let go of me! Let go of me."

He covered his face with his hands and rolled on the floor. "No!" Claire screamed. "*Let me go!*"

Two men rushed into the room on the other side of the fire and threw a blanket over the burning man. He disappeared. Claire fell to the floor.

She woke up screaming. It was happening again. She'd seen him burn again. She fought to free herself from the harsh-scented, rough sheets. She couldn't breathe. Why was it always so hard to breathe? She sat up gasping.

"It's okay," a familiar voice soothed. "It's okay. It's okay, Claire. I'm here. It's okay."

Toby's sweet face came into focus, along with the

eggshell-brown walls, gaudy flowered curtains and the hard stink of disinfectant and disease.

Claire whipped her head around to face him. "How long have I been here?" she asked furiously.

"Only since last night," he said, standing practically on top of her.

"What did Ian tell you?" she demanded. "What did he tell that doctor about me?"

"I don't know what he told the doctor," Toby said, sitting on a hideous red vinyl chair near the bed. "He told me you came to his apartment last night, incoherent but not drunk, babbling about Harcourt Abernathy."

Claire's eyes widened in shock.

Toby sighed. "He said you threatened to set yourself on fire."

"It isn't true," Claire shot back, prepared for Toby to be totally freaked out and to take Ian's side.

"I know," he said.

"What?" Claire asked. "How do you know?"

"Because I know you, Claire," Toby said. "I know what happened that night, and I know you didn't try to kill yourself. That isn't you. What I don't know is why Ian thought he had to do this."

Claire leaned back on the thin pillows and metal bed frame. "I told him the truth," she said, exhaling voluminously. "Obviously that was a big mistake."

"Don't joke, Claire," Toby said.

"Why?" she asked. "Will the bad karma fairy come and bite me on the ass?"

Toby grinned slightly and leaned back in his chair to look out the window.

"What time is it?" Claire asked.

Toby checked his watch. "Ten o'clock."

"In the morning?"

"*Yes*," Toby gestured incredulously to the daylight streaming in through the unattractively wide window.

"Of course," Claire said, shaking her head and getting out of bed.

"What are you doing?" Toby asked.

"Going home," Claire answered. She dug through a pile of stuff on a bigger black chair and found her clothes. "Turn around." Toby turned his head. Claire stripped off the flimsy hospital gown and put on her clothes from last night. She sat on the gray metal heater near Toby's chair. "Tell Ian I'm not going to report him for what he did."

"You should report him," Toby said. "It was illegal and unethical."

"I know," Claire agreed. "But I don't want to. So I'm not."

"It's your call, Claire," Toby said, standing up. "I'm just glad you're okay." He hugged her.

"You're uncharacteristically mellow about this whole thing," Claire said. "I would have expected you to be hovering over me." She ran her fingers through her hair and gazed at him. He looked different. Happy. And complete. It had to be Miranda. As hot as Toby was, he had never been in love before, never committed his heart to anyone. Claire felt a grin break over her face. "Love has changed you, Toby Cavanaugh."

Toby blushed. "Stop it." He put on his leather jacket. "I had a nice talk with a guy down the hall when you were sleeping." He picked up an outdated magazine. "I took this photograph three years ago." He flipped through the pages, then dropped the magazine on the table. "You know you can't just walk out of here, don't you?"

"I know," Claire said. "I also know that in light of my obvious stability, Ian will have a harder time making a case to keep me here." She ran her fingers through her hair again, as if she expected it to be longer. "And if he doesn't, I'll re-think not reporting him." She sat back down on the heater. "Who was this 'nice guy' you talked to while I was drugged against my will?"

"Claire." Toby winced. "Don't."

She smiled. "Sorry. I always forget you don't like gallows humor. Who did you talk to while I was sleeping?"

"I don't know what his name was," Toby said. "He was visiting his sister."

A giddy buzz hummed around Claire's eyelids and down her nose—probably some aftereffect of whatever drug Ian had forced through her veins. Anger at him muddied her focus. She massaged the back of her neck. Time softened its grip as a flood of warmth spread through her, parting her lips and making the grim hospital room smell like May air.

Toby smiled and glanced over her shoulder to the Boston skyline, then gazed back at her. "Well, for whatever reason, you look great."

The fizzy warmth washed around and through Claire. She felt Harcourt's presence near her. But he wasn't the warmth circling in her chest; that warmth felt, of all things, as if she was filling herself with herself. Thank God she didn't have to explain that to anyone.

Toby narrowed his eyes and smiled again. "What are you *thinking* about?"

"Nothing," Claire answered, in a high-pitched, I'm-totally-lying-voice. She rubbed the orpine on her ring. "What did you and the mystery man talk about?"

"Not much," Toby said. "We played cards."

Claire groaned.

Toby colored. "I didn't lose any money, if that's what you're thinking, but that was another weird thing. You know how much I love to play, even though I'm a terrible card player. I won every hand. He was playing to let me win, and I don't have any idea how he did it. After a while he asked about you." Toby flushed. "I hope it was okay that I talked to him about you." He stammered slightly. "I'd just gotten here. Ian was nowhere around. You were completely out of it. This guy seemed genuinely concerned."

"Don't worry about it," Claire interrupted. "I'm not ashamed or anything."

"I wasn't thinking you'd be ashamed," Toby said, running his fingers through his hair.

"Well," Claire said, "what did you tell him?"

"Everything," Toby said softly.

"What do you mean 'everything'?" Claire asked.

"Everything," Toby repeated. "The nurse said you'd be out for a while, so we went to the cafeteria to play cards and get a cup of coffee, which was unbelievably fabulous, by the way, like coffee you'd get in Italy or France. And real cream, thick and almost yellow." Toby shivered at the sensual memory. "Amazing."

"And what does your caffeine orgasm have to do with telling my story to a stranger?" She bit her lip.

"Everything," Told said again. He sat in the black chair near her, his feet touching hers. "He felt familiar. I asked him if we'd met before, but he said he didn't think so." Toby reached for Claire's hand. He turned it so he could see her ring. " 'Love is enough.' Right?"

"Right," Claire answered, not having any idea where this was going.

Toby sighed and gently dropped her hand. "I was pretty freaked out when Ian called me, as you so delicately surmised earlier." Nervously, he ran his fingers through his hair. "Ian left a message at the studio around three in the morning, when he knew I was unlikely to still be there. I heard it first thing this morning and rushed here in a state of panic over you."

He looked down at his shiny Italian shoes. "I was a little rough on the nurse. I lied and said I was your brother. She was about ready to kick me out when this guy came over and assured her I wasn't crazy or difficult, which at that point from my behavior I'm not sure how he knew. But anyway, he calmed her down, calmed *me* down, and asked me to get coffee with him."

"I still don't understand why you had to tell him everything about me," Claire said.

Toby laid his palm across his broad, pale forehead and rubbed his hand over his hair and down his neck. "He seemed like he knew you, Claire. Without my saying anything, he asked questions he only could have known to ask if he knew you."

"Questions about what?" An icy mix of fear and excitement ran like water down Claire's back.

"About flowers. About that Milton poem you named your store after. About the fire, about Vermont." Toby gazed directly at Claire. "About love and relationships," he said quietly. "About whether or not you were married or had plans to get married."

Ian walked into the room.

Claire jumped off the heater. Ian was visibly distraught and clearly unprepared to find Toby here. He glared stonily at Toby, then stared at Claire. "Before you say anything, Claire . . ." he began in a hard, defensive tone.

Claire stood up straight. "I don't think that's the way you want to begin, Ian."

He directed his gaze briefly to the scuffed metal door-frame. The muscles of his delicate face twitched.

Claire waited patiently.

"I was wrong," Ian said, facing her again.

"You were more than wrong," Claire said.

Out of the corner of her eyes Claire could see Toby step forward, everything he wanted to say vibrating angrily across his lips.

"I know," Ian said quietly. "I'm sorry."

"Get me out of here, then," Claire said.

"Dr. Harvey has to discharge you. Tell him I made a mistake. I've already spoken with him. Tell him I misdiagnosed what was happening to you. Explain, however you want to, why you fainted in Sonsie and why." Ian sucked in a ragged breath. "And whatever you want to say about why you told me what you did about the monograph and you'll be released. You're not a danger to yourself or anyone else. They can't keep you here for believing in something."

He glanced away from her. Claire tentatively stepped toward him, but he backed away.

"I have rounds this morning." For the first time, he nodded civilly in Toby's direction. "I'll call you later." Ian laced his fingers behind his long white coat. Claire stared at him and waited. He gritted his teeth. "I'm not going to let you go, Claire." He left.

The clicks of his heels on the linoleum floor bubbled together in Claire's ear until they sounded like horse feet. She felt dizzy and spun around to Toby, who sat with a magazine opened in front of him and a long silver pen in his hand.

Cowpe dipped his pen into the inkwell and began to write. Kate waited for him to finish. The hope for an early success had proven false. Mr. Oldman had died this morning and his young son was doing very badly. Dr. Cowpe handled all such losses with a practical air and a soothing presence, but within his guiding hand and healing voice was an inviolable thread of confidence. Kate tried, and failed, to emulate him.

"It is not that I have never made a mistake," she confided to Cowpe after he stopped writing. "Or that I have never worked tirelessly only to see a morning's patient perish before the afternoon, but more and more I feel a lack of understanding at why they slip through my hands."

She crossed to their shared desk and sat in her chair. Cowpe had spent most of the night at Mr. Oldman's bedside. Exhaustion colored and creased his face. Kate was reluctant to confess further disappointment. She didn't want him to think of her as an emotional woman who could not separate her feelings from the rational understanding of a problem.

Cowpe took a deep swallow of what had to be thoroughly cold tea. He curled his lip away from the bitter taste and wiped his mouth with his hand. "I too thought Mr. Oldman would come round," he said at last, rising noisily from his chair.

The clock struck ten.

"I promised Mrs. Cowpe I would help her choose a new color for the parlor before noon today," he said, smiling wearily. "Send for me if there is any news of young Oldman."

"I will," Kate said.

Cowpe left for home.

Kate read his notes, then opened her journal to record her response. She dipped her pen to write, but the idea of Harcourt Abernathy stayed her hand. The memory of his presence was so vivid she could taste his mouth on hers. She closed her eyes and remembered the pleasurable heat of his hands on her waist. She wanted nothing more than to rest her head on his breast and feel his strong arms surround her. She breathed deeply and shook her head.

Was this what she could expect of herself from now on: a constant state of divorce from reason, fueled by a girlish desire for passionate embraces? Kate swore a silent oath, pushed herself away from the desk and stood up. Had her attachment to Harcourt already diluted her power to think clearly? Was this the cause of her mistakes these past few days? Was Mr. Oldman's death due to her inability to concentrate? She crossed to the window but turned from the view before gazing out.

Such an idea was ridiculous, but it was proof of how disjointed her thinking had become. Kate longed for her sister Lydia, for a woman's counsel and point of view. She was terrified to acknowledge her deepest fear: that *this was* the nature and definition of a woman, that a need to submit was woven into the fabric of the female brain, that an inherent weakness made a woman dependent on a man.

"Not for me," Kate spat, and strode to the desk to work. She reread Dr. Cowpe's notes and picked up her pen once more.

Mr. Oldman's death was a sad and unexpected blow. The shame and responsibility I feel because of it threatens to soften my abilities, but I will not allow an emotional response to weaken my devotion to the research.

Harcourt silently entered the room behind Miss Ishingham. Earlier this morning Cowpe had told him about Mr. Oldman. He had planned to try and cheer Kate, but he would wait until she'd finished her writing. He sat in a hard chair near the door.

> *As I read Dr. Cowpe's clear, unsentimental description of the human body, how the musculature works together, how the nerves communicate, indeed how the whole lovely piece is fitted together with such precision and intricacy, I am moved by the hand of God and I remember why I started on this path. Every thought of condemnation slips away and is replaced by awe in the presence of the construct of life.*

Kate exhaled and dipped her pen in the inkwell. "Mr. Abernathy," she said when she glanced up and saw him.

He smiled.

"Forgive me," Kate said, touching her cheek to make sure it was neither warm nor pink. "I had no idea you'd come. Is Miss Abernathy in health?"

"She is, thank you," he said kindly. "It is you I have come to see. Dr. Cowpe told me the sad news of Mr. Oldman's death."

He gazed pityingly at her, as if he knew how hard she had taken Mr. Oldman's loss, but he said nothing else. A need to touch him was like a vise around her fear-filled stomach.

"Celia has asked me to invite you to accompany her to the Leightons' on Saturday," Harcourt said, attempting to lighten the air. "Do you ride?"

"I do not," Kate said abruptly. She had never told him about Lydia's death. The tightness in her voice made Harcourt lean forward in his chair.

"My sister Lydia," she said quietly, "whom you painted so beautifully, died after a fall from a horse."

"I'm sorry," he said, rising and crossing the small room to sit near her.

Sunlight poured in through the window and burned the

back of Kate's neck. Briefly she ran her fingers over her skin there to block the sting of heat. She glanced at the door and tried to think of what to say. It had been nearly three years. She should be able to speak of it.

"When Lydia died I sat with her body until we left for the churchyard. She looked the same and yet different—heavy, as if all the lightness had gone out of her, devoid of internal space and spaces, as though she were filled to the bursting point with lifelessness. There she was, without herself, and I, as lost as the ancients, half believed she had left to cross the River Styx, accompanied by the ghostly boatman."

Harcourt drank Kate in.

"I had seen death before," she went on. "I'd watched death arrive and life depart from the old and the young. Those experiences were pierced with grief for those left behind, but my consciousness never lay with the dead, only with the living until Lydia. I could not believe she would lie in the ground. That she would submit to the darkness of the coffin and the dampness of earth. Where had her fight gone? Where had her spirit gone? What air held her now?"

She looked up at him. "Where does brightness go when a candle is snuffed out?"

Harcourt held her hand tightly. He wanted to take her home with him tonight, to take her to his heart and his bed and never let her go.

"Perhaps that is what heaven is," Kate said. "A realm of the light of souls, and of stars, and of fire. A place of light and only light."

She felt Harcourt's attention penetrate her skin. She thought she could taste him in her own mouth. *I have seen the inside of a human body,* she thought. *I've seen the pink and shining gut of health and the sad misshapen color of diseased innards, but I cannot imagine where that feeling lives, when I see you, or think of you, or know you are seeing me. It is a connection more powerful than that of fragile flesh to fragile flesh, a connection invisible and palpable, formed of other matter.*

Harcourt watched Kate as she sat quietly beside him, content to breathe the air that held the perfume and substance of her skin.

Kate let the heat from his fingers course through her for a moment and exhaled. "I must record my thoughts of what happened to Mr. Oldman while they are still fresh."

He pressed her hand once and then released it. "Of course," he said gently. "I shall take my leave." He gazed at her, then rose from his chair. "Dr. Cowpe is not here, is he?"

"No," Kate said. "He is at home."

Harcourt frowned slightly. "He is not at home. I called on him before coming here."

"Would you like me to deliver a message?" Kate asked.

"A boy is waiting to see him. His mother is ill."

"I'll go to her." Kate rose from her chair.

"No," Harcourt said, laying his hand on her shoulder. "The family lives outside Painswick."

"Painswick is not an hour's ride from here," Kate said, pulling away from his hand and glancing around the room for her kit.

Harcourt took her by the shoulders. "You will not go, Kate. It is too far. No one knows you, or will expect a woman to come as a physician. You may not go."

"May not?" Kate repeated. "I will go, Harcourt. I will *never* stand by while someone suffers needlessly if I can help. And I can help. I will go."

She had never said his name before, Harcourt thought. The sound of it opened something within him that he hardly had time to recognize. He breathed deeply and spoke as gently as he could. "Your devotion to others moves me immeasurably, Kate. I shall go to Painswick and find a surgeon. The boy's concern is money. I think Cowpe would have treated her for nothing. I'll find the Painswick doctor and pay him."

"That is noble of you . . ." Kate began.

"It is good," he interrupted. "Not noble."

Kate stepped back. Mr. Denton had teased Harcourt

about despising the peerage. Why? She had forgotten about it in her overreaction to the discussion of the horrors of a female scientist. Harcourt had risen to her defense then. Why would he support the idea of a female doctor but not the practice?

"Kate," he said softly, "I do not wish to pain you. My concern is for your safety and your reputation. And Cowpe's as well."

He stood taller and breathed deeply. Despite herself, for a moment Kate could think of nothing but the broad strength in his chest, and the light of intelligence and kindness in his eyes.

"It would take more than the brief expanse of this moment to express the depth of my admiration for your work and your courage to continue it," he said, taking her hand in his. "And I shall never forget how you cared for Celia. I would never presume to offer advice on matters concerning putrid pox or your research with Dr. Cowpe. I only ask that you allow me to protect you where you are less sure."

Harcourt's words were lovely, but his face was immovable. He was asking her permission only to make her feel better. He had no intention of letting her go. If she defied him now, would that signify the beginning of the end of his affections? If she acquiesced, would it mean the beginning of the end of her autonomy? She hated the consequences of each.

The door opened. A female servant entered the room. "Miss Ishingham," she said, "a letter has come for you with instructions that you open it at once." She handed over the letter, nodded at Harcourt and left.

Kate held the letter lightly between her fingers. She bit her cheek and breathed deeply. "I will not go to Painswick if you agree to find the best possible care for the boy's mother. But do not mistake me, Harcourt—I am only agreeing to remain here in deference to your opinion, which I do not share, and because I trust you to be true to your word. I am reasonable, but I will not be swayed if I believe I am right and someone needs my care."

"I have no intention of stopping your care of others, Kate," he said. "But do not mistake me, I will never be prevented from protecting you, however I see fit."

Before Kate could respond Harcourt moved to the door. "I shall leave you to your letter. Remember me to your hostess, Mrs. Ansley." He left.

Claire felt Toby squeeze her shoulder. The doorway of her hospital room came into focus.

"I could fucking kill Ian," Toby said. "Are you okay?"

"I'm fine," Claire answered, shocked by the steely calm in her voice. "You can go." She turned around and faced Toby, who looked overfamiliar: as if she knew him twice. "I'll be fine. I know you have a busy week ahead."

"Okay," he said, then blushed. "Actually, I'm helping Miranda pick out a paint color for her living room today. Call me as soon as you get home."

"I will," Claire said.

Toby kissed her head and left.

Harcourt Abernathy materialized outside Claire's hospital room. He watched Toby stride down the hall as confidently as Cowpe. Harcourt could be anywhere he had been while he lived. This hospital stood on the foundation of a tavern he had frequented with Pickney before they traveled to Vermont. Harcourt had never materialized so that Claire could see him; she'd want to follow him and he didn't know how he would stop her again. But he had not come to see Claire. He had come to see Charles.

Ian Gilbertson strode down the appallingly bright corridor. When he came near, Harcourt moved in front of him.

"Excuse me," Ian said, not looking up.

Harcourt stood still.

"Excuse me," Ian repeated, then swore.

Harcourt did not move.

Ian froze, then recaptured himself. "Get out of my way," he whispered, "or I'll call security."

"Call for whomever you wish," Harcourt said, grinning icily.

Recognition shivered across Ian's face like a silverfish in an empty basin. "What are you doing here? How did you know to come here?"

"Leave her alone," Harcourt said.

Ian's face darkened. Fury lit his green eyes. "I don't have to listen to you."

"Who are you talking to, Dr. Gilbertson?" a nurse asked.

"Leave her alone," Harcourt said again, his calm face inches from Ian's trembling visage.

Ian stared at the nurse, who obviously couldn't see Harcourt. "No one. I'm talking to myself!" He walked past Harcourt and strode toward Claire's room.

Chapter Sixteen

Kate read the first line in the letter from Charles. Her heart caught in her throat.

> Dearest Kate,
>
> I regret to be the bearer of sad tidings, especially against your father's wishes, but I am compelled to write. (I know you will not resent me when you know my reason.) Your father is ill. He will not, nor will your mother, tell me much of the nature or the severity of the illness, and he has expressly forbidden me to write to you, but you will remember how deeply it pained me not to be informed of the extent of Lydia's injuries until it was too late for me to return home in time.

The shaky, uneven hand so unlike Charles's customarily flawless penmanship terrified Kate. She scanned the remainder of the brief missive. Charles was lodging at an inn in Painswick and had come to take her home. Kate left a brief note for Dr. Cowpe explaining the situation and rushed to Fretherne to pack her things. Mrs. Ansley kindly offered the use of her phaeton, which reached Painswick in the early afternoon. Kate thanked the driver and hurried to the Falcon Inn, where Charles was staying.

The door of the venerable inn groaned in protest when she pushed it open. The heavy scent of dust and bodies and ale poured into the warm air outside. Kate smoothed her dress, pulled her gray gloves tighter and walked in.

Charles, who was speaking with a tall, handsome, expensively dressed young man, spotted her and crossed the room. "Kate."

"How is Papa?" Kate begged.

Charles gestured to the man in the corner. "Oh, Kate," he murmured. "He keeps to his bed. He eats almost nothing."

Fear contracted Kate's throat. "But what has the surgeon said?" she demanded in a thin voice.

Charles turned once more to the narrow gentleman who was now easily making his way through the crowded tavern without touching any of the less well-dressed patrons. "Your father has refused to see anyone." He glanced at his feet for a moment. "I think he is waiting for you."

Kate stifled a cry and took Charles's arm. "Let us go home at once," she said, pulling him toward the door.

"Kate," Charles urged soothingly, "wait. You cannot imagine I would convey you on horseback to Warwickshire."

"You have no carriage?" Kate asked, incredulous.

"I have a carriage," Charles sniffed in a voice of light indignation. "But I shall not journey home with you."

Charles's thin companion, who appeared less pleasing upon closer inspection, came up to her cousin and stood beside him. His features were even, but something unsettling lingered beneath his clear skin like dark fluid through muslin.

"Your mother sanctioned my journey to retrieve you when she realized your father would see no"—Charles choked on the word like an emetic—"*physician* save you. She asked that I travel by horseback in order to ease your father with the news of your assured arrival."

Kate glanced at the blue-eyed gentleman who waited patiently at Charles's side. "How am I then to return to Greydon Hall?" she asked.

"Lord Harvey," Charles said in admiration, "may I present my cousin, Miss Ishingham?"

Lord Harvey made a sober bow. Charles drew in a ragged breath. For a moment Kate saw a thread of hesitation in his eyes, then Charles stood taller and closed any vulnerability in his expression.

"I have happy news to soften the burden of your father's illness," he said in a penny-bright voice.

"What news could soften such a blow?" Kate asked, suddenly feeling the heat of the day and the close air of the room.

"I have become engaged to Lord Harvey's sister, Miss Forester," her cousin said, smiling at Lord Harvey, who beamed solemnly at Kate.

"What?" Kate asked. "When? Why did you not write me?"

"I have not written for reasons I have no intentions of airing in a public house," Charles said, a flash of anger darkening his honeyed tones.

"Miss Ishingham," Lord Harvey interjected softly, "if I may speak on Mr. Ishingham's behalf . . ." He waited for a sign of approval from Kate.

She glared at Charles, then nodded.

"This trying time of Lord Greydon's unfortunate illness has deeply pained Mr. Ishingham," Lord Harvey said, in a hushed voice so as not to draw any attention to the conversation between the three of them.

"I don't understand why . . ." Kate interrupted.

Charles stared furiously at her, but Lord Harvey drew back, a nearly imperceptible grin fluttering over his thin, beautifully shaped mouth. "Of course you do not," he murmured soothingly. "Allow me to explain." He smiled pityingly at her and continued. "Although Mr. Ishingham has been engaged to my sister for but a brief time, I have already come to regard him as a brother, and I flatter myself

235

with the hope he regards me in a similar fashion." Charles smiled weakly in assent and exhaled, as if he were relieved to relinquish the task of talking to her.

"Mr. Ishingham has asked that I escort you home to Greydon Hall whilst he journeys home in haste in order to comfort Lady Greydon until we two arrive tomorrow evening," Lord Harvey said. "And I have happily agreed." He smiled in satisfaction, his straight teeth shining like paste pearls.

Charles stepped closer and took Kate's hand. The heat in the room pulled the scent of starch and sweat from his throat. Kate felt sick and turned away. For an absurd moment she imagined the two sour-faced men lumbering through the tavern door had come to take her away with them, but they moved past Charles and Lord Harvey as silkily as maids at a ball.

"It is the only way, Katie," Charles said.

A distant alarm sounded in Kate's brain. Charles had not called her Katie since childhood. She rooted her feet to the floor and breathed deeply, drawing in the heady scent of warm ale mingled with urine and body odor. Gracefully, she turned to Lord Harvey, who had not taken his eyes from her.

"I cannot begin to adequately express my gratitude for your kindness to me and my family at this uneasy hour," she said. A ripple of what looked like anticipation unfurled Lord Harvey's noble brow as he nodded in understanding. "With your leave, Lord Harvey," Kate said in her most submissive tone, "I should like to speak briefly with my cousin in private."

"Of course, Miss Ishingham," Lord Harvey said eagerly before Charles had a chance to protest. "I shall wait outside." Distaste shaded his features for the first time. "The air in this room pleases me not at all." Lord Harvey nodded to Kate and to Charles, then left through the creaking door.

"What's going on?" Kate demanded. "Tell me the truth, Charles. I have always been able to tell when you are lying."

Charles glanced nervously around the crowded room and took her hand. "Come to my rooms, Kate. I will not discuss it in the presence of all these people."

"Very well," she said. "But do not attempt to deceive me."

Once upstairs, Charles closed the door. The iron clasp snapped into position. Kate heard the click echo as if he had shut the door twice.

"Please," Charles said, gesturing to a leather chair near the window. "Sit."

Kate did as she was told.

He breathed uneasily and sat in the chair opposite Kate's. "Lord Harvey, although he carries the decidedly unsavory air of a rogue, comes from an impeccable, slightly impoverished family. You will not fare any better, Kate."

Kate's chest tightened, and she resisted the urge to cool her throat with her hand. "I am happy you have allied yourself with such an honorable family, but what has it to do with me, or more importantly, with Papa?"

Charles moved his chair closer to Kate, then changed his mind and rose to stand nearer the door. "Your father is not ill. He is perfectly well, save his utter misunderstanding of what is best for you." He laced his fingers behind his back. "You sullied your chances for any better man when you decided to abandon your place and follow this deplorable path. Lord Harvey wishes to marry you and I have given my consent."

"What!" Kate screamed. "You have no right to speak for me."

"When your father lost perspective on what is right and good for you I took it as my duty to protect you, Kate," Charles hissed. "You cannot begin to know how near you have come to total ruin. The circumstances of your existence and the sick men and women with whom you are in disgustingly intimate contact make your life hardly better than that of a whore's. That a man such as Lord Harvey is willing to wed you is a blessing I never dreamed possible, and when the opportunity arose I took it for you. Your father will come to my way of thinking. I am certain of it."

Kate reeled in her chair and tried to quell the sense that she was drugged or falling. Charles sat beside her and took her hand. "Forgive me, Kate. It was the only way."

Disbelief curdled like old cream in Kate's throat and she couldn't speak.

Charles stroked her hand impossibly gently, as if it were a newborn kitten. "You are free to refuse him, Katie," he said in a near whisper, "but I would beg that you at last come to your senses and choose what is right for you."

A soft knock like the thump of a dog's tail sounded on the door. Lord Harvey.

"I will leave you to it," Charles said, rising to open the door. "I trust you to make the right decision.

Claire got up. The metal frame of the hospital bed groaned uncomfortably. Ian walked in and shut the fat door behind him.

"We need to talk."

"You are not in a position to order me around," Claire said.

Ian clenched his teeth. "Please sit down and talk to me."

She sat on the red chair. Ian hesitated, then lowered himself slowly into the black chair as if it were a hot bath and he was in pain. Claire reached for his hand. "I'm not going to lodge a complaint or anything else. I know you only did what you did because you thought it was best for me." She clasped his fingers. "It *is* a weird thing to take in. I know you hate that kind of airy-fairy stuff. But I had to tell you."

Ian stared intensely at her with so much need, for so many things Claire didn't want to try to identify. But it was over. Ian would never be able to accept her for who she was. And if she tried to make herself into what he wanted, she would lose herself along the way.

He glanced down at their joined hands and breathed heavily. "I meant what I said, Claire," he said, gazing up at her.

She waited.

"I won't let you go," he said.

Claire pulled her hand away. "Ian."

He exhaled forcefully, then composed himself. "I won't let you go for something that's never going to happen again. If you want to believe you had an . . . an affair with a ghost—well, I can't do anything about that. But if you think you're going to get rid of me, *of us,* because I don't compare to a *fantasy,* you really are crazy!"

Claire shut her eyes for an instant, then turned toward the unmade bed and ugly floor tiles. This was how Ian thought he could win her back? She rested her chin on her palm, then took both her hands and briefly massaged her neck and shoulders. The only thing to do was to be quiet and let him say what he wanted to say. Whatever nasty things popped out of his mouth sprang from hurt and fear. It was over. She had to let Ian get over it in his own way and then they could both move on.

"What are you? Dead?" Ian yelled. "How can you just sit there and say nothing? Jeez, Claire!" He jumped out of his chair. "I don't know why I bother!"

"What the hell do you want from me, Ian?" Claire asked. "Because if you want to get back together you couldn't have picked a worse way to go about it!"

"I want you to be normal, Claire!" Ian shouted. "I want you to be like everyone else and understand the world as it is, not as you wish it was. I want you to want *me* and not some vibrator fantasy in a Merchant-Ivory costume!"

Claire stood up. "That's it. I'm leaving. Tell Dr. Whatever-the-hell-his-name-is whatever the hell you want, but I'm out of here."

"I burned that monograph," he said.

"What?" Claire said, astonished. "What are you talking about?"

"You of all people should know, Claire," he said cruelly. "I burned it. I threw it in the fireplace and waited until it turned to ashes."

Claire heard a knocking sound, like a distraught patient

239

pounding on an empty tray, or a huge dog wagging its tail against a door. She pressed her tongue to the bone behind her front teeth. Her heart raced in her chest.

"I had to," Ian said imploringly. "It was making you crazy. There was no other way. I didn't know what else to do."

Claire closed her eyes. She felt herself sit down on the red chair, then leaped out of it as if it were made of sharpened nails. "It doesn't matter. The monograph doesn't matter. Thousands were printed. I could find one anywhere." She strode over to Ian. "What I can't find anywhere is . . ." Claire stopped. The words died in her throat. She couldn't say it. She couldn't say what she wanted. She steadied her breath and rubbed her teeth together like flint and tinder. "Good-bye, Ian."

"I won't let you go," he said, grabbing her arm.

Claire ripped her wrist from his grasp. "You can't stop me," she said coldly.

The door opened. Ian paled and dropped Claire's arm. Claire turned around and saw Harcourt Abernathy standing in the doorway. She stared at Ian's terrified expression.

Ian *saw* him. He knew!

Charles passed from the room like smoke, letting Lord Harvey close the door.

"From the flush of indignation on your face, Miss Ishingham," the aristocrat said in perfectly shaped vowels, "I am forced to presume you have been apprized of our little ruse." He waited for Kate to sit, then pulled a chair from the wall to the center of the small room and sat down.

"Forgive me," he said creamily and utterly unapologetically, as if Kate didn't exist, save for his perception and wants. "But Mr. Ishingham described your nature in such a way that no ordinary means seemed likely to win you. The deception, such as it was, was my idea, though I easily won Charles to my way of thinking."

Lord Harvey leaned gracefully forward. The sun glinted

on the snow-white cuff at his wrist. "Charles is besotted with my sister," he purred. "I do not blame him. She is more than passing fair." He grinned. The paste pearls in his mouth shone like small gray moons. "He is lucky to have her," Harvey continued, balancing the word *lucky* like a toy between his tongue and his teeth.

Kate felt that luck had no connection in Harvey's mind to Charles actually deserving the woman in question. But if Harvey's sister was anything like her viperish brother, she would never deserve a man like Charles—despite the dreadful position into which her cousin had so foolishly and cruelly put Kate.

Kate rose from her chair. Harvey slunk up to a standing position. Kate smiled and breathed slowly and confidently. "Although I cannot approve of the thoughtless way in which you and Charles contrived to bring me here," she said, keeping a tone of disgust from her voice, "I am flattered you thought highly enough of me, despite never having met me, to ask for my hand."

She waited for any response from him, but Harvey— though his attention was decidedly fixed on her—seemed not to hear her at all. His eyes traveled from her neck to her feet and he swayed a little, as if his bones were formed of viscous fluid. Kate glanced at the door. "I appreciate Charles's concern for my happiness," she said, trying not to stare at the door handle. "And your kind interest, but I must decline your offer of marriage."

Harvey raised a perfectly formed eyebrow.

Kate's heart began to race. She planned how to get to the door. "I am certain Charles did not tell you everything about me—"

Lord Harvey grinned slowly, his mouth closed this time. "He told me enough to make me want you for my own."

Kate stepped back.

"I have surprised you," he clucked. "Good. Then we are well suited to one another, Miss Ishingham."

241

He'd said her name. Kate thought of a snake's warning hiss.

"I am not," he said, stepping no nearer to her but crowding her all the same, "as other men would be, offended by your dalliance with science or medicine. Instead, your charming foray into the world of men was the very thing that excited my interest in you, Miss Ishingham."

Lord Harvey elongated the consonants so that her name sounded like water spraying from a chink in a dam wall. He slid so close to her, Kate could see the pores and hair follicles on his throat. She froze in her place on the floor. He smiled.

"I have no desire for an ordinary wife," he purred, his breath thick on her face. He ran a cold finger down Kate's cheek. She couldn't move.

"We are alike, you and I, Miss Ishingham," he said. "Set apart from the world, indifferent to convention, unbound from the concerns of others." His finger moved to her jaw, then slipped under her chin to her neck. "Others too weak to indulge in pleasure or pain."

Kate snapped to attention, backed away and walked around him. "You misunderstand me, Lord Harvey," she said fiercely. "Our conversation is finished." Furious, she ran for the door.

Harvey grabbed her wrist and held it fast. "Our conversation," he murmured, "has just begun."

"Release me," Kate growled.

Harvey hummed and squeezed her wrist tighter as she tried to pull away.

"Release me!" she shouted, pulling with all her might.

He let out a kind of feral grunt and yanked her to him, slamming his fluttering lips on hers and shoving his tongue into her mouth. Kate bit down hard. He cried out and slapped her with enough force to knock her to the floor. Gently he touched his tongue with his finger and checked the tint of blood on his skin. He pulled her to a standing position. She fought back but couldn't free herself from his grasp.

He stood still, watching her struggle uselessly against him. Kate saw an erection press against his pants. Harvey moaned and pushed her to the wall, grinding himself against her. Kate tried to force him away. He licked her throat. She smelled his breath, sticking like venom on her skin and almost vomited.

"Katherine," he said, breathing heavily, reaching to un-button his pants with one hand while holding tight to her with the other. "We are meant for one another. You do not weep or submit as a weaker woman would." He shoved his tongue down her throat again while pressing his fingers so painfully on the muscles of her jaw she couldn't close her mouth.

"You," he moaned, taking his erection out of his pants and pushing Kate harder against the wall so she couldn't break free. He held her wrists above her head and stepped on her skirts so she couldn't raise her knee to kick him away.

Kate bit at the air, trying to catch his flesh. "Get away from me!" she screamed.

He laughed. The door slammed open. Harvey shoved his erection back in his pants and turned, swearing furiously.

Harcourt grabbed him by the shoulders and threw him down. Harvey's head slammed against the floor with a crack like a dropped pot. Harcourt smashed his fist repeat-edly on Harvey's mouth; blood poured out and ran into his ears.

Kate slid to the floor.

Lord Harvey cried out, choking on the blood in his throat. Kate shook her head and turned to them. She jumped to her feet.

"Harcourt," she pleaded, her hand on his shoulder. "Stop." Kate pulled on his arm. "Stop."

Harcourt hardly heard Kate's voice. He hardly felt her

hand on him. The bloodied face beneath him had ceased to be the monster who was hurting Kate and had become a memory from the past: the monster who had let his father die, who had verily murdered his mother and had turned his sisters, *three children,* out onto the London streets with nothing to sustain them. The man stopped fighting but Harcourt kept hitting.

Kate dug her fingers into Harcourt's shoulders and pulled him back. She grabbed his face and turned his head so he could see her. His eyes were wild. He stared at Kate as if he hardly recognized her.

"Enough!" she said. "You'll kill him." Kate brushed the hair from his brow. "Enough," she whispered. "It's over." She stood silently for a moment, then took Harcourt's unbloodied hand and kissed it. "It's over."

Harcourt stared in disbelief as Kate knelt beside the beast on the floor and wiped the blood from his face. She pulled the man's eyes open and gently ran her fingers over his face. The man moaned in pain. "You've broken his nose. But otherwise he seems unharmed." She stood up. "Call for a surgeon to be sure," she said, wiping the blood from her hands with a cloth on the table.

Harcourt stood strangely, as if he was unsure how to remain in an upright position.

Kate walked to him and took his hands. He shook uncontrollably and she gathered him into her arms.

"Kate. Kate," he whispered again and again.

She pulled him closer and opened her hands on his back. "I am unharmed. Thanks to you." She laid her head on his chest. "I'm fine."

Harcourt ran his fingers over her loosened hair, then took her face in his hands and locked his eyes to hers. *I can't lose you,* he thought but couldn't say. "I can't," he started. "I can't . . ."

Kate slid her hands inside his waistcoat. He kissed her softly, clenching his teeth so he would not cry.

"The surgeon," Kate said gently, pulling away from him.

Harcourt glared in disgust at the man moaning on the floor. "He can wait," he said bitterly. "Are you certain you're not hurt?" The idea that this demon had injured Kate inflamed him again. Instinctively Harcourt whirled toward the man, ready to fall on him and finish the job.

"I'm not hurt," she said gently, turning his face to hers.

Harcourt pulled her close. Kate realized she was shaking. "Please send for a surgeon," she said. "I'd like to sit."

He led her to a couch near the window, then crossed to the man on the floor. "Get up," he said, pulling Lord Harvey up. "Get up."

"You'll hang for this," Lord Harvey snarled, spitting blood onto the floor.

Harcourt laughed bitterly. "You'll be lucky if *you* don't hang," he said pushing Harvey toward the door. "Get out and find yourself a surgeon."

Harvey stepped threateningly close to him. The quiet violence in Harcourt's eyes terrified Kate. Lord Harvey stilled where he stood, as if the air in the room had turned frigid.

"If you ever come near her again," Harcourt said in an ice-cold voice, "I *will* kill you."

Disgust curled Lord Harvey's bloodstained mouth, but fear stole the color from his pale face. Harcourt stopped him before he could speak. "Get out now." He opened the door, pushed Harvey out and closed the latch.

Kate sighed in relief. Harcourt crossed the small room and sat beside her on the couch.

"How did you know I was here?" Kate asked. "Why did you come? You couldn't possibly have known Charles lied to get me here."

"He lied?" Harcourt said. "Your father is not ill?"

She shook her head.

"He allowed this—this monster to come near you?" Harcourt jumped from his chair.

"Wait," Kate said. "Harcourt. Wait."

His name in her mouth unhinged him and he sat down.

"Charles could not have known Lord Harvey's intentions. He thought . . ." Kate stopped and shook her head, as if the movement would somehow clear Charles's thinking. "He thought he was helping me by finding me a respectable husband."

White-hot anger flared in Harcourt's breast. "Respectable men don't . . ." He couldn't finish the thought.

Kate touched his arm. "It's over," she said softly and definitively. She wove her fingers through his.

He raised her hand to his mouth and kissed it.

"Now," she said, "tell me what made you come."

Harcourt exhaled heavily, feeling the rage begin to drain from his body. "After I left you I called on Cowpe again to ask about a physician for the boy's mother. He told me your father had fallen ill and you had left for Painswick to meet Mr. Ishingham and to return home. I saw your notebook open on the desk and thought you would want it. I decided to try to reach you before you left for Warwickshire."

He pulled Kate's notebook from a small valise on the floor. "I met Mr. Ishingham next door in a coffeehouse. I recognized him from his portrait and from the chatter on the streets."

Kate took his hand. "What made you come find me? You could have given Charles the notebook."

"I attempted to give it to him," Harcourt said. "He wouldn't take it. He said you wouldn't need it."

Kate let go of Harcourt's hand and reclined on the couch. The last of the afternoon sun spilled over her face.

"I knew you'd want to work harder now that poor Mr. Oldman had died. I thought you would need your notes. And so I came to return it to you." Harcourt paled and shuddered slightly. "When you weren't in the tavern," he said, grinding his teeth together, "I was struck by a sense of dread and ran upstairs." He inhaled heavily. "I heard you scream and broke open the door."

Kate watched him run his fingers over the notebook. She met his eyes as he laid the book softly in her lap. Every emotion she had fought against when Harvey attacked her, when Charles lied, when she'd thought her father was ill, leapt to the surface and closed her throat.

Harcourt understood why she'd want her notebook. He saw her for who she was, for what she was, and he loved her anyway. For the first time since Lydia's death, Kate wept.

"Love," Harcourt said, moving closer to her and taking her in his arms. "Love," he whispered into her hair.

Kate threw her arms around his neck and cried until her throat swelled and she couldn't speak. When her heart had stopped racing and her breath had slowed to a regular pace, she laid her head on Harcourt's chest and felt the heat of his flesh warm her skin. She listened to the beating of his heart, and the sense of belonging to someone filled her. The awareness of his body against hers awakened a desire Kate had only felt flashes of before. A distinct need for him, not just to touch her or to kiss her, opened inside her with a force and weight of its own. She wanted to touch *him*. To feel him warm and heavy against her. She wanted him to push himself inside her.

As if he could sense her thoughts, Harcourt stirred and lifted her face. Kate opened her mouth and he lowered his face and brushed his lips against hers. She flicked out her tongue and caught him behind his teeth. He pulled away slightly and gazed at her, taking in every feature as if he would draw her. She ran her hands up his chest and sat on his lap. He sucked in short mouthfuls of air and moaned softly. She repositioned herself on his lap. His flesh hardened beneath her and she undulated against it.

Harcourt breathed raggedly. "Kate," he said hoarsely. "Love." He moaned and raised himself to meet her soft flesh more tightly. "Kate," he said as she writhed on his thighs. Whatever he wanted to say, it went unsaid as he kissed her fully on the mouth, catching her darting tongue with his, following the movements of her hips with his own. His body throbbed threateningly, demanding release. He pulled away and sucked at the air in the room. "Not yet," he said softly. "Not yet."

Kate dropped her head to his shoulder but stayed on his lap, his erection hot and hard between her thighs.

"Marry me now," he said. "I cannot wait for your father's permission."

"Take me home," she begged in a whisper.

In one swift movement, Harcourt lifted his bride-to-be in his arms and carried her out of the room. They walked downstairs and out onto the street. Lord Harvey was nowhere to be seen, but Charles sat at a table in the tavern. He wore an expression of wild-eyed regret. Harcourt would deal with him after he and Kate were wed. He glared for a moment at Charles, who did not see him, then offered his arm to Kate.

"I rode," he said, when they were outside at the stable, "to reach you before you left for home. I have no carriage."

Kate eyed the brown mare and stroked her soft, broad side. She smiled. "Help me up."

Harcourt lifted her up, then mounted the horse himself. Kate wrapped her arms tightly around his waist as they rode into the blackening sky toward Ledwyche.

Chapter Seventeen

Harcourt Abernathy stared at Ian in the buzzing white glare of the hospital room. It seemed he had learned nothing after a lifetime and a half. Harcourt saw no regret in Ian's eyes, only blind arrogance. "Leave Kate alone," he growled.

Claire snapped her head around at the sound of his voice. *She could see him.* He looked as he had at the Black Hound but no longer solid or formed of flesh. Her mouth fell open. Harcourt ignored her. Claire turned to Ian. An expression of terrified recognition glittered in his eyes. *They knew each other.*

"Or have you forgotten what nearly happened because of your arrogant interference?" Harcourt snarled, moving nearer to Ian, who jumped back.

Wait, Claire thought thickly through a swirl of discordant sounds and memories too blurred to identify. *It isn't his fault,* she thought, reaching through the fog of images to establish herself in the present moment. "He thought he was helping," she blurted out, surprised by the steady calm in her voice. "Don't blame him. I can take care of myself. I'm not hurt."

Harcourt turned to her, sad affection softening the tight edges of his mouth.

"It's over," Claire said soothingly. "It's over. He didn't hurt me."

Ian moved to go. Harcourt snapped to attention like a cat and blocked his way. Claire stared at Ian, whose features shifted to reveal an expression she had never seen.

"You can't leave me," Ian said in a strained voice. "I don't care what *he* thinks or what you say. You can't leave me. You don't belong with him. You belong with me."

Harcourt stepped closer.

"Wait," Claire said. She stepped between them. "Ian. Calm down. You don't want me. You don't even really know me. Not all of me, at any rate." She flipped her hair over her shoulder.

Ian stared at the movement, fury straining the delicacy of his features. He glared at Harcourt, clenching his teeth as if willing himself not to believe.

"Being wrong about something isn't a sin," Claire said, ignoring the fear and rage in Ian's eyes. "Unless you insist on believing you're still right after the truth is unavoidable."

Ian shuddered violently. Claire reached out to him. She wasn't afraid. And for the first time in seven years, the sickeningly thick urge to submit, to slide under what Ian or Toby wanted, was gone. Ian turned away. Claire felt Harcourt disappear. She whirled around to the doorway. "No!" she begged. "Don't leave."

"Don't drag me into your craziness, Claire," Ian muttered through his teeth.

Claire stared at the empty space where Harcourt had stood a minute before. "Don't go."

"Don't ignore me, Claire!" Ian shouted, grabbing her shoulders.

She shimmied easily out of his grasp as though he had no strength or power in his body. "Don't go," she said again, but it was useless. Harcourt was gone. Claire pulled in a long breath and turned to Ian. "How long have you known? How long have you known he was real?"

"I don't know that he *is* real," Ian spat.

"You saw him," Claire said, pissed as hell that Ian still thought he could lie to her without consequence. "You spoke to him."

"You made me!" Ian whined like a child.

"You're acting like a little boy," Claire said.

"Fine!" Ian snapped. "Fine. If you want to fool around with a dead guy *who doesn't even know your name* be my fucking guest. Just don't come crawling back to me when you find out you can't marry or have children with a freaking ghost!" He stormed out of the room, throwing Claire's signed discharge papers on the floor.

"What are you talking about?" Claire called after Ian, but he'd disappeared into a crush of med students. "What do you mean he doesn't know my name?"

A scissoring sense of splitting in half sliced through Claire. She felt as if her bones and blood were separating from the ribbons of surrounding muscle. *Kate*. Harcourt had called her Kate. Claire hadn't felt a split this intense since she was a very young child and her dreams of a big house, a wide lawn, lovely dresses, pulled at her so deeply that she felt her skin tear when she got out of bed. "Kate, not Claire," she said to herself. She stood still and tried to connect her feet to the hard tile floor.

The light in the room turned pink, but it was too early for sunset. Street sounds below and voices within melted into themselves. Everything in the room—the ugly chair, the gold plastic water pitcher, the bed, the curtains, the suspended, chunky black television—existed separately, distinctly unto itself, as if it had gained an additional dimension or lost a vital one. Claire swayed where she stood, trying to catch a thread of connection to something. He'd called her Kate. And it had sounded like her name.

"Kate," Harcourt whispered.

Claire turned but couldn't see him. "Where are you?"

A vibration in the air like a soundwave made visible shimmered in front of Claire as Harcourt materialized.

She sucked in air like water. "You called me Kate."

Sorrow darted across his eyes like a snake in a pool. "I cannot stay," he said, his voice rough.

"Why?" Claire cried out. "Why?" She reached for his hand, but he wouldn't let her touch him.

"I cannot," he said. "You know I cannot."

"I don't know!" Claire said.

He gazed intently at her, as though he wanted to sketch her. "You see what I am," he said.

"I don't care," Claire pleaded.

"This is what you would have become if I had let you follow me," he said. "A fragment. A half-self."

"I don't care what you are," she said, stepping closer to him.

He walked away with his eyes fixed on hers. Claire felt as if a thread that kept her insides together was being ripped from her chest, taking with it bits of bone and muscle. She expected to see blood on the floor.

"Don't go," she begged, following him. "Please. Please don't go."

"I cannot stay, Claire," he said.

"Don't call me that," she demanded.

"I should have left you alone when I saw you at the inn," he said, a ferocious desperation scratching at his voice. "Forgive me," he said and folded into the air of the bright hospital room.

The swaying stopped. The floor rose up and met Claire's feet. The room and the objects inside settled into the background. Fluorescent white burned away the pink light. The familiar-as-skin impulse to run and hide dripped from Claire's limbs like lather. *I am so tired,* she thought—tired of taking in, tired of swallowing, tired of being a waiting receptacle, tired of offering nothing back. She never had any control. She gave herself over to everyone, melted for fucking everything. Anger, unfamiliar and cleansing, rose inside her, filling her veins like fierce music. Her muscles ached for movement. She wanted to dance in ecstasy like the Bacchantes who descend on Orpheus, after Eurydice is sucked back into the underworld and his mournful song makes all the animals on earth weep.

Kate. The name of the girl in the dream. The girl with a sister and parents. The name of the woman Harcourt Abernathy loved. Her name.

"You choose when to come and go," she said, hoping Harcourt, wherever he was, could hear her. "You came to *me* in Vermont. You found me. I will follow you. I will go where you are. I'll find you. I'll find where you lived, where we lived, and go there. Because I cannot stand being haunted and teased like Tantalus and the grapes for the rest of my fucking life. I want *all of you* and *all of me* or nothing!"

Claire sucked in gulps of air and left the hospital, icy air peeling back her unbuttoned coat like the torn skin of an open wound.

She ran across Tremont Street and devoured the cold, wet February air as if she had two mouths, two throats and two sets of lungs to fill. Twice alive, two hearts pumped the blood that flowed from her veins to her arteries. But she didn't want two. She wanted one. One self. One life. One love. Or nothing. A police siren screamed like a banshee. Claire had to save herself.

She slammed her apartment door behind her, glad of the ringing echo in her ear. She left a message on Toby's voice mail, then unplugged her phone. The red light on the answering machine went out. Claire shivered in the sunlight filling her kitchen. She started a pot of coffee.

Toby would hate that she'd unplugged her phone. If he didn't have Miranda he'd probably come over tonight no matter how late he finished at work. Thank God he *did* have Miranda. She'd make everything easier for him. Claire sat down at her computer and Googled "Kate Abernathy."

A woman in Kansas who sold vintage dresses online.

A teacher at a prep school in Maine.

A teenager's blog with quotes from obscure artists and the lyrics to Sponge Bob in French.

And under WOMEN IN MEDICINE: *In 1823 Dr. Thomas Cowpe of Ledwyche, England, began successfully innoculating people against perithisis, which was eradicated in 1974. In 1885, more than twenty years after Cowpe's death, the unnamed colleague who'd helped him discover what would be the vaccine was revealed to be Katherine Abernathy, the wife of botanical illustrator Harcourt Abernathy and the daughter of revered physician Lord Greydon.*

Claire lifted her fingers from the keyboard. She strained her ears to concentrate on anything other than the silent scream in her own head: voices in the hall, the sounds of Mr. and Mrs. Nathan downstairs, car horns, dogs and yelling on the street.

"Claire," Toby called, banging on her door. "It's me. Let me in."

Claire sighed and got up to answer.

"Why is your machine turned off?" Toby asked, waving his cell phone at her.

Claire heard her voice message on Toby's phone.

"Why didn't you pick up the phone?" he asked. "How long have you been home?"

"Not that long," Claire said.

Toby searched her apartment nervously. He stopped at her desk and read the lighted monitor.

"What are you looking for?" she asked.

"What the hell is this?" he demanded, ignoring her question. "Why are you looking up Kate Abernathy?" He leaned on Claire's desk so he could read the screen. He was wearing a black jacket, black pants and a white shirt with long cuffs. The paragraphs on the screen reflected on Toby's shirt in a shape like an oversized vest or a waistcoat.

Claire stared at him, and a thread of comprehension unfurled inside her chest. "Why did you call her Kate? The site says Katherine."

"What are you talking about?" he asked impatiently. "It says . . ." Toby's voice trailed off. He slammed the laptop cover down. "Don't."

"Don't what?" Claire asked.

"You know what I mean," he said.

"What?" she asked. "Don't use a computer? Don't turn off my answering machine? What?"

"I don't want to run your life, Claire," he said.

"I know," she said.

Toby pushed past her and searched frantically for a place to sit among the entirely empty chairs and couch. He finally stood with his back to the wall and window.

Claire walked to the green and silver silk couch and sat down.

"What did you mean when you said on the message that you were going away?" Toby asked.

"I need to get away," she said. "This thing with Ian has totally freaked me out."

"Listen to your voice, Claire," he said. "You're the world's worst liar." He played with an antique silver pen and ink set she kept on the windowsill. "I know what you're doing."

"You don't," she said tersely.

"Yes," he said. "I do." Toby took a long, deep breath. "Don't go. For me. Don't go." His voice rose. "Do you think you're the only one haunted by what happened to you in Vermont? I saw you, Claire. I listened to you scream until they got you out of that room."

Toby moved to sit beside her but instead sat on the arm of the couch. He sucked in a soul-quaking breath. "Maybe we do live other lives," he said in a soft voice, as if he were coaxing a child from a tree. "Maybe we do have other loves. Maybe there is more than what we see or comprehend. All that energy, all those lives, must go somewhere. But there is no crossing over, Claire. Time moves in a straight line. If we do live again and again, we don't move back and forth between."

His words echoed in Claire's head. She brushed them away. "If you are so convinced I'm wrong," she spat angrily, "what are you so afraid of? If nothing's going to happen, what could happen?"

"I don't know, Claire. You tell me," he said beseechingly. "You scared me in Vermont. You scared me in Sonsie. You scared me today when you weren't in the hospital and you weren't home."

She closed her mouth.

"Claire," Toby said, getting off the couch, "everyone has fantasies. That's why there are books and movies and music. And therapy. But anyone who refuses to see the difference between what is real and what is wished for is in trouble. And that," he said in a broken voice, "is what I'm afraid of for you."

Claire leaned her whole body toward his and made certain to keep her emotions in check. "I've spent my entire life pretending to be someone I wasn't. Trying things on and acting in a way I imagined was appropriate or fitting. But everything I did was a game. Nothing and no one I touched had consequence." She stared out the window, bit her tongue and tried to control her voice. "Except for my grandfather. And you. You are my only connection to anything real in me. The one part of my life where I feel like myself."

She breathed deeply. She'd never said that out loud before, never been able to articulate her connection with Toby. That small confession opened something inside her and she could breathe. "In my whole life I have never been more grateful for anyone or anything than I have been for your friendship."

"Claire," Toby said. He sat beside her. "No matter what happens in my life, no matter what happens with Miranda, I'll always be there for you."

"I know, Toby," Claire said. "I know that. But I have to find the truth. About Harcourt. About Kate. About me."

"And then what are you going to do?" he asked. "Lie around and wait to die so you can be with him? I won't let you."

Claire stood up. "I have to know."

"So find out here," Toby begged. "Go to the library. Find a women's studies program where some angry woman has codified and categorized every minute of her life and demonized Cowpe for taking credit when she *expressly* wanted none. Have you thought this through at all, Mrs. Abernathy? Does such a course of action seem reasonable or practical? It won't bring her back and it won't send you anywhere."

Claire stared openmouthed at Toby, a resonant chill awakening every slender nerve. "Didn't want credit? And you called me Mrs. Abernathy."

On the night of their wedding, Kate gazed up at Harcourt, who held himself above her in their bed, his skin golden in the candle glow, shadows and light at play on the muscled contours of his chest. He lowered himself gently to her, until his skin brushed hers. He kissed her brow.

She closed her eyes. The wedding had gone smoothly, she thought, trying to distract herself from what was about to happen. Distraught by the crime Harvey had almost committed, Charles had spent the wedding day in a state of alternating fury and contrition, sometimes in the same moment, on the same breath. In the days before the wedding Lord Harvey had tried to make a case against Harcourt. He failed when Charles spoke out against him. Thankfully for Charles, Harvey demanded that his sister break off their engagement.

"Kate," Harcourt whispered, "don't think. Your brow is furrowed." He kissed her forehead again and rested his weight on his elbows. He slid his hands under her shoulders so his fingertips caressed the nape of her neck. "Be present," he murmured, kissing her ear. "Be here. Now. With me."

He kissed the length of her throat. Kate's body lit up and breathed with pleasure. Tentatively she raised her hips up to his.

He moaned softly. "Yes," he said, moving against her. "Trust me."

His erection throbbed between Kate's legs; she closed her thighs together and slid closer to his hard flesh.

He breathed slowly and deliberately. "My Kate," he said. "My wife."

A hum of pleasure flowed to the tips of Kate's fingers and settled achingly between her legs. Harcourt kissed her neck. Each tender kiss echoed deep inside her. She pressed her legs tightly to his hard shaft. Harcourt moaned low and long, and took her taut nipple into his mouth. A thrill she couldn't control made Kate cry out. She opened her eyes wide and tried to concentrate on the white ceiling. He circled around her sensitive nipple with his tongue and she almost lost herself.

Harcourt stopped and raised himself so his face was level with hers. He brushed Kate's hair from her cheek and gazed into her eyes. "Love," he murmured. "What are you afraid of?"

His sex throbbed lightly against her wet center. She tried to steady her breath and clear her head. He pressed his waist to hers, making Kate moan in spite of herself.

Harcourt kissed each eye. "Are you afraid it will hurt?"

"No!" Kate said fiercely. "No. I'm afraid to let go. I'm afraid to lose myself. I'm not in control of my thoughts or my reactions when I'm with you. I don't know myself."

Harcourt tried to reposition himself so he wouldn't be too heavy on her, and the tip of his shaft pushed inside her. Kate moaned in reluctant ecstasy.

Harcourt shuddered and exhaled forcefully. "We don't have to. I can wait."

Kate grinned. She had never heard a less convincing statement. She ran her finger down his spine.

"Please," he said, desperation coarsening his rich voice. "If we are not to . . ."

Kate sucked in a shallow breath. "I am unaccustomed to being unable to direct my thoughts or feelings exactly as I wish."

Harcourt gazed at her. "Then direct me," he said. "I am happy to do whatever you wish. But you"—his breath was ragged—"you must tell me what you want."

Kate felt as if she'd been bathed in warm water. Desire for him hummed in every part: her mouth, her breasts, her legs, her fingers and the center of her body so close to his.

Harcourt waited.

"I want to see you," she whispered.

He moaned, writhing on top of her. He couldn't speak. He rolled off her, his back propped against the pillows, his erection huge and rock hard.

Kate gazed openmouthed at him. What she wanted, what she needed, shocked her.

Harcourt sucked in little, short breaths.

Kate couldn't close her mouth. She licked her lips, and a throbbing ache pushed her forward. She leaned toward him and took him in her mouth. Harcourt cried out. Kate ran her tongue under the hot curves of his flesh.

He breathed wildly beneath her. "God, Kate," he moaned.

She pulled more of him into her mouth, running her tongue up and down the length of him. He tasted salty and rich. She sucked him to the back of her throat.

"Kate. Kate," Harcourt said desperately as he throbbed and pulsed in her mouth. "Wait. Stop."

Slowly she drew her mouth off him. She circled her tongue around the tip and kissed it.

"God," he said on a shallow breath.

He pushed her onto her back and gazed intently at her

with a mix of love, desire and admiration. He kissed her deeply. She wrapped her tongue around his. His erection throbbed against the wet ache between her legs. He steadied his breath enough to say, "I love you. I love you. I love you." He threaded his fingers through the soft hair covering her maidenhead.

A sharp thrill shot through Kate. "Now," she said. "I'm ready."

He smiled slowly and kissed her brow, her eyes, her nose, her mouth. "Not yet."

Harcourt circled his thumb on the plump, wet flesh beneath her tight curls. Kate felt a shock of pleasure shoot to her head. He smiled and kissed her. His thumb circled until he found a place she never knew existed. She sucked in bites of air that never seemed to reach her lungs. With an impossible lightness and aching slowness, Harcourt caressed her until Kate thought she would die from wanting something she couldn't name. He slid his finger in and out of her slick wetness and circled the tiny spot again and again. Kate heard a deep cry pour from her throat like water. Her flesh, her body, her self, blossomed and opened under his sure hand as wave after wave of pleasure resonated inside her.

"Love," he whispered in her ear. "Love."

Harcourt's words washed over her as the vibrations continued to cascade within her. She opened her eyes and took his hard shaft in her hand. He sucked in mouthfuls of air as she caressed the hard, hot length. Harcourt opened his mouth and kissed her. Kate took his tongue inside her and released her hand from his erection. Harcourt moaned and gently thrust inside her.

It did hurt.

He was so big, she could hardly believe he fit inside her. Kate cried out as a sharp pain cracked her open.

"I'm sorry," he whispered on borrowed breath. "I'm sorry." He stopped moving.

"Don't stop," she whispered into his ear.

His hair brushed against her face.

"Don't stop," she said again.

He breathed steadily and slowly thrust again. Kate moaned softly as the same sensation she'd felt when he'd touched her with his hand started to build again.

"Harcourt," she whispered.

He moaned, kissing her and pulling so slowly in and out of her. Kate raised her hips to his and he thrust deep inside her.

"Faster," she said. "Move faster."

Harcourt moaned lightly and thrust harder and faster. The sound of his voice melted in Kate's ear. He stopped moving and let out a long, shuddering cry. Kate felt him explode inside her. She opened against him, opening and closing around him again and again as waves of ecstasy splashed inside her. The last reverberations of pleasure vibrated between them.

Harcourt raised himself onto his elbows and gazed at her with so much love in his eyes that Kate realized she could die at this moment, for she would never be happier than she was right now.

"What?" Toby said to Claire, who sat still as water on the green and silver couch. "I did not call you Mrs. Abernathy."

"You did," Claire said, leaning back on the thick cushions.

The dreamlike sensation of her throat clogging with mucus and her chest contracting crept in, but she was breathing easily. Wasn't she? She ran her fingers over the back of her neck and swallowed slender droplets of air purposefully, as if each slow breath was her last. She sealed her teeth together for a moment, then looked at Toby. "And you said Kate did not want recognition. How could you know that?"

"Fuck you, Claire," Toby said desperately. "I did not!"

Claire jumped forward on the couch and stared at him.

"If you go to England . . . ," Toby said through clenched teeth.

"I didn't tell you I was going to England," she said.

Toby ignored her. "If you go through with this death-lust hunt," he said, "I'll never speak to you again."

"What?" Claire said, astonished by the whiplash of his emotional shift.

"I mean it," he said. "I won't talk to you if you go. I don't know how else to save you from yourself." Toby stepped closer to her, the afternoon sun framing his outline in yellow light. "Choose," he demanded.

"Choose what?" Claire asked trying to focus on his face.

"To save yourself or to throw your life away," he said.

Sunlight illuminated the dust in the air. Claire watched tiny particles floating aimlessly around her friend, hanging and diving like breath. "I've already made my choice."

Toby moaned softly, as if he'd arrived too late to retrieve something he couldn't lose. He stared away from her. "Why did you ask for my help?"

"I didn't ask," Claire said. "You found me. You came to me."

Toby shook his head. "I don't know what to say," he said, his voice thin with too much air.

Claire walked to him. She stood in the broad beam of sunlight that spilled out beyond Toby and warmed her fingertips. "You've forgotten what I look like. You've forgotten how to see me."

"I won't watch you kill yourself, Claire," he said.

"I'm not going to," she said.

"Then stop chasing something you can never catch," he implored in a voice like a silver bell.

Claire pulled in all the air she could hold. "I have stopped."

"I don't see it," he said sadly.

"I know," she said. "I'm going."

Toby stood unmoving, quaking in his skin.

Claire waited.

He stepped forward and ran his hand through the air around her head, as if he wanted to touch her but couldn't.

He left without saying another word. The door shut behind him. His feet lightly hammered each carpeted stair in the hall. Claire walked to the window and watched him until he turned the corner and disappeared.

Chapter Eighteen

Cowpe opened the door to his office a week after Abernathy's wedding. He pulled back slightly when he saw Kate at work at their shared desk. "Good morning Miss . . ." He stopped. "Good morning, Mrs. Abernathy. I did not expect to find you here." He sat down without looking at her and pointedly opened a volume of Dr. Adbaston's to a chapter on the benefits of emetics.

Kate returned her pen to the silver inkwell and sighed. "Did you think I would abandon myself, and you when I became a wife?" she asked more tartly than she meant.

Cowpe leaned back in his chair. "Did you ever think I might desire you to do so?" he asked, impatient already with this interchange.

"No," she said. "I did not."

Cowpe exhaled and closed his book. "The situation is different now that you are married, Kate."

She smiled. "You have never called me Kate."

Irritation that he had done so without thinking laced Cowpe's agreeable features uncomfortably close together. "Forgive me. I assure you it was unintentional."

Kate sighed and pushed her book away. "What do you want me to do? I'll leave if you ask it."

Children's voices came in through the open window. Kate folded her hands on the desk and turned her silver wedding ring around on her finger.

"Abernathy showed me the ring," Cowpe said. "He had it made by a silversmith in London. Did he tell you?"

Kate nodded.

"If I had known earlier," Cowpe said, "if I had known what to expect, if I had heard it from Abernathy—or from you—instead of Jenny Greeley, I might have known, I might have been better prepared to make a decision as to whether our partnership should continue. But you have me at a disadvantage, Miss Ishingham." Cowpe glanced away from Kate. "Mrs. Abernathy," he corrected himself. He spread his fingers wide on the green surface of the mahogany desk. "The situation is different now."

Kate let go of the ring and held her hands together. "If you ask me to, I shall leave, but I will not abandon the work."

Cowpe sighed. "It isn't as if I expected you to choose differently," he said quietly.

"Shall I work at home?" Kate asked.

"At this point, does such a course of action seem practical or reasonable?" Cowpe asked heatedly.

"No," Kate answered. "But neither does abandoning a successful partnership because I—like you—am now married."

"But you are a wife," Cowpe said too loudly.

"Mr. Abernathy does not wish me to quit the partnership, Dr. Cowpe," Kate said.

Cowpe shook his head, and his long curls woke up the dust in the sunbeams. "The truth is, Kate, that your husband is more radical than you are. And more immovable in his views than you shall ever be."

Before Kate had a chance to ask Cowpe to explain such a statement, he changed the course of the conversation. They spent the remainder of the day, and the weeks after, as they had before Kate was married: inching closer to a safe, effective means of variolation.

Claire landed at Heathrow at seven o'clock the next morning and checked into the small hotel she and her grandfather stayed in whenever he had lectured in London. After Toby left the day before, she'd gone online again and learned that Harcourt Abernathy married Kate Ishingham on October 12, 1823. They had lived in Ledwyche, Gloucestershire. Claire called Toby before she went to the airport, and then again at Logan before the flight took off.

He'd refused to take her calls.

Kate left Cowpe's office after seven o'clock on a very dark November night. She heard shouting as she opened the door of the honey-colored stone cottage.

"I do not like it, Celia," Harcourt shouted up the stairs as Kate walked into the hall.

Celia's bedchamber door slammed.

"Damnation!" Harcourt cursed, turning furiously toward the parlor door. "Kate," he said on a thunderous exhalation. "Forgive me. I did not hear you come in. Did you walk? Why didn't you send for the carriage?" He kissed her nose. "Your cheeks are red from the cold. Come in. The fire is ready." Harcourt offered his arm, saying nothing about his argument with her sister.

Kate kissed him, then removed her bonnet, cloak and pelisse. She handed them to Mrs. Week, who smiled nervously at her. The housekeeper glared almost imperceptibly at Harcourt, who ignored it. Kate threaded her arm through Harcourt's and followed him into the warm, well-lit parlor. She sat on the gray damask couch near the blazing fire. "Come, love," she said softly. "Sit beside me."

He looked as if the last thing in the world he wanted was to sit. Kate watched him stare longingly, if briefly, at the black night outside the window.

"Harcourt," she said, smiling slightly, "it is too cold and too dark to walk."

He exhaled and softened his tense posture. "Too dark and cold for me," he said, sitting close to her on the couch. "But not for my charming wife."

He slipped his arm around her waist and kissed her on the mouth. The reaction in Kate's body was immediate and intense. He pulled away from the kiss and smiled at her. She shuddered and leaned into him, kissing him again. He slid his tongue into her mouth and raised his hand to her breast, where she already ached for him to touch her. The door clicked open. Harcourt pulled away with a groan.

Celia strode in, pink with anger and oblivious to her intrusion. "Kate," she snapped briskly, "I wish to speak privately to Harcourt."

"Celia!" Harcourt chided.

The girl narrowed her eyes and glared at him. He ignored her. Kate rose to leave.

"Stay where you are," Harcourt said.

Kate sat.

"It is not your place to ask Kate to leave her own parlor," he said to Celia, whose blue eyes flashed.

"Harcourt," Kate said softly.

"Please," he said before turning back to Celia. "You are not permitted to come downstairs clothed only in your dressing gown. And you are most certainly not permitted to spend another day in bed pining for anyone."

"I am ill," Celia protested heartily. "I pine for no one!" She sat heavily on a striped chair far from the heat of the fire.

"You are trying my patience, Celia," Harcourt said, rising from the couch in frustration and crossing to her.

Celia sat up slowly and folded her hands in her lap. She gazed at Kate, then turned to Harcourt, fierce purpose on her soft face. "I shall write to Grandmother and ask her permission," Celia said quietly with a light quiver in her pretty voice. "She'll approve of Edward. His uncle is an earl."

Harcourt went white. He stood violently still. Kate stared at Celia.

"I'm sorry, Harcourt," Celia stammered, all her confidence vanished. "I'm sorry. Please don't be angry with me. I only said it because, because—"

Harcourt seemed to suck at invisible fire. "You are never," he said in a low growl, "never to mention her again." He threw open the door and stormed out of the room.

The front door of the house slammed with a resounding crash. Celia burst into tears. Kate glanced at the door, then sat in a chair beside her.

"Celia," she murmured, taking the sobbing girl in her arms. "Don't. Harcourt won't be angry for long. Don't. Shhhhh."

Kate had not known Harcourt's grandmother was alive. He never spoke of any family at all, other than his sisters, Anna and Elizabeth, and their husbands and children. Celia wept uncontrollably.

"Shhhh," Kate said.

Slowly, Celia quieted, but she kept shaking in Kate's arms.

"I've been writing to her for two years," Celia said at last, in a tiny voice. "Dorothea Leighton sends and receives the letters for me." She gazed up at Kate with huge, wet eyes.

Kate breathed deeply. "Does Harcourt know?"

Celia shook her head, and sighed haltingly before speaking again. "She is ill. Grandmother, I mean." Celia glanced nervously at a noise from the hall. "Her servants have all left her, save a few. Grandmother will not see a surgeon." Celia sat up straighter and steadied her breath. "She trusts no one."

"I don't understand," Kate said. "Does Harcourt know your grandmother is ill? Does he know she is alone?"

"Harcourt knows nothing!" Celia said in an excited voice. "And you cannot tell him, Kate. Promise me you will not tell him."

"I'll make no such promise, Celia," Kate said. "Whatever

ill will Harcourt bears toward your grandmother must be forgotten."

"Please!" Celia begged. "Do not say anything to him!"

Kate lost her patience. "Harcourt will not hurt you when he finds out."

"I am not worried for myself," Celia protested fiercely. "It is Harcourt I fear for."

"Why?" Kate asked.

Celia rose from her chair and buttoned her loose robe. "I've said too much." She took Kate's hand. "Thank you for your kindness and your affection."

"You're welcome," Kate said in confusion.

"Edward Stackpoole has asked permission to marry me," Celia said.

"Sixteen is still young," Kate said. "What does Harcourt think?"

Celia gazed at Kate. "You have made Harcourt happier than he has ever been." She let go of Kate's hand. "No one deserves happiness more than he does, but I want to marry Edward Stackpoole."

Kate did not know what to say. She had hardly been able to keep up with whatever it was that was going on. "Celia, you must speak with Harcourt."

"I want to marry Edward Stackpoole," Celia said calmly. "I want my own life."

The front door of the cottage slammed open, albeit more quietly than earlier.

Celia paled, then stood taller. "Say nothing," she begged Kate. "I shall tell him soon. I promise."

"I shall say nothing of Mr. Stackpoole," Kate said. "That is your affair. But I must inform Harcourt about your grandmother, if for her sake alone. It is inhuman to knowingly allow someone to suffer because we find them objectionable. I will not do it."

Celia flushed.

Harcourt entered the room, calmer than before but still

distraught. He glanced longingly at Kate, who ran to him and took his hand.

"Forgive me," Celia said, almost in tears again.

Harcourt kissed her brow. "We'll talk later," he said kindly, but in a strained voice. "For now please give me leave to speak with Kate."

Celia threw Kate a desperate, pleading glance and left the room.

Harcourt embraced Kate, then stepped back. He waited for her to sit by the fire before he sat in a chair at a small writing desk in a corner of the room. "I regret . . . ," he began in a halting voice. "I'm sorry you had to see me behave in such a manner."

His voice was sincere and pained, but Kate realized Harcourt had no intention of speaking of his grandmother. She glanced at the flames in the hearth. When she turned to address him, Harcourt's eyes were shut tight and he held up his head with his hand.

"Love," Kate said, rising from the couch to stand behind him. She ran her hands over his broad shoulders and down to his chest. He grabbed one hand and kissed it fervently. She buried her face in his thick hair, still cold from the night. He smelled of smoke and November air.

"I suppose that Stackpoole fellow wants to marry Celia?" he asked.

Kate stood up. "I-I . . ." she stammered. "You must ask Celia yourself."

Harcourt stood up and smiled sadly at her. "Mrs. Week tells me supper is ready. Shall we go in?"

Kate stood still. "Harcourt, wait. I must speak to you—"

"Kate," he said. "Love. Light of my soul. You may ask anything of me. I will make it my life's work to make you happy."

"You have already done so," she said.

He smiled softly at her. "But there is one thing," he said, "which you may never ask of me, for I will never grant it." Harcourt exhaled. "Let us go in to supper. Cook has made potato soup and roast beef."

"Wait," Kate said.

"No," Harcourt said softly. "I will not."

"But—" Kate began.

"My darling," Harcourt said as gently as he was able, "my grandmother is not a fit subject for discussion. Ever."

Kate sighed in frustration.

"I have made allowances for you," he said in a closed voice. "Allowances few men would make. I have made them gladly and willingly, for I love you, Kate, more than I could say in a thousand lifetimes. I ask of you only this." He didn't wait for an answer.

"She is ill," Kate said.

Harcourt whirled around in such fury that Kate staggered back in fear. For a moment no sound, no speech came from his open mouth. Then he turned to the door and shouted.

"Celia!"

"Claire!"

Claire whirled around on the unfamiliar London street only to be embarrassed to find the caller speaking to a woman in front of her. Claire felt herself blush. She shook her head and grabbed the back of her neck. She should have taken a train to Ledwyche this morning, but something had held her back.

Walking down the crowded street, Claire glanced disinterestedly at absurdly expensive shop windows. After Ledwyche, there would be no more chances to take. Whatever happened would end all possibilities of anything else. If she couldn't find Harcourt in Ledwyche, if she couldn't change his mind, she would finally have to stop hoping they could ever be together in any kind of meaningful way. That was what she couldn't explain to Toby: that going to Ledwyche wasn't some kind of cliff-leap into the impossible but an end of trying to make the impossible come true.

"Shit!" Claire swore when her heel caught in a crack in the pavement. Stupidly, she'd only brought one pair of shoes, and now this red heel flapped uselessly from its smooth black sole. She snapped the heel off the other shoe and hobbled into the closest shoe store, where she bought a lovely pair of soft, sage green boots.

"Ooh, I love your boots," a gentle, American-accented voice cooed when Claire stepped outside the shoe store.

"Thanks," Claire said, glancing up to see a lovely teenage girl.

"You're welcome." The girl smiled and looked Claire up and down. "That blue jacket suits you. Great color. Sky blue, not tacky blue. *Celestial blue*," she added dramatically.

Claire grinned. "Thanks."

The girl smiled back, then bounced up the street to join a round-shouldered, pink-faced boy who looked as if he'd lie down in front of a train for her. She kissed him, then laced her arm through his, and disappeared into the crowd.

A group of women chatting in jewel-bright voices and pushing strollers jammed with fat babies took over the pavement. Claire jumped back to avoid having her new boots run over by dirty gray stroller wheels. She banged her head on a shop window. "Shit!" she cursed again and rubbed the back of her head.

"Careful," an old man warned in a stern voice. He held open the bookshop door.

Claire was too embarrassed not to walk in. "Thanks," she said, reddening like an adolescent who is suddenly and intensely aware of her presence in the world.

I need a drink, Claire thought, wandering around the crowded bookshop. Or a huge cup of coffee. "Is there somewhere around here I could get coffee?" she asked the red-haired flirt behind the counter.

The young man, who wore a green T-shirt with Tom and Jerry on it, smiled slowly. "We have coffee here," he said, leaning close to Claire. "But it's shite. Go two doors down. It's much better."

A woman pushed Claire out of her way. "I'm in a hurry,"

she said, glancing nastily at Claire for taking up space at the counter and not buying anything. She handed the clerk a softcover book with silver lettering.

"Was this the last copy?" the clerk asked.

"Yes," the woman snapped briskly.

He turned the green book over in his hand. The title caught Claire's eye like a tiny fish hook: *Botanical Illustrators of the Romantic Age in Britain*, by Celia Stackpoole.

"May I see that?" Claire asked, taking the book from the laughing-eyed man behind the counter.

"What do you think you're doing?" the impatient woman barked.

The man rang up the purchase. The woman handed over a credit card while Claire read the back cover.

The publisher's first reissue of Celia Stackpoole's delightful observations on botanical art of the Romantic Age gloriously reproduces the original illustrations in flawless color.

Celia Stackpoole, who lived to the age of ninety-two, was the sister of botanist and botanical illustrator, Harcourt Abernathy. Shortly before her death in 1910, Mrs. Stackpoole donated Abernathy's house, with its extensive collection of plant specimens and botanical illustrations, to the village of Ledwyche in Gloucestershire. The Abernathy house is now a museum honoring the contributions of British artists and scientists of the Regency.

The book's buyer pulled it from Claire's grasp. "Get your own copy," she snapped and left the store.

The man behind the counter watched the woman prance away with an expression of mild disgust on his face. "If you really want a copy, the museum in Ledwyche has loads," he said to Claire. "My mum volunteers at the shop on weekends."

"How far is Ledwyche from here?" Claire asked.

She really should have had coffee earlier. Her voice sounded weird, as if it were on a three-second delay to prevent curse words from being uttered unexpectedly on TV or radio.

"Not far," he said. "About an hour and a half or two hours, depending how you go. Or how fast you drive." He raised a reddish eyebrow and grinned.

"Is there a train?" Claire asked dreamily, aware of her voice traveling much slower than her thoughts.

"From Paddington Station," he answered distractedly, eyeing a very pretty dark-haired young woman standing behind Claire and smelling of patchouli.

Claire watched the man blush at the black-eyed girl and smiled. "Thanks," she said and pushed the fat door wide open.

Harcourt flung open Celia's door, but she was nowhere to be seen. "Celia!" he shouted furiously. "Celia!"

Kate ran up the stairs. "Harcourt."

"Do not speak to me, Kate," he said sharply. "This matter lies strictly between Celia and me." He strode angrily out to the landing and searched the other upstairs chambers. "Where is she?"

"I do not know," Kate answered coldly. "But I should not come out if I was being summoned like a disobedient hound."

White rage flickered over Harcourt's countenance. "You do not understand," he said slowly, as if each release of consonant and vowel was dangerous.

She cut him off. "I don't need to understand the particulars," Kate said, "to know that you are neglecting your duty to—"

"*Stop!*" Harcourt shouted, his eyes wild with a kind of desperation Kate had never seen before. "Stop."

Kate stepped back.

He walked around her, almost panting. "Celia," he called, not shouting any longer. He walked downstairs.

Kate stood in disbelief on the landing. The door of the chamber she and Harcourt shared creaked open. Kate turned to see Celia fully dressed.

"Tell Harcourt I am sorry," the girl said softly.

"Celia," Kate said severely, "do not leave. If he is angry you must allow him to speak to you about it. Don't leave. It is cowardly."

Celia screwed up her young, determined face. "I only wrote to her because I didn't want to forget. Mama's face and Papa's as well were starting to disappear from my memory. I wanted to remember them; I wanted to remember our house and London and life before. Harcourt, Anna and Elizabeth refused to speak to me about anything." Emotion rose in Celia's clear voice. She breathed deeply. "It was Edward's idea that I ask Grandmother about it."

Kate glanced at the stairs. "Is there no one to look after your grandmother?"

Celia shook her head. "No one. The servants who remain are nearly as old, or older, than she is."

Kate rubbed the back of her neck, but the tension stayed, stubbornly clinging to the slender muscle. "Where does your grandmother live?"

"In London," Celia said.

Kate smiled sadly. "Yes. I remember what you said earlier. I meant, where in London."

Celia gave Kate the fashionable address.

Kate slid her teeth together, listening to the coarse, wet scrape. "Do not leave this house without speaking to Harcourt. He couldn't bear it if you left like this." Without waiting for an answer, Kate turned and walked into her bedchamber.

Before she climbed into a cold bed, Kate packed a small valise with clothes, her leather medical kit, and copied pages for the monograph. On impulse she took Charles's poem, "Ode to Eurydice," and slipped it into the bag and got into bed. Scared, upset and hungry, Kate stared at the ceiling. She waited for Harcourt and tried to fall asleep.

* * *

Claire grabbed her suitcase and checked out of her hotel. She reached Ledwyche a little before dinner and checked into an old inn called the Horn and Powder.

"You're lucky," the innkeeper, a slim, vibrant woman in her forties, said as she and Claire climbed the narrow stairs. "Your room overlooks the garden."

The innkeeper unlocked the door, and Claire felt as if she'd been punched in the chest. It took all her concentration to speak normally.

"Lovely, isn't it?" the woman purred, gazing affectionately around the charming chamber.

"Yes. It is," Claire said a little breathlessly.

"Good," the woman chirped. "Don't hesitate to ring downstairs if you need anything." She closed the heavy door behind her.

Claire sat down on the bed but jumped off almost immediately. She couldn't stay in here right now. The breath of hundreds of guests clotted in her throat, making her long to scream. She left her suitcase unpacked on the flower-patterned, Turkish carpet and ran downstairs.

Harcourt trudged wearily up the stairs after a discussion with Celia that seemed to have taken years off his life. He hated that Kate had gone to bed without speaking to him, but he was relieved not to have to talk any more about anything. Painfully and slowly, he pulled off his clothes. Moonlight shone in slices of gray light across Kate's sleeping form. He just wanted to lie against her. Recklessly, he decided not to wear a dressing gown or anything at all and climbed into bed, hot and distraught and naked. Sleepily, Kate pulled him close to her.

He nestled his face gratefully to her neck and felt himself fall asleep.

Ledwyche reminded Claire of Beacon Hill—low, charming buildings warmly lit and seemingly full of happy secrets.

She wandered up Beckwith Street and had dinner in an adorable restaurant on the second floor of a gray building with a romantic stone terrace. She knew from a guidebook she'd read on the train that Harcourt's house was at the end of Beckwith Street. It would be easier to see it at night first, she thought, when no one was trudging through it, asking ridiculous questions, or showing off what they knew about history.

Claire zippered her blue jacket. Celestial blue, she thought, smiling at the memory of the girl in front of the shoe store that morning. God, that seemed like a lifetime ago.

The street sloped gently. From the top, Claire could see lights in every window of a honey-colored stone cottage. She felt a sugary swirl of warmth invade her skin, as if she'd drunk a glass of wine on an empty stomach.

"What's going on?" Claire languidly asked a well-dressed couple hurrying past.

"There's a party at the museum celebrating the anniversary of Mr. and Mrs. Stackpoole's wedding," the gentleman said brightly.

Claire turned her head toward the cottage windows twinkling against the dark blue sky. A lush sense that the air was thick as water pleasurably slowed her movement. She grinned—too foolishly, she worried, then turned back to the couple who were politely waiting. "Thanks."

They hurried down the street like rabbits in a children's book. Claire watched them disappear into the winking house, then followed.

Chapter Nineteen

The following morning Kate woke before Harcourt. His sleeping face was still lined with the vexation of the previous day. She dressed carefully and waited for him to awaken. Mrs. Week knocked at the door with tea and toast. Kate sent her away.

Sunlight flooded across the floor and onto Harcourt's face. He groaned and turned away from the brightness. When he realized Kate wasn't in bed with him he jumped to a sitting position. She walked swiftly to the bed and sat down beside him. Kate ran her fingers through his tangled hair, gold streaks glowing in the morning light.

"Kate," Harcourt said thickly, sucking in air as if he'd been held underwater. "I've had the most unsettling dreams."

She kissed him.

"Why are you dressed?" he asked. "What time is it? Is Celia here?"

"It is eight-thirty and Celia is downstairs," Kate said gently. "She is going to call on Mrs. Miller later this morning.

She is starting a book of alphabet letters for Mrs. Miller's son William, who is learning to read. Remember?"

"I had forgotten." Harcourt sat up straighter and rubbed his eyes and face with the heels of his hands. He swung his muscular legs over the side of the bed and stood up.

Kate stared at him, adorably naked and sleepy, and smiled.

He grinned possessively and took her into his arms. Her skin responded vibrantly, like an echo after a resounding crash. Harcourt moaned lightly and thrust himself forward into the soft muslin of her gown. Kate sucked in the earthy scent of his skin and sighed.

He kissed her throat. "You have dressed too early," he murmured into her ear.

Kate couldn't think straight; he touched her and she lost all sense of anything except his skin and his hands and where she longed for him to touch her. Harcourt raised her skirt and reached for the soft skin of her thigh and the damp flesh above it. Kate's knees gave way as he slid his finger inside her.

Someone knocked on the door.

Harcourt growled. "Ignore it," he moaned on a ragged breath. He slowly pushed his long finger in and out of her. Kate's breath came in intermittent bursts, echoing the building tension that chased the rhythm of his finger inside her.

The knocking continued.

"In a minute," Harcourt barked.

The rapping ceased, and the tap of footsteps on the stair sounded, then disappeared.

Harcourt undulated against Kate, his erection almost painful against her belly. He gently increased the speed of his hand. Kate tried to catch her breath. She pressed her hips to him and moaned. He answered her and kissed her deeply on the mouth until the movements of his finger and tongue unlocked her, and she came, vibrating and pulsing against him.

In one swift, graceful movement, Harcourt lifted Kate from the floor and laid her on the bed. He slid into her. She came again almost instantly. He ground his forehead to hers and thrust hard inside her.

God, she thought, trying to grab at any coherent idea, but the sense of his huge, hard shaft sliding in and out of her erased any idea but keeping him there as long as possible. Harcourt moaned forcefully and thrust harder. Kate raised her hips and moved faster. He penetrated so deeply, she felt as if he touched the back of her neck.

Harcourt threw his head back and moaned loud and long. Kate grabbed him and pulled him closer. He thundered against her soft flesh. His shuddering release flooded her with hot liquid, which ran warm and wet down her thighs and over her gown.

Out of breath and heart pounding, Harcourt sank his damp face into her neck. "I love you."

His mouth at her neck and his breath on her skin enveloped a connection still so new and fragile. Blissful satiety hummed in Kate's muscles and blood.

Harcourt let his weight softly melt into her. His sex was still hard and lightly throbbing inside her. His skin was warm, and his chest and legs were firm against her softer body. "I love you," he said again.

Kate turned her head to let him kiss her, and she spotted her packed valise on the floor near the door.

"What?" Harcourt asked as she stiffened suddenly. He pulled out and rolled off of her. "What is it?" Alarm replaced the languid thrill in his voice. "Why were you dressed so early?"

Guilt slashed through Kate's heart. She bit the inside of her cheek until she could taste blood.

Harcourt stood up. "I demand that you tell me what you are planning, Kate. As my wife, it is your obligation."

Kate sat up. "Forgive me," she said quietly.

"Forgive you for what?" he asked. A sickeningly familiar sense of dread made his heart beat faster. He could not allow himself to believe she would defy him. Not about this. "Answer me, Kate," he said when she did not respond.

"I am going to London—" she began.

"*What!*" he said.

"I am going to London," she said again.

"I heard you," he growled. "I'm not deaf."

"I'm not trying to defy you," she said. "We need never speak of it and I will never ask you to justify or explain your feelings."

"What in hell are you saying, Kate?" he shouted. "Are you mad? You are most certainly not going to London. This discussion is over!" Harcourt stormed to the door, then realized he was still naked.

"I warned you before we were married that I would not be swayed from what I believe is the right course of action," she said. "I shall go. You cannot stop me."

"You shall not!" Harcourt moved to grab her shoulders, but she stopped him with a glance.

"Do not underestimate me, Harcourt. I will not be moved." She swept the creases from the skirt of her gown. "I shall be but a few days. I'll come home when I am certain—"

"I have no wish to know why you're going," he seethed. "Or what you seek to accomplish while you are there. Because you are not leaving this house!"

"I'm sorry," Kate said. She breathed painfully and walked to the door.

He blocked her path.

"No one, Harcourt," she said. "No matter what their crimes—"

"My grandmother, my family, is not a fit subject for discussion. *Ever!*" He felt as if he had been struck in the face without provocation. "You do not understand—"

"*I do not care what your grandmother did to you,*" Kate shouted. "The decision to help cannot be predicated on the actions of others! No one, no matter what their sins, deserves to die alone. I will not stand by while an old woman suffers unattended. *It is not in me.*" She picked up her valise from the floor. "I'll never speak of her to you again, but I will go."

Blinding anger flashed in Harcourt's head. He hardly heard Kate. The walk across London that hellish night ten years before came flooding back. He and his young sisters had not been to their father's house since he discovered their mother's body. He had been the one to cut the rope from the ceiling and lay his mother's cold body on the couch. The heavy stiffness of her flesh and the frozen desperation in her empty eyes filled the well of his hands now. He pressed his palms against the warm muscles of his bare thighs as if he could suffocate the memory from his skin.

It had almost killed him to return to that house. The image of his grandmother's red spitting face had followed him for the whole of the journey, and the echo of her obscene screaming, so loud the glass in the chandeliers trembled from the force of it, had scorched his ears as he walked the London streets with his terrified sisters.

Elizabeth was hysterical, but Anna dead silent. Celia, who was almost six, was so frightened that she vomited all over Elizabeth's dress. Elizabeth had wailed that it was now her only gown and she did not know when she would have another. Celia's trembling voice whispered over his shoulder as he carried her. "I'm sorry. I'm sorry. I'm sorry."

"I'm sorry," Kate said. "I'm sorry to upset you. But I will not be someone or something I am not to appease anyone. Not even you."

"Appease me?" He crossed to the window, his fists in tight balls. "I have not asked, nor will I ever ask you to be, anything other than what you are. I would not have married you if you were anything else. Do not confuse my *single* request of you with an irrational, unwarranted, fearful conviction that has nothing whatever to do with *me!*"

Between Kate's skin and her heart a thin shell crumbled and fell away. She felt as if she were straddling an abyss and whatever direction she chose would seal her fate. She couldn't move. She gazed pleadingly at Harcourt as if she were falling.

He took her into his arms and held her. She laid her cheek against his chest. "I would never ask you to sacrifice who you are," he said. "You must trust that."

Kate kissed his bare skin. His heart beat against her mouth. He held her tighter to him.

"I'll stay," she said. Harcourt shuddered violently in relief. Kate drew her fingers across his cheek to his mouth, where he kissed them. "I'll stay," she said softly, "on one condition."

He did not answer. She ran her hands over his naked back and tried to catch her breath. "You must send money and help. I do not care who it is, but you must make certain your grandmother is cared for."

Harcourt pulled back. "No," he said quietly. "And you may not ask me again." He turned away and began taking clothing out of a fat, square dresser.

Kate watched him. The muscles in her chest and stomach trembled and contracted. She bit her lip to keep her voice from shaking. *Forgive me,* she begged silently. *Please forgive me.* "I shall come home when I have done everything I can," she said. She took her valise from the floor and left.

Harcourt spun on his heels and watched the white door close. He searched frantically for a dressing gown, then ran after her, but it was too late; Kate had already boarded an unfamiliar coach, which made its way swiftly up Beckwith Street.

Claire made her way unsteadily down Beckwith Street. Her new boots had begun to pinch her toes. A car passed too close to the pavement, tossing up dust from the road. She choked. For an instant, panic that she'd never be able to breathe again gripped her irrationally. She sucked at the night air until oxygen flowed easily into her lungs.

The cottage seemed to grow larger as Claire approached; laughter floated onto the street like the buttery fragrance of a bakery. Over the years the stone walls of the house had darkened from honey to caramel. A small hand-lettered sign reading PRIVATE PARTY stood outside the front door.

Claire stopped. She pressed her aching toes into the soft gravel. There were so many people crowded into the parlor and the kitchen and the dining room and Harcourt's study. Well-dressed strangers were chatting upstairs in Celia's room, in Anna and Elizabeth's room and her bedchamber. Why were there so many people here? A shrill, shrieking giggle hooked Claire's ear, and she felt as if she were lifted off the ground and dropped again. Partygoers streamed past like river water over a stone. She shouldn't be here. She stumbled back and ran up the street toward the Horn and Powder.

Dissonant scents of car exhaust and ale and fried food swam in the cold air as she ran up Beckwith Street. Her stomach shook violently and fear contracted her throat. Claire ran toward the hotel, praying not to vomit on the street.

She slammed her room's door shut behind her and ran to the bathroom. Her stomach lurched. She held tightly to the door handle and sat on the cool floor with her head in her hands. In a panic, she began reflexively telling herself she was crazy. *Crazy, crazy, crazy,* she chanted to herself. She was wrong to come, wrong to think anything could ever be any different than it had ever been. He couldn't live when she lived. And she had nowhere else to go.

But *crazy* wasn't sticking. It peeled off her like pages in a storm. A light rain began to fall. Action on the street sped up, as people shouting to each other and cursing the weather rushed to cars and shops to escape the coming downpour. Claire heard an old woman yell and choke. A heavy odor of unwashed sheets wafted in through the bathroom window.

* * *

Kate found Harcourt's grandmother's house in London the following day. She sealed herself from any thoughts of him. Whatever consequence would fall because of her actions, would fall. A sudden image of the shattering relief in his eyes when she told him she would stay made her want to cry, but she clenched her teeth together and knocked on the door of the dilapidated townhouse. If any servants remained, none came to the unlocked front door. She knocked loudly again, then let herself in and called for help. No one answered. It was a miracle the house hasn't been stripped by thieves, she thought. A faint stench of unwashed linen grew more pungent as she walked up the staircase.

"Who's there?" A surprisingly vital voice choked from the chamber nearest the landing.

Fear clamped Kate's chest. *This was a mistake,* she thought. *To come here alone was a mistake.* She had behaved exactly the way Harcourt said she had. In a desperate attempt to assert her sense of reason she had acted entirely on fearful, weak emotion. Kate drew in a deep breath and a sickening premonition closed its hand around her throat.

"Who's there?" the voice repeated.

Cautiously, Kate entered the cavernous, foul-smelling room.

Lady Clotbur—Celia had told Kate that was her grandmother's name—sat surrounded by layers of bedclothes lit by the bright morning sun.

"My name is Mrs. Abernathy," Kate said firmly, walking toward the bed.

The old woman leaned forward, her long hair matted to the sides of her head. She stared Kate up and down. "You are not Mrs. Abernathy. Get out of my house!"

Lady Clotbur was seized by a fit of choking and fell back onto the pillows. Kate took the cleanest bit of cloth she could find in a linen press in a small adjacent room and wiped the thick dust from the table near the bed.

"Get out of my house!" the old woman demanded.

Kate opened her kit on the table. Footsteps sounded on the landing. A servant entered the room.

"There is no one in the house, my lady," the man croaked irritably before spotting Kate. "Who are you? What are you doing here?"

He didn't seem alarmed, or more than mildly interested in Kate's answer. Kate trembled internally. She wished Harcourt had come with her, then shoved that thought away; wanting him only made her feel weaker and more incapable. "I am Mrs. Abernathy," Kate said as calmly as she could. "I am Harcourt Abernathy's wife."

"You'll get nothing from me!" Lady Clotbur seethed from the bed.

"I have not come to take anything," Kate said, disgusted that that was the old woman's first thought. "I have come to care for you."

"I don't need your help," the old woman snapped back.

Kate ignored her and turned to the man. "Please find a clean pitcher and basin. Fetch water and clean muslin."

The servant stared at her. Kate held her ground and stared him down. "Go!"

He muttered something unpleasant but left the room.

"I don't want you here," Lady Clotbur growled phlegmily.

"When did you last have anything to eat or drink?" Kate asked.

"How dare you address me, girl?" Lady Clotbur hissed.

"I will ask your servant when he returns," Kate said.

The old woman began choking again, more violently this time; Kate sat on the bed and helped her to a sitting position. "Does your chest hurt when you cough?" she asked, feeling Lady Clotbur's head for fever.

Lady Clotbur's lip quivered angrily. "Yes," she spat.

Kate touched her shoulder and arm. "Your gown is damp. You must allow me to change your clothes and these linens."

"Why are you here?" the old woman asked, slightly less

venomously, though suspicion brightened every word.

"Celia told me you were ill and alone," Kate said simply.

The old woman turned her head away, like an infant refusing a spoonful of peas. Kate saw what must have once been a handsome face, now surrounded by a halo of nestlike gray hair. "You'll need to eat or drink something," Kate said.

The woman whirled her head around. "Where is Harcourt?"

The sound of her beloved's name in his grandmother's acidic mouth flushed Kate with sudden anger. "He is with Celia."

Lady Clotbur's mouth trembled in anger again. "Weak."

"No," Kate said furiously. "Not weak. Enraged."

The servant came in with the cloth and water and stood in the doorway.

"As you are enraged," Kate added. She turned to the servant. "What is your name?"

"Turner," he answered coldly.

"Well, Mr. Turner," Kate said, "if there is no female servant in the house, you must help me. I will bathe and change her, but you must help me with the linens. When and what has she eaten recently?"

Mr. Turner did not answer.

Kate sighed and took money from her valise. "Fetch meat and potatoes and bread. Is there a fire?"

He nodded.

"But no one in the kitchen?" she asked.

"No one," he said peevishly.

Kate exhaled again. "Hurry, then."

Mr. Turner left with the money.

Lady Clotbur was quiet when Kate pulled the disgusting clothes from her. Her thin, dry skin was covered in purple sores, which Kate did her best to treat. When Mr. Turner came back, Kate had him make a fire in Lady Clotbur's room. She started a kettle of soup in the kitchen and made tea. Mr. Turner helped her change the linens.

Lady Clotbur devoured the bread and tea Kate brought while the soup was cooking. She eyed Kate menacingly and said nothing.

Night fell and Lady Clotbur's fever returned. Kate stayed at her bedside, cooling her hot skin and listening to her rave incoherently. Three days later she died, without a word for Celia or Harcourt, or a breath of thanks to Kate.

Mr. Turner came into the room.

"I think it was influenza," Kate said wearily. "How do you feel, Mr. Turner?"

"I?" he croaked. "I am as strong as an ox." He stood up taller, as if to prove the veracity of this hearty pronouncement.

Kate smiled slightly to herself. She felt exhausted and a little light-headed. "We must make arrangements."

Mr. Turner interrupted her. "Mr. Sloan's been sent for, and the coroner too."

Kate drew her head back at Mr. Turner's initiative and resourcefulness. "Good," she said, feeling more light-headed. "I shall return to Ledwyche and inform Mr. Abernathy and his sister."

Turner watched her leave, and locked the huge door behind her.

Kate's head began to ache before the carriage reached the outskirts of the city. To distract herself from worries about Harcourt and from an increasingly insidious spread of fear in her veins, she reached into her valise for the copied pages of the monograph to work on. A letter stuck between the pages fell to the floor of the carriage. Kate bent over to pick it up and felt sick. She stared out the window until the feeling passed and opened the letter. It was from Celia.

Ledwyche, 8 November 1823

Dearest Kate,

Please do not judge Harcourt too severely for his reaction to me last night. Although I cannot regret writing to my grandmother initially, or continuing to write for her advice on marrying Edward, I did not expect Harcourt to respond differently, nor do I blame him.

He will never tell you what happened and so I shall. I have never been one to hold my tongue on important matters and I see no reason to begin the practice now. Forgive my bluntness and understand that it is for Harcourt's sake that I am writing to you. You have made him happier than I have ever seen him—almost as happy as he deserves to be.

Harcourt sacrificed everything he wanted for Anna and Elizabeth, and for me. He raised us alone and gave up what he thought his life would be in order to do so. I am sure you see he was made for more than lovely flower sketches, though he has raised that simple delicate task to an art.

Ten years ago our father was imprisoned for a debt that was not his. Our grandfather, who could have paid the debt, refused to help. Grandfather was a peer. Papa was a merchant, and Grandmother despised him for it. Six months later our father fell ill of an infectious disorder and died without ever seeing our mother again. She hanged herself in the parlor of our house. Harcourt found her and took her body down. He was eighteen years old.

Over the useless protests of our weak and grieving grandfather, Grandmother refused to allow her daughter to be buried in the family burial plot. Our mother was buried in a pauper's field. Her children were not present. We still do not know where she is buried. Harcourt confronted our grandfather, who took to his bed and would not be seen. Grandmother made certain Harcourt would be disowned. She pulled us from our beds and demanded we choose: stay comfortable and cared for with her, or leave now with Harcourt and be barred forever from the house and family. We all chose

Harcourt and left the house that night. After our mother was buried, Grandfather refused to stand up to or defy our grandmother. Harcourt has never, and will never, forgive either of them. Grandfather died five years ago. I began writing to Grandmother three years later.

The next time you see me I shall be wedded to Edward Stackpoole. Harcourt has refused permission until I am eighteen, but I see no reason to obey him and wait. He will forgive me. He knows I love him and am only choosing what he would choose for me if he were not so blinded by anger.

Tell Harcourt I do love him. Very much. More than I can say. Tell him Edward is good and kind and loves me and I only want the chance to make someone happy. Please tell Harcourt that much.

Yours in love and affection,
Celia

Kate stared into the dark interior of the carriage. A sense of being cut in half traveled the length of her spine. She sucked in breath as if the air in the enclosed space was disappearing. Would it have mattered? she thought, clinging to the letter as the coach lurched violently forward. Would it have mattered if she had known what Harcourt had endured? Would it have mattered if he had confided the story to her and begged her not to go instead of commanding her to stay? Would she have stayed behind to be with him? The pain in her head grew hotter and her neck began to feel stiff. She could not pretend not to know herself any longer. She could not stop thinking or feeling.

No matter what Harcourt said or what his grandmother did, Kate would have left. Her belief in herself and in the soundness of her decisions had always been immovable. Charles was exactly the same. It was a fault she forgave in herself and not in him. He never questioned a decision or judgment after it was made, even when he was faced with obvious consequences. But Kate knew she was just as bad, just as stubborn about her own opinions as he. She would have still gone to London, and she *still believed it was the right choice*. How could it be otherwise? Wasn't she responsible for caring for people when she could?

But what was her responsibility to Harcourt? Here she had failed. She knew she had. How could he forgive her? And she had failed his grandmother as well. In a blind effort to preserve a vital part of herself, Kate had risked losing everything. The coach shook. She had to bite the insides of her cheeks to keep a sense of sickness from overpowering her. She stared out the window. Broad swaths of grass seemed to undulate under the soft gray sky. She closed her eyes and leaned her cheek against the cool, vibrating glass. Celia's letter fell from her lap and onto the floor.

Kate felt sicker and sicker. By the time they reached the Ledwyche village gate she felt fevered and heavy, as though her limbs were filled with water. The coach stopped in front of the Horn and Powder. Kate's stomach lurched. She held tightly to the door handle. She turned to the window; thick air slowed her movements.

She stepped out of the coach. The driver laid her valise at her feet. Kate glanced dizzily down Beckwith Street. She would never make it home. Leaving her valise, which seemed uncommonly heavy, on the footpath, Kate made her way purposefully toward Cowpe's office.

"Dr. Cowpe's at the Eastons'," his servant said when Kate entered the room. "Are you unwell, Mrs. Abernathy?"

Kate opened her mouth. The words, what she wanted to say, stuck in the back of her head like a cart without a horse.

"Here," the woman said kindly. "Sit down. Dr. Cowpe will be back soon."

"I want to go home," Kate said.

"What would you have me do?" she asked.

"I want to go home," Kate said, as if no other phrase or idea was possible.

The woman glanced around the room. "All right. I'll fetch Mr. Abernathy."

Chapter Twenty

Harcourt sat in his small open carriage, beside himself with fury. He did not know how he could ever forgive Kate. He'd asked for *nothing* but this. And Celia would betray him too. Though she denied it, Harcourt knew she planned to run off and marry Edward Stackpoole. He had lost control. Of everything and everyone of any importance to him, and all because of an unspeakably heartless woman who had stood by while her daughter took her life. The carriage was moving impossibly slowly. "Faster!" he shouted.

Harcourt felt as if a hissing snake undulated up and down his spine. He couldn't think. He wanted to run. He could have run and reached Cowpe's office sooner. He should have followed Kate to London. He shouldn't have let her go. He couldn't have stopped her. He had made one request and she had refused him.

Since the moment of his own death across the ocean at the Black Hound in Vermont, the spirit of Harcourt Abernathy had returned to his own time only once. He chose the day Kate came home from London, as if he could somehow alter the outcome, as if he could change the course of Kate's short life. But he only succeeded in reliving the helpless horror of hearing her cry out and coming to her too late.

Observing one's life after it has passed is an ecstasy too potent for most to endure, but Harcourt chose this day again. So here he sat, in a moment long passed and ever present, beside himself, in a carriage slow as lead, waiting to witness his wife fall into his arms only to come home and die.

The carriage lumbered along Beckwith Street. Harcourt's stomach filled with dread as Cowpe's office came into view. Helplessly, he watched Kate step out of the door and walk toward the tavern. The carriage stopped. Harcourt alighted. He watched himself walk toward Kate. He shuddered as he saw Kate fall into his arms. Impotent grief tore at his stomach like a frenzied animal. It was only a matter of time. Harcourt turned from the scene. He heard Kate scream about the Horn and Powder.

"My valise," Kate wailed as Harcourt took his wife into his arms. "My valise. My kit. My kit. I've left it. It's at the Horn and Powder. I need it."

"Shh." Harcourt murmured, carrying Kate to the carriage. "I'll get it, Kate. Don't shout. I'll get it for you." He helped her into his carriage. Her skin was burning.

"Please," she muttered and dropped her head to his shoulder.

Harcourt watched his carriage disappear down Beckwith Street. Acid-mouthed sorrow corroded him from the inside. He turned away. In a few hours Kate, his Kate, would be dead. The inevitability hit him like a brick in the face. Kate's valise still sat on the footpath in front of the inn. In a fit of desperation after Kate died, he'd tried to retrieve the valise, as if it held some magic elixir to bring her back. But it was gone. Stolen, most likely, and then abandoned, for there was nothing of value within it.

He walked slowly to the brown leather valise, not yet

stolen or lost, and picked it up. A grieflike song of Kate crying for it swelled in the middle of his ears. He lost his sense of equilibrium. Feeling dizzy, Harcourt sat on the steps in front of the old inn.

Mr. and Mrs. Gedge walked by. Mrs. Gedge chattered bitingly. Her husband listened, stony-faced. They gazed through Harcourt as if he wasn't there, which, of course, he wasn't, and walked into the Horn and Powder. He breathed in the overfamiliar Ledwyche air and opened Kate's valise. He found a few articles of clothing, her kit filled with glass phials and small tools, her notebook, Charles's poem and the leaves of paper that would become the monograph.

If these stolen pages would comprise the monograph, and he knew they had, how had Cowpe published the book? Were these copies of their work? Harcourt paged through the sheets, proud of Kate's clear, forward thinking and powers of precise expression. Between the pages was a letter to Cowpe describing Kate's wish not to be credited for the monograph, for fear of damaging her husband's or Dr. Cowpe's reputations in any way. She needed the work, not ephemeral recognition. Harcourt breathed deeply. No one could ever sway Kate from what she wanted, no matter what the consequences.

And in the chance of a second lifetime, Claire had made the opposite mistakes. Instead of standing up to Charles or Ian, or whatever the hell his name was, she'd let him decide who she could be. She chose to hide rather than find the strength to be herself. Kate died rather than be someone she could not. Harcourt knew that now, but he'd been too angry to see it then.

Now he was going to live through it again. And Claire, despite his efforts to prevent it, would continue to live a half life, trapped between two worlds, living in neither.

He should have been stronger. He should have left the Black Hound as soon as he realized the woman in the red dress was Kate. He should have let her go when she offered to find another room. But he could not have stopped himself.

Two boys ran by, kicking up street dirt into his eyes. He pressed the heels of his hands to his eyes and squeezed them shut. Kate had wanted him to get her valise before they returned home. She had screamed and reached for it as they climbed into the carriage, but he had refused her. All he had wanted was to get her home, where she would be safe.

Harcourt opened his eyes and leapt to his feet, the valise still in his hand. The self-propelled carriages he'd seen when Moulton told him Claire had been in the room for three days, sped noisily past. People, talking animatedly to small objects they pressed to their faces, crowded Beckwith Street. Excessive light and noise filled the air. Harcourt walked onto the footpath and turned around. The HORN AND POWDER, EST. 1727 sign was still hanging.

The door of the inn opened and closed behind him. Men and women dressed all in black, or in garish colors with skin exposed, bits of silver pierced through their mouths, passed by him. An enormous red coach, lined with windows and spewing gray smoke, stopped in front of the inn. A oversized likeness of a nearly naked man, gazing both at himself and out at the viewer, was painted on the side of the red carriage—if it had indeed been painted, for it seemed an exact mirror of a face, more like a calotype or a salt print than a painting, save that the colors of the man's skin and hair were more true to life. The text above the Hyacinth-beautiful man's face read *NARCISSUS TRANSFIXED*. THROUGH DECEMBER. AT THE NEW ADELPHI THEATRE. Harcourt dropped Kate's valise and stepped into the inn. Claire was here.

Claire stood up. Waves of nausea and dizziness swirled inside her. She lay on her bed and closed her eyes. Faces from her past and from her dreams began to blend together like a book with moving parts. Toby. Ian. The kissing couple in Sonsie. The red-haired boy in the bookstore. And Celia, who had admired her blue jacket.

Claire's knees and hips stiffened. She stretched, and crossed the small room to the window. An old suitcase sat in the middle of the sidewalk like a single glove in a surreal painting. Claire waited for someone to claim it or steal it, but no one came. She shivered and walked away from the window.

Raucous laughter bubbled in from the hall. She started pacing and then stopped. *I'm turning into Toby*, she thought. He paces madly whenever he's angry or upset. An ache of regret that they had parted on such bad terms swelled in Claire's throat. She sat at the desk and took a pen from a reproduction dip pen and ink set. She could write him a letter, try to explain why she had to come. A glossy-paper guidebook, *What to See in Ledwyche*, took up too much space on the small desk. She pushed it out of the way. It fell. As she jumped to catch it she knocked the inkwell to the floor. Purple ink, like violet smoke, spread out on the flowery carpet.

"Oh, my God," Claire said, unsuccessfully trying to blot the ink with a sheet of stationery. She stained her fingers, then her arms and neck with purple spots. She shook her hands and the ink sprayed everywhere. She groaned and wiped her hands on a clean piece of stationery. The guidebook had fallen open to a broad color photograph of Harcourt Abernathy's house. She picked it up.

"*. . . built of honey-coloured stone, native to the surrounding Cotswolds. Be sure to visit the Abernathy House and Museum . . .*" Blah, blah, blah. She'd read the same things on the back of Celia's book. She turned the page. "*Botanical illustrator Harcourt Abernathy lived in the house with his wife, Katherine Ishingham Abernathy, until 1823. Mrs. Abernathy, who helped Thomas Cowpe discover what would become the vaccine for perithisis, died after visiting London during an outbreak of meningitis. Abernathy died of an infection after a fire in America, less than one year later.*

Claire knelt in the wet ink. *In a fire, in America,* she thought slowly, as if the words or the idea behind them had to be dragged reluctantly from the back of her brain. *He died trying to save me. Because I tried to follow. He wanted to leave, to save himself, and I forced him back.*

The laughter in the hall rang louder. The sound stretched wide like Silly Putty—misshapen sound like misshapen text imprinted on the rubbery toy.

Claire felt a buzz in her mouth and fingers, but it wasn't Harcourt. She felt it in her legs and breasts and belly, but it wasn't Harcourt. He wasn't here. He was still in Vermont, or in Boston. A memory of when she was little and Mr. Moulton lived with them slapped Claire's brain back to speed. Mr. Moulton told ghost stories of London, where he had lived as a young man, and of the Black Hound Inn. The story Claire asked to hear again and again was about an Englishman who died in the hotel. Mr. Moulton couldn't remember how the man died, but his ghost remained behind: crying in a chair near the fireplace, his head in his hands, his family, his wife, an ocean away and he trapped forever on a foreign shore.

Claire ran for the door, her mouth and fingers and toes, the backs of her knees and her hair buzzing with some presence. Her skin felt damp and hot. The door opened before Claire grabbed the handle.

"Kate!"

"Mrs. Week," Harcourt said as he helped Kate into the house, "send for Dr. Cowpe." He led Kate to the couch in the parlor and sat beside her. Her skin was damp and hot. He felt frozen. "What is it? What's wrong?"

Kate looked through him. "Get Celia out of the house," she whispered fiercely.

Could she be angry with Celia? His Celia? Harcourt roughly grabbed Kate's shoulders. "What did that evil woman tell you? What lies did she spread about me and my family?" He released her and stood up. "I told you not to go! I made one request of you, Kate. One! But you had to have your own way! You are incapable of thinking beyond your own needs, Kate. I do not know you."

He stopped talking and walked to the window. Kate lay down. She felt her blood and fluid and life pouring from her too-loose, ill-fitting skin. She turned her face to the back of the couch and began to let go.

Harcourt felt as if his eyes were on fire.

Kate took in shallow, panting breaths. "She died. Your grandmother. She died."

Harcourt sighed and shut his eyes for a moment. Kate breathed slowly. Mrs. Week entered the room.

"Get Celia out of the house," Kate said again. "You should leave as well, Harcourt."

Comprehending what she meant, Harcourt stared in disbelief. He felt as if he was drowning. "Take Celia to the Leightons'," he said to Mrs. Week. "Where is Dr. Cowpe?"

"No one knows where Dr. Cowpe is," Mrs. Week said, glancing nervously at Kate. "He was at the Eastons' this morning, but no one has heard from him since then."

Harcourt swore. Kate made a small cry of pain. She tugged at her swelling fingers and pulled off her wedding ring. He took it from her hand before it fell to the floor.

"Go!" he shouted to Mrs. Week. "Tell me what's wrong," he begged Kate, in a voice he didn't recognize.

"I don't know. My head is throbbing. My neck aches." Kate stopped talking. She groaned and took shallow breaths.

Harcourt stood up and quickly fetched an empty basin. When he returned, he sat beside her and placed the basin on the floor.

"Where were you?" Kate asked. "Why did you leave?"

"I'm here," he said. "I'm here."

"I think I'd like to see Dr. Cowpe," she said in an uncharacteristically small voice.

"Cowpe's been sent for," Harcourt said, pushing her hair from her face.

Kate groaned. Her breathing became shallower and faster. Harcourt picked up the basin and gently helped her up so she could vomit into it. She finished and fell back onto the couch.

"Is that better?" Harcourt asked.

She didn't answer. Purple spots had begun to appear on her skin. Harcourt opened her dress.

"It's not putrid pox," Kate said, her voice coarse from the acid in her throat. "Your grandmother had purple lesions. I thought they might be bedsores. But they weren't." She stopped and vomited again. Harcourt was ready with the basin.

Kate raised her hand and tried to rub out the stiffness in her neck. "It was dark and filthy in the house. I could hardly see." She shut her eyes again.

Harcourt raised her gown to see if the spots had appeared anywhere else. Huge purple lesions covered Kate's knees, as though she'd knelt in violet ink.

Kate took a deep breath and sat up. "I thought your grandmother was stricken with influenza, but this is too severe and sudden in onset. It is something else." She raised her hand to her neck again.

"Let me," Harcourt said. He gently massaged her neck. Kate sighed and lay back down. She fell asleep. He got up to empty the bowl.

"Don't leave," Kate said suddenly from the couch.

"I'll be right back," he said.

"Please," Kate begged. "I don't want to be without you."

Harcourt left the basin on a table and sat beside her. He took her hand and held it, and sat with her while she slept.

Cowpe arrived long past nightfall. He'd traveled to Painswick to call on the Dentons. Harcourt waited while Cowpe examined Kate, who was still sleeping. After a few minutes Cowpe stepped away from the couch. He pushed his fingers through his hair and did not face Harcourt.

"What?" Harcourt asked. "What is it?"

Cowpe didn't say anything.

Harcourt ran to Kate. She was breathing. Sleeping. Was she not? Cowpe could see that. Couldn't he? He turned wildly to Cowpe. "What do you see?"

Cowpe breathed deeply and turned.

"No," Harcourt said, retreating from the terrible expression in Cowpe's eyes. "She'll be fine. She is young. She wasn't ill at all when she left for London. No," he said, shaking his head. "No."

Cowpe stared at the doorway. "Forgive me."

"Whatever for?" Harcourt asked, fear thinning his voice.

"Forgive me," Cowpe said. "Though I don't know what I could have done had I been at her side all day."

"Tell me what the devil is going on!" Harcourt demanded.

Kate groaned. He turned to her. "Shhh, love," he said and kissed her brow.

"I don't know how long she'll last," Cowpe said very softly.

"What do you mean?" Harcourt asked. "I don't understand what you mean."

"Come and talk with me outside," Cowpe said.

"Why?" Harcourt asked. "No. I'm staying with Kate."

"We are disturbing her," Cowpe said, suddenly severe. "Sleep is the only thing that can help her." He led the way to the door.

Harcourt turned back, and for an instant all the light was sucked from the room like water down a drain.

"Toby!" Claire said, holding open the door of her hotel room. "What are you doing here?"

"What happened to you?" Toby asked, staring her up and down. "What is all that purple?" He grabbed Claire's face.

"I spilled ink," she said. "You called me Kate again."

She shut the door. Toby sank down onto the plump cushioned chair near the door and didn't answer Claire's implied question.

"How did you find me?" Claire asked.

"Where else would you be?" Toby said, sighing and running his fingers through his hair. "I looked up Kate and Harcourt Abernathy online and flew out on the flight after yours."

"So, you didn't refuse my calls?" Claire asked.

"What?" Toby said. "No. I told Sally I had a personal emergency and not to give anyone any information. She's so literal." He gazed wearily around the room. "What are you going to do?"

"What do you mean?" Claire asked.

"You know what I mean," Toby said. "Do I have to say it out loud? Past lives, reincarnation. What are you going to do? You were Kate Abernathy in a previous life. The ghost of Harcourt Abernathy found you again in Vermont. So, what now? What are you going to do? Sit in this room forever?"

Claire flashed on an image of Harcourt at the Black Hound, his head in his hands. She bit hard on her lip. "Why are you calling me Kate?" she asked angrily.

"I think," Toby said softly, "I think I knew you somehow." He stood up and gazed intently into Claire's eyes. "From the first moment I saw you at school, poring over that ridiculously old book in the library, I was seized—as I have never been in my life—by a desire to take care of you. As if I had failed to once before. I can't explain it." He walked away and sat on the bed. "I've always thought of you as Kate."

"What?" Claire asked. "Why didn't you say anything before now?"

"What should I have said? That for the first two years we knew each other I couldn't remember your name?" Toby asked. "Why do you think I always called you sweetie? That ink is all over you, you know."

"I know," Claire said.

"You still haven't answered my question," he said.

Claire walked to the chair near the door. She had a headache and her neck felt stiff from the long train ride.

She massaged her neck, then pressed her fist to her mouth and bit on her silver ring. "I have to let go."

"What does that mean?" Toby asked.

"This isn't me," Claire said quietly.

"Who is it, then?" he asked.

The door opened. Toby turned his head in a languid sway, like an oar in a river. Harcourt Abernathy stood in the doorway, an old suitcase in his hands. "Claire."

Claire ran to him.

"I don't understand," Toby said to Harcourt.

"I don't understand," Harcourt said, grabbing Cowpe by the arms. "How could she fall so ill so quickly?"

"It is an inflammation of the brain," Cowpe said softly. "She may survive it."

"What do you mean, *may?*" Harcourt squawked in a voice he hated.

"I am sorry," Cowpe said.

Kate moaned something from the parlor.

"Let her rest, Abernathy," Cowpe said, taking Harcourt's arm. "She has to sleep."

Harcourt stood in the hall, Cowpe's hand on his arm.

Kate cried out. Harcourt couldn't hear what she said. The mournful sound of her voice reached for him. It brushed across his face like a lash formed of feathers. He pulled his arm from Cowpe's grasp and ran into the room where Kate lay. When he got to her she was dead.

Claire screamed. Fluid clogged her mouth and throat and stopped her breath.

Harcourt and Toby ran to her.

"Forgive me," Toby said to Harcourt as they led Claire to a chair near the window. "Forgive me."

"It wasn't your fault," Harcourt said.

Claire stared at Toby. Cowpe's face shimmered beneath his skin. She understood. He thought he had failed her,

303

that it was his fault she had died, because he wasn't there soon enough. She met Toby's eyes and held his gaze until he actually saw her. "It wasn't your fault," she said. "It wasn't your fault. You have to live your own life. You found Mary again when you found Miranda. You have to live your own life, Toby. And I have to live mine."

She could breathe again. A hum of life and presence buzzed ferociously in her limbs, strength and weight gripping her from the inside. "It's me," she said quietly to both men.

Harcourt took her hand. "Claire. You cannot go. Tell her she cannot go," he said to Toby. "Tell her what will happen if she tries to follow me. Tell her."

Toby was silent for a moment. "What about Ian? What am I going to tell Ian? That I let you destroy yourself in Ledwyche because you can't think beyond your own convictions?"

Claire breathed deeply. She felt simultaneously desperately ill and vitally strong. Waves of nausea and a throbbing headache fought with a fierce compulsion to run and a sense deep in her muscles that she could accomplish anything at this moment if she tried. Pushing away an overwhelming dizziness, she turned to the window and stared down at the dark and dormant garden below.

"Did Jenny Easton have a son or a daughter?" she asked.

Harcourt glanced desperately at Toby. "Help me," he mouthed, then turned to Claire. "She had twins, a girl and a boy. But Claire—"

Claire whirled around. "Don't call me Claire."

The valise stood on the floor between Harcourt and Toby.

"Please," Harcourt begged.

"Did you bring that for me?" she asked, pointing to the valise.

"What?" Harcourt asked, turning around. "No. I picked it up . . ." He stared at the valise and then at Claire.

"It's mine," Claire said, taking the valise from the floor. "Isn't it? I asked you to get it for me."

"Claire," Harcourt implored.

She ignored him and opened the valise on the bed. The battered leather softened into newness in the same vibration of atmosphere that produced Harcourt seemingly out of nothing. Scuffs and scratches peeled away like sunburnt skin. Claire recognized everything inside: the gray gown she'd worn when she'd first arrived in Ledwyche, a book of Charles's poetry, her kit, her tools, her vials, her notebook and, at the bottom, the copied pages for the monograph. Her pages. Claire took the letter to Cowpe that explained her desire not to be credited and why and handed it to Toby. Harcourt stepped closer.

"It's me," she said. Heat and vibration spread like a fire inside her. "It isn't you." She held the pages. "It's me. It's Kate."

Harcourt smiled sadly at her. "Yes, love. I know. I've always known. But you must go home."

The hot energy intensified inside her. Claire began to feel sicker. Her throat filled up again. She panicked that she wouldn't be able to breathe. But she was breathing. And standing. She wanted to run.

"It's me," she said, trying to grab Harcourt's coat. Her hand melted through it, as if he were formed of water. "Why can't you see that? It's me!"

"Claire," Harcourt said.

"No!" Claire screamed. The mournful sound flowed out of her mouth as if she was bleeding, blood and fluid and life streaming out, and she couldn't stop it. Twice alive, two voices poured from her throat. But she didn't want two. She wanted one. One voice. One life. One love. One self. "I am the ghost," she said to Toby. "Not Harcourt. I am the fragment, the half-self. And I want to be complete."

Toby took her hand, then let it go.

"If I stay here I'll disappear. I don't belong. I want to go home." Claire took the book of poetry out of the valise. "Give this to Ian. Tell him to find his better nature again. Tell him he doesn't have to compete with me anymore. Tell him my father loved him better as a poet and wouldn't have wanted him to be a doctor. Tell him that the boy in the poet is the Charles I love and will always love. And read my letter, Toby. You will not miss me."

Toby opened his mouth to protest.

"You will not," Claire said. "Because you will not worry anymore that you failed to save me. I need to save myself." She kissed Toby's cheek and turned to Harcourt. "I love you. Follow me."

Claire ran from the room and out of the inn, onto Beckwith Street.

"Aren't you going to stop her?" Toby asked.

"No," Harcourt said, trying to catch his breath.

"Do you have any idea what she's capable of when she sets her mind to it?" Toby said in a strained voice.

Harcourt turned to his friend. "I do, which is why I will not try to stop her." He had no right to keep her from herself any longer. He had to let her go, even if that meant watching her die again. He would follow her home and kiss her for the last time. Harcourt took Toby's hand. "Thank you for watching over her." He moved to go.

"Wait," Toby said, in a voice like one awakened from a drunken stupor by a pail of water. He folded Kate's letter and put it in his pocket. "I'm coming with you."

Claire grabbed the Abernathy House Museum door handle and shook it. The partygoers had all gone. The door wouldn't open. Claire could hear voices through the windows, which were layered in both darkness and light, like a negative on top of a photograph.

"Tell me what the devil is going on?" Harcourt's voice demanded. "Shhh, love."

"I don't know how long she'll last," Cowpe said.

"What do you mean?" Harcourt asked. "I don't understand what you mean."

"Come and talk with me outside," Cowpe said.

Claire felt above the door for a key. She searched under stones and the mat. Nothing. A bronze plaque above an urn carved with orpine told a brief history of the house and its inhabitants. Below the date of the museum's most recent renovation were the last lines of Charles Ishingham's famous poem. "Death and rebirth weave time on a single thread. Eurydice saves herself."

Claire slid her finger behind the plaque. She pulled out a key on a chain attached to a card with the alarm code and instructions for the museum docents. Claire whispered thanks and good-bye to Ian. She unlocked the door and entered the dark parlor. It was empty.

She lay on the damask couch, closed her eyes and opened her mouth. A sensation of bright metal sliced the length of her spine, cutting through inflammation and infection. All ambient noises faded, as if flesh or water filled her ears. She was falling. The metal sheet expanded inside her, splitting her in two. She felt as though she was dying and being born on the same breath. A great shattering sound echoed through no end of space. The icy metal tore itself from her body and she was depleted, gasping for breath, grasping at her long skirt.

Harcourt entered his house in time to see himself and Cowpe leave the parlor where Kate lay dying. Toby followed him inside. Harcourt saw himself take Cowpe by the arm.

"I don't understand. How could she fall so ill so quickly?"

"It is an inflammation of the brain," Cowpe said softly. "She may survive it."

"What do you mean, *may?*"

Kate wailed from the parlor. Harcourt recognized the sound. It was the same cry that poured from Claire's mouth at the Horn and Powder. He listened, dumbstruck, unable to move or think past the terrible song pouring from his wife's throat.

Toby stared at Claire, pale and gasping on the antique couch in the dark museum. "Go to her," he said to Harcourt. "She's given you a second chance as well."

"What?" Harcourt said, as Cowpe and Toby spoke simultaneously.

"Go," Cowpe said again. "Go to her. You have a second chance."

Harcourt melted into his own solid body and ran for Kate. She turned her face toward the door and opened her mouth. He lay on top of her and caught the mournful song in his mouth.

He kissed her, pouring a part of his own life force into her. He kissed her again and again, and drew from her the part that belonged to him, the part of her soul that was his to watch over. He kissed her and she was safe inside him.

Claire opened her eyes and gazed at him. She drank in his scent and savored the warm weight of his body. Harcourt smiled, lovely, loving, sweet and deep. He kissed her again.

She turned her head and saw the polished wood walls of their parlor and smelled the smoke of the fire. A far-off kiss touched her hand. "This is what I want," Claire whispered to Toby, who she couldn't see. Silence roared into the vacuum of her head.

Toby felt Claire's wrist and wept.

Cowpe felt Kate's pulse and sighed with relief.

Harcourt laid his cheek near hers. She raised her hands and pulled him closer. His thickly muscled back sprang to life under her touch, and his mouth convulsed on hers. Tears poured into her eyes and ears. She held on tighter. The kiss grew deeper. He opened his mouth and fell inside her. She embraced his kiss with her own, life and blood coursing through her veins.

"Kate," he said. "Kate, Kate, Kate."

She took his face in her hands.

"I am here," she said, and smiled. "I am home."

STILL LIFE
MELANIE JACKSON

Snippets of a forgotten past are returning to Nyssa Laszlo, along with the power to project her mind. Each projection thrusts her into a glowing still life of color and time, and her every step leads deeper into undiscovered country. Things are changing, and dangerously so. She is learning who she is—whether she wants to or not. She is also learning dark things are on the rise. From the Unseelie faerie court to Abrial, the dauntless dreamwalker who pursues her, the curtain is going up on a stage Nyssa has never seen and a cast she can't imagine—and it's the final act of a play for her heart and soul.

𝓛AUREN'S EYES
𝓝ORAH WILSON

There is going to be a murder, and the eyes of Lauren Townsend have foreseen it. But the authorities refuse to take her seriously. Working alone, Lauren follows the clues—to an almost bankrupt dude ranch in Calgary and its desperate owner, Cal Taggart. The man's kisses promise paradise, yet his ex-wife is the one Lauren has seen strangled. Is Cal capable of murder? Lauren longs to speak, but if she confides in Cal, will she lose him forever? She will risk everything—her happiness, her future, her very life—to save the man she loves. But the outcome is one thing she can't see.

Winner of the National New Voice in Romance Contest sponsored by Romantic Times BOOKClub *and Dorchester Publishing!*

KATHERINE GREYLE
ALMOST AN
ANGEL

Carolly Hanson is training to be an angel, or so she believes. It is
the only explanation for why she keeps dying and reappearing in
different places and times. Clearly she is intended to help people—
and clearly the best way to help people is to find them true love.
Never mind that it hasn't worked yet.

This time she awakes in the arms of James Oscar Henry
Northram, Earl of Traynern. The handsome noble is charmed by her
odd sense of humor, strange forthright manner and complete lack of
interest in trapping him in marriage. But he also thinks her a
Bedlamite and isn't the least bit cooperative with the women she
pushes in his direction. So, just who is James's true love?
